'Funny, fast, witty and brutal . . . Whenever he's got a new book out I drop everything, knowing that the next couple of hours are going to be pure gangland bliss.' David Bowie

'An ironic, postmodern morality tale that I found the most compelling in the series . . . The acid-house scene, the rave scene, new lads meeting old lags, Brit gangster films made by mockney directors, ecstasy, the teenage girl whose death after taking it filled the tabloids: Arnott marshals these seedier elements of the last decade in superb style.' Erwin James, *Guardian*

'Arnott pinpoints with devastating accuracy how today's world leads to the survival of the shallowest. His ear for low-life patois is as sharp as ever and the narrative proceeds at a cracking pace.' Michael Arditti, *The Times*

'Arnott earned his spurs in [his] first two novels, both pin-sharp and tough as hide . . . [the conclusion] only furthers Arnott's credentials, allowing his ear for dialogue to cut through . . . The prose is as hard, stylish and memorable as our antihero himself.' *Arena*

'Probably the most astringent satire yet on what was probably the slimiest of decades, the Nineties.' Mark Simpson, Books of the Year, *Independent on Sunday*

'A fast, stylish and unexpectedly angry book that ultimately rails against the crime-as-glamour period it details.' Andrew Holmes, *Scotland on Sunday*

'[An] incredibly accurate social history of Britain in the Eighties and Nineties . . . A superb, profound and thoughtful response to the *Lock, Stock* generation.' Ally Fogg, *Big Issue in the North*

'Arnott's satire is right on the money.' Peter Guttridge, *Observer*

'Chilling, funny and caustic . . . he manages to pull off the difficult trick of satirising a decade while maintaining

realism through careful and sometimes brilliant detailing'
Peter Watts, *Time Out*

'Arnott has established himself as a writer able not just to spin a good yarn, but to place crime in its social and historical context; and it is that alertness to detail which gives the writing its edge . . . an adroit and thought-provoking fable' Max Davidson, *Sunday Telegraph*

'Arnott manages, in a way not seen since Martin Amis, to make the city of London a character in itself, a brooding, windswept place where the ghosts of crimes past never seem to fully go away, and nobody is ever afraid to do you a bad turn . . . inventive, witty and enjoyably referential' Ian O'Doherty, *Sunday Business Post*

'Astonishing . . . *truecrime* very knowingly and accurately reflects our celebrity-obsessed culture, and wonders, with a puzzled laugh, at the fascination reserved to real-life violent criminals and the feverish fame, acceptance and faux-respectability now bestowed upon them . . . [it] is undoubtedly Arnott's *tour de force*; a brilliantly constructed, hard-edged and humorous novel that works on many different levels, not least as a damn good and thoroughly gripping, page-turning read.' Joe Storey Scott, *Gay Times*

'By far the best of his trilogy . . . one of the most thrillingly nihilistic novels I've read, deserving several literary prizes for sheer bravado. If this makes the book sound at all off-putting, I feel duty-bound to add that Arnott's experimentation is always entertaining and incredibly readable.' Matt Thorne, *Waterstone's Books Quarterly*

'Arnott has pulled off the difficult task of writing a book which has a uniquely British voice but can stand up to the best of the crime books from across the Atlantic.' Matt Hall, *Word*

JAKE ARNOTT

truecrime

SCEPTRE

Extract from *Nineteen Eighty-Four* by George Orwell
(copyright © George Orwell, 1949) by permission of Bill Hamilton as the
literary executor of the late Sonia Brownwell Orwell and Secker & Warburg Ltd.

Extracts from *The Good Person of Szechwan* by Bertolt Brecht translated by
John Willet by permission of Methuen Publishing Ltd.

Extract from *Brave New World* by Aldous Huxley originally published by
Chatto and Windus. Reprinted by permission of the Random House Group Limited
© the estate of Mrs Laura Huxley.

First published in Great Britain in 2003 by Hodder and Stoughton
A division of Hodder Headline

The right of Jake Arnott to be identified as the Author
of the Work has been asserted by him in accordance with the
Copyright, Designs and Patents Act 1988.

A Sceptre paperback

5 7 9 10 8 6

A CIP catalogue record for this title is
available from the British Library

ISBN 0 340 81857 3

Typeset in Sabon by Palimpsest Book Production Limited,
Polmont, Stirlingshire
Printed and bound in Great Britain by
Clays Ltd, St Ives plc

Hodder Headline's policy is to use papers that are natural, renewable and
recyclable products and made from wood grown in sustainable
forests. The logging and manufacturing processes are
expected to conform to the environmental regulations of
the country of origin.

Hodder and Stoughton
A division of Hodder Headline
338 Euston Road
London NW1 3BH

1
ghost writers in the sky

In Newspeak, euphony outweighed every consideration other than exactitude of meaning. Regularity of grammar was always sacrificed to it when it seemed necessary. And rightly so, since what was required, above all for political purposes, were short clipped words of unmistakable meaning which could be uttered rapidly and which roused the minimum of echoes in the speaker's mind. The words of the B vocabulary even gained force from the fact that nearly all these words – goodthink, Minipax, prolefeed, sexcrime, Ingsoc, bellyfeel, thinkpol and countless others – were words of two or three syllables, with the stress on the first syllable and the last.

George Orwell, *Nineteen Eighty-Four*,
Appendix: *Principles of Newspeak*

Transcript of taped conversation between Tony Meehan and Eddie Doyle

5/3/95

TM: You OK to start?

ED: Yeah, sure. But look, I do want to talk about how this whole thing is going.

TM: Fine. But let's try and get some ground covered first.

ED: It's just that I'm, well, I'm not happy about some of it, you know?

TM: I understand. It's a difficult process. But if we can just get something on tape.

ED: OK. Yeah. Well, where do you want to start?

TM: I thought we could talk about the Hounslow bullion job. If that's OK.

ED: That (laughs). Right, well, there's some things I can't talk about, you know that, don't you?

TM: I know.

ED: Never saw a penny of my cut. Twelve fucking years. Kept my mouth shut and all. For what?

TM: Let's talk about the events on the day.

ED: That fucking security guard we had on the inside. First whiff of trouble and his arse drops out. Fucking joke. Sorry, you want to talk about the day?

TM: If we can.

ED: Well, let me tell you something about that day. We had no fucking idea what we'd got. How fucking big

3

it was. Maybe if we'd just got what we'd been going
for in the first place, if we'd just got the money,
well, maybe it wouldn't have turned out so bad.

TM: How do you mean?

ED: Well, it was cursed, you know. That gold. Opening
up that vault was like opening up the tomb of
Tutankhamun or something. It cursed us, that gold.

TM: You know, that's not a bad angle for the story.

ED: And I'll tell you something else. You know all
those films when they open the vault and there's
all the gold bars all neatly stacked up and
gleaming like fuck? Well, it wasn't like that.

TM: No?

ED: No. They were all in these cardboard boxes with
metal tapes around them. Like fucking shoeboxes.
We wouldn't have noticed them if we hadn't had
trouble getting the safe open. We were going after
the money, you see. If only we'd got that safe open.
The money, that would have been easy. Used notes,
unmarked. Just divvy it up after the job. Instead we
end up with all that fucking gold. And that's when
the grief started.

TM: What happened with the safe?

ED: Well, we had trouble getting the combinations out
of the guards. They were shitting themselves but
maybe we'd put the frighteners on them a little too
much. They couldn't concentrate, could they?

TM: Well, you had doused their private parts with
petrol and threatened to set light to them.

ED: Yeah, well. Hang on.

TM: I'm only going by the trial report.

ED: Yeah, well, let's talk about this.

TM: Yes let's.

ED: Let me tell you about the petrol. It was watered
down. It wouldn't have ignited if you'd put a match

to it. There was enough of a smell to make them think that. But that was the point. To scare them into giving us the combinations.

TM: I see.

ED: But this is where it all goes wrong. You know?

TM: I'm not sure I do.

ED: I mean the way you're telling my story. It's like you're always dwelling on anything nasty and brutal. Like I'm some sort of a thug.

TM: I can assure you I'm not trying to do that, Eddie.

ED: And some of the stuff I've seen. It makes me sound, well, inarticulate. You're supposed to be a writer, for fuck's sake. It all comes across as really trashy, you know?

TM: Well, the public do go for a brusque style.

ED: Fuck the public. I want my story told properly.

TM: We both do, Eddie. Look, it's early days. Once we're at the editing stage we can go through all this. But we really do need to get it all down first.

ED: It's like all you're interested in is the violence and the scandal.

TM: Well, that is what's going to sell copies, you know.

ED: And all the Ruby Ryder stuff.

TM We did talk about that.

ED: Well, I don't know, Tony. I don't know.

TM: It is a crucial selling point of your story. You were married to her, after all.

ED: But she's trying to get her career going again. I know she won't be happy having the past dragged up again.

TM: Look, can we try and get back to the story? We can go over this later.

ED: No. I want to sort this out now.

TM: Eddie . . .

ED: Turn the tape off.

TM: We are behind schedule, you know.
ED: I said turn the fucking tape off . . .

Tape ends

'There.' I pressed the stop button. Eddie looked liked he was about to grab the tape machine. 'It's off.'

'Right.'

Eddie sits back in his chair, folds his arms and gives me that well-practised glare of his. A look I've seen on countless villains and old lags.

'So.' I sigh, trying to soothe the situation. 'Let's talk, then, shall we?'

'Yeah,' he replies with a grudging shrug.

And I knew I was in for another difficult session. But I had to try to get him to talk. Because, well, this is not my story. I'm the 'as told to' or the 'with'.

I'm the ghost. The ghost writer.

Once, when drunk at some dreadful book launch trapped in that soul-destroying 'and what do you do?' small talk, I slurred my nomenclature as 'ghost rider' rather than 'ghost writer'. It conjured up that old country and western song 'Ghostriders in the Sky' where howling echo-chamber cowboys are doomed to chase a spectral herd across the firmament.

Yippy-ay-oh, yippy-ay-eh.

Ghost writers in the sky.

Doomed is right, like the Flying Dutchman or the Ancient fucking Mariner. Tony Meehan, twenty years crime journalist for the *Sunday Illustrated*, erstwhile editor of *Murder Monthly*, author of *Cop Killer: The Billy Porter Story* (remaindered after one edition), I am condemned to ghost-write sickening boastful memoirs of retired villains for the Groombridge Press. And having hacked away my meagre writing talents down the decades, to indulge in childish word games and perverse etymologies.

Though Eddie Doyle seems quite capable of unnecessary semantics himself.

'Thing is,' he says, 'you're supposed to be my ghost writer but I'm the one that feels like a ghost. It just doesn't seem real.'

Christ, a professional criminal getting all existential on me. That's all I bloody need.

'Well,' I reply, 'we just need to get the tone right.'

Get the tone right. Well, we know what that means: lower it. True Crime, what a racket it is. I prefer to rearticulate this term into a lower case composite: *truecrime*. Like George Orwell's newspeak words *thoughtcrime* or *sexcrime*, the coining of the term *truecrime* came to me from that ancient Stalinist logic – the manipulation of vocabulary to ensure correct thought. But this newspeak is imposed not by a totalitariarian state but by my publishing dictatorship, the Groombridge Press. True and Crime, words that were once at odds with each other as much as alibi and detection, now conspire to create trashy bestsellers. Another newspeak conjunction, *prolefeed*, comes to mind, but these days, with the decline of the proletariat, it strikes me that, rather than feeding the proles, we are now serving them up for suburban consumption. Fetishised masculinity, the stories of hard men to provide vicarious thrills for the boring lives of white-collar strap-hangers. 'Get the tone right,' that's what Victor Groombridge, my boss, insists is my job as ghost writer. 'Make it sound authentic.' That is to say: make this intelligent, emotionally complex, deviously manipulative, professional villain sound like an engaging thug, a curious monster.

'Yeah, but it's my story,' he almost pleads with me.

'Of course it is,' I say, nodding hopefully.

I mean, Eddie Doyle seemed an easy enough prospect when Victor Groombridge signed him up and passed him over to me for the treatment. Jewel thief, bank robber, known associate of most of the major gangland faces. Got sent down in 1983 for the Hounslow bullion job – twelve years served and he never divulged where all that fifteen or so million went missing. But one of the biggest hooks for his story was that he was Ruby Ryder's husband in the sixties and seventies. Ryder's career has seen more downs than ups but at the moment her kitsch has attained a kind of cult status. Rumour has it that she is in the frame for a major part in a TV soap opera. So, it's all there: gangland iconography, showbiz gossip, heist stories, the lot.

But the problem is Eddie. He has his own ideas, far too many of them. He's been away too long. Years of emptiness filled with nonsense, courtesy of some half-baked liberal prison education scheme. He is far too well read. And he is painfully aware of not being the author of his own memoirs. He's not happy being put through the mill. With most of the villains I've done, they're only too glad to let you do all the work. They're happy to just cough it all up on to the tape recorder and let you hack it out. When the book comes out they're so pleased to see their name on the cover with some suitably menacing picture that they imagine somehow they've written it. A good ghost will never disabuse them of this. It's always their book. You just content yourself with a split in the royalties and everybody's happy and they don't realise about the money until after it's all been sewn up. They don't realise how they've been stitched up until after the game's over. They imagine publishing to be some gentlemanly practice, not realising that they're up against the most heinous form of organised crime, of organised lying, until it's far too late. But even here, Eddie is questioning.

'And what about this advance?' he asks.

'What about it?'

'Well, I've not seen much of it.'

'I told you.'

'You told me twenty grand. I've only seen two and a half thousand.'

'I told you, we don't get it all at once. A quarter on signing.

A quarter on delivery. A quarter on hardback. A quarter on paperback.'

The familiar litany, the vagaries of the racket.

'Christ,' seethes Eddie. 'And I thought that I was fucked over by gangsters. But a quarter, that means I'm due five grand on signing, not two fifty.'

'I told you, it's a fifty-fifty split.'

'Jesus. You lot are good. You're fucking lairy.'

'So look, Eddie. Going back to the bullion job. You say the gold was cursed. What do you mean by that?'

'I mean that we weren't up to dealing with it. We were just a team of blaggers. Good ones, mind, South-East London's finest, but blaggers nonetheless. We were after a substantial haul of used notes with no problems. But that gold, I mean, we couldn't believe our luck when we realised what we were sitting on, and we were right, it was luck all right, bloody bad luck. It meant we had to find a way of getting rid of it. And you know what that means, don't you?'

'You tell me.'

'It meant approaching certain people. People who could fence that kind of amount. And that's when the trouble really started. There was so much more at stake than we'd bargained for. Pretty soon all that lovely gold had more than a bit of blood on it.'

'You want to talk about that?'

'Hm. Probably not a good idea, you know.'

'The tape's not running.'

'Look, Tony, I did twelve years and kept my mouth. I'm not going to start yakking now, am I?'

'Well, you wouldn't have to name names.'

'Just tell the story?'

'It sounds like a good one.'

And it did have a ring to it. An archetypal narrative, wealth corrupting those who find it, death coming in the form of gold. Like the Pardoner's Tale.

'Look, I'm serious,' Eddie insists, becoming more agitated. 'I don't want a bullet in the back of my head, you know.'

'Don't worry,' I try to placate him.

'Don't worry?' he cuts in. 'Let me show you something.'

He leads me furtively to a window, standing to one side of it and peering down at the street below. He cocks his head.

'See that parked car – don't get any closer to the window – see it?'

'Yeah.'

'Don't lean forward like that. Come over here. See? That bloke. See him?'

'I'm not sure.'

I try to get a proper look but Eddie pulls me back.

'Don't. Oh, for fuck's sake. Come on, get away from the window.'

'Do you mean to say you're being followed?' I ask him as we sit back down again.

Eddie nods. An intent look on his face. Paranoia, probably.

'Who do you think it is?'

'Don't know. Now that I'm out it could be that certain people are getting a bit jumpy. Might think that I want my money.'

'And do you?'

'What?'

'Want your money.'

Eddie smiles.

'Well, what do you think? But I don't want to get myself killed. I was hoping that I could make some gelt from this racket, you know, selling my story. But I kind of figured that I might get a bit more up front, though. I mean, two and a half grand? Maybe I should stick to what I'm really good at.'

'Well . . .'

Eddie gives a dry laugh.

'Don't worry, Tony, I'm fucking redundant. No one robs banks any more. It's all drugs now. The Hounslow job, well, that was supposed to be my pension. My final coup. And it was all taken away from me.'

'So how are we going to tell the bullion job story?' I ask him.

Eddie sighs.

'Up to when I went away, I guess. I kept my mouth but others didn't. That stupid fucking security guard, our bloody inside man, he starts to bottle it, doesn't he? As soon as he gets a tug he starts coughing.'

'Can I put the tape recorder back on?'

'Yeah, but I ain't saying anything about where the gold went. And I want it told intelligently, not like we were just a bunch of thugs.'

After the session, as I'm coming out of Eddie's flat, I go past the car that he pointed out to me. There's no one in it. Eddie's probably imagining things. It's hard adjusting to the outside world after such a long stretch. But I have a quick scan around. No. Nobody's following me. Some chance.

Ghost life. Make my way back home. *Yippy-ay-oh, yippy-ay-eh.* Nobody knows. I've managed to control myself all these years. I got away with it all.

Get an *Evening Standard* by the Underground. The headline is: GANGLAND KILLER RONNIE KRAY DIES A PRIS-ONER. The first paragraph heads, *Notorious gangland killer Ronnie Kray died today in hospital, two days after collapsing in his ward at Broadmoor. Police said 61-year-old Ronnie – the madder and badder of the feared Kray Twins – died at 9.07 a.m. . . .* The Beast is dead, that'll be good for business. I bet Victor is already buying somebody up, some crony or associate to squeeze another drop out of the tired old Kray legend.

Back at the flat I check the tape and go through my existing notes on Eddie Doyle. Somebody else's life. Try to muster some enthusiasm for this book. I like the cursed-treasure angle, something allegorical about that. Victor will, however, want it all done to the *truecrime* formula.

truecrime is a beast with two backs. It has two main forms. There are the nasty murderers, the rippers, the sex killers, the mass murderers: *sexcrime*, if you like. Then there are the gangsters, the villains, the Kray associates. All hoarded together in that furtive corner of the bookshop, a section that is expanding: *truecrime* is booming. Victor Groombridge has done very well out of it. Though this book with Eddie is way behind schedule and he isn't happy with me. I've got lunch with him tomorrow.

I'm not that interested in villains' memoirs but I made a conscious decision to work in that field rather than explore the awful killers. Conscious, well, if you knew my proclivities you'd understand why it seemed safer to be employed in this way. Too much of a temptation for me to indulge myself in the *sexcrime* branch of *truecrime*. I have gone straight, as it were.

I haven't killed anyone for almost ten years. But I thought it best to avoid anything that might arouse my dormant desires.

Besides, that end of the field has the danger of becoming respectable. Gordon Burn, Brian Masters, Gita Sereny. It's this modern thing about psychology. I blame Colin Wilson, this existential obsession with the self. I used to believe in all of that, of course. But that was before I became a killer myself.

Everybody now is obsessed with the 'serial killer'. In my day it was more blunt: mass murderers, that's what we called them. But in the eighties the FBI Behavioral Science Unit asserted a new *truecrime* paradigm. Psychological profiling, offender signatures, victimology. But this new 'science' has a whiff of pulp fiction about it. Robert Ressler, the FBI profiler, claims that he was inspired to coin the term 'serial killer' out of a sense of cheap drama. 'Now that I look back on that naming event,' he is quoted as saying, 'I think that what was also in my mind were the serial adventures we used to see on Saturday at the movies.' The dissatisfaction of the cliff-hanger ending that increases rather than lessens the tension. It's certainly what kept the readership of *Murder Monthly* going. And this new pop psychology approach has an inspiration all of its own. In 1993 a rather dreary psychopath called Colin Ireland picked up masochistic homosexuals at the Colherne leather bar in Earls Court, took them back to their flats and strangled them. JACK THE GRIPPER, the *News of the World* called him. *The Sunday Illustrated* went one better: THE FAIRY LIQUIDATOR. Sid Franks, the news editor in my day, he would have loved that one. I was intrigued, for a while, since his modus operandi seemed so familiar. So similar to the circumstances of that time I throttled a homo back in 1966.

It turned out that the Fairy Liquidator was actually inspired by Ressler's book on serial killers and indeed, along with a useful forensic awareness he had acquired in the execution of his crimes, his very aspiration was simply to join the hallowed ranks himself. Once he had gone past the required score of victims he was ready to retire. 'I have read a lot of books on serial killers,' he declared in a phone call to the police. 'I think it is from four people that the FBI class as serial, so I may stop now I have done five.' Tabloid celebrity secured, he had realised himself, with the help of all that wisdom from *truecrime*. Self-help for serial killers.

But I have been able to control myself. I was never one for getting carried away, after all. And nothing can be traced to me. My crimes are all cold cases now. Indeed, that is what I have become: a cold case. I'm as dead as they are. All my sins remembered but nothing much left inside. I have no desires left to enact except to watch and record. And I console myself with this fact: I am not a serial killer. Neither in inclination nor statistics. Remember, I only killed three. That queen in Earls Court, the whore in Shepherd Market. And Teddy

Thursby. And of course the 'victimology' of Lord Thursby of Hartwell-juxta-Mare doesn't really count on the profile. I got no pleasure wringing his flabby neck. Christ, no. No *sexcrime* there. No, the FBI *Crime Classification Manual* clearly defines my opportunistic strangling of Teddy Thursby as: *108.02 Situational Felony Murder. Property crime (robbery, burglary) is the primary motivation for felony murder, with murder the secondary motivation.* I killed him for his diaries. For my own gain. Though in some way the acquisition of them has all the hallmarks of acquiring a 'fetish object from the victim' that all these serial killer books bang on about. I have so much of him in my possession, after all.

Teddy Thursby's diaries, oh yes, quite a treasure is my little wordhoard. Of course, I can never fully exploit them, not publicly, I mean, that would implicate me. But then I'd rather not have them published and pored over by the grubby-fingered masses. They're mine. A wonderful reference work they are too. Incomplete, though. Thursby and Julian, his 'official biographer', destroyed some of the more damaging material when they were working on that dreadful whitewash that was to be his memoirs. But there's still plenty of scandal and ignominy recorded by the poisoned pen of that dirty old peer. Particularly entries in the sixties – Teddy really was feasting with panthers back then. Bits of underworld stuff that could be useful for what I'm working on now, you never know. There's even a reference to the Hounslow bullion job somewhere, I'm sure of it.

Thursby was definitely my last killing, I think I was finally cured of it by suffocating him. It was a means to an end, I wasn't being driven by some frenzied passion, I got no enjoyment from it, in fact it rather disgusted me. No, what really did give me a thrill was taking those diaries. I was taking a life, you see, that's what I'd always wanted to do. With that pile of battered journals in my grasp I realised that I wasn't really a murderer. I was a biographer.

My first book on Billy Porter, the notorious Shepherd's Bush Cop Killer should have been my big break. It had been my story right from the start. Victor Groombridge commissioned it but we argued for a long time over the manuscript. It was 'over-written', he said, whatever that was supposed to mean. He wanted a brash, sensationalist account but I felt that there was something deeper in the story. Our discussions became quite heated: at one point Victor said: 'I can't believe that you can make this terrific material so boring and drawn out.' We made some compromises in the end and it was published but it didn't sell and Victor blamed me.

And I ended up ghost-writing for him, which is all right, but you don't get that control over the subject that I really want. The book with Eddie started out with some promise – he is intelligent and articulate, at least, not like some of these moronic thugs Victor has had me ghost. Of course, this makes it difficult to come up with the standard Groombridge Press treatment on him. With that and all the other troubles we've been having, I don't know how this book is going to work.

Eddie's tape and my own notes reveal a myriad of theories about what happened to the loot, how it was disposed of – money laundering, dodgy gold dealers, offshore banking fraud, and so on. Some crooked businessmen and gangsters put away for receiving but rumours of a bigger internationally coordinated operation. A number of murders and disappearances associated with the bullion job. Although I like the notion of how wealth destroys and corrupts I'm not sure how I'm going to make it work as a story.

I'm weary of it all. I'm tired of having to eke out a miserable living with all this hack work. Something Eddie Doyle said about the bullion job: *it was to be my final coup, something to retire on.* That's what we all dream of, I suppose, to be at rest. I was looking forward to retirement myself until I found out what the useless pension scheme I had been conned into buying into in the eighties was going to be worth. Absolutely bugger all. I dread to think about being left to the mercies of the state in old age.

I need one more chance to write a proper book. Not just a ghosted memoir, something that will secure my reputation, something that will sell. A *truecrime* classic, something big and definitive like John Pearson's *The Profession of Violence*. That's all I want now, but will I ever get another chance?

Bedtime. Brush my teeth and stare into the looking glass. Ugly old queen. But I'm not a monster. Am I? My crimes were not so bad. The dead don't miss much. I think about all that cursed gold and men dead because of it and it gives me a bit of a thrill. Can't think why. I've kept myself clean all these years, for what? A ghost's life, a monster in captivity, a specimen in the jar. A face in the mirror. All this psychological profiling is a bit like a return to Cesare Lombroso's notion of the criminal type, *L'Uomo delinquente*. Physiognomy, external signs from which we can read guilt. But my face betrays nothing.

I wipe a bit of toothpaste off my chin. Turn the light out.

Lunch with Victor. The publishing world marches on its stomach. Any problem, any issue to discuss, any deadline looming, any problem with a manuscript, they leap into action and sit down to feed. Victor Groombridge had been the gossip columnist on the *Sunday Illustrated* before he set up on his own. He was known for his finesse in buying up people and quickly getting a story out of them. I tell him about my angle on the Eddie Doyle story. He is not impressed.

'The fucking Pardoner's Tale? What are you talking about now?'

'Well, it's a universal story, of how money corrupts. It's like a parable.'

'Do me a favour, Tony, drop all these fucking literary pretensions, will you? We're well behind schedule as it is.'

'I just thought it would give it some shape. He doesn't want to name names on who got rid of the gold so I thought that if we had a sort of moral-to-the-story element, well, that could be the hook.'

Victor sighs and shakes his head.

'He doesn't want to name names on the bullion job, he doesn't want to dish the dirt on Ruby Ryder, just what have you two been talking about all this time?'

'Well, he's not the easiest story I've had to ghost. And I can see his point with the bullion thing. There's been more than one murder connected to that job. But he does want to tell his story. He's just a bit sensitive about how he comes across.'

'Yeah, yeah. Look, much as we'd really like some redemptive, moral-of-the-story angle, how I rehabilitated myself with a sociology degree or whatever, it ain't what's selling. The public want lovable monsters. Unspoiled monsters.'

'Yeah, well.'

'And now that Ronnie Kray's croaked, well, it's just the right time. End of an era and all that bullshit. There must be plenty of old faces to buy up who'll trot out all that nostalgia trip. If it isn't working with Eddie Doyle, well, maybe, I don't know, maybe we should drop him.'

'You mean . . . ?'

'Well, we're way behind and Eddie isn't exactly being cooperative, is he?'

'Well, no, but . . .'

'So, I want something by the end of May or we forget about it.'

I don't know what to say. I want to tell him to fuck off but I need the work. I need the money.

'Victor . . .' I begin.

'Just get on with it, Tony. You fuss around too much. Just hack it out.'

'So, is that all you think I'm good for?'

Victor sighs and shakes his head wearily. We carry on eating for a while without talking.

'Look,' Victor says finally, 'get him to the funeral at least.'

'What?'

'Eddie. Get Eddie to the funeral.'

'What funeral?'

'Ronnie Kray's, of course. I'll get a photographer. It's going to be the social event of the calendar for retired villains. He'll have to be seen there. Get him lined up with a few faces from the sixties. That'll look good. And try to get him to talk about Ruby Ryder.'

So a week later and we were in the press huddle in front of St Matthew's, Bethnal Green. A monster's funeral, the church-yard teeming with old lags and young wannabes. A phalanx of bouncers, the cream of London's doormen, formed a guard of dishonour around the lich-gate. A police helicopter buzzed overhead. The hearse arrived. A black-and-gold glass-sided carriage, drawn by six black-plumed horses. Victoriana kitsch, just as he would have wanted. The Last Empire Hero. Wreaths and flowered tributes to the grand old psychopath: RON and THE COLONEL. One from Reggie, his womb-mate: TO THE OTHER HALF OF ME, like a floral expression of schizophrenia.

I was there with Eddie Doyle, a reluctant mourner. *I never had much truck with the Twins*, he protested. But Victor was insistent: *Get a picture of him with some other celebrity villains. Reputation, that's what it's all about.* And sure enough our smudger Geoff was on hand, patiently setting up a small aluminium stepladder to get a good angle over the crowd.

Also with us was Piers, a young journalist with the Groom-bridge Press's latest publishing venture, *Sorted* magazine. *Sorted* is aimed at what Victor assures me is a fresh and growing market: the 'New Lad'. I have no idea what this means. Apparently it's all about postmodernism, post-feminism. It's 'ironic', according to Piers. Well, it's all newspeak to me.

And this Piers character, well, he was just full of it. All these hard men giving him a hard-on. His lazy, public-school vowels droned on in my ear, wanting me to put names to faces. Faces. Yeah, I know them. Yes, Piers, that's Mad Frankie Fraser.

He turned his tape recorder on Eddie.

'Can I ask you a question, Eddie?' he said, pointing the little gadget in his direction.

'Uh?' Eddie seemed distracted, looking around, a bit twitchy.

I started to worry about Eddie and his paranoia. He still thinks he's being followed and he's not used to such a big crowd. He did his full stretch in closed conditions, high security. An hour or so a day in the exercise yard or association for twelve years doesn't exactly prepare you for something like this.

'What do you think?' Piers continued. 'It's the end of an era, isn't it?'

'What do you mean?'

'Well, you know, the old school of crime. Codes of honour, that sort of thing.'

Eddie winced and turned to me.

'What's this cunt fannying on about?' he asked me.

Piers gave a nervous little laugh.

'Oh, that's good,' he declared. 'I might well use that.'

Geoff teetered on his perch, screwing a huge lens into his camera.

'Ready when you are, chief,' he told me.

So, the idea was to get Eddie up to the doorway of the church, but he was hesitant, looking out into the crowd.

'Christ,' he muttered. 'Look at all this lot. It's like fucking *Jurassic Park*.'

'Come on, Eddie,' I urged him. 'We need to get you up near the front.'

It had all been sorted, Eddie had got an invite. Flanagan, a blonde-haired ex-Page Three girl, was doing the guest list and his name was on it. All we had to do was get him up by the door, through the crowd, then Geoff could start snapping away. I tapped Eddie on the shoulder.

'Hang on,' he said. 'Look.'

He was looking at somebody in the crowd. I tried to see who but there was just a mass of solemn faces. He nodded at someone.

'There,' he whispered sharply at me.

'What?' I tried not to sound impatient.

I didn't really care who he was looking at. I needed to get him moving.

'Come on, Eddie,' I begged, hoping to encourage him. 'We're on.'

'Wait a minute,' he insisted. 'It's . . .'

I tugged at his sleeve. He was in some sort of trance or something. He turned around, briefly, his face incredulous. I thought I'd got his attention but just at that moment Reggie Kray arrived, handcuffed to a prison warder. The crowd was suddenly roused and started surging forward.

'I don't fucking believe it,' Eddie declared, then looked back. 'It's . . .'

The mob was pushing towards the church, the doormen were holding everyone back, keeping the path clear for Reggie and the other guests. I had to get Eddie up there but he was working his way in the other direction, against the momentum of the masses.

'Eddie!' I called after him.

I watched him make for somebody who was standing stock still in the moving throng. A thickset man, swept-back hair, reminded me of someone but, so I thought at the time, only in the way so many of these dinosaurs do. A face, familiar. But the churchyard was full of them. I remember seeing a granite face break into a smile as he saw Eddie trying to reach him. And then his back turned and he was away. Eddie still tried to barge his way through in pursuit.

Shit.

The funeral party were filing into the church and I was losing sight of Eddie. Geoff called down to me.

'What's happening? Where's our bloke gone?'

'Stay there,' I said, mounting the stepladder. 'I'm coming up.'

'What? Wait a minute, I don't think this thing can hold the both of us.'

'Don't worry. Just hold on.'

I clambered up. The ladder creaked and teetered a bit but I made it to the top and grabbed hold of Geoff.

'Steady on, chief,' he complained.

I scanned the crowd. I could just make out the man Eddie was following. He was dodging around an outside broadcast van on the other side of St Matthew's Row. I pointed him out to Geoff.

'That bloke,' I said.

'Yeah?'

'Get him!'

The stepladder wobbled again as Geoff strained to get a good shot. He suddenly understood my urgency and let fly with a barrage of shots, his camera whirring like an angry cicada. I crouched down to steady the ladder for a second then stood up to see Eddie come into sight, emerging from the throng, looking around. I saw him catch sight of the man he was following and move towards him.

'There's Eddie,' I said to Geoff. 'Try and get them both together.'

The two men stood looking at each other for a moment and Geoff carried on clicking away. Then one of the funeral Daimlers moved slowly between them. When it had passed Eddie was alone. The other man had disappeared. Eddie looked around, then started making his way up towards Bethnal Green Road and we soon lost sight of him as well.

'What was all that about?' Geoff asked.

'I don't know. But it certainly isn't what was planned. Let's get off this thing before we break our necks.'

And we both got down.

'So, what do we do now, chief?' he asked.

I sighed.

'Don't know. Wait until it's over and there's people coming out. Might be able to get something then.'

I didn't have much confidence in that. Victor was going to be furious. The funeral service was in full swing. The strains of Frank Sinatra singing 'My Way' could be heard coming out of the church PA system.

When it was all over and the funeral procession, a vast column of Daimlers packed with recidivists, was on its way to Chingford Mount Cemetery, Eddie staggered back into the churchyard. He looked flustered and scant of breath.

'Well,' I declared, 'there goes our little photo opportunity.'

Eddie just looked at me blankly.

'Are you all right?' Geoff asked, looking up from packing his camera bag.

'Yeah, yeah,' he muttered. 'Look, I'm sorry, chaps.'

'Eddie, what the fuck was all that about?'

With a nod of the head he motioned for me to follow him off a bit, out of the earshot of Geoff and Piers. Eddie caught his breath.

'It was him,' he whispered, as if to himself. 'I'm sure of it.'

'What do you mean?'

'I mean, maybe that's what's been going on. Who's having me followed. It would make sense. He wants to know where all the missing gelt went too.'

'Will you just tell me what the hell you're talking about.'

'That bloke. The one I was chasing. It was Harry.'

'What?'

'Starks,' he hissed, his eyes wide and crazy. 'It was Harry fucking Starks.'

2
camp classic

The old, they say, find little fun in hoping.
Time's what they need, and time begins to press.
But for the young, they say, the gates are open.
They open, so they say, on nothingness.

Bertolt Brecht, *The Good Person of Szechwan*

Little Julie, aged ten, creeping out on to the landing, hearing gruff voices downstairs in the kitchen, thinking: maybe Dad's come back after all. Sitting on the stairs listening . . .

There she is.

There I am. In a dream. Well, not quite dreaming. Halfway between sleep and being awake, lucid but not yet conscious. A memory. I reach out to hold it, to know more, but motion becomes struggle, reverie turns into wilful thought.

And I wake up. Before I can work out what it meant. It was about Dad, that much was for sure.

Dad. I do miss him, even though I can hardly remember him at all. I didn't see much of him. He was away until I was seven. Inside. Visiting time didn't add up to much. Then when he did get out he was soon away again. Spain. *Timeshares*, that's what Mum told me he was doing out there. Not much time to share with me, though. Then he was gone for ever. And there was another little lie Mum had to make up. Another alibi. But I do miss him. And the worst thing is there's so little to hold on to. Just a big gap where he should have been. And all the memories tainted with badness.

You know how you can go through life with all these bad feelings, fears and doubts that you can't quite explain? Insecurities that nag at you and eat away at your confidence. You figure that it's just because you're neurotic. What was it that student counsellor had said? Yeah, you *internalise* all the things that have gone wrong in your life. You turn them in on yourself and make them all your own fault. And that eats away at you until you feel that you have to find out what is really to

25

blame for your unhappiness. The one thing that could make sense of all of these confused emotions. Something you could put a name to.

I'd buried Dad deep for a long time. The only way I had to deal with the shock of it was to pretend it had never happened. Pretending, that's what I did, Mum had always encouraged me to do that. It was her that had got me started with acting in the first place. She was projecting her own ambitions on me but it was also a way of us avoiding the truth. A dreamworld. And that's what I thought it was, like entering a world of other possibilities where you could become other people. Of course, when I went to drama school all of a sudden acting was supposed to be about reality, about channelling real feelings. We did what were called 'sense memory exercises' where you use recalled emotions to give truth to a performance. In one particularly intense session we were supposed, in turn, to relive a traumatic experience of our lives in front of everybody. Well, I couldn't do it. I just froze. I couldn't think about anything else except what I felt like when I found out about Dad and I couldn't go through the lies that I'd always used about what had happened to him. I just walked out of the class. The next day my acting teacher sent for me and went into this lecture about how an actor has to confront their demons in order to be any good. I would have to deal with whatever it was, he insisted, otherwise it would block me as a performer. He spoke to me in such a concerned tone that I was filled with dread, to be honest. When he suggested that I go and see the student counsellor I agreed more to reassure him than anything else. But I didn't tell her the truth either. Instead I used the story Mum had concocted all those years ago. And this counsellor woman talked about *bereavement* and *loss* and *closure* and all these modern words that made no sense to my ancient grief. She mentioned something called *recovered memory syndrome* which I didn't like the sound of at all. I went along with these sessions just to make everybody happy. Except me. Therapy was no good. I mean, where would that get me? But I did learn a new litany of terms that I could use to cover up what I really felt. And from then on I learnt to fake this internal stuff if I ever needed it.

I felt more at ease with the externals of acting, the technical side of things. Voice production particularly interested me at drama school. More than anything I wanted to be able to speak quite differently from Mum, to become quite a different person to the one my background had determined. And when I went about building a character I always approached it from the outside in rather than the other way around.

Maybe this inability to really let go in a part was the reason that I haven't been as successful as I might have been. Though it mostly seemed a matter of chance. Some of my peers went on to do really well after drama school, others hardly got any work at all. I've fallen somewhere in the middle, become what they call a 'jobbing actress,' and I seemed quite happy with that. I had a simple sense of purpose, I enjoyed what work I managed to get and I felt in control of my life.

I got depressed from time to time, especially between jobs – 'resting', some people call it, though it never feels like that. I think for a while I blamed Dad for this, or rather the lack of him. Him not being there. One great big negative that made it easier to block things out. But it wasn't his fault, not really. It was someone else. I knew that deep down. I had just spent so much of my life covering it all up.

And that was how I wanted it to be. I had reinvented myself as a confident young woman with middle-class manners. When I'd got enough acting contracts I applied for an Equity card with a new name, a stage name. Julie McCluskey became Julie Kincaid. I felt a bit guilty, getting rid of Dad's name like that, but I wanted to leave the past alone. And for a few years I felt quite free of it all.

Then it all started to come back. Lost memories clicking into place like a ratchet. I started having that dream

– well, that half-dream – in the mornings, just as I was coming up to the surface. About being little and hearing voices downstairs, talking about me. And something else happened.

The counsellor at drama school had once told me that traumatic memories could be sometimes triggered by quite unexpected stimuli. Some seemingly harmless detail in day-to-day life could suddenly throw you off balance.

I remember coming out of the Gate cinema in Notting Hill with Jez, I don't know, some time in the spring of 1995. We'd been to see *Pulp Fiction*. Jez was raving about it. It was a *bloody masterpiece*, he announced in that lazy drawl of his. I didn't really like it, but I didn't think that I was much bothered one way or another. But when he asked me what I thought I remember I said:

'I don't really like films with guns and gangsters in.'

I hardly thought about saying it, but once I had I suddenly felt very cold. Jez didn't notice I'd gone quiet. He was still talking about the film. He was never happier than when he was rattling on about a film he liked.

I hadn't been that impressed by it, or so I thought. It was smart and slick, a *bloody masterpiece* all right in that it was modern *grand guignol*. It was the audience's reaction that had been really perturbing. There was a great deal of laughter at the violence displayed. There were groans, too, but they sounded disturbingly like groans of disappointment. As if all the blood had not been enough.

But out in the street I realised that the subject of the movie had made an impact on me. Perhaps because of the very frivolousness of its treatment, which rendered cool something that I had a deep and painful fear of.

Guns and gangsters.

Dad. I'd spent all those years holding it together and now that stupid Tarantino movie had brought it all back. The horror of it all.

'Julie?' I heard Jez say my name, softly. It sounded distant. 'Are you OK?'

I turned and forced a smile. I didn't want Jez to know about it. I'd told him that Dad had been killed in a car crash. Not a hard lie to tell. It had been the official family line for years. What Mum had told me to tell people. I had only been ten at the time. Mum hid the newspapers from me. Told me not to take any notice of what people said. We didn't talk about it, not properly, so a lot of it got mixed up in my mind. Over the years, I'd just about got to believe it myself. But something had clicked, that was for sure. I knew then that I would have to go back over it and work out what had really happened. But I didn't want Jez to know about any of it, not yet.

'What's the matter?'

'I'm fine. Really.'

We were standing in the street looking at each other. There was something sweet in that little frown of concern beneath Jez's mop of blond hair. It meant that I could smile properly and look him in the eye.

'You're coming back to mine?' he asked.

'Yeah,' I replied. 'Sure.'

I'd been seeing Jez for about three months. We'd met on a short, no-budget film I had a part in and he was directing. It was his first real break. His *calling card*, he called it. He loved to think of himself as a struggling Young Turk. The fact was that he had contacts. He had worked as a runner in a film company owned by a friend of his father's. He'd done a few music videos. Now he was trying to get a screenplay together for a feature film but he was having trouble with it.

The strange thing was that Jez was as keen to cover up his background as I was mine. He had started to pick up this wide-boy demeanour, this silly fake cockney accent. He was quite good at it actually. I mean, he was a good mimic. But I knew what hard men were really like and he wasn't it. I think, in a way, that's what endeared me to him. There was something awfully vulnerable about the way he puffed himself up. He seemed utterly harmless and that's just what I wanted in a man. There was a sense of security I felt with him, something safe that I had always longed for.

He made a big thing of the fact that he had left school at sixteen. Public school, that is. While it had been quite a struggle for me to get into drama school. Mum hadn't wanted me to go, she'd thought that stage school was enough but it hadn't really taught me much except all the eyes and teeth show-business stuff. I'd got a speaking part in *Grange Hill* when I was fourteen and she'd been so chuffed, so happy to see me on the telly. But Mum's ambitions were never enough for me. I had wanted to be a proper actress, with classical training and received pronunciation. I didn't want to be stuck with an accent, the voice of my unhappy childhood. I wanted to escape in spite of all the teacher's talk about 'reality'. The real point of acting for me was the opportunity to be someone else. And it had worked, in that I could fool people. I mean, Jez took me for a well-bred girl. And although I hadn't been so lucky with actual jobs since drama school, I'd done small parts in a couple of plays at the Royal Court Upstairs, lots of profit-share fringe work. I'd got away, that was the main thing. I had made a break with my past. The thought of having to go back over it made me feel a bit sick. And frightened.

We got back to Jez's flat, the second storey of a Georgian house just off the Portobello Road. His father had bought it for him. He still had that quizzical look on his face as he opened a bottle of Chardonnay.

'Look,' he said, handing me a glass, 'what's up?'

'It's nothing, really.'

But my brain was bursting. I took a gulp of wine. His pale blue eyes stared into me. I sighed, relieved by the distraction of his prettiness. And he was pretty, much prettier than he was comfortable with. I suddenly felt that if I could summon up an urgent desire for him then I could stop thinking about anything else.

I kissed him on the mouth. My lips were cool, wet. I knew that I looked quite impressive. Long red hair that I'd inherited from Dad. A friend of Mum's once remarked that I looked like Maureen O'Hara. And my height, I got that from Dad too, he had been a big man. I was a couple of inches taller than Jez. He didn't seem to mind me towering over him; in fact, I was pretty sure that was one of the things he liked about me. He always liked me being on top when we had sex.

'What's this?' he said, still curious.

'I want you,' I murmured.

And I did. I wanted him. I wanted to empty my head of all the bad thoughts. To feel a simple bodily desire for life. To be in control of it.

'Yeah?' Jez whispered, his face close to mine.

'Yeah,' I breathed, all husky. 'Right now.'

We went into the bedroom. He let me take off his clothes and push him on to the bed. I stripped off and straddled him. I felt anger mingled with the desire and I clawed at him as I felt a wave of release come over me. Afterwards he touched the marks I had made on his chest. He sucked in a little breath.

'You hurt me,' he moaned.

And yes, there was hurt in those baby blue eyes of his. I smiled with cruel joy.

'I thought that's what you public schoolboys liked,' I taunted him.

'Leave it out,' he complained, sulkily. *Leave it out*, his fake vowels flat. He was such a give-away when he was angry.

And I felt another little jab of meanness inside of me. I was annoyed by how he imagined, in some way, that he was wider than me. I knew more than him and I never let on. I didn't have that weakness, that middle-class guilt. So whenever I felt that Jez was getting close to me, I mean close to finding out about my past, I would go on the offensive. Tease him about his own background.

'So what did you get up to in the dormitory?'

'What do you mean?'

At first I had thought there might be something gay about Jez. The way that he so desperately wanted to project this exaggerated masculinity. His obsession with hard men even though he was pretty and quite fey really. But it was more complicated than that.

'You know,' I went on, 'you and the other boys,'

Jez sat up in bed.

'Look,' he said, all indignant, 'I never . . .' He trailed off, not knowing the ending.

'Well, it must have gone on.'

'Yeah, well.'

'So didn't you ever . . . I mean, with another boy.'

Jez stared at me. His blue eyes had gone all steely.

'No,' he said, flatly.

'Not ever?'

'No.' He sighed. 'Never.'

It seemed such a definite. Such a definite sadness. Something else in his expression. Resentment. A wistful look suggesting that he had somehow missed out. That he lacked some knowledge, some sense of initiation. It was then that a thought occurred to me that almost made me laugh out loud, though I managed to restrain myself since I didn't want to hurt his feelings *that* much. I thought that maybe Jez was a public schoolboy who had been traumatised because he *hadn't* had a homosexual experience.

He found sleep sooner than I did. I lay there in the darkness, trying to empty my mind. Noises of street life outside harsh and malevolent. Exhaustion finally overwhelmed me but in the morning the half-dream came for me again.

Little Julie, aged ten, creeping out on to the landing, hearing gruff voices downstairs in the kitchen, thinking: maybe Dad's come back after all. Sitting on the stairs, listening. But it's not Dad. It's Dad's friends, those big friendly men who'd come to the house sometimes. Speaking low and soft, trying to calm down Mum who is angry and tearful.

'And what about Julie?' Mum is saying. 'I've had to tell her she can't go to stage school now.'

Little Julie blushing, hearing that they are talking about her. The low voices mutter something consoling. Little Julie gets up and tiptoes down the stairs . . .

A low thumping noise. Jez was already up and padding around the bedroom clumsily. I groaned.

'Sorry,' Jez whispered. 'Do you want a cup of tea?'

I groaned again and turned over in bed. I thought about the dream, tried to work out what happened next. But it was gone.

I took a shower and got dressed. Jez was in the front room tapping away at his laptop. He looked absorbed.

'You working on the screenplay?' I asked.

He hadn't written anything for weeks. He looked up and grinned, shook his head.

'Nah,' he said. 'I'm starting a new one.'

'What?'

'Yeah. And this time I think I've really got something.'

'Well, that's great.'

I had meant that to sound encouraging but it came out flat and bitter. Jez looked up and frowned.

'What's the matter?' he asked.

I sighed. I didn't want to talk to Jez about what was going on in my head.

'It's nothing. Sorry, I mean it. Everything's great.'

I gave him a big warm fake smile.

'I'll let you get on,' I said.

I went into the bedroom and called my agent. There was

an audition for a small theatre company doing a tour with a Brecht play. Equity minimum. I took down the details. Jez was still at it when I came back through.

'Look,' I said, going over to him, 'I'm going to get off.'

'OK,' he replied, hardly looking up.

He looked happy, occupied, his face held in childlike concentration, blue eyes twitching. I smiled for real this time and ruffled his blond hair.

'I'll see you,' I said, and kissed him on the cheek.

I went back to my flat and mooched about. Tried to busy myself. Put my CV up on the computer screen and tried to rearrange it so it looked convincing. After an hour or so it still read like a desperate alibi. I went through a new audition speech. Constance from *King John*. But I could distract myself only for so long. I knew what I had to do. Who I had to talk to.

Mum. I know so little about Dad but far too much about Mum. We know each other all too well. Her thwarted ambition foisted upon me at such an early age. She wanted me to be the person she could have been. If only. Expectations and disappointments were measured out through the years. And yet so little was said. Like there was vowed silence between us.

I knew that it wasn't going to be easy. I phoned to say that I was coming over, hoping that my voice would not betray that something was up. I didn't want her on the defensive.

'How's work?' she asked me, almost before I was through the door.

She always wanted to talk about work, about 'the business'. As long as I can remember this was what we talked about. Or rather, what she talked to me about. Ballet and tap classes almost as soon as I could walk. A fish-finger commercial when I was four, for God's sake. Always telling me to 'have a big smile and lots of personality' or whatever. I found out at stage school that I wasn't alone. Most of the girls there (and some of the boys too) had been propelled into 'the business' by pushy mothers. Frustrated women who'd never made it themselves. I always felt slightly guilty thinking of Mum in this way. She wanted so much for me, after all. And although I somehow knew that she was projecting her own desires on to me, I felt that I was being cruel and ungrateful if I didn't go along with it.

I told her about the auditition for the tour but she wasn't impressed.

'Do you really want to bother with that, darling?' she said. 'Nobody's going to see you in that.'

She was right, of course. A medium-scale tour of studio theatres and community art centres probably. I wasn't sure I wanted to do it myself. But maybe I needed the work more than ever now. Something to focus on that wasn't . . . well, wasn't all this stuff going on in my head about Dad. Acting had always been a refuge for me, I'd never cared much one way or the other about success as long as I could escape.

But she had this unreal notion that somewhere, just around the corner, was my big break. This, for her, meant television or film. In her mind theatre wasn't worth bothering about unless it was West End.

'I saw Ruby the other day,' she announced, proudly.

Ruby Ryder, she meant. I cringed a bit, embarrassed that my mother couldn't resist name-dropping, even with her own daughter, about someone who was, at best, a C-list celebrity. But they did go back. They'd met in the sixties when Mum had worked as a showgirl in a club in Soho. Well, a stripper really, not that she would ever quite admit to that.

'She's being considered for a big telly part. In a long-running series. It's all a bit hush-hush at the moment. She asked after you. You should go and see her. She might be able to help you, you know, casting directors and that.'

'Look, Mum, I really don't need any help.'

'Baby, you've got to take what breaks you can in this business. I should know.'

I felt an awful sense of panic that we'd end up going over her failed career, the breaks she'd never had. There was something she seemed to relish about her misfortunes, as if they formed some great tragic role for her. She indulged herself in regret. She'd talk about the struggle it had been to put me through stage school. The sacrifice she'd made. And I was supposed to redeem all of this somehow. She'd never seemed to understand what I wanted. I felt resentment and something else. Urgency. I just didn't want us to end up having the same old conversation.

'I want to talk about something else, Mum.'

'What do you mean, something else?'

'I mean something other than the business.'

'Fine,' she said petulantly.

I had wanted to ease gently into this somehow. In the end I couldn't help just blurting it out.

'I want to talk about Dad.'

Her eyes widened. I cursed myself inwardly for being so brusque.

'Oh,' she said, with a sigh of disappointment. 'Oh.'

Oh, the big O. I knew then that I had sod-all chance of getting much out of her. Her face froze over and I went from resentment right back to guilt again. I knew how much she'd suffered. How much she'd had to hold in all these years.

'Sorry, Mum, it's just . . .'

I didn't know what to say. She lit a menthol cigarette and let the smoke sigh out in a long stream.

'Oh, love,' she moaned. 'What do you want to know?'

'Well, you know, about what happened.'

The awkwardness was almost unbearable. This had been a big mistake. Mum's lips trembled. She sucked on the pith of the cigarette hungrily. Smoke hissed in. Out.

'You mean about . . .'

'Yes. About.'

About. It had always been *about.*

'About him being killed,' I said.

There, I'd said it. Mum just stared at me.

'Julie, please,' she chided, as if I'd said something rude.

'It's just we've never really talked about it.'

'But what good . . .'

'Mum.'

'I mean, I'm sorry, I know I should have . . .'

'Don't.'

'I know, I know. But you were so little. I wanted to protect you from it all. I wanted . . .'

There was a catch in her voice. A little forlorn sob. Her eyes brimmed with tears.

'I only . . . only . . .' she stammered, throatily. 'I only wanted the best for you.'

'Mum, please don't cry.'

I got up and went to her, held her as she quivered with grief. I spent the next hour or so calming her down. Eventually she was done and I talked of other things, changed the subject. While I had been comforting her all I could feel was a frustration that she wouldn't talk to me about what I needed to know. But when all of that was done, after all the mascara-streaked smiles and fake happy goodbyes, when I left the house to go back to my flat, my feelings changed into something quite different. A slow-burning anger inside me at how both our lives had been ruined.

Dad. What could I remember myself? Jock McCluskey. 'Big Jock', that's what everyone called him. A big man with a soft rough voice. Smooth and abrasive at the same time, like sandpaper. Singing to me gently as he tucked me in. 'Strangers in the Night' in a thick Glasgow accent. *Do be do be do.*

Away. Inside. Vague memories of prison visits. The smell mostly. And all the clattering noise of confinement. Mum and Dad talking across the table. Him winking at me, calling me 'princess'.

The rest was keeping up appearances. Me and Mum putting on a brave front. Blotting out things even back then.

Then he came out and there was a big party. I do remember that. I was seven so it must have been 1977. The function room above a pub. Tables laden with sandwiches and booze. Me in a party dress with my long red hair up. Lots of well-dressed men with big hands covered in jewellery, smiling down at me.

Uncle Tam down from Glasgow. Feather-cut hair and huge lapels on his suit jacket. CODY tattooed on the knuckles of his right hand.

'Who's Cody?' I asked him.

'Come On Die Young.' He spelled it out, his voice warm and gruff like Dad's, holding up the inked letters on his battered fist for inspection.

Dad out on parole. Straight life. Going out to work during the day. Always coming home late. Sometimes not coming home for days on end. Mum and Dad arguing at night. I thought they were going to split up or something.

But then Spain happened. Dad went away to Spain on business. He came back with pictures of the villa. He went back after only about a week. Dad lives in Spain now, I remember thinking. In a villa in Marbella. Me and Mum went over there in the school holidays. A big white building, a tower with inlaid coloured glass. Pink marble floors and Moroccan wall hangings. A stone fireplace with a driftwood sculpture above it. Wrought-iron gates at the end of the drive. A fairy-tale castle. Blue skies. Happy holiday memories, bright and clear as home-movie colour film. *Dad works in timeshares*, that's what Mum told me. *Timeshare*. Back and forth through Málaga airport. Our place in the sun. It seemed to work out, Mum seemed happy enough. A new routine. A timeshare life.

Diving into the swimming pool. Showing off for Dad. Breaking the still, turquoise water. Feeling the cool silence as I came to the surface in a perfect arc. I loved that swimming pool. The . . . oh Christ, yes. The pool. Diving into the past, falling. I'd forgotten that. No, the swimming pool. Dad falling . . .

The swimming pool. They found Dad face down in it. His blood diffusing from the bullet wounds. Turning the water pink.

We were back home when it happened. Crowds outside the house. Cameras with huge lenses. The press. Mum tried to shield me from it all. Hiding me from it all. Keeping the newspapers from me. But, shit, yes, I remember it now. That headline in the *Sunday Illustrated* that I managed to sneak a glance at: *GANGLAND SLAYING IN SPAIN. 'Big Jock' shot in Marbella.*

It was all too much. Memories after this point are memories of trying to block things out. News hounds and strange messages we got in the post or through the letter box. Anonymous phone calls. *Your dad was a grass*, somebody hissed once when I picked up the receiver. Mum disconnected the phone. And everything else. We moved house. She went through what we were to tell people about ourselves. We rehearsed it, we got our story straight.

Then later on, the night when I heard the voices downstairs. The gruff voices of men like my dad. The dream I keep having. It meant something. And it wasn't just about Dad. It was about Mum too. And me, something about me going to stage school.

I just felt so exhausted. Too many memories flooding back. My head was bursting and I needed to talk to someone. I just couldn't think who.

I still couldn't talk to Jez about it. I still didn't want him to know the truth about my past. I wasn't quite sure why. But I suppose I just wanted to hold it all together for as long as possible. I was scared of what I was now facing up to and there seemed certainty in deception. If I could carry on fooling Jez at least I would be in control of that. And I needed to be sure of something.

The bizarre thing was that Jez was becoming more and more fake wide boy with every passing day. It was all to do with the screenplay he was working on. That Tarantino film had really set him off. A 'classic British gangster movie', that's what he said he was working on, and he'd got a writing partner now, Piers, a journalist friend of his. Piers claimed to have met some real 'faces' in the line of duty. He was a serious coke-head as well so, like most of the London media world, it seemed, he had a recreational link with organised crime. But Jez's research was more corporeal. The barrow-boy voice and the cocky little swagger started to take him over. Though with his cherubic face and, well, his *gentleness*, this was all a bit contradictory. He was trying to toughen himself up, working out at the gym, going to Thai boxing classes, but it couldn't alter the essential fact of himself. That he was a nice, well-brought-up young man. Which is what I loved him for. This yobbishness was all a bit silly, but harmless, playful. I didn't like it when he and Piers started hanging out with a drug dealer friend who took them to dodgy pubs and drinking clubs. For research purposes, Jez insisted, though it was easy to tell that he was excited by it all. Not that I worried about him getting into drugs, Jez was far too clean cut for that. I just didn't want him to get into trouble.

And I would feel a little left out when I was with Piers and Jez. They would go into this routine, repeating lines of dialogue at each other. It could be infuriating but boys will be boys. Once they started bantering about me, calling me a 'posh bird'. Well, I nearly lost it that time.

And I thought, well, that's ironic. Not that I was certain that my predicament conformed to the rules of irony. It was just that word seemed to be everywhere at the time. Piers was always using it. He worked for *Sorted*, a new glossy magazine for men. For the 'new lad', that was the new market niche, apparently. Along with football and fast cars there was the usual timid soft porn. But it was deliberately tacky, Piers insisted, it was 'ironic sexism'. It was a joke, he explained. I didn't get it.

But maybe that was it, my situation was a joke, it was just part of all this 'ironic humour' that was so fashionable. But it didn't feel comic. It felt tragic. Jez was quite different when he was alone with me, sensitive, affectionate, but I couldn't talk to him about what I was going through. Not until I felt strong enough about it myself. But his current obsession didn't exactly help.

I needed to talk to someone. Someone who would have some idea of what I had been through. There was Joe Patterson, an actor I knew from when I'd worked at the Royal Court. Joe's dad had been a serious South London villain. Joe had had a lot of success in the late seventies and early eighties, he'd played the lead in the punk film *Borstal Breakout* in 1979, but he'd not had much work since. There were rumours that he'd been following in the family business. I'd already suggested him to Jez and Piers for their film project. Some of the Royal Court lot loved the fact that he knew real criminals and he'd indulge them with all sorts of stories, but he was always discreet when it came to me. He knew about my past but kept quiet about it, which I appreciated. Joe never really talked to me directly about my dad or anything, he knew that I wanted to keep shtum about that, but I always felt that he understood somehow. I got to know him fairly well but we lost touch after the run. But that's always the way with the acting business. The business and the other business. They had a lot in common in some ways. A lot of people I knew had one foot in each of them.

I'd really messed up with Mum. If only I'd spent more time listening to her instead of jumping in with 'I want to talk about Dad'. She'd wanted to talk, after all. What had she been going on about? Oh yeah, Ruby. Ruby Ryder. Well, there's one for you, I thought. And then I realised that there was someone I could talk to after all. Ruby Ryder.

> I am not mad: this hair I tear is mine;
> My name is Constance; I was Geoffrey's wife;
> Young Arthur is my son; and he is lost.
> I am not mad; I would to God I were,
> For then 'tis like I should forget myself.
> O, if I could, what grief should I forget!

Sometimes you know when you've got them, when the speech you are doing is absolutely captivating them. The most difficult thing about any audition is that you are taking something out of context, a speech that in performance would have the whole play to build up the intensity that it needs. But in an audition you have to do it cold and usually in some God-forsaken church hall at eleven o'clock in the morning. But I wasn't cold. I was burning. I was channelling all the stuff that had been going on in my head the last few days into Constance from *King John*. This was sense memory all right, I had grief down pat. And it was working, I could tell. I had them.

Red Rag was a feminist theatre company that had been set up in the seventies. They had had a good reputation but were now in decline. Their Arts Council grant was due to be cut and they would have to apply to the Lottery instead. Radical theatre was a thing of the past.

They were doing a production of Brecht's *The Good Woman of Szechwan*, three weeks' rehearsal, six months touring. I was tempted to point out that *Der Gute Mensch von Sezuan* translated more correctly as The Good Person (or even the Good Soul) of Szechwan, and that to apply a gender could be misleading. But this could have stirred up some pointless debate about sexual politics, and besides, I was being very working class with this lot, instinctive rather than intellectual. I knew that would go down well with them (I found myself talking like Mum). But I did know the play. I'd done Brecht at drama school. And I liked it, especially the part I was up for, the lead, a good-natured prostitute, Shen Te, who pretends to be her own ruthless male cousin in order to protect herself from people who take advantage of her kindness.

I somehow had a soft spot for Red Rag too, although they did seem a little ridiculous. Out of date. A bit humourless and worthy, despite their name. Piers would have deemed them an 'irony-free zone'. But they stood for something, which was becoming very unfashionable these days. Maybe it was a sense of a lost cause that I had an affinity with. They told me they'd let me know the next day. Did I want the job? I wasn't sure.

'And what about Julie?' Mum is saying. 'I've had to tell her she can't go to stage school now.'

Little Julie blushing, hearing that they are talking about her. The low voices mutter something consoling. Little Julie gets up and tiptoes down the stairs.

Walking into the kitchen in her pyjamas. Mum and a lot of grim-faced men sitting around the table. They don't notice her at first. Then one of the rough faces lights up.

'Aw,' he goes. 'Here she is.'

'Aww,' they all go, smiling down at her.

Julie does a few ballet steps, lifting up for a pirouette. The men clap and laugh.

I met Ruby Ryder for lunch at Elena's on Charlotte Street. Ruby was half an hour late. She swept in looking a bit wild about the eyes but still managing to radiate charisma. I stood up to greet her.

'I'm sorry, love,' she said, kissing me on both cheeks. 'I've had a hell of a morning.'

Her trademark blonde hair looked immaculate, cut in a simple bob. Probably a wig but you really couldn't tell. She let a waiter take her topcoat. She wore a skirt suit with large pink and black checks. Gold buttons and lots of jewellery.

'Gerry Wilman's croaked,' she explained as she sat down. 'Found him in his flat yesterday. Dead as a doornail. An overdose, apparently.'

Gerald Wilman was a comedian, famous for his long-running radio series *How's Your Father?* and much TV work. Ruby had done a film with him, *A Bird in the Hand*, back in the sixties.

'Had the press and the TV on the phone all morning wanting some fucking eulogy. I'm sorry, love, I'm all wound up by it. I can't even remember what I said.'

The waiter handed her a menu. She stared at it blankly for a moment then looked up again.

'I mean, what is there to say? Gerry, I mean, I loved him to death and everything but he was a bitter old queen really. Sad and lonely. Sorry, I'm in a bit of a state. I've had to say about a hundred times what a marvellous performer he was, a warm person and all that shit. Well, he ain't warm any more.'

She started a chuckle that ended in a groan.

'Maybe this isn't a good time,' I said.

'Don't be stupid. It's lovely to see you.' She looked at the menu again. 'You know what you're having? Good, let's order now then we can talk.'

A smile and a slight nod of her head brought the waiter over. He took our orders and then Ruby leaned across the table slightly.

'So, you working?'

My agent had phoned that morning to say that Red Rag had offered me the tour. I told Ruby about it. I still wasn't sure whether I was going to take it.

'Do you want to do it?'

'I like the part, yeah.'

'Then do it, darling.'

'But I'll be out of London for six months and playing places where no one's going to see me.'

'Then don't do it.'

She grinned at me.

'Sorry, Ruby, I know, I've got to decide myself.'

'I know what it's like, you get to your mid-twenties and nothing's really happened yet and you start to worry. But there's nothing you can do about it. You never know what will come up. All that trashy stuff I did in the sixties, that film with Gerry, that stuff's getting me work now. They're calling it "camp classic".'

She shrugged.

'What goes around, comes around,' she declared, picking up a piece of bread.

'Mum says you're up for a big TV part.'

'Yeah, well, she should have kept her trap shut. It's all touch and go and I'm supposed to keep quiet about it. I think they're worried about my past. My first husband, Eddie, he's out of prison and he's selling his bloody story, isn't he? It's all I bloody need. I tried talking to him but there's something up with him. Seeing ghosts or something. Reckons he saw Harry Starks at Ronnie Kray's funeral—'

Ruby's butter knife clattered to the floor. She sat stock still for a moment, staring.

'Sorry,' she muttered. 'I didn't mean to bring up . . .' She trailed off, slowly gesturing with the piece of bread. '. . . all that.'

That name. I hadn't heard it in years, but I'd always known it. Off by heart. Newspaper reports that Mum tried to hide from me: *Starks, the double murder suspect in the 'Costa del Crime' killings* . . . A name always whispered, just out of earshot. Harry Starks. He was the one that . . .

'Anyway, as I was saying,' Ruby continued nervously.

He was the one that killed Dad.

'No, Ruby, that's just it. That's what I want to talk about.'

'What?'

'The past.'

'The past?' She frowned at me.

Yes, I thought, the past. I want it back. Starks. He was the one that took it all away from me.

'I want to know about Dad,' I said, flatly.

'Jock? He was a lovely fellah. Really lovely. A real gentleman. Some of those stories in the press, you know, they really exaggerated.'

'Please, Ruby,' I broke in.

'What?'

'I don't want a bloody alibi. I know Dad did bad things. But I want to know the truth. So much has been messed around in my head about it. Mum won't talk about it. But it's driving me crazy. I keep having this dream and I can't work it out.'

'Well, you've got a right to know about these things,' Ruby said. 'But be careful, dear. It's all . . .'

'I want to know, Ruby. About all of it. I want my life back.'

'What?' She frowned at me again.

I couldn't explain what I meant.

'Just tell me what you know,' I said.

'Where do you want me to start?' Ruby shrugged.

'I don't know. The beginning, I suppose.'

'Well, Jock was with Harry Starks' firm when your mum was working at the Stardust Club. That was Harry's club. That's how they met.'

'When Mum was a stripper?'

'Yeah, well.' Ruby shrugged. 'It was a revue-style show. It wasn't obscene.'

'And she got pregnant with me and they got married.'

'Well, that's being a bit blunt. Your dad was quite a charmer, you know.'

'But it was all a bit of a rush, wasn't it?'

'Well . . .' Ruby sighed. 'Jock was on remand by then. I remember the wedding. Brixton Register Office. He was handcuffed to the biggest copper they could find from the Serious Crime Squad.'

The sad beginning of my existence, I thought. Barely legitimate. Dad being taken away when I was still *in utero*. Then taken away for good. By him.

'So, why did Harry Starks kill my dad?' I demanded.

Ruby flinched slightly.

'Julie, I . . .'

'I need to know, Ruby.'

'I don't know, love. Business. Your dad was looking after Harry's money through business deals in Spain. Something went wrong.'

'Something went wrong? Business? Christ, Ruby, you make it sound like an administrative error or something.'

Ruby squirmed in her seat a bit.

'Well . . .'

'Just tell me,'

'Harry Starks was very, very heavy. So was your father, for that matter. They were bad times, Julie. Things got messed up. There was this bent copper, Mooney. Now he was a really nasty piece of work. It was horrible.'

She was hunched over now, as if she were going into herself somehow, trembling slightly.

'Ruby?'

A shaky hand came across the table and held on to mine.

'I'm sorry love. I've seen some bad things myself, you know.'

'Tell me.'

'Nah, I can't talk about some of it. Look,' she said, glancing up at me, pulling herself together, 'I don't know what happened between Harry Starks and your dad. I know that something was settled with your mum afterwards.'

'What?'

'I don't know any more. Sorry. I'm in a bit of a state. What with Gerry dying and everything. I'm still in shock.'

She was holding something back, I felt sure of it.

'You know what the worst thing was about Gerry?' she

went on, carefully changing the subject. 'He was dead two days before they found him. It was only because a neighbour noticed a funny smell coming from his flat. Isn't that terrible? Him a household name and all.'

I thought about asking her more about Dad's death but I left it at that. It was about as much as I could hope to get out of her for now anyway. And more than enough for me to think about.

'Ladies?'

It was the waiter arriving with our orders. Ruby suddenly had her for-the-public smile. All eyes and teeth.

I left the restaurant with a peculiar sense of relief. The unspeakable had been spoken and maybe I could now start to make sense of things. It was him, he was the answer to it all. Mum would never allow that name to be uttered. It had been a secret word for me, a curse that I'd never completely known the meaning of. I'd spent so much of my life turning hatred on to myself, carrying around an absurd sense of guilt about what had happened to my family. Now I felt the beginnings of a kind of calculation. The deep sense of loss I had always felt, the emptiness, well, I had a name for it now. Harry Starks. This was something to focus my anger on. This could be a way of sorting myself out, dealing with some of my neurotic and insecure feelings. I would have to find out more, remember more. And maybe I could start to work out what the dream meant. Then what? I didn't know.

So other decisions came more easily. I took the Red Rag tour. I certainly needed something to concentrate on so I wouldn't just explode. I needed to work or I would go crazy.

The first day of rehearsals was the following Monday. I still hadn't told Jez about the job. About the fact that I would be away for six months. After all the introductions, the director gave a short speech about the production then we settled down to the first read-through.

The Good Woman of Szechwan is a parable. The gods come down to earth searching for a truly good person (unless they can find one the world cannot continue to exist), but of all the people of Szechwan, only Shen Te, a prostitute, offers them shelter. She is rewarded with money with which she buys a small tobacco shop.

But when news of her good fortune spreads a whole horde of parasites, would-be relatives and creditors, descend upon the shop. To protect herself, Shen Te assumes the personality of a ruthless male cousin, Shui Ta, a tough and implacable young man who drives away all those who prey on the goodness of Shen Te.

Back as Shen Te, she falls in love with an out-of-work pilot who is only after her money. She loses her money, and him, but it is only when she realises that she is pregnant that she takes action. Back comes the bad cousin Shui Ta to sort things out again, utterly pitiless where Shen Te has been the soul of generosity. When Shui Ta is accused of killing Shen Te (she has been missing for such a long time suspicions are aroused), there is a trial in which the gods act as magistrates. Shen Te finally reveals that the bad Shui Ta and herself are one and the same person. Only under the guise of greed and cruelty can the good person of Szechwan hope to provide for herself and her unborn child. For the good cannot live in our world and stay good.

The gods depart, content that the one good person they found still exists. When Shen Te confronts them they evade the issue; somehow, they insist, she will manage. The epilogue implores the audience to make its own happy ending; a world in which the good cannot survive without becoming bad must be changed.

After the read-through the designer showed us a model of the set we were going to tour with. Then we broke for lunch.

I met up with Jez at the end of the day. He was having a

drink with Piers at the Atlantic Bar in Piccadilly. On the way there I remembered something Ruby had said: *something was settled with your mum afterwards.* What the hell could that mean?

I had the play to think about now as well. The good woman Shen Te becoming the bad man Shui Ta, that had a sense of foreboding about it. Memories of the past had made me feel weak and vulnerable. In the future I would have to find strength from somewhere. I would have to become bad, I thought, without really knowing what that could mean.

When I arrived at the bar, Jez and Piers were having martinis. Piers was holding forth, speaking very quickly in a confident manner. Coke talk, obviously. As I joined them and Jez stood up to kiss me, Piers seemed to lose his flow.

'Ah.' He nodded in my direction. 'Julie, we were just . . . what were we talking about?'

Jez laughed and shook his head.

'All right, babe?' he murmured to me.

'Yeah,' I said. 'I've got some good news.'

'That's great,' said Jez.

'Well, good news and bad news.'

Piers stood up.

'Er, just got to powder my nose,' he said, and wandered off.

'He should really go easy, you know,' I told Jez.

'Yeah.' Jez shrugged. 'I guess. So, what's the good news?'

'I've got a job.'

'What?'

'You know, a part.'

'That's fabulous. What is it? TV or film?'

'It's theatre.'

'Oh.'

The conversation suddenly fell flat. Despite Jez's very expensive middle-class education and upbringing he seemed entirely unscathed by bourgeois values. He had absolutely no interest in the theatre. He loved popular culture. That was what he wanted to understand.

'That's really good,' he added quickly, trying to summon up as much enthusiasm as he could.

He smiled and kissed me again. I liked the way he always tried to be sweet to me, tried to show interest, even if there was none. He was the sort of boy you could take home to your mum but I'd never done that. If he met my mum, well, that would give the game away.

Piers re-emerged rubbing at his nose and sniffing. His pupils were like pencil leads. He came up behind Jez.

'I've put money in your pockets,' he announced in a *faux* East End drawl. 'Even when you was out of order. Well, now there's been an eruption!'

Jez poked him in the stomach.

'You're a big man,' he replied. 'But you're out of shape. With me it's a full-time job. Now behave yourself.'

And they both burst into laughter.

When we got back to his flat I felt light hearted. For the whole evening I'd managed to forget about everything. I still had something to tell Jez, though.

'You haven't asked me what the bad news is yet,' I said.

'What?'

'I told you I had good news and bad news. I haven't told you the bad news.'

'Oh.' (I bet he thought that the bad news was that it was a theatre job.) 'What is it?' he asked.

'It's a tour. I'm going to be away for six months.'

'Shit,' he said.

'Yeah, I know.' I shrugged. 'It's work. Come here.'

He moved close to me.

'You won't be getting rid of me yet, you know. We've got three weeks of rehearsal first.'

'Good,' he said, and kissed me on the mouth.

'Hold me,' I said.

He put his arms around me.

'I'll miss you,' he said.

Yeah, I thought, *you will. You'll hardly know me. But just hold me for now*. I felt Jez's body. His muscles were firmer and more defined than when I'd first known him. He was hardening up, on the outside. All that exercise and weight training. But I was hardening up inside.

Little Julie gets up and tiptoes down the stairs.

Walking into the kitchen in her pyjamas. Mum and a lot of grim-faced men sitting around the table. They don't notice her at first. Then one of the rough faces lights up.

'Aw,' he goes. 'Here she is.'

'Aww,' they all go, smiling down at her.

Julie does a few ballet steps, lifting up for a pirouette. The men clap and laugh. Mum turns and smiles. Her eyes are red.

'It's all right, Julie,' she says. 'It's going to be all right.'

'Yeah.' One of the battered faces looms down at her. 'You're gonna be a star, darling.'

I woke up with a start and woke Jez up too.

'What's the matter?' he muttered.

'Nothing,' I said. 'Just a bad dream.'

I sat up in bed and thought about it again. About Dad, about Mum. About me going to stage school. I remembered something.

'Hey,' said Jez, trying to pull me back under the covers.

I pushed him back. I had to think.

'Go back to sleep,' I told him.

After Dad died, Mum had told me that I couldn't go to stage school, that we couldn't afford it now, and I remembered that I'd felt relieved. I knew that I really should have felt disappointed, like Mum was, but I wasn't. I didn't have to take all of that seriously any more, that's what I had felt. I could just be a normal girl, go to a normal school.

I got up, showered and got ready to go to work. I had to think about that now. But I was distracted. *Something was settled with your mum afterwards*, that's what Ruby had said.

The second day of rehearsals and we were going through the Prologue, where the gods have come down to Szechwan and Shen Te has given them refuge. There is a bit of comic business where the gods offer payment to Shen Te for her hospitality. The joke is the embarrassment of the Illustrious Ones being seen giving money to a prostitute. I didn't have any lines but I remember where we were in the script:

> THE FIRST GOD, *awkwardly, to Shen Te:* We understand that you have no money to pay for the rent. We are not poor people, so it is natural that we should pay for our lodging. Here you are. *He gives her money.* But please let nobody know that we paid. It might be misinterpreted.
> THE SECOND GOD: Only too easily!

'What do you want me to do?' I asked the director

'Just stand there and take the money,' she said.

So I stood there as the gods went through their exchange and it suddenly hit me. The money. That was what the dream was all about. The money.

It hadn't come from heaven. *They* had paid for me. The gruff-voiced men downstairs. *He* had paid. Starks. The man who had killed my dad. That was what was *settled*. And Mum had taken it. Blood money.

I can't remember much of the rest of the day. I kind of walked through it, in character, thank God. But as soon as it was over I knew what I had to do, who I had to see.

Mum. All that bullshit about 'sacrifice'. All that guilt-tripping, years of betrayal. This time we really would talk.

'Who paid for me to go to stage school?' I demanded almost as soon as we'd sat down.

'What?'

'You heard. Who paid?'

'Well, I did, of course.'

'No you didn't.'

'What do you mean, Julie? I can show you the check stubs if you like.'

'Where did you get the money?'

'Look, Julie, love . . .'

'You took money from them, didn't you?'

'Please.'

'No. I'm sick of being good little Julie. For you. For them. I want to know the truth.'

'OK.'

She lit a cigarette, her nicotine-stained fingers fumbled with the lighter. Her eyes started to well up.

'I'm sorry darling,' she said. 'I just wanted . . .'

'Don't start all this, Mum.'

'What?'

'All this I'm sorry, I only wanted the best for you. I only wanted you to have the breaks I never got. I'm fucking tired of it, Mum. I just want to know. I just want what's mine.'

'What's yours?'

'Yes. Mine. My fucking life.'

'What do you mean, dear?'

'I mean it's all been taken away from me, hasn't it?'

She stared at me, baffled.

'Oh, it doesn't fucking matter,' I snapped. 'Just tell me what happened.'

'Your father didn't leave us with very much when he died. The timeshare business, well, that was just a front. I didn't have any money coming in and I had you to look after.'

'So you took money from the man who killed Dad?'

'Well, not him directly, of course. But some of his, you know, business associates, they . . .'

'You bitch,' I cut in coldly.

'What else was I supposed to do?'

I stood up to leave.

'Julie, please, you've got to understand.'

'You fucking bitch,' I said, and walked out.

Seething, I was seething with rage. I got back to my flat and it was all I could do not to smash the whole place up. *Bitch, bitch, bitch*, went through my head for hours. But that wasn't it. I was seething but it boiled down to something else. It would take me a long time to forgive Mum but I couldn't hate her, I couldn't blame her. In a way what I felt towards her was a sense of release. I was free of any guilt now. And it wasn't her fault. *What else was I supposed to do?* she had said. What she had done wasn't right, but it was for the best, in the only way she could understand. No, my seething boiled down to something else. Someone else. Starks. It was his fault, he had taken away Dad and determined the course of my life, he had paid for me to go through stage school, made me what I had become. I had no choice but then neither had Mum; that was all she knew, after all. I could have been a normal girl. But I wasn't. I was a fucked-up actress full of rage. And it would all turn in on me if I wasn't careful. And I had to get on top of this otherwise it would destroy me. I had to understand it, try to work it through somehow.

I briefly thought about trying therapy or counselling again. Maybe there was a talking cure that could mend some of the damage that had been done to my life. But I was hardly convinced of that. At least I could concentrate on work, on the only thing that I had ever really known, on performance.

I was trying to develop the physicality of my character. Of how Shen Te becomes Shui Ta. A woman becoming a man. Posture, the way she held himself as him. The walk, the gestures, the arrogance. How a hard man moves. I remembered Joe Patterson, at the Royal Court, talking about 'shaping up', the display of aggression, the assertion of power that is often the defining moment in conflict. I had a long way to go. In rehearsals I'd only managed a kind of comic swagger, which got a few laughs but wasn't what I wanted. I'd tried to move like Dad but ended up looking like Jez. He was another male impersonator, after all. I'd have to do better than that.

And I was too busy to see much of Jez. He was hard at work, too. When we were together he'd tell me about the screenplay and I'd nod and grin. It sounded pretty stupid but I didn't want to be discouraging. I was more concerned about the 'research' he was doing with Piers. Collecting characters and stories that 'had an edge', as they put it, as if reality for them existed *in extremis*. They went on about 'authenticity', whatever that was supposed to mean. They had talked to 'real villains' and believed every word they'd said, which seemed a very foolish policy indeed from what I knew. Of course, I was worried about them getting close to my own past. I would have to tell Jez some time but now, more than ever, I needed to keep it all close to my chest. But I did wish that they would realise how horrible and brutal that world really was. They saw the glamour not the ugliness. And I didn't trust Piers. His cocaine-fuelled bravado would get them out of their depth if they weren't careful.

And I felt compelled now to do my own research on the subject. I found a couple of well-thumbed paperbacks on Jez's desk. *The Profession of Violence: The Rise and Fall of the Kray Twins* and *London Underworld*. True crime books. I picked up *London Underworld* and looked through it. There were photographs in the middle. Blurred black-and-white shots of men like the ones that were in the kitchen in my dream. There was an index. I looked up Dad. *McCluskey, 'Big Jock,' 201, 203, 207.* I looked up the last entry.

Then, on 5 December 1979, 'Big-Jock' McCluskey was found dead in the swimming pool of his villa in Marbella. He had been shot in the chest. The next day, in nearby Llanos de Nagueles, retired Detective Superintendent George Mooney was shot dead on the balcony of his house. A ballistics report indicated that the same gun was used to kill both men. Although both murders remain officially unsolved by the Spanish police the main suspect for them has always been Harry Starks, who is still on the run after his spectacular escape from Brixton Prison that year.

McCluskey was, of course, part of his firm for many years. George Mooney took early retirement from the Met in 1973 having received numerous commendations during his service, though there were rumours that Mooney was part of the 'firm within a firm' of corrupt police officers . . .

I checked all the other references but Dad was just listed with others, just part of a litany of villains. I dropped the book back on to the desk. It was all laid out with such detachment. My father in this cheap history. Men. Bang bang you're dead. Never mind what happened to their families. It was all here, the 'truth', True Crime in black and white. But there was a surprising amount of information in these kinds of books about Harry Starks. Part of me wanted to obliterate that name from my mind but another part of me was fascinated. I started to study him, I even began making notes. I became obsessed by him, wanting to find out everything I could. Ruby had said that her ex-husband Eddie had seen him recently, at Ronnie Kray's funeral of all places. The thought of his presence made me uneasy. There were simple feelings of fear but something else that I couldn't fathom, a sense of excitement, of expectation

We were coming up to the last week of rehearsals, getting to that stage when the production starts to crawl, blinking, into the light. It's a nerve-racking time for a company. All the major decisions have been made and if you haven't got something by then it's unlikely that any amount of reworking is going to save it. We did a first run-through. It was laborious but it was coming together. All the elements other than the acting were being put in place. Costumes were being made, the set was being built. Music and songs were worked into the play. It was an ensemble piece and there was an atmosphere of intense collaboration. It gave an illusion of belonging to something and that was comforting in a way.

Part of me remained distant, though, from the rest of the group. I had a selfish sense of concentration on my role. A ruthlessness about it that I felt the other actors must have noticed, though nobody said anything. I had got Shui Ta now. I had broken through the comic effect of a woman pretending to be a man and found something convincingly dangerous. Bits of costume helped, and he now had a manner and deportment of flamboyant callousness. I could understand why Jez and Piers could get obsessed with a person like this. The sense of power, the lack of conscience. I knew who I was playing now, who my subject was. It was him, of course. It was Harry Starks.

I still had a way to go with Shen Te but I was getting there. I found that I had really made a breakthrough with my acting work on this job. I had finally achieved some sort of deep engagement with a character, an emotional truth I had never hitherto thought possible. Of course, it was hardly Brechtian, full of passion and an insistence on empathy that he had always railed against. But I didn't care. I had put something into practice, eked something out of my sad, sorry experience. At times I felt a cold fear that he, Starks, had become my motivation, along with all the other unwarranted menaces he had subjected me to. I couldn't avoid that terrifying fact but I tried not to think about it, intellectualise it or follow any implications from it. It worked, that was all that mattered, and my role could soar above all the fears and doubts I had. It was something I could use.

And there was a sort of happiness in my work. I felt that it was the best thing I'd ever done and I was looking forward to getting into theatres with it. I was even confident enough to bully some casting directors to come and see it when it came back to London.

I'd be out of town for a few months but, looking at the schedule, I figured that I'd be able to make it back for some weekends. And maybe I'd be able to get my career going a bit. I was in control again and had a clear sense of purpose, of calm occupation. Then something awful happened.

I was in bed asleep when I got the phone call. It was about 3 a.m. Saturday morning.

'Er, Jules, um, is that you?'

It was Piers. He sounded out of it as usual. But nervous. I tried to clear my head of sleep.

'What's the matter?' I murmured.

'Look, you better get over here, it's Jez.'

'What's happened. Where are you?'

'Er, Casualty, St Thomas's.'

'Shit. He's had an accident?'

'Yeah, um, something like that. He's going to be all right. Can you come over?'

I got dressed and called a minicab. Piers was outside reception, having a cigarette.

'It's all right,' he said. 'He's being seen to.'

'What do you mean? What the fuck's happened?'

'He's just had to have a few stitches.'

'Oh, Christ. What's he gone and done?'

'Well . . .' He gave a horrible, nervous giggle. 'It was mad. It all happened so quickly. It all just kicked off.'

'You got into a fight?' I asked incredulously.

'Not exactly. It was more of, er, a kind of altercation, really. Then someone came at us with a Stanley knife.'

'What? What have you done?'

'Calm down, Jules. I mean, we didn't mean to start anything. We were just having a laugh. Then it all turned nasty.'

'You wanker. You stupid wanker. I blame you for this, Piers. You think you're so fucking clever.'

Piers was backing away from me. He'd never seen me this fierce nor heard me talk like this. My 'posh bird' voice disappeared and the harsh sound of my past poured out of my mouth at him.

'Oh, Jules, look,' he was protesting. 'I'm sorry. OK?'

'So. Where was he cut?'

'In this club. Well, it was more like a drinking den, really.'

'No. I mean where. On him.'

'Oh. Yeah, heh-heh. No. Um. Well, er, on his face, actually.'

His face. His beautiful face. I saw him come out of the treatment room with a dressing all down the side of his left cheek. He looked dazed, still in shock. We got a cab back to his flat.

I tucked him into bed.

'I'll sleep on the sofa,' I suggested.

'No,' he said softly. 'Don't go.'

'But your face. I don't want to hurt it.'

'Please,' he implored. 'I'm . . . I'm scared.'

I got under the covers and carefully nestled up to him. He was trembling.

'It's all right,' I whispered.

He started to cry. I held on to him and he sobbed away in the darkness.

The next day he was quiet, sullen.

'Do you want to talk about it?' I asked.

He shook his head.

'I want to go home,' he said, like a little child.

'But Jez,' I replied, 'you are home.'

Then I realised what he meant. He wanted to go home to Mum and Dad.

They lived in a big pile out near Chalfont St Giles. Jez

hadn't introduced me to his parents before then and this wasn't exactly the best of occasions on which to meet the folks but they were friendly enough. He called them by their first names, which seemed a bit odd to me. Alex was an advertising executive, Caroline had been a successful model in the sixties. They were seriously posh but they had this assumed air of casualness. I realised that this was the key to it. My middle-class act had always been a bit too earnest, too serious.

The mood in the house, though, was a little edgy. Jez had told them that his wound was an accident, that he had fallen on some broken glass. They hardly seemed convinced by that but they didn't say anything. Jez was quiet and brooding and I had to try to make conversation. At one point, when Jez was out of the room, Alex said:

'We're worried about Jez. He is all right, isn't he?'

'We know things have been difficult for him,' Caroline added.

And I tried to reassure them. I held back the feelings of resentment that I had. Jez had misspent his youth and pretended to rebel against privilege but there was always this safety net here for him. I'd walked a tightrope with a sheer drop below all my life, it seemed.

But then I remembered that I did have a wealthy benefactor. Starks. A gangster's trust fund, what a dreadful thought. That any precarious sense of self I might have had was tainted by the influence of his blood money. He had added insult to injury. He was not a benefactor, I reasoned, he was a malefactor.

On Sunday Jez's grandfather came to lunch. He had been a war hero, a major in the marines, decorated for gallantry in a rearguard action at Dunkirk. I was expecting some sort of terrifying old patriarch but he was nothing of the sort. He was a charming old soldier with a mischievous, almost camp manner. Jez was happy to see him; they were obviously very fond of each other.

'Lovely to meet you, Julie,' he said with a twinkle in his eye. 'Lucky old Jeremy, eh?'

He was clearly the only one in the family allowed to call Jez 'Jeremy'.

'Goodness me, Jeremy, you have been in the wars. What?'

'Jez had an accident,' Caroline explained.

'Hm,' the major went on. 'Looks like a bit of rough house to me. I know my old Jeremy. Always getting into scrapes, aren't you, boy?'

'Dad, you really shouldn't encourage him,' Alex complained.

'Nonsense, make a man of him. He'll have quite a duelling scar.'

Jez's mood lightened a bit at this. Later, as we were getting ready for bed, I caught him examining the line of stitches in the bathroom mirror, his blue eyes wide with wonder at his new face. I suddenly thought, maybe this is what he wanted. A war wound. A sign of manhood, of proof. A mark of initiation.

Back in London he was more sullen. He didn't want to go out at all, the noise and the bustle of the streets below seemed to frighten him. He moped about his flat during the day and slept badly at night. I spent as much time with him as I could but I was busy. There was a technical rehearsal, then a dress rehearsal, and we were previewing the play at the end of the week. Jez's wound was starting to heal; he had a cicatrice of scar tissue down the left side of his face. His prettiness now had an edge to it. His expression began to change, becoming colder, saturnine.

By the weekend I was off on tour. I'd felt for some time now that a great change was happening in my life, though I had no real idea what it might be. But I hadn't imagined that Jez might be changing too. I'd hoped that I could rely on the certainties of his life, a sense of stability I felt about him, of balance. Now I wasn't so sure. We said goodbye and made all kinds of promises to each other. But I was scared. I was worried about what we were both becoming.

3
essex comedown

Soma *was served with the coffee. Lenina took two half-grammes and Henry three. At twenty past nine they walked across to the newly opened Westminster Abbey Cabaret. It was a night almost without clouds, moonless and starry; but of this on the whole depressing fact Lenina and Henry were fortunately unaware. The electric sky-signs effectively shut off the outer darkness. "CALVIN STOPES AND HIS SIXTEEN SEXOPHONISTS", from the façade of the new Abbey the giant letters invitingly glared. "LONDON'S FINEST SCENT AND COLOUR ORGAN. ALL THE LATEST SYNTHETIC MUSIC".*

Aldous Huxley, *Brave New World*

The snow has started to fall. Yes, the weather forecast is right for once: snow is general all over Essex. Watch it through the window. White dots against the black. Like an old telly gone on the blink. Interference. Like the fuzziness in my head.

The phone goes and I sort of jump a bit. I'm so fucking edgy. Pick it up.

'Yeah?'

'Gaz?'

It's Beardsley.

'Yeah. What?'

'The coma girl's dead.'

'Yeah?'

'Yeah.'

'So?'

'Look, Gaz, this isn't good. No. This is very bad. The press are going fucking crazy. This isn't inner-city lowlife. This is middle fucking England. And you know that her old man . . .'

'Yeah, I know. Used to be a cozzer.'

'Well, then. The fucking Essex Constabulary are going to be coming down heavy on all of us. We've got to sort a few things out.'

'Yeah, well, do you think . . .'

'Look, we shouldn't be talking on the phone. I just wanted to let you know, that's all. Let's meet in our usual place.'

'Right.'

Then he's gone. I put the phone down and try to think. I chop out a couple more lines on the coffee table, roll up a note and give it both barrels. More snow. Outside and inside. It's a fucking joke. My head is like a fucking snowstorm. You know, those little plastic domes filled with fluid and these little bits of white in them that swirl and fall tinkle tinkle tinkle when you turn them over.

I try to think. But everything seems blanked out. Like the landscape outside. Pick up the phone again and call Karen.

'Hello,' she says.

'Karen? It's me. Gaz.'

She sighs.

'Look, Gaz. I've got an injunction.'

'I know, I know. Look, you didn't have to do that.'

'Well, it's done.'

'Yeah. I'm sorry. Please. Come home.'

'Gaz, I can't cope with this. I can't cope with you.'

'It won't happen again, babe. I promise.'

'No. I can't trust you. You've got to sort yourself out. You know what? You need help, that's what you need. Professional help.'

'Look, I ain't going to see no shrink.'

'Well, you've got to do something. You've got to change.'

There's a bit of a pause. Can't think what to say.

'How are the girls?'

'Fine.'

'Do they miss their dad?'

'I can't deal with this, Gaz.' Her voice goes into a sob. 'I can't.'

The line goes dead. Hold the dialling tone against my head for a bit. Then put the phone down. Change. She's right. I've become a monster. I didn't mean to lash out. The snow's beginning to settle on the ground outside, white as uncut charlie. Need to talk to someone. Not a fucking shrink, that's for sure. A friend. Someone like Dan. He always seemed to know what was going to happen next. But I haven't seen Dan in five years.

*　　*　　*

Dan was my oldest and best friend. He'd settled down and I'd just carried on being naughty. It had always been just a bit of a laugh with Dan. Something I guess he always knew he'd grow out of. For me it was always serious.

We grew up together in Stepney. The East End was a shithole back then, don't let anyone tell you any different. Luftwaffe playgrounds. Bombsites that were never cleared with TEMPORARY OPEN SPACE council signs on them. Dad was a docker until he got laid off in the seventies. Worked hard all his life for some poxy redundancy pay-out. Then another job when we moved to Dagenham. Factory robot slave. They'd go on strike every so often to remind themselves they were human. That they could disobey orders. I decided early on that I wasn't going to be a mug like him.

Not that there were that many opportunities. But there were stories and rumours. People who had made something for themselves without ever being told what to do. Villains and gangsters. The Kray Twins. Harry Starks. Flash bastards. Legends.

I wanted to be someone. I wanted that kind of power and respect. I remember going to Madame Tussaud's on a school trip with Dan. I remember being overwhelmed by this idea that if you were famous enough they'd make this life-sized copy of you that people would come to gawp at.

'Fucking amazing, ain't it?' I said to Dan.

'They're only waxworks, Gaz,' he said. 'A bunch of fucking dummies.'

'Well,' I declared, 'I'm going to be in here one day.'

'The only way you're getting in here is when they put you in the Chamber of Horrors. You evil bastard.'

Dan started cackling and I went to give him a smack. But I remember thinking back then that he was probably right. I wanted to be someone. And if it was from doing bad I didn't care. I felt apart from other people. A tearaway, Mum called me. Torn away, more like. Never felt I could fit into a crowd.

Never wanted to. A problem child, school called me. Even sent me to this school shrink. Never did any good. Once, when he was out of the room, I took a butcher's at something he'd written down: *Gary Kelly's disruptive behaviour is an obvious ploy to get attention.*

But maybe they were right all along and there is something wrong with me. Maybe Karen's right and I need to have my head examined. I don't know.

The next day I'm driving out to a service station on the M25 to meet Beardsley. Get a paper and a cup of tea and sit in my usual place. On the front page is this picture of the girl that died after banging a pill at a party in Basildon. A tangle of tubes coming out of her face. *LOOK WHAT DRUGS DO*, screams the headline. *The picture her parents want Britain to remember.*

Beardsley arrives. He picks up the paper and looks at it. Shakes his head and sighs.

'Isn't that terrible?'

I nod. He drops the paper on the table. Stares at me.

'You don't look so good yourself, Gaz.'

'I'm all right.'

'You wanna sort yourself out, son.'

'Look, I just had a rough night. OK?'

'OK, OK. So. What do we know about this?'

He points at the paper. I shrug.

'The pill was bought at a club in Basildon. Some people are saying it was contaminated.'

Beardsley shakes his head.

'No. It wasn't a snide one. I've heard that for sure. It was an Apple. You know what that means, don't you?'

Apples were a new batch of Es from Amsterdam. Extra strong, they were. Beardsley had smuggled a load of them in only a couple of weeks before.

'It means they could trace it to us,' I say.

'Yeah, us or Tony Tucker's firm. They were dealing them as well. Look, Essex Old Bill are going to want a body for this and there'll be no peace for the wicked until they find someone.'

'So?'

'So, we keep our heads down until it all blows over. Yeah, and maybe someone should give them a clue. Let Tucker's firm take the blame.'

'You saying we should grass somebody up?'

'Well, it doesn't have to be like that, does it? It could be done, like, indirectly.'

'How?'

'I don't know, do I? We'll think of something, eh?'

'Yeah.'

'One thing is for sure. The happy smiley time is over.'

'Beardsley,' I said. 'The happy smiley time was over long ago.'

I never figured I'd know about fashion, let alone be able to make a lot of money out of one. Fact is, in the past, fashion always caught me out somehow. No, it was Dan that knew about style and that. Right from the start. He'd follow the trends, be up with whatever the thing was that week. Aged twelve and he was a baby skinhead. Orange Ben Sherman, white Sta-Press, braces and cherry-red Astronauts. I wasn't so flash. Monkey boots, jungle greens and a collarless shirt. We were too young for it first time around. We tried following around the older kids but they'd tell us to piss off. One thing I have to say: I fucking loved the music. Ska and bluebeat. Dad would always complain: 'Turn that fucking jungle-bunny music down!' he'd shout. I could get lost in it, the mad skanking rhythm of it.

The fashions moved and Dan moved with them. Always one step ahead of the other kids in our school. The seventies. He grew his hair out. Suedehead then a shoulder-length Smoothie.

Had it done in a feather cut. Platform shoes. Oxford bags. Tank tops with silver stars on. He followed the football too. West Ham, of course. The Under Fives. They were like an apprentice firm for kids who wanted to prove themselves and would spy on rival fans for the older hooligans. I used to go along to home matches. But I couldn't really understand it all, you know. I always thought that if you were going to get into trouble it should be for some sort of gain. Hooliganism, vandalism, Paki-bashing, these things were done just for the buzz. There had to be more to it than that.

And I'd started to notice the real villains around my way. The clothes, the gold, the cars. They had got something out of life. Something more than cheap thrills at the weekend and some shitty job for the rest of your days.

Well, we moved to bloody Dagenham. The old man got a job on the assembly line at Ford, building 1600E Cortinas. New school and I had to prove myself. But I was a big lad, even then. I could handle myself. Age fourteen and I was already scaring the teachers. I didn't have Dan around to get me into normal teenage trouble. So the trouble I got into started getting serious.

Next time I saw Dan was five years later, 1979. I'd just got out of Youth Detention for the second time. Burglary. I'd liked the idea of it but I was no good at it. I was a big clumsy fucker. You needed to be light footed and nimble to shin up drainpipes and balance on window ledges. I kept on getting caught, didn't I? Ended up in the juvenile courts. Probation, approved school, borstal, the lot.

After a while Mum and Dad didn't want me back home any more. Can't say I blamed them, I'd caused them enough grief and I wanted to get away from them and all. So I found myself looking for clues back in the East End and that's when I bumped into Dan. It gave me a shock when I saw him, though. It wasn't that I didn't recognise him. It was like he'd become too familiar. The long hair, the lairy big collars, the flared trousers – gone. He'd got a number-one crop, bottle-green Fred Perry, straight-leg Levis and a pair of Doc Martens. Like all the seventies had been cut away from him and there was just a big version of the little Dan I knew ten years ago. I mean, time plays tricks when you're away inside. Every time you come out you have to try and catch up. New money, new governments. But this was like time had gone backwards. I shook my head.

'What's happened, Dan?'

He gave me this big nutty grin.

'The skinheads are back, Gaz,' he announced.

He played me this new record. It was a version of 'Skinhead Moonstomp' by this local group called Earthquake. *Yeh-yeh-yeh-yeah, yeah, yeaah, yeaah, yeaah, yeaaah*.

I laughed. 'Fuck me. This takes me back.'

He told me that this was the new thing now. Two Tone, they were calling it. Ska bands like The Specials and The Selecter from the Midlands and Earthquake who were from Upton Park. They were playing at the Music Machine in Camden Town that very night.

'Come along,' Dan said. 'It'll be a laugh.'

It seemed a bit odd. A bit too young for it first time around and a bit too old for it now. But then I'd missed out on my youth what with borstal and probation and that. And I'd always loved the music. I grinned at Dan.

'Yeah, all right,' I said.

'Just one thing we've got to sort out.'

I still had long hair, of course. Everybody had it when I'd gone away last. So Dan got his electric clippers out and shaved it all off in the kitchen. Funny, it's a treatment you expect going into Youth Detention, not coming out of it.

So we went to this gig mob handed. All these new skinhead types. West Ham, most of them. The InterCity Firm they were calling themselves these days, on account of the fact that they had started to travel in this fashion to away games instead of on the poxy football specials that were laid on for the plebs. Made it easier to avoid the Old Bill or being ambushed by rival home fans, and it was a helluva lot more flash. And they did like looking flash. The ICF/Earthquake look was boots, red-tag Levi's and tasty-looking green MA1 flight jackets. Lots of familiar and half-familiar faces. Lots of drinks bought for me when Dan told people where I'd just come from. It was more of a homecoming than I got from Ma and Pa, that was for sure. Had a line of sulphate with Dan in the bogs and I was raring to go.

Earthquake took the stage and we all went mental. I felt the speed rush come up as I was bouncing around in this crowd. They played ska dead fast, drums, bass, guitar, organ, saxophone and two guys out front. A white guy who did the singing and this black kid in a porkpie hat and wraparound shades who called out on the rhythm, went *chicka chicka chicka chicka*, or talked his talk over the songs. It's funny, because there was a bit of *sieg-heiling* between numbers from some of the skins. I saw some NF and British Movement badges on the arm pockets of some of the MA1 jackets in the crowd. And when they did 'Skinhead Moonstomp', this black guy, Caleb he called himself, called out, NOW REMEMBER, I'M YOUR BOSS SKINHEAD SPEAKING. HUH? REMEMBER, I'M THE BOSS, and most of the skins cheered but there was some monkey-noise taunting and *sieg-heiling* from the crowd as well. I didn't try to understand this. I just felt the buzz of it all. It was like having my childhood back after being banged up and confined.

Some poxy punk band were on next so we went on the rampage. Scared the fuck out of all of these punk rockers, even though they outnumbered us about four to one. They didn't want to know. Went back to Dan's afterwards. He let me kip on the sofa, said I could stay for a bit, until I found a place of my own. He was working as a plasterer and he said he'd keep a lookout for any labouring work that might be going. Well, I didn't fancy that but I didn't say anything because he was just being a good mate, looking out for me and that. I hung about with his group of friends, brought the gear, went to the Earthquake gigs. It was a bit of a laugh and, I guess, a bit like being in a gang but I didn't think that it was a thing that I really belonged to. But then I met Beardsley.

Earthquake were doing this gig at the Hope and Anchor on Upper Street and some trouble kicked off. There were these North London skins there that were acting like they owned the place. Someone got shoved and a fight broke out. I waded in and started to put it about a bit lively. It was this mob instinct, I guess. Them and us. I can be big and nasty if I want to be, and I was. I led the charge and we ran them out of there.

Afterwards I was standing about having a drink and I was kind of like the centre of attention for a bit, the others standing around me, and it was then that Beardsley came over. The group around me just parted to let him through, lots of respect, that's what Beardsley got, and there he was, suddenly in front of me, looking me up and down. Simon Beardsley was Earthquake's manager. A skinhead legend, he was. Rumour had it that he started the whole thing back in the sixties. He'd only shot a couple of Hell's Angels in the Golden Goose amusement arcade in Piccadilly back then. A real face. A real villain too, in his time. He'd worked with Harry Starks and Jack 'The Hat' McVitie. And he'd done a lot of porridge. He was supposed to be legitimate now but the music business always was a front for all kinds of naughtiness and everybody knew that he'd never really retired. And there he was, shaped up in front of me, staring me out. He gave this little grin – just showing his teeth, mind, the eyes stayed cold.

'Think you're fucking tasty, don't you?' he asked flat, all matter-of-fact.

I shrugged. Nodded.

'Yeah,' I replied.

He smiled, eyes and all this time.

'Good. Want a job, rude boy?'

'What?' I gave a little laugh, surprised at the question. 'What you mean?'

'I mean working for me. Earthquake are going on tour. We're going to need extra security. What you reckon?'

That's how I first teamed up with Beardsley. All that time ago. I've learnt a lot from him over the years. Now he thinks I'm losing it. *You wanna sort yourself out, son.* Yeah, yeah. So everyone's on my fucking case now.

I go home and crash out. Wake up around seven and make myself something to eat. Watch a bit of telly. The news comes on and there's more about the girl that died. Grieving parents. Kind of shakes me up a bit. Think about my daughters. Charlene and Donna. Karen won't let me see them. Pour myself a drink and brood about it. Can't help thinking about the coma girl. What if something like that happened to one of my kids?

Snap out of it. Got to go into Southend tonight. Have a couple of lines to sharpen myself up. Drive to Tiffany's, this Sharon and Tracey club near the seafront that's started doing House and Jungle nights for the last couple of years. I run the doors there, which also means controlling who does the dealing. But it's the legit stuff to sort out tonight. I've got all the invoices so that the doormen can get paid.

Frank, the manager, is out front, expecting me. Friday night is usually busy as fuck but tonight it's a fucking graveyard.

'How's it going, Frank?'

He rolls his eyes.

'This business with this girl,' I say, shaking my head.

'Well,' he replies, 'I think we can forget about our four o'clock licence for a while.'

Frank had applied for an extension at the weekends.

'Speaking of which,' he goes on, 'had a bloke from the

council in here earlier. Looking for you. Wants you to phone him.'

He fishes out this business card and hands it to me. *Roger Wilbey*, it says, *Environmental Health Registration Scheme*. This could be hassle over my licence to run doors. There's been complaints against me. Fuck. That's all I fucking need.

I pay off the doormen and have a quick chat with George, the head bouncer. He nods at a bloke over at the bar.

'See him? Well, there's something dodgy about that one.'

I look around slowly. Short ginger hair, lime-green Ted Baker shirt worn on the outside, a pair of dark blue Dockers. Eyes darting about, as if looking for something.

'He's been asking around, wants to "score", apparently.'

'And has he?'

'Nah, I've told everyone to act innocent.'

'Good. What you reckon? Cozzer?'

George frowns.

'Don't think so. Don't know what he is but he just doesn't look right. Shall I chuck him out?'

'No. I'll deal with it.'

I go over and stand beside him at the bar. Now I ain't exactly inconspicuous so he soon notices this big fucker looming over him.

'You sorted?' I ask him.

'Er, no,' he replies.

'Well, I've got Apples. Dead strong. Ten pound each.'

His little eyes light up. He reaches into his pocket.

'Not here,' I tell him. 'Follow me.'

I lead him out to the fire escape at the back, beckon him to go up against the bar on the double doors, then give him a big shove into the alleyway beyond. He tumbles over into this pile of boxes and rubbish. I wave to George to come and close the door after me and I go out myself. I pick this bloke up. He's whimpering a bit.

'Please,' he says. 'Please don't hurt me.'

'Who the fuck are you?'

'Press,' he wheezes.

'What?'

'Journalist,' he goes on, still out of breath. '*Sunday Illustrated.*'

I laugh and let go of him.

'What's the story? How the evil dealers have taken over the clubs?'

'Yeah. Well, something like that.'

Then it hits me. This could be it. Beardsley saying how we need to hand somebody up for that girl dying. Well, this could be the way. Don't have to go to the cozzers. Do it through the papers. I laugh again.

'You want a story?'

He nods.

'Well, I'll give you a story.'

We go back to his hotel room. I say: you can put that fucking tape machine away for a start. Just write it down. You want an exclusive? Well, he goes. No, don't worry about payment. This is a favour (and remember I'll want one back in return). Just get all of this down.

I go through the lot with him. Give him a couple of Tony Tucker's dealers. That should keep the cozzers off our backs for a while. Give him some leads to follow up in time for a big juicy story on Sunday.

Help myself to the minibar. Start to flag after a while and I get the charlie out.

'Fancy a toot?' I ask.

And this little hack, Keith is his name, he sort of looks all wide eyed for a bit and gives this silly little grin that middle-class wankers give when they think they're doing something naughty.

'Oh, yeah, all right, then.'

These media types, they're the fucking worst, if you ask me.

Drugs. The big story. Never thought it would ever get this big. Me and Beardsley thought we could just retire to Essex and live off the fat of the land. But it got so fucking competitive. Villains moving in from everywhere. No one's going to bother with over-the-pavement stuff when you could make so much money dealing. Thing is, we'd been at it for quite a while, Beardsley had been selling uppers way back in the sixties. But we never figured it would get this big.

Back in 1979 when I first worked with him it was just 'extras'. I didn't know what he meant when he'd employed me as a minder for Earthquake. He just said:

'Well, it's a ton a week plus extras.'

So I ended up going around the country with the band in this battered old coach. My job was to look after them. I'd meet up with whoever was organising the stewards for whatever venue we were playing to let them know who I was. It was their job to look after the hall. I'd be with the band backstage and then down the front when they were playing. Then afterwards, when the road crew were getting the stuff out, I'd be about in case there was any trouble. I made sure I was tooled up. A bottle of squirt, ammonia that is, and a Stanley knife.

During a gig it would get pretty mad. Most nights I'd find myself on stage near the end to stop the local crowd storming it. I'd be pretty whizzed up by then and I'd end up doing this funny kind of boot stomp to the music as I pushed or kicked out at any potential interlopers. After a while it became part of the act, me getting up to do this nutty dance. I got known by the hard-core Earthquake followers and they'd chant 'Gaz, Gaz, Gaz' at me. I even ended up being featured on the video for the band's second single, 'Ska Train InterCity'. I liked that. Showing off. Having a bit of recognition.

And I found out soon enough what Beardsley had meant by 'extras'. He had this amphetamine factory somewhere out in Canning Town banging out kilos of speed and he had me look after shifting it to the audience every night. Kevin, one of the roadies, did the dealing and I'd be his minder in case there was any hassle or any rival dealers to be dealt with. Beardsley didn't want the band to know about it or get caught up in it in any way. They already had an 'image problem', as he called it. The NF and British Movement elements of the band's following were doing them no favours at all. There were these stupid press stories calling them 'Nazi Hooligans' and shit like that. So I was to make sure that the speed business was all done discreetly.

It was sweet. I was having fun and making a load of money out of it. There were groupies here and there, too. Girls skins with peroxide fringes around the crop. And with the side racket I was running I had a way into the dodgy side of Beardsley's activities. Something I felt sure would come in handy for the future. I was thinking of the long term, see? After the tour.

We did the North, and the Midlands, then made our way South again. But it was at the Queensway Hall, Dunstable, that's when things kicked off really badly.

There was a big fuss by the front entrance. This mob had arrived who were out to get any NF or BM skins. Now some of them were weedy-looking lefty types, there were some Anti-Nazi League placards and that, but with them were a bunch of real nasty, pikey-looking greasers. One of the Queensway Hall stewards said he thought they were the South-East Outlaws, a local biker gang. This chant had started up, *Fascists out! Fascists out!* Now there wasn't much point in trying to reason with this lot, pointing out that there was a black guy in the group, for fuck's sake. The greeboes were here for a ruck, that was for sure.

The stewards were keeping them out for now, but for how long? I got on the phone to Beardsley and begged him to get some back-up to us. Dan and some of his ICF mates were at the gig so I got him to round up some of the tastier ones among them and get them to tool themselves up with whatever came to hand. Kevin the roadie had equipped himself with a short scaffolding pole. So I assembled my troops and gave them a bit of a pep talk.

Half an hour later, just as the support act was going on stage, there was this banging noise from below. The greasers were kicking at the fire doors in the downstairs foyer, where the cloakroom and the bogs were. We rushed down the stairs mob handed just as they stormed in. Some of the skins who were quick on their toes got caught up in the charge and took a right pasting. I shouted at the others to hold back so that we could make a proper stand.

This ugly bearded greebo was coming forward slowly, a rusty cut-throat in his hand.

'Who wants some?' he taunted, his little eyes gleaming.

Behind him some poor fucker was being kicked about like a rag doll. I looked around. A lot of the skins had bottled out and made for the girls' toilets. Kevin and Dan were beside me and a few others behind.

I took my squirt bottle out and let the cut-throat geezer have it right in the eyes. He started squealing. Another bloke came forward and Kevin whacked him out cold with the scaffolding pole. More and more of them were coming through the fire doors and we moved back to the stairs to get some high ground, lashing out desperately at anything that moved. This biker was swinging a chain about at us, which actually kept back some of his own side, he was going so wildly with it. We were just about holding our ground but it couldn't last.

Then there was this loud boom. A shotgun, no doubt about it. Fuck, I thought, this is it, they've got fucking shotguns. But there was a commotion outside. Someone shouting and the greasers legging it. A whiff of cordite and suddenly Beardsley appeared through the fire doors in a sheepskin coat with some other geezer behind him holding a sawn-off. And the rest of the greeboes scarpered.

After the gig I drove back to London with Beardsley and the bloke with the shotgun, Declan he was called.

'I owe you a drink,' Beardsley had said.

We ended up in an after-hours club he ran in Tottenham. Rock steady music playing in the background.

'So,' he said. 'You fancy some more work once this tour's over?'

'What, with Earthquake?'

'Nah. I don't think there's going to be many more gigs for a while the way things are going. All this trouble that's been kicking off. Bookers don't want to know, to tell you the truth. The band is going to have to clean up its act if they want to go anywhere now. I'm trying to get them to change their image, become more like a comedy band, sort of, you know, music-hall stuff. A novelty record, that would be good. Get a younger following, drop all of this heavy skinhead palaver. It's been bad for business.'

'You mean stop being a ska band?'

He frowned, shrugged. A new track came over the sound system. 'I'm In A Dancing Mood' by Delroy Wilson. Beardsley smiled at it.

'Listen to this,' he said. 'This is the real stuff. Earthquake are just plastic compared to this. Look, I'm as honky as the next guy but white boys just ain't got it. All the music I've ever loved has been spade music. R&B, Tamla Motown, reggae. White kids, well, they try to copy it but they just ain't got the soul. You know what I mean?'

I nodded vaguely. Wasn't quite sure what he was on about to tell you the truth. He'd mentioned work and I wanted us to get back to that subject.

'So,' I said. 'This "work", it wouldn't be with Earthquake?'

'No. I reckon you've done your apprenticeship. I was thinking of something more, well, serious.'

I liked the sound of this.

'Yeah,' I replied, nodding, grinning. 'Sure.'

And so I started doing jobs for him on a regular basis. There was the speed racket that was turning over nicely and Beardsley branched out into coke and hash. There was this bloke who smuggled it into Essex from Amsterdam in this big fuck-off power boat. Beardsley would use me and Declan as minders on meetings when big quantities of drugs and cash were being exchanged.

Beardsley was still officially in the music business. It was a useful front for all the dodgy dealings he was up to. I learnt from him that it was always important to have some sort of legitimate front. Earthquake released their last single at the end of the year. It flopped and they split up but Beardsley carried on doing stuff. 'Management and Promotions', he called it. He also ran various hookey companies, not in his own name, of course. Long-firm frauds that would be set up and then dissolved, with a load of unpaid for goods going missing. These would need front men, 'business associates', he called them, that would sometimes have to take the rap if there was a proper investigation. Sometimes his unfortunate 'partners' would want to tell all about who was behind the scheme when they got a tug from the Old Bill. And that's when me and Declan would be called in to give a little gentle persuasion, as it were. And that's when I got into trouble again.

This bloke, Douggie Kennedy, he was adamant that he wasn't going away for this warehouse load of electrical goods in Wood Green. So we went around to see him. Well, it got pretty nasty and he ended up hospitalised. Then he grassed us all up. In the end they couldn't get a result on the long firm itself so we would have all been all right if only he'd held his mouth. But me and Declan ended up going down for two counts of making an unwarranted menace and one count of GBH.

So I went away again. It was proper bird this time. Two years. Prison was a real education for me. Approved school, borstal, that had been like O-level stuff. But this was the university. The Royal College of Useful Knowledge.

I did my first couple of months in the Scrubs. This was an allocation period when they work out what category you are and where to put you. An overcrowded Victorian gaol, three to a tiny little cell. A real mix of cons during allocation. I was banged up with some nutter who had been robbing sub post offices and this timid little white-collar bloke who was in for embezzlement. Everybody's trying to front it out in their own way, working out what the pecking order is. You're in with some really horrible people and some proper arseholes too. You learn quick how to look through people, to know whether someone is genuinely dangerous or just full of bullshit.

After about six weeks in the Scrubs I was allocated to Coldingley, this modern nick in Surrey. Electronic doors and cameras everywhere. I got to know some proper faces in there. Tommy Patterson, this South London villain with a real reputation. One of the chaps, as they say. And Chris Lambrianou, who had been on the Kray firm.

I was a bit wary of Chris at first because he was in for being part of the murder of Jack 'The Hat' McVitie, and Beardsley and the Hat had been a team back in the sixties. Prison paranoia – you're always aware that there might be grudges, scores to settle, shit like that. I needn't have worried. Chris had found God and put all of that Kray stuff behind him. He was this big, mild-mannered, born-again Christian who worked in the prison garden. Chris was a clever bloke, wise, I guess you'd call it. He did me a favour once and I thanked him for it. He smiled and said, 'A brother is born to help in time of need.'

But, to be honest, I wasn't after that kind of wisdom. I wasn't ready to be saved, I was up for more villainy once I was out. Tommy Patterson was well connected. He knew

Beardsley and some of the other faces I'd got to know on the outside. So I learnt from him. About how reputations are made and used. How to get to know the right people. And how to get to be known by them. Prison is full of nasty, devious people for the most part. You find out who to trust and who to steer clear of. You get to spot what bad is really like, I mean real bad, not just naughty bad. So when I got to the end of my sentence I thought I was a little bit cleverer than when I had first gone in. I'd done a little bit. Just a little bit of time at the start of my career that could stand me in good stead.

'You know,' I say to this Keith bloke in his hotel room, 'I got loads of stories I could tell you. Tricks of the trade, faces I've known, stuff like that.'

'Yeah,' he replies, nodding. Looks a bit wired.

'I could tell you stories, Keith. Look, fancy another line? Shit. I run out. I could go and get some more.'

'Look, Gaz. I better get some sleep. I need to get on with this story. But I hear what you're saying. I'm always interested in a good story.'

He hands me his card.

'Let's keep in touch,' he says.

Go back to the motor. Freezing night air clears the head a bit. Don't want to go home. Don't want to go back to a poxy empty house. Run out of gear anyway. Christmas lights on everywhere. Feel so fucking lonely. Need to get out of it. Out of my head.

Phone Martin on the mobile. One of our dealers. Come on over, he says. Like I'm welcome somewhere. A semi-detached council house out in Braintree. Martin's been saving up to buy it on the discount. Then maybe sell it on. Get on the property ladder, so he says. Only he's worried about this negative equity thing.

Martin stays up all night watching satellite. Works the night shift drugs-wise. Always reliable like that, and he can afford to charge a little bit ·extra for the availability. Like those twenty-four-hour Paki grocers.

Of course, I'm a discount customer. But I always give Martin something just for the service. My nights have been so fucked recently I've needed it badly.

Get in the door and he's already talking about the girl that died.

'Leave it out Martin,' I say. 'I've heard enough about her.'

We go in through to the lounge and there's this young bird on the settee. Eyes dark rimmed, filmy and blinking, like little screens reflecting the gloomy light of the telly.

'But it was an Apple, wasn't it? That's what done her, I heard. I've been dealing them myself.'

'Look, Martin, just give it a rest for a bit. I've had enough.'

Martin shrugs, hands up like an apology. Scared of me like most of them. Without being asked he gets the gear out and starts chopping out big long lines of it on the powder-smeared mirror on the coffee table.

I sit down next to this girl. She turns her head slightly and gives me a fucked-up smile.

'Natalie,' says Martin. 'This is Gaz.'

'Hi,' she sighs.

We hoover up the coke. Martin skins up some skunk weed. A bottle of Jack Daniel's. This is good. Feel numb. Warm. It's started snowing again outside. Time goes whizzing past. Grey morning comes. Kids' cartoons on the telly. Natalie giggling on the settee.

We have some ketamine. *Special K for breakfast*, Martin jokes. I'm lying on the floor as the horse tranquilliser takes hold. *I could tell you stories*, I mutter to myself. I feel so heavy, sinking into the stained white shagpile like I weigh a hundred tons. The world is spinning, falling, turning. Body dead. Mind racing. Thinking. Remembering. Coming out of prison that first time.

Coming out, well, you're never prepared for it. Release date is all you ever think about inside but it doesn't make you ready for it. Outside seems extra manic and bright after being in the grey world inside. And there are all these changes, things that have happened to remind you that everything has moved on while you've been standing still. It was June 1982, three million on the dole and there'd been a war with Argentina. But it was the little things that took me by surprise, as per fucking usual.

I was on the Underground, Central Line going east, off to see Dan in Mile End. Now I was wearing what I wore before I went inside. Doc Martens, red-tag Levi's, green MA1 jacket. And I'd just had a number-one crop, almost the first thing I did when I came out. Well, this bloke gets on at Liverpool Street dressed exactly the same, skinhead just like me, and sits opposite. I clock him, thinking maybe he's a face I know, someone from the Earthquake days or one of Dan's ICF mates. But when I look up: nothing. Don't know him from Adam even though it's kind of like looking in the mirror. He's a big bloke, like me. I sort of give him a slight nod and he nods back slowly. A half-smile on his gob but a cold stare. Like he's saying: *Yeah, I know you*. But I don't know him. And I think: shit, maybe he's Millwall or one of the North London skins I had a row with that time. I look away. I don't want to get into a row with this geezer. I've only just got out, for fuck sake. I look back and he's eyeing me up and down like he's thinking about how he's going to do me. I give him the fiercest eyeballing I can muster but he's screwing me back, still with this stupid smile on his face. I decide to ignore him. I think to myself: I could have this cunt but he's not worth it. It's not worth the bother. Unnecessary aggro. That's one of the things I learnt to avoid inside.

So we get to Mile End and I get up to get off. I give him a last *fuck you* look and step out on to the platform. As I'm going up the steps I glance back to see he's only got off himself, hasn't he. I try to think nothing of it, maybe it's his stop as well. But as I'm going down Burdett Road I look back and there he is. He is definitely following me. I start to get ready for the off. Thinking. Maybe he's tooled up. I haven't got a thing on me. I start looking around, for a brick or something.

I go into the waste ground by Mile End Park and shape up. I am definitely going to have this fucker, I decide. I'm by some manky bushes waiting for him.

'Over here,' I call out to him as he comes by.

He sees me and smiles, walks up to me.

'Isn't this a bit open?' he asks.

It was then I realise that something is wrong. Very, very wrong. His voice doesn't match his clothes. It's soft, a bit posh.

'What do you mean?' I say.

He comes right up close to me. I don't fucking believe this.

'Well, if we're going to, you know . . .'

He is touching me, the fucker is only stroking my fucking leg.

'Get your fucking hands . . .'

I push him away. I shape up to give him an almighty punch but he's still staring with that silly smile on his lips like maybe this was something he was into too. So I draw back. I don't want to touch him.

'Fucking queer!' I shout at him.

But he just carries on smiling. Lets out this queeny sigh.

'Oo, we are upset, aren't we?'

'Look, just fuck off, OK?'

He shrugs and turns to walk away.

'Another time, then,' he calls out.

I was fuming. I felt like going after him and kicking the shit out of him but I knew that would make things worse. I felt dirty. And confused. What was a queer doing dressed up like that?

When I met up with Dan he explained it all to me, as usual. As usual, the fashions had changed while I'd been away. They'd gone fucking haywire.

I mean, now Dan looked like a poof. Floppy hair in a side parting. A pink polo shirt and V-neck golf sweater, for fuck's sake. Slacks and these silly slip-on loafers and white socks. This was what the ICF lot were wearing now, apparently. I told him the story. I was embarrassed, to tell you the truth. Dan just laughed like a drain.

'Well, Gaz, it's only poofs that are wearing stuff like that these days,' he said, pointing at my clobber. 'That and the diehard Nazi lot.'

'You mean homos are dressing like skinheads?'

'Yeah. Crazy, isn't it?'

And all the hooligans were now going for this poncey look. Designer stuff. The casual look, Dan explained. Obsessed with labels. Pringle, Fila, Sergio Tacchini, Diadora, Ellesse, Lacoste. All trying to outdo each other with all this expensive gear. Like a bunch of girls. All with this floppy side-parted hairstyle, the Wedge, they called it.

I don't know, poofs dressed like hooligans, hooligans dressed like poofs. Well, I thought I'd seen it all now. I thought that if I ever went away and came out again fashion would never change in such a crazy way. I was wrong, of course. The next time it would be even weirder, but we'll come to that later.

So, I started wearing this designer stuff, didn't I? Got rid of my old gear. I mean, I didn't want people to think I was a bum-bandit or some NF loony. But I kept the hair short. It suited me. All this label stuff was like a sign of the times. It wasn't just about looking flash, the label showed it cost a lot of money too, it proved you had cash. The East End was changing, all that proud-to-be-working-class stuff was over. The docks were being redeveloped, there was real dosh to be made, legitimate too. Some of Dan's mates even worked in the City, for fuck's sake. It was a funny time. A lot of people were out of pocket while some were flush. There was a lot of selling-off going on and money sloshing about in the trough.

I went back to work for Beardsley. I'd kept my mouth shut and done my time so he owed me work. Business was booming for him too. Though it weren't exactly legit.

He had a new scam. Gold. He was smuggling it into the country and selling it to a reputable dealer. The buyer would be liable to pay VAT, fifteen per cent of the cost price. Of course, Beardsley's 'company' would just be a fake firm with short-let office accommodation with some headed notepaper with a moody VAT number on it that would fold in a couple of months without making any returns. So he could pocket fifteen per cent of all the deals he had made. It was quick money. And simple.

'You mean you're actually collecting tax?' I asked him.

'Yeah,' he said with a big grin. 'On behalf of Her Majesty's Customs and Excise. Except her lot doesn't exactly get to see any of it. Good, ain't it?'

So Beardsley got to know a lot about gold. And when the Hounslow bullion job happened he was well placed to have a bit of it. Fifteen million pounds' worth of gold blagged. The whole of the underworld started buzzing about the bullion and where it might be going. Of course, Beardsley was well placed for a touch but he played it all very carefully. There was a lot at stake and it got a little bit hairy, I can tell you.

I got to work out what was happening by the little things he told me when I was running errands. And I put some of it together myself as well. I knew that the gold had to be resmelted first before it could be sold on. And there was this front man, Solly Blumberg, who ran a jeweller's in Hatton Garden who would do the selling to legitimate gold dealers and fix the paperwork so it looked like it was kosher. Me, Beardsley or someone else on his firm would courier the stuff down to Solly bit by bit.

We'd have to be extra careful because Beardsley figured that there was a lot of surveillance going on. C11, the Met's Criminal Intelligence Unit, or customs investigators. I've never exactly looked inconspicuous so I went for this disguise. I'd dress up like some Aussie backpacker with a stupid hat on to cover my features and the trademark crop. I'd come out of Farringdon Station with this rucksack on which was, of course, stuffed full of resmelted gold bars. Weighed a fucking ton. I'd walk down to Hatton Garden and into Solly's shop. I'd announce in this stupid accent I'd rehearsed in front of Beardsley that I was looking for an engagement ring for my sheila back in Wogga Wogga. Solly would start showing me trays of stuff and I'd take off the backpack. Then, while we were fannying on, the rucksack would be swapped for an identical one with just clothes and stuff in it.

Solly was a real talker. Never knew what the hell he was on about half the time but he could be dead funny. Always telling these Jewish jokes.

There was this other bloke involved too. Manny Gould, an ancient bent accountant who dealt with the money that was made from selling the bullion. Laundering, offshore banking stuff that was well above my head. Once, I took a whole suitcase of £50 notes down to southern Spain. Fuengirola was the drop, at 'Pete's English Bar', run by a cousin of Beardsley's. There was an international organisation that was running things. I had my own ideas about who might be behind it all but I kept my mouth shut and tried not to think about it too much. It doesn't pay to know too much sometimes.

Anyway, we were raking it in. Beardsley bought this huge

mansion in Essex with a swimming pool and everything. And he was paying me a fair whack. But the money I earned during that time soon went. Motors, flash clothes, tarts, a bit of charlie from time to time, gambling, going out and showing off. I knew in my mind that I should be putting some of this gelt aside, investing it or whatever. But in my heart I always felt that it was bad money. Money that had to be spent.

I still kept in touch with Dan. He was doing all right for himself and all. There was a lot of building work going on in Docklands. He'd settled down with this bird Marcia and they'd had a kid together. But the funny thing was he was still running with the ICF at weekends. And they were so fucking organised. Blokes pushing thirty still acting like hooligans. Like military planning how they took on their enemies. They even printed up calling cards to leave on rival fans that they'd done, *Congratulations, you have just met the ICF*, stuff like that. I couldn't understand it given that they weren't making anything out of it.

Then we got some bad news. Beardsley had been doing some surveillance of his own. Apparently Solly had been visited by the Flying Squad at his Hatton Garden premises and had kept shtum about it. Then some gold went missing. Beardsley reckoned that Solly might be making a deal with the cozzers. Returning some of the stuff officially or using it as a bribe. Whatever, it looked bad. If Solly coughed we could all be fucked.

Beardsley and me went round to his shop as he was closing up. Solly acted all jovial and friendly. You could tell he was scared, though.

'Simon,' he greeted Beardsley, his arms raised palms upward. 'And young Gary. I didn't recognise you without your wild colonial boy disguise.'

Beardsley was worried that Solly might be wired up so the conversation was all sort of coded.

'I told them nothing,' Solly insisted.

'Really?' said Beardsley. 'Then why didn't you tell us that you'd had visitors?'

'I didn't want to worry you. This I can deal with myself.'

'Deal? You've made a deal?'

'No, you misunderstand me. No deal. No talk. No nothing.'

'So where's the stuff gone?'

'Well, I had to put it somewhere safe for a while. I can't say right now where it is.'

'You won't say, you mean.'

'No, no. Can't. Some things cannot be said. Or rather they are explained in another way.'

'You're talking in riddles, Solly.'

'Yes. Well, that's it. That's exactly it.'

'Look, Solly. You really shouldn't be fucking us around like this. There's far too much at stake. We need to know where it is.'

'No, please, Simon, try to understand. It's hidden but' – he leaned forward and whispered – 'there's a map.'

'What are you talking about, a map?'

'That's what makes it safe. Just give me some more time.'

'I can't promise you any more time. Sorry, Solly. It's not just down to me, you know. Come on, Gaz.'

'Please, Simon,' Solly begged as we walked out of the shop.

Two days later Solly Blumberg was shot dead as he was opening up his shop in the morning. A motorcycle with a pillion passenger pulled up beside him and three bullets were fired into him.

Beardsley never made any direct comment on whether it had been him that had ordered the hit. 'Shame about poor Solly,' was about the most he'd ever say on the subject.

And after that the bullion thing got really quiet. The missing gold never got found, either by the cozzers or people on our side. Rumours went round about it being hidden somewhere.

Buried treasure. Beardsley stopped being involved and tried to make sure that there was nothing that could link him to it. And I tried to forget it all. To deliberately not remember things and to work out all sorts of alibis for that time. Bit by bit a lot of the dodgy businessmen who had been handling the Hounslow bullion got pulled but Beardsley remained in the clear. One thing stayed in my mind, though. Solly had got done. I could get done one day.

So it made me a little edgy. But that's a natural thing, isn't it? I mean, you look at an animal in the wild and their little head is going to be darting about all the time, checking out if some bigger fucker's going to do them. And at the same time they're looking around for something to pounce on themselves.

Open my eyes and I'm looking up at the ceiling. Little swirls of textured paint. Move my head to look around. Natalie asleep on the settee. No sign of Martin. I'm fucking lying on the floor. Weak as a kitten. I try to sit up a little but I'm pinned down, like I'm on a fairground ride, as the whole of Martin's council house goes whizzing around through space. I'm fucking helpless. Anyone could come in and do me.

I look around the lounge. There's a sheath knife under the coffee table. I crawl over and grab it. I've got to get up and get on. But I've got to rest for a bit more. I just need a little more time.

A little more time.

In 1985 I got into trouble again. My flat got spun by the Drugs Squad at seven in the morning. They didn't find what they were looking for but they came across a handgun I kept under a loose floorboard by my bed. So I went away again, this time Parkhurst, on the Isle of Wight. Reggie Kray was there and I got to know him a bit during evening sessions in the gym. I was a bit worried, again because of Beardsley's connection with the Hat. But all these old scores seemed forgotten. Inside it's different, you're more likely to have a grudge with someone over an ounce of snout or a lump of blow.

Reggie seemed very gentle really. Mad keen on weight training, but very soft spoken. He was always going on about this friend of his on his wing.

'He's going to be a star, you know. He's got a terrific voice and he's a fantastic mover. He's won medals for disco dancing.'

It was strange, this famous gangster going on like a schoolgirl. And there was a lot of gossip going around. *It's nothing like that*, said one of the old lags, but with a kind of glint in his eye like you weren't sure whether he was taking the piss or not. It got me thinking. Of course, a lot of *that* went on inside, I knew that. But it wasn't the sex. It was something else. Being close to other people. I mean, I'd always found it hard. Inside you don't have any choice. You can't feel properly alone, just properly lonely. One time, when I got in a row with another con, I was glad to be on chokey block, in isolation for a while. But sooner or later you have to deal with other people.

Outside, who had I been close to? Dan? Yeah, well, I'd never been that close to even him. Birds? Well, tarts I'd paid for. Earthquake groupies, skinhead girls that might as well have been boys the way they looked.

I wouldn't tell anyone but I got to thinking about all sorts of shit on that stretch. Disconnected, that's how I felt. Now I'm swimming, it's that out-of-body feeling, nothing is happening from the neck down or the waist down for that matter. Just thinking. Not knowing fuck-all really. Mind reeling away. The way that queer at Mile End looked at me, like he knew something. I wish I fucking knew.

But I don't. A kind of lovely numbness. A dullness that soothes bad memories. Thank fuck I'm out of there. Out of it.

When you're banged up, wanking away and running out of things to think about, as I said, it ain't just sex, or rather the lack of it, it's coping with being crammed together with all those people. Having to fight for that space around you that you take for granted in normal circumstances. That space that you need to protect yourself. It becomes part of the prison.

Tired.

Curled up. Quiet and warm. Safe.

No.

Feel the floor move slightly. Someone is creeping up on me. Fuck. Grab the handle of the sheath knife. Hope that I can move fast enough.

A hand touches my shoulder and I roll over. Grab at the legs and pull this fucker over. I'm on top of them. Knees on their arms, hand on their face, blade at their throat.

A loud scream. I look down. It's the girl. It's Natalie. I let go of her face and take the knife away from her neck.

'What the fuck are you doing?' I shout at her.

Her mad little eyes staring up in terror at me.

'I, I . . .'

She's trembling. I get off her and stand up. Help her up on to the settee. She lights a fag shakily.

'I was . . . I was just going to wake you up,' she finally says. 'I didn't mean to freak you out.'

'Yeah, well. I thought it was someone else. Sorry.'

She's already scraping a couple of lines together. We both have a bit of a pick-me-up and she puts the kettle on for a cup of tea. It's dark outside again. I haven't seen the light for days. What time is it? I look at the timer on the video but it's just flashing 00:00. Come to think of it: what fucking day is it? I ask Natalie when she comes back through with the tea.

'It's Saturday. It's five o'clock.'

'Where's Martin?'

'He had some business to attend to. Said that I should look after you.'

'Oh yeah?'

She was pretty. Skin and bones, though. And scarcely more than a kid. I got my mobile out and switched it on. Two messages. Both from Beardsley. I played them. Number one: *Gaz, it's Beardsley. Call me.* Number two: *Where the fuck are you? Look, call me. Something's come up.* I start to dial his number. Natalie's come over. Standing right up close to me. Touching me.

'You want a blow job?' she says.

'What?' I scowl at her. Move her hand away from my crotch. 'No,' I say. 'No, no, no, no.'

'Go on. Twenty quid.'

'How old are you?'

She gives this stupid grin.

'Sixteen.'

Look down at her face. Knowing smile marked out in lipstick. Old before its time. Think about that other girl's face in the papers with tubes coming out of it. Think about my girls. Charlene and Donna.

Natalie's walked around me and put the telly on again. I wander out into the kitchen and make that call to Beardsley.

'Where the fuck have you been?'

'I've been busy.'

'Yeah, sure. Busy getting off your face.'

'Look, I've sorted something out. What we talked about.'

'Oh yeah?'

'Yeah.'

'What have you done?'

'Never you mind. Just check out the papers on Sunday.'

A pause. I can tell Beardsley's intrigued. I've caught him on the hop. Thinks I'm fucking useless.

'What is it?'

'No,' I say. 'You tell me.'

'What?'

'You phoned me. So. What is it?'

'Meet me tomorrow night,' says Beardsley. 'I'll let you know where.'

Drive home. There's a letter from this bloke Roger Wilbey from the Environmental Health Registration Scheme informing me of a review of my licence to run doors in the district on Wednesday and requesting my attendance.

I've still got Dan's phone number even though we haven't spoken to each other for all this time. I want to talk to him now. I pick up the phone and dial. For all I know he's moved or changed his number or whatever. It rings six times then an answerphone message. Dan's voice recorded. He's still there. Can't think of what message to leave so I just put the phone down.

I got out in the summer of 1988. This time I thought I would be ready for whatever lairyness fashion could throw at me. But as I said before, I was wrong. It was a shock, I can tell you, especially after coming out of the most drab and grey place imaginable.

I went to see Dan. He said he wanted to go out and celebrate, as we always did. He looked a right fucking state when he opened the door to me. He was wearing dungarees, for Christ's sake. Some hippy tie-dye T-shirt, a pair of scruffy baseball boots and to top it all a fucking paisley-pattern headscarf.

'Dan, what the fuck is this?' I said.

'It's all right, Gaz,' he said, kind of patting me on the arm, like. 'It's cool.'

We just sat and talked for a while. Tried to catch up with all the years. It was getting late and we'd just had a couple of beers. I was ready for a skinful.

'We ought to be getting ready to go,' I said. 'It's nearly ten.'

'Don't worry,' Dan insisted. 'We're going to this club later.'

I assumed that he meant an after-hours drinking place.

'Ain't you going to get changed?' I asked.

Dan laughed and shook his head.

'You mean, I'm going to have to be seen with you going out like that?'

'Don't worry, Gaz. Some of the old firm will be there.'

Well, we got to this club around midnight. It's a bloody warehouse. A half-derelict dock building on the south side of the river between Southwark Bridge and London Bridge. Weird electronic music with this thumping beat blaring out.

'What the fuck is this?' I ask Dan.

'Don't worry,' he replies, and holds something up between his thumb and forefinger. 'Take this.'

It's a pill. He goes to put it in my mouth.

'Uh-uh,' I say, grabbing his hand.

I take the pill off him and look at it. It's a big white thing.

'What is it? Speed?'

'You'll see,' says Dan.

And so I put it in my gob and swallow it.

We meet up with some old ICF mates of Dan's and some of them look as lairy as he is. They all look really pleased to see me and are dead friendly. All talking to me at once: *Good to see you, Gaz. Nice one, mate. Fucking blinding. Get on one.* And so on. They're all huddled around me. A bit too close really. I put up my hands.

'Easy now,' I say to them.

Dan clocks me looking a bit uneasy and he ushers me through.

'Come on, lads,' he says, laughing. 'Let the dog see the rabbit.'

We walk through the warehouse. It's filling up with kids, young and old. All doing this spastic dance to this thump-thump-thump music.

'You feel it yet, Gaz?' he asks.

'What?'

'You know, the pill.'

I shake my head. We're moving through the crowd and people are letting us through, smiling. Dan seems to know a lot of people here because they're like patting him on the arm as he passes them. People are wearing all kinds of things: smiley-face T-shirts, over-sized jumpers, there's even someone in a fucking poncho. *Can you feel it?* this voice keeps saying on the record. No I fucking can't, I think. Then I see a couple of tasty-looking geezers looking over in our direction. I nudge Dan.

'Dan', I say. 'Those blokes over there.'

'Where?'

I try to nod at them surreptitious, like. But they've already noticed that we've noticed them. They're coming towards us. I get ready to shape up. Dan's just grinning.

'Dan, they're fucking Millwall, aren't they?'

I'm thinking, here we go. I'm looking back to see where the rest of the ICF lot are. But Dan's just going up to these geezers and shaking their hands.

'Gaz,' he says, turning to me. 'Meet Billy and Johnno.'

They both grin at me and I manage a smile back. What the fuck is going on?

'I need a drink, Dan.'

'Stay here, I'll get you one.'

This new record starts. Boom-boom bass drum with harsh high hat. Piano chords. Then: *all right* chanted on the beat. *All right. All right. All right.*

Dan's back and he hands me my drink. I take it off him. It's one of those little bottles of Lucozade. I hold it up.

'What the fuck is this, Dan?'

This is the last straw. I'm livid, or at least I think for a second that's how I feel. Then I start laughing. It's so fucking stupid. Lucozade. What Mum used to give you as a treat when you were sick, I mean really sick, not just bunking off school. I'm grinning like an idiot. Like a kid again. I take a swig from the bottle, all the bubbles rising in my head. Lucozade Aids Recovery, I think, grinning away. *But it's gonna be all right,* says the record. *'Cos the music plays for ever*. And bosh, my head is lifted. All that pressure, that aggro, that loneliness, it just falls away on to the filthy warehouse floor. *On and on and on and on and on*. And, yeah, I know now. What all these silly fuckers were saying. I'm on one.

Shoom! It all happened for me at once then. *All right*. I'm moving like a spastic, too. *All right*. I'm among the crowd, dancing. *All right*. I'm letting go of that solid block of space around me. *All right*. I'm smiling, touching people.

Five o'clock in the morning and we're outside by the river, watching the sun come up, passing a spliff around. I'm sat cross-legged on the floor.

'Look at Gaz,' Dan says. 'He looks like the fucking Buddha.'

I was happy. I ended up hanging around with Dan and his mates for a bit, going to all these different Acid nights. There were plenty of Es around. This bloke Brian was supplying. He was a normal fellah, not a proper dealer or anything. He'd come across the stuff in Ibiza the year before and he'd get hold of enough to sort his mates out. It was good to relax and let go of it all for a bit. Especially after being inside for a while. And I felt that I could connect with people. Feel warm towards them.

But you know what, after a while I thought: so what? Maybe I was getting less of a rush from the pills. Maybe I was just getting bored with being happy. It's not my style, to tell you the truth. It was time to get back to work, I thought. And this scene had given me a few ideas.

I was at this thing called Spectrum on a Monday night. It was in a proper club under the arches at Charing Cross. I'd gone up on the balcony to get away from the crowd for a bit. I remember watching the light show. A green laser fanning out over the crowd, like a thin film of scum on a pool. Hands reached up to break the surface as all the pond life wriggled below. I started to think about how much cash I could make out of all of those happy mugs.

Of course, I'd be lying if I told you that I was first in thinking how much could be made out of this racket. Already people were making their moves. The ICF and other hooligan firms were muscling in to a lot of the clubs that were springing up all over the place. But it was early days and with a bit of organisation someone could make a killing. I knew who I had to go and see.

There's a photo of one of Tony Tucker's dealers on the front page of the *Sunday Illustrated*. *EXCLUSIVE: WE REVEAL MEN QUESTIONED IN ECSTASY DEATH INQUIRY.*

Beardsley is well pleased.

'You have something to do with this?'

'Yeah,' I reply, and tell him about my meeting with Keith.

'Nice one, Gaz. That ought to keep things off our backs for a bit. Which is just as well 'cos I've got other things to worry about.'

'What?'

'Well, a certain face seems to have reappeared. Either that or someone's seeing things.'

I know better than to pry. Just let him rabbit on.

'It's that fucking gold, Gaz,' he says with a pained look. 'I thought we were done with it but . . .'

He lights a fag. I realise he's nervous.

'Remember Solly?' he asks.

I nod.

'I don't know, Gaz.' He sighs. 'We might have made a very big mistake.'

'What's this all about, Beardsley?'

He holds his hand up and shakes his head.

'You keep out of this, son.'

He turns the paper back over.

'Well done with this,' he says, tapping the front page. 'Maybe now's the time for taking Tucker and his friends out of the game for good.'

'What, grassing them up?'

'What you take me for, Gaz? Nah.' He laughs. 'I was thinking of something more permanent.'

Beardsley and Tucker aren't exactly on good terms although they still do bits of business together. There's supposed to be an agreement about how things should be organised but Tucker is always pushing his luck. He has a reputation for fucking people over in drug deals. And now his main partner Pat Tate is out of prison they're getting more and more lairy. Beardsley resents people like Tucker and Tate as opportunists who've jumped on a bandwagon while he has carefully built up his own organisation and avoided trouble or attention being drawn to his activities.

'Easy come,' he says, 'easy go. I should never have let them move in on my racket.'

'Our racket,' I remind him.

'What?'

Beardsley pisses me off sometimes. He's the guvnor and I've never minded that but sometimes he forgets how things were. It was me that got him started in all of this, after all.

I had taken Beardsley along to this club in Charing Cross back then.

'What the fuck is all this?' he said, looking down from the balcony at all the mad ravers waving their hands in the air.

'They're calling it the Second Summer of Love.'

He turned to me with a sour look on his face.

'Well, it's horrible,' he said.

I shrugged.

'It's business,' I told him. 'The Es, the pills these kids are taking, they're twenty quid a throw.'

'Really?'

'Yeah. You want to try one?'

'Not if that's what it does to you,' he said, nodding at the throng below.

'It's a good buzz.'

'I'll take your word for it.'

'Thing is, the dealing is all a bit laid back. There doesn't seem much organisation to it. If we could get a proper supply we could undercut everyone else and clean up.'

Beardsley thought about it for a while.

'I don't know, Gaz. This so-called Second Summer of Love, well, it's going to be over soon. Thank fuck. After that this whole scene might just blow over. Then we'll be left in debt with a load of unsold drugs.'

'I don't think so.'

'No?'

'No.'

'Well, I'll tell you what. Prove it.'

'What?'

'Prove to me you can make some gelt out of this. Then we'll talk. Now, I'm getting out of this place. It's giving me a fucking headache.'

I went around to see Brian with Dan. He was dead friendly, sort of making a show of it. Bringing out the champagne and the charlie and being all cool with it. He was obviously coining it a bit from selling pills but he was dead slack about it. Didn't seem to have any proper back-up and Brian wasn't what you'd call heavy himself. And he'd let far too many people know what he was up to.

I asked him about the pills.

'Well,' he said, 'I only deal to my friends.'

We talked and talked but I couldn't get him to tell me who

his supplier was. He wasn't that stupid. In the end I just put it to him straight.

'Could you get me two thousand?'

'That's a lot of friends, Gaz.'

'Yeah, well, I . . . well, we was thinking of having a bit of a party, like.'

'Hm.'

He went a bit quiet. Suddenly out of his depth.

'Well?'

'Yeah, sure,' he said, fronting it all casual. 'Take me a couple of weeks, though.'

'How much?'

'Um, er, fifteen, er, fifteen grand.'

I wondered what the real mark-up was. I'd soon find out.

'Sweet,' I said. 'Let me know when you've got them.'

Ten days later and I got the call. I went around there with Dan again. Brian had the pills.

'There you are, geezer,' he says, all cocky, holding up this bag full of them. 'Yellow Burgers, the best that's around at the moment.'

'Thanks, Brian,' I replied, taking them from him.

'So,' he said with a grin. 'Um . . .'

'What?'

I think he knew then that something was wrong.

'Well . . .' he said.

He was getting very, very edgy. I thought: get it over with. I took out my squirt bottle and did him in the eyes with ammonia. He clutched at his face, with a horrible squeal.

'Sorry about that, Brian,' I said.

'What you do that for?' he moaned, stumbling about the flat.

'I need to know your supplier.'

He was heaving and groaning, panting and wheezing. Cursing.

'Fuck! You fucking bastards!'

'Now, Brian,' I went on, 'you don't want me to hurt you any more. Do you?'

I grabbed him by the hair and got him down on his knees. It didn't take long. Though getting this name and address was a right palaver. Dutch. Luckily Dan was there to do the spelling. We dragged him into the bathroom and put him under the cold tap, phoned an ambulance and got out of there.

'That wasn't very nice,' Dan told me.

'Taught him a lesson. If it hadn't have been me it would have been someone else.'

'But fucking hell, Gaz. You didn't have to.'

'What's the matter with you?'

Dan sighed.

'I don't know, Gaz. I thought you'd calmed down.'

I shrugged. I would have told him that I was calm. That this had been business, not me being out of order. But I knew he wouldn't understand. He wouldn't even take a proper cut from the pills we'd nicked. Silly cunt didn't want to know.

It was then that me and Dan sort of fell out with each other. We didn't have a row or anything, we just stopped spending time together. He had his family and he had stopped all that ICF stuff. And I was getting busy with something.

I set up some guys I'd met in these clubs who I thought I could trust. I sold the pills on to them at a tenner each so I made just about twenty grand. Beardsley was well impressed when I dropped the pile of money on his desk.

'Well, I'm impressed, Gaz,' he said, holding up the money like he was weighing it or something.

I gave him the name and address of Brian's contact but Beardsley said he was planning a trip to Amsterdam to have a word with some of his own friends out there. He went to hand me back the cash. I shook my head and put up my hand.

'Nah,' I said. 'That's an investment. In our new business.'

Beardsley smiled.

'You're learning, son.'

There were a lot of rumours going on at that time about who was running what on the acid scene, as it was called back then. Hooligan firms getting organised, various faces and well-known families wanting to move in. But it was hard to keep track of. Clubs were coming and going. Warehouses would be squatted in for one night and then the promoters would move on. Everybody was talking about this new Acid House thing but no one was quite sure what was going to happen next. Beardsley had his own ideas about what we should be doing.

'It's about power and control,' he said one night when we were having a bit of a coke session.

'Yeah.' I nodded. 'Of course.'

'You know, when I was inside I did a bit of studying.'

Beardsley always started with the clever talk when he'd had a bit of charlie.

'This Roman,' he went on. 'Juvenal, he was called. He said: *quis custodiet ipsos custodes*.'

'Oh yeah?'

I didn't know what the fuck he was on about now.

'You know what it means?'

'Nah.'

'It's Latin. It means, who will guard the guards themselves.'

'Oh,' I said, like I understood what he was fannying on about. 'Yeah.'

'What he meant, Gaz, is that those entrusted with power by the state or whatever, they're the ones that can end up running things. You know, like those African countries where the army takes over the government.'

'Yeah.' I still didn't get what he was on about. 'Right.'

'It's who runs the doors, Gaz. That's what this thing's going to be all about. It doesn't matter who runs the club, who promotes the event or whatever. It's who's in control of security, that's going to be the thing. That way you decide who can bring in drugs and deal inside the place. It's the guards, Gaz, *ipsos custodes*.'

Custodis Security, that's what I call my door firm now. Sounds classy, doesn't it? And I made sure that it all looks above board. Tax, VAT, national insurance, the fucking lot. When I settled down with Karen the whole idea was that I'd go straight. I didn't want our kids to have a daddy away in prison.

Of course, the business was a legitimate front for lots of naughty things that I've been up to and it's also been a way of laundering money, but I've always been really careful to make it look kosher. Then I get this grief from the council. This Environmental Health Registration Scheme thing. There's been complaints against some of my doormen and me personally about 'using excessive force' and suspicions that my staff have allowed drugs to be brought into premises.

Needless to say this girl dying hasn't helped. It's Wednesday morning and I'm sat in front of them all. A couple of blokes from the Police Licensing Unit, some local councillors, this twat Roger Gilbey who sent me the letter and this woman from Environmental Health who announces that she's chairing the meeting. Kangaroo court, more like.

She starts off droning on in this foreign language about policy and procedure, monitoring and guidelines. I nearly doze off. Another bad night and my head is fucked. I just nod along to it at first. It's them trying to be all reasonable and shit before they start to have a go.

Then the aggro starts. Complaints. Persons assaulted by my doormen. Evidence of drug dealing apparently sanctioned by some of my doormen. The criminal records of some of them. My criminal record. I butt in and say:

'Hang on a minute.'

But this woman stops me and says:

'Mr Kelly, please do not interrupt. You will have your chance to answer these allegations in good time.'

And she looks at me like I'm a fucking naughty schoolboy or something. I try to stay calm. Think about how I can talk my way through this when the time comes. But then it all goes horribly wrong.

'And we understand,' one of these cunts is saying, 'that your wife, Mr Kelly, has served an injunction against you as part of proceedings in a complaint of assault on her person.'

Well, I lose it now, don't I?

I'm shouting. I'm on my feet and I'm shouting at them.

'What the fuck has this got to do with you?'

'Mr Kelly, please calm down.'

'This has got nothing to do with you!'

I've really blown it now. It's funny, part of my brain is taking in this fact, while the rest of me is going ballistic. I'm going to lose my licence and half of Essex knows that I'm a wife-beater. Great. Fucking great. No point taking any more of this shit so I just walk out.

I'm going to lose my licence. There goes my legitimate livelihood. And with Beardsley shutting everything else down what the fuck am I going to do for money? It goes so fucking quickly. The dodgy cash just gets burned up and the clean money I've put through the firm, well, the fucking taxman's going to be after most of that.

The thing that really nags at me is that I'm damn sure they mentioned the injunction Karen got served on me deliberately to wind me up. Get me angry and justify their opinion of me as just a mindless thug. And it was horrible all of that coming out in the open. Embarrassing. Worse than that. Shameful.

I've had a few drinks and I find myself welling up. I'm so fucking sorry. I'm in a fucking sorry state. Got to snap out of it. Have a wash and a shave. It's getting late. A couple of lines and I feel a bit sharper. And it numbs things out a bit, does the old charlie.

Got to go out. Got to prove that I can hold it together. Need to know what's happening too. If Beardsley isn't up for anything maybe I'll just find someone who is. Drive over to the Epping Forest Country Club. Bit of a flash place. Know the guys on the door. Some of them have worked for me. Have a bit of a chat.

Wander in and see a few familiar faces. Cautious nods all round. Everybody wary of each other since this girl dying. Loads of dealers have been busted, clubs raided. Tons of Class As flushed away in panic. Essex Drugs Squad extra proactive. Essex gangland completely paranoid.

Spot Tony Tucker and Pat Tate in the corner. Hard to miss them, they're both fucking huge bastards like me. First thought is: avoid those two, they'll have the hump about that story I fed to the press. Then I think: wait a minute, they don't know it was me, do they? And I don't want to make it look like I'm blanking them.

Send a bottle of champagne over. Kind of flash gesture they'll go for. Get a nod from Tucker and I go over.

'All right, Gaz?' says Tony as I join them. Friendly enough. Bit of an edge.

Pat Tate is gibbering away. Gurning. Off his face obviously.

'We're going to do them,' he's saying. 'Fucking take the cunts.'

'Take it easy, Pat,' Tony mutters.

'All right, mate?' Pat grins at me. 'How's Beardsley?'

'He's fine.'

It doesn't look like they suspect a thing and everything's all right with their arrangement with Beardsley. I stay and have a drink with them. Tate is really hyper. Making up for lost time. Only got out a month ago. He wants to make up for lost time in other ways too. He's talking about how he's missed out on making lots of money because he's been away so much. Looking around and seeing how well some people have done. Know how he feels. Beardsley's got a big mansion and I've got a Barratt home that's worth less than what I paid for it.

Tate's just got back from Holland. Went to get his money back on some bad puff he had smuggled in. Now he's got some cash and him and Tucker are about to do some sort of deal. He's talking far too much. Tony Tucker's quiet. Asking me questions. Obviously wanting to know what me and Beardsley are up to.

'Beardsley's keeping well quiet until this thing with the girl what died calms down a bit,' I tell him.

'And what about you?' Tucker asks.

I shrug. Don't tell them about losing my licence to run doors. What am I going to do? Got to start making money soon. Bills to meet and cash running out. Tax and VAT to pay on the legitimate front of Custodis Security. Don't know what's going to happen with Karen but I want the girls to be properly looked after. So many things to worry about and so much of my money going straight up my nose.

Everybody's taking far too many drugs. Tate especially. His body all pumped up with steroids and all. Pat's got a right reputation in Essex. Back in 1988 he'd got into a row in a Happy Eater and robbed the till. He got arrested and they found a load of gear on him. Two weeks later at a remand hearing at Billericay magistrates' he jumped the dock and made a getaway on a motorbike waiting for him outside. He hid out in Spain for a while but made the mistake of going to Gibraltar and got pulled there. Ended up doing six years for what started as an argument in a cheap restaurant.

He's talking to me later, going on about his plans. Bragging about how much money he's going to make. Flying in consignments of coke from the Continent in a light aircraft.

'Everybody's made a fucking fortune while I've been away,'

he's saying. 'Well, now it's my turn. And if you aren't doing anything with Beardsley at the moment, why don't you come in with me?'

'What do you mean?'

'Put some money up. I've got something lined up. You put something up and I could double it.'

'How much?'

'I don't know – say, thirty grand. In a week I could double that for you.'

'I don't know, Pat.'

'Come on, Gaz. You should start making money for yourself. Don't be Beardsley's fucking junior partner all your life.'

'Yeah, well. I'll think about it.'

'Do that. But make it quick. As I said. Something's lined up.'

Drive home. Think about it. Thirty grand turned into sixty. Could buy myself some time. Sort things out with Karen. Get away from all of this for a bit.

Think about what Tate said about me and Beardsley, too. I'm sick of being in his shadow. He's done so much better than me out of all of this yet I was the one that really saw how much could be made out of the rave thing.

It was late on in '88 and I'd gone to this outdoor rave held in this disused aircraft hangar in Kent. It was at a secret location, the precise address was left on a phone bank answering service just a couple of hours before the thing started. A huge convoy of motors all turned up at the appointed hour. 'Paradise', this thing was called, and it was fucking incredible. Flares lining the side road that led to the gig. Dry ice all over the floor and lasers flashing into the night sky with a mammoth sound system throbbing away so hard you could feel it in your bones. There was fairground rides and even a fucking bouncy castle, for Christ sakes. The ravers looked even more lairy than usual, white gloves and goggles, fluorescent face paint, some bloke on stilts wandering about, all holding their hands up in the air like they were worshipping some god. I was coming up on one and feeling well happy. Most of all I was high on the numbers. There must've been near on ten thousand punters at this thing, all of them pilled up. Fifteen quid to get in and fifteen quid a pill – well, my mind was buzzing at the pure mathematics of it all. If we could move into this one we'd be laughing.

I reported back to Beardsley and we spent a bit of time finding out who this Paradise lot were. Turns out it was run by this public schoolboy type called Ben Holroyd-Carter. He was using ex-squaddies as their security, not any London faces, out-of-towners, yokels. We put together an extra-tasty team of heavies together for the takeover. Then we kidnapped him and took him to this lock-up that Beardsley used for such purposes.

We tied him to a chair and knocked him about a bit. Beardsley let him know of the new arrangement. We'd take fifty per cent of the takings and control all the drugs at the raves.

'Well, thank you for your kind offer,' Holroyd-Carter said in his posh voice, trying to act all cool. 'But we've already got our own security arrangements.'

I held my Stanley under his nose.

'How'd you like a permanent smiley face?' I asked him.

Beardsley waved me back. He had this big mobile phone in his hand.

'Look, give me the number and I'll call up your guys. Tell them to come here and you can let them know what's going to happen from now on.'

'Well, they're not going to like this. What if they take it out on me?'

'Don't you worry about that. We can deal with these country bumpkins. One thing is certain, though. If you don't deal with us you're gonna get your throat cut.'

So Holroyd-Carter called them up and they arrived team handed. We had all of our firm there, tooled up to the back teeth. Baseball bats, CS gas, shooters. We outnumbered and outgunned this ex-army lot. They were fronting it out a bit but we had the upper hand.

'Look.' Beardsley was talking to Holroyd-Carter. 'You knew it was only a matter of time before a London firm would take over. You think that every villain in the Smoke hasn't been looking to move in on this racket sooner or later? We can give you proper protection, better than this bunch of fucking swedes. So tell them.'

Holroyd-Carter sighed.

'I'm sorry, boys,' he said to the squaddies. 'I'm going to have to go with these new guys.'

The yokels kind of looked around at us and each other. For a moment it looked like they might make a move. Then suddenly their leader kind of shrugged and said:

'Oh, fuck it, lads. Let's go.'

And they walked out of there.

So Paradise was ours and all through the next year Holroyd-Carter put on all these big fuck-off raves all around the South-East. He was a clever little cunt, was Ben. Beardsley thought that he would have some kind of input, him knowing about music promotion and so on, but he ended up learning from him. He knew about money laundering too. Paradise Incorporated was registered in the Virgin Islands, a nice little tax haven, so the authorities couldn't touch it.

'Never underestimate a rich rid,' Beardsley said to me. 'Business sense, well, they get it in their mother's milk.'

And Ben had a lot of useful friends in high places, clever lawyers to do all the paperwork, moody leases on sites and so on. A lot of the punters reckoned what they were attending was all very anti-Establishment but Holroyd-Carter was a right little Tory.

'It's enterprise culture, Gaz,' he said to me once.

'Yeah, fucking *Starship Enterprise* culture, more like,' I replied, looking around at all these gurning space cadets.

He was clever with technology, too. He used the British Telecom Voice Bank system, which meant he could put loads of phone lines into one answering machine. That meant he could leave a message telling everyone of the location from his mobile phone at the last minute and keep the Old Bill off the trail.

And the M25 had just opened. All the raves were set up somewhere close to it. Because it was a big circular motorway it was harder for the cozzers to set up a roadblock on it. There would be this long convoy of party people on it on the night of the rave, waiting for the signal. 'Keep it orbital' was what Ben would say.

I felt dead clever. There was plenty of money about and this time I was ahead of the game. Fashion had always played tricks with me in the past. Well, now I was getting my own back. I got to learn some of the words that these rave people would use. 'Dibble' for the police, 'cool' for about almost everything, and so on. And I got a nickname of my own. 'Geezer Gaz' was what they called me. At first I thought they were taking the piss but I came to take it as a mark of respect. That I was the top geezer, as it were.

Friday and I've arranged to take out thirty grand from the tax account of Custodis Security. Doesn't leave very much in the balance. Fuck it. Might as well dissolve the company. Put the cash in a sports bag, take it home and stash it. They're burying the girl that died today. Hear about the funeral on a news bulletin on the car radio. The priest groaning on about how she was not to blame but rather the guilt lay with a society that allowed the creeping cancer of drug abuse to destroy so many lives. And so on.

In the afternoon I've got this appointment with the doctor. It's a group practice and I suppose I assume it's going to be

Jake Arnott

a bloke that I'm going to see. But it's not. Dr Hanson turns out to be a woman.

So it's difficult to talk about what the matter is. Embarrassing. What do I say? I've knocked the wife about and she's got an injunction against me and thinks that I've gone psycho and can I have some treatment please?

I start off saying that I've had trouble sleeping and had nightmares and that. I tell her that I've found it hard to control my temper and that there are times that I feel paranoid. And she's just sitting there nodding. In the end she says:

'So, Mr Kelly, what do you think the problem is?'

'Well,' I reply, 'I don't know. You're the doctor.'

'Hm, yes. Do you think it's a medical problem?'

Oh Christ, I think.

'I don't know,' I say.

'Because I could refer you to a community psychiatrist. If that's what you want.'

'A shrink?'

Dr Hanson gives a little laugh.

'Yes, a shrink. Do you want me to do that?'

'Not really.'

'You see, Mr Kelly, there may be many ways of looking at this. You have problems with sleeping, feelings of anxiety, issues with aggression and violence. Would you say that you were a violent person, Mr Kelly?'

She looks up, staring me right in the eyes.

'Yeah,' I say. 'I guess.'

She stands up and goes to a filing cabinet and starts rooting around in it.

'Look,' she's saying, 'there is something. Now, where did I . . . ? Oh yes, here it is.'

She's got a little pamphlet in her hand. She gives it to me.

'MOVE,' she says.

'What?' I almost jump up out of my seat.

'Sorry,' she goes on. 'Men Overcoming Violence in Essex. It's a support group for people in your predicament. It meets every week. Why don't you it a try?'

Jesus fuck, I'm thinking. A fucking support group. Let's go around the circle and introduce ourselves. 'Hi, my name's Gary and I'm a professional thug.' But I nod and look at this leaflet like I might be interested. Maybe I can convince Karen that I'm doing something to change. Maybe it'll look good if anything goes to court.

Dr Hanson is writing something on a prescription pad.

'I can give you something to help you sleep as well. See how it goes and come back and see me if it doesn't work out.'

Pick up the prescription from the chemist's and drive home. Lots of traffic. Everybody out shopping. Less than four weeks to Christmas. All the houses in my street have got their decorations up. Only our house is dark. Decide to put some fairy lights up around the windows. Don't want burglars to think the house is empty. Don't want neighbours to think that my wife and kids have left me.

Drag the Christmas box from the cupboard under the stairs. Sort through the lights and the decorations. Think: maybe I should get a tree. Think: what's the fucking point? Put the lights up and the effort of it all makes me exhausted for some reason. Depression, I suppose.

Order a takeaway and have a few drinks. Decide to stay off the gear tonight. Get an early one, yeah. Check out the pills the doc gave me. Temazepam. Yeah, I'll have a few of those.

Have a look at this pamphlet. Shit. I don't want to talk about my personal problems with a load of blokes I never seen before. Still, maybe I should tell Karen about it. It was her idea that I should go and see someone, after all.

Phone her up. It rings a couple of times then this recorded voice comes up. *The number you have dialled has not been recognised. Please check and try again.* Shit, must have dialled the wrong number. I phone her again. Same poncey voice telling me I've not been recognised. Fuck. Karen's changed her number.

But I want to talk to her. Not sure what I'll say. That I'm sorry, I guess. That I miss her? Well, we don't really feel very much for each other any more. But it was good once. I miss that. Take another handful of temazepam and stumble off to bed.

It was in the summer of 1989, at one of the raves, that I met her. It was the morning after and the sun was coming up over this field full of lunched-out punters still at it. I was having a walk around, checking up on things. Sometimes people we knew would give us the nod if anyone else was dealing other than our people. Then we'd grab them, chuck them out and nick their drugs so we could sell them on. I was walking around the edge of this field that the rave was on. The birds were making a right old racket like they were competing with the thump of the bass line in the background. I noticed this girl crouched down by the hedge. I thought she might be sick from banging too many or something so I went over.

'Are you all right?' I asked, standing over her.

She looked up with this amazing smile on her face. Green eyes luminous in the low sunlight. Pupils like pinpricks.

'I'm just picking flowers,' she said. 'I ain't done this since I was a kid.'

I sat down next to her. The grass was wet with dew but I didn't care.

'It's nice, ain't it?' she said.

'Yeah,' I said. 'Nice.'

She'd made a daisy chain and she put it over my head like a little crown.

'Leave it out,' I said, laughing.

'No. It suits you.'

'What's your name, love?'

'Karen.'

'Hello, Karen. I'm Gaz. Geezer Gaz.'

She laughed at this then we sort of stared into each other's eyes for a bit, then started kissing. I felt all warm and tingly, buzzing from the pills. 'Loved up', as they say, and at that moment I knew what they meant. It wasn't really sexual. I felt I wanted to be close to this girl, to touch her gently and delicately.

We walked back to the party holding hands. *It's just the sun rising*, went this song. And it was. Me and Karen looked at each other and laughed like we suddenly thought the same thought together at the same time. Like we were connected. A woman's voice wailing these strange notes over the top of the music. Repetitive. Hypnotic. Murmur murmur murmur. *Love is just a state of mind. You leave behind.*

We ended up back at my gaff at about three in the afternoon and went to bed. It was sweaty and clumsy but it was good. It was nice just lying next to each other, both completely knackered. Empty and quiet. Just a little warm buzz to take us into sleep.

Wake up to a cold grey morning. Gloomy. But the temazepam did the trick. Slept through without any bad dreams. Head a bit thick, though.

Get up and make a cup of tea. Letter on the doormat from the Environmental Health Registration Scheme. Have a look at it ... *officially informing you that after due consideration we have decided to suspend your licence to provide security for entertainment premises forthwith* ... Chuck it in the bin.

The house is a tip. Try and tidy it up a bit. Phone rings and I pick it up. Little jolt of hope: maybe it's Karen. Stupid. It's Frank, the manager at Tiffany's.

'Gaz, what's going on? I just heard you lost your licence.'

'Yeah, that's right.'

'Well, what am I going to do? Who's doing the door tonight?'

'I don't know, Frank. You'll have to sort it, I guess.'

'But Gaz, it's Saturday night. I mean . . .'

'Well, it's not my problem any more, is it? They've taken away my fucking livelihood, haven't they?'

He's droning on. Doesn't give a fuck about my situation.

'And what do I say to your door staff when they turn up tonight?'

I really don't need this grief.

'I don't know, Frank, and I don't fucking care.'

'But Gaz . . .'

'Look, Frank, you useless cunt, just fuck off and leave me alone, OK?'

Put the phone down and think. Fuck. Every fucker is going to be phoning me up. Club managers, doormen I employ, geezers that pay me to use my company as a front so they've got legit invoices to give to people paying for their services and so on. Well, fuck them. Custodis is going into liquidation. I'll have to have a word with the accountant next week.

Of course, this means we won't be able to control who deals the drugs in all these clubs. Beardsley's not going to fucking like this. Anyway, I've decided, I'm going to make as much money as I can and fuck off out of it. Make a new start somewhere.

Phone Pat Tate and tell him I'm in. Arrange a meet at a café in the Lakeside Shopping Centre in Thurrock. Put the sports bag in the back of the car and drive over there. The sky looks cold and grey and heavy. Looks like it's going to snow again.

I hand over the money.

'How about coming in with us for good, Gaz?' he says.

'I don't know, Pat.'

'Beardsley's got you running around doing his dirty work but what have you got to show for it, eh?'

'Well . . .'

'We're going to be the main firm in Essex. We're going to take over the fucking manor. You want to make sure that you're on the winning side, Gaz.'

I shrug. Don't know what to say. I get up.

'I've got to be going,' I say.

'Think about it,' Tate calls after me as I leave.

Get back and there's a load of messages for me. Ignore all of them except Beardsley. Give him a call. Wants me to go over to his place.

It's dark when I get there. Talk to the intercom and the wrought-iron gates slowly swing open. Crunch up the gravel drive to the front of his huge gaff. Spotlit columns and Greek urns. Beardsley comes to the door with one of his Rottweilers. He looks edgy.

'You on your own?' he asks.

'Yeah, 'course.'

He gets rid of the dog and shows me through to this big lounge with a bar attached. He goes to fix the drinks.

'Cognac all right?'

'Sure,' I say, sitting down on this big white suede settee.

Beardsley comes over and hands me this huge glass. Grabs an armchair.

'So,' he starts, no fucking about. 'What's going on?'

'What?'

'What's this about you losing your licence?'

I sigh.

'It's these fucking Environmental Heath people.'

'So you lost the fucking doors in Southend?'

'Yeah.'

'Great. That's fucking great, Gaz. So what am I going to do now?'

'I don't know.'

'Well, I'm going to have to find someone else to deal with. You're no fucking use to me now.'

'Thanks a fucking lot, Beardsley.'

'It's fucking true. You're no fucking use to anyone these days. You're off your face most of the time. Look, I know you've been having personal problems but I'm running a fucking business here.'

'I thought we were supposed to be laying low what with this girl dying.'

'Yeah, but I didn't mean just to roll over and die. And what's with you getting involved with certain people?'

'What are you talking about?'

'You know what I mean. You're up to something with Tucker and Tate, aren't you?'

'So you been checking up on me?'

'Look, that firm ain't exactly being discreet themselves. They're going to fuck up really badly one of these days. Well, I've had enough.'

'What?'

'It isn't working out any more. You're a fucking mess. And I can't trust you any more.'

That is well out of order.

'You fucking what?' I demand.

'You heard.'

'You cunt. You fucking ungrateful cunt.'

'What?'

'After all I done for you.'

'You done for me?'

'It was me that got us started in this thing. Me. You always made more money than me but it was my idea in the first place. Well, fuck you, Beardsley. Thanks for fuck-all.'

And I walk out of there.

'I picked you out of the gutter when you were just a little hooligan!' he calls after me.

Fuck him, I think. I don't need him. I can take up Tate's offer and go in with them. Drive home and think: fifteen years working for Beardsley and it comes to this. Diabolical.

It seemed so easy back then. So simple when we were just doing the big raves. A bit of a laugh.

Everybody came to Paradise. I mean all sorts. From pikey-looking kids who kind of lived the life to yuppie twats who just wanted to get monged out of their skulls every weekend or so. There wasn't any overall style. Sure, there were odd little things some of the hard-core ravers picked up, white gloves, kids' dummies, face masks with Vicks Vap-O-Rub smeared on them which was supposed to boost the buzz, but there didn't seem to be any big fashion thing going on. A lot of the people who came were quite old really. I remember looking out at this mixed crowd with a feeling that something was over, that fashion was over – well, in terms of it being about youth and rebellion and that.

Of course, all these grinning people being happy with each other would no doubt be kicking the shite out of each other if it wasn't for the pills. The music got faster and harder. 'Mental', that's what everyone was doing that summer, 'going mental'. But they were easy enough to keep under control. Docile. We hardly ever had to do much real security work at the raves. Just organise the drugs and keep ready eyed for any rival firms that might want to muscle in.

Beardsley told me that he'd read this book set in the future where the government gave happy drugs to everybody to keep them in order. *Soma*, this stuff was called, and he reckoned it sounded just like E. He said that the state should dole it out on the National Health if they wanted to keep things nice and quiet.

He grinned. ''Course if it was legal we'd be out of a fucking job, wouldn't we?'

The powers that be didn't see Beardsley's point and they were getting a bit edgy. *SMASH THESE EVIL ACID PARTIES* were typical headlines in the press. *Evil dealers openly peddling drugs to the background of mind-bending music and lasers.*

The cozzers started organising themselves so that they could close down the raves. Dibble was getting wise. This special squad was set up to deal with all the raves – the Pay Party Unit, it was called. Now they had to stop the party from actually taking place. I mean, once there was ten or twenty thousand people in some field or warehouse it was going to be bloody difficult to arrest everybody, wasn't it? Undercover officers would go around clubs and record shops and pick up flyers. They'd listen in to pirate radio broadcasts, they even started sending out broadcasts themselves, sending potential punters to the wrong places. They'd have police helicopters buzzing the M25 on the run-up to Saturday night, looking for anything big and suspicious on the move like fairground rides.

Holroyd-Carter was smart but he was running out of luck. One night the Pay Party lot followed Paradise's lighting riggers to this venue and closed it all down at about six o'clock. There was a reserve site, this warehouse in the East End, so everyone made for there. But the cozzers were having a good day because they managed to track that one down too. It was about ten and the Paradise lot had set up and there was about a thousand kids in this building. Suddenly a whole convoy of plod vans turn up, riot police, dogs, the lot. Holroyd-Carter tried to reason with them with his moody paperwork and posh manner but they were having none of it. A bloke with a megaphone told everyone to disperse. Some of the kids tried to steam in but they got beaten back pretty quickly. I had to get out of there because I had a shed-load of Class As on me.

Holroyd-Carter called a meeting with me and Beardsley the next week. It was bad news.

'I'm getting out, I'm afraid,' he told us.

'What do you mean?' I demanded. 'A little bit of trouble and you're getting frightened.'

'Look, I'm under so much surveillance I can hardly fart

without them knowing about it. They've got the Tax Inspectorate and the Customs investigating me. I can't afford this much grief.'

'So where does that leave us?' I asked.

'Well, gentlemen, it's been a pleasure doing business with you.'

'How do we know that you're not having us over?' Beardsley cut in sharply.

Ben started to look a little flustered. 'What do you mean?'

'I mean, how do we know you're not going in with another firm or something?'

'Really, I can assure you.'

I grabbed him by his neck and pulled him up out of his chair a bit.

'We ought to do him anyway,' I said to Beardsley.

He was wheezing and going a funny colour. Beardsley started laughing.

'Let him go, Gaz.'

'You sure?'

'Yeah.'

So I dropped him back on his arse.

And that was it. By the end of 1990 it was all over. Most of the other raves closed down about then too. Some people reckoned it was the cozzers and this Pay Party Unit but it was us too. The villains, I mean. It had got all a little heavy for some people. But one thing changed for ever – drugs. Everyone was taking them now. So there would be a lot of money from that up for grabs.

But something really big in my own life was happening. Karen was pregnant.

'Gary is it?'

'Yeah, well, everybody calls me Gaz.'

I'm at this Men Overcoming Violence thing. Dingy community centre, plastic chairs in a circle. Tea and coffee things on a table in the corner. I'm early and it's just me and this guy I spoke to on the phone.

'I'm Bob,' he says.

'You the teacher?'

He sort of laughs at this.

'No, I'm the group facilitator.'

'What does that mean?'

'Well, it's my job to try and get people to talk, to share with each other. MOVE is about men taking responsibility and supporting each other. The group has to belong to the men in it for it to work. I'm just here to get this rolling.'

Fuck me, I think. Bob can tell I ain't too keen.

'It's not easy, Gaz. But remember, one of the hardest things is having the bottle to come to this group in the first place.'

I go and make myself a cup of tea. People are starting to turn up. I look at them all. Wife-beaters probably. Like me. Why don't they just call it Wife-Beaters Anonymous. Oh, fuck. Someone I know. I don't fucking believe this but someone I know has just walked in the door. It's Trevor something or other, used to work as a doorman for me a couple of years back.

'Good to see you, Gaz,' he says to me.

I lean close to him.

'Look,' I say softly, 'this isn't my idea coming here and if anyone finds out about this I will fucking kill you.'

'It's all right, Gaz.'

Then we're all sat in a circle. There's this big pad of paper on a stand next to Bob with GROUND RULES written at the top of it. Bob introduces me and everybody says their name. Then we're supposed to come up with these rules that Bob writes on the chart with a big marker pen. Things like not interrupting each other or making judgements. One of them is called GROUP CONFIDENTIALITY and Bob explains that it means that anything we say in the session is not to be repeated anywhere else, and I make sure that I catch Trevor's eye at this

point and give him a bit of a nod and a glare. The last one is
<u>BE POSITIVE</u> which Bob underlines twice. I get this horrible
queasy feeling.

Now we are all taking turns to talk. Going around the
circle. All these confessions. People saying about how they
were knocked about as kids and how they were taught to see
violence as acceptable. Everyone seems to have worked out
why they've done bad things. One bloke going on about it
being like an addiction, the adrenalin rush and that. Someone
else says he always felt powerless and aggro was a way of
asserting himself.

Everybody's yapping away about themselves. It's like those
daytime TV shows that Karen likes to watch. I can't understand it, these blokes grassing themselves up, going QE on
all the bad things in their lives.

It comes around to me and I don't know what to say.

'I don't know what to say.'

'It's all right, Gaz,' says Bob. 'Just maybe share a few
things.'

Shit. *No comment*, that's what I usually say when someone's asking questions. *I ain't saying anything without a
brief*. They're all looking at me. Waiting for me to cough
something up.

'I don't have an alibi,' I say at last.

There's this pause.

'Go on,' says Bob.

'Well, I don't know why I'm a big nasty bastard, I just
am. My old man might have clouted me a few times and
my mother certainly did but that didn't make me what I
am. I can't blame anybody. I've done some horrible things
and I'll probably do some of them again.'

'So why are you here?' This is from one of the blokes in
the group.

'Well, I lost it, didn't I?'

'Lost it?'

'Yeah.'

I suddenly feel giddy. The circle turning like a fairground ride. Surrounded by all these faces.

'I lost it completely. I can't remember all of it. Some of that was the drugs. You see, I was off my face. Off my fucking face at four in the afternoon. But I've blanked some of it out as well. It was so fucking horrible. I remember the voices. The kids crying. My wife screaming. And somebody shouting. I remember that. I remember thinking: who's that shouting? Then I realised it was me. And I stopped. And I looked around. Karen on the floor and me over her. And it suddenly went quiet. And she just looked up at me, face all swollen where I'd hit her, all swollen with hatred for me.'

Head spinning. In a cold sweat. Panting like a dog. And now it's quiet in the room. Here. That horrible quiet. Somebody coughs.

'You say you lost it, Gaz,' Bob is saying. 'Is that how you feel? Do you feel lost, Gaz?'

'Yeah,' I croak.

And then the others start talking. Saying things to me. Like they are trying to encourage me and that it's a difficult process and so on. And I'm not really listening, just trying to get my breath back and to get this fucking merry-go-round to slow down a bit. And then somebody else starts talking about their problems and I can relax a bit.

The session ends and I'm out of there as quickly as possible. Bob follows me out into the corridor.

'Gaz,' he says. 'I know that was hard. But I think you made a real breakthrough there. Well done. See you next week, I hope.'

I get to the motor. Well done? That's a good one. I'm still shaking from it all as I drive away. Put the radio on. Weather report: another big freeze expected. *Do you feel lost, Gaz?* I feel lost, all right. Lost in space.

Flashbacks of me beating Karen up. Need to blot it out.

Need to stop that video nasty playing in my head. Get hold of Martin on the mobile and head over there.

When I get there him and Natalie have been chasing the dragon. Bacofoil all over the coffee table.

'Fancy some?' asks Martin.

And my first thought is: no, I'm not a fucking junkie. But then I think: why not? No harm in just smoking it.

'Me and Nat just do it from time to time,' says Martin, like he's reading my mind.

'Yeah, all right, then,' I say.

And before you know it I'm sucking up this smoke from this line of smack on the foil as I'm burning it with a lighter underneath.

'Tell Gaz the story,' Martin is saying.

Feel sick. Go and puke up in the downstairs bog. Stomach retching away but I don't feel it. Wash my mouth out in the kitchen and come back through.

'A friend of Nat's heard this story. Go on, tell him.'

I collapse on to the settee. Feel warm, calm. Numb.

'You mean the pizza story?' Natalie is saying.

'Yeah. Listen to this, Gaz, this is the latest on Pat Tate. Tell him, Nat.'

'Well, according to Sharon last night Pat Tate's girlfriend was ordering a pizza from this pizza place in Basildon and she wanted this pizza with different toppings on it.'

'What, different pizzas?' I say.

'No, different toppings on the same pizza, you know, on different slices of it. Anyway, this bloke says they don't do that sort of pizza so Pat Tate grabs the phone and starts shouting at this geezer saying, "Bring us the fucking pizza we want, you cunt, or we'll come and get it," stuff like that, and the bloke puts the phone down on him. Well, then Pat Tate goes fucking mental. He turns up at the shop and throws the till at this bloke. He presses the panic button and Tate jumps the counter and smashes this bloke's face against the draining board in the kitchen, then fucks off before the police arrive.'

Shit. If Tate's been pulled I'm screwed.

'So then what happened?' I ask.

'Well, they can trace the call to Tate's house. But this pizza bloke, a few of this friends let him know who it was that beat him up, you know, what kind of bloke Tate is, and surprise, surprise, by the next day he don't want to press charges.'

Well, thank fuck for that.

Have a couple of lines and decide to go home. It's started to snow again. Get some gear off Martin to keep me going. Some charlie and some K.

'Want a bit of this?' Martin asks, holding up the bag of smack.

I shrug. Nod.

Why not?

It does take away the pain, after all.

Drive home through flurries of snow. Delicate little flakes of it melting on the windscreen. I'm thinking about the fact that I've given thirty grand to a maniac who beats people up because of disagreements over pizza toppings. What the fuck have you gone and done now, Gaz? Still, the drugs keep me calm and numb. I'll think about it tomorrow.

Home. Fairy lights flashing on and off in an empty house. Get inside and put the central heating on. Think about the group tonight. Me saying all those things in front of strangers Shudder with embarrassment. And all that stuff coming back about what happened.

Have a bit more of the smack. That stuff does the trick, you know. All the things I worry about fade out. Don't care. Don't have to care. Mmm. A yawn goes all tingly inside of me. Put the telly on. Lie on the settee and let it all wash over me.

When Karen was a few months gone she moved back in with her parents in Southend. Then I bought us the house here.

I'd put enough money aside to buy it outright. Put it all in Karen's name just to be on the safe side. We were married in July 1990 at Southend Register Office. I'd wanted Dan as my best man but we'd lost touch with each other. So Beardsley did the honours. He'd done really well out of the rave thing, much better than me. But I didn't mind back then. I had more than I'd ever imagined I'd get out of life. My own house, a woman that I loved, money in the bank and, to top it all, on 1 September that year Charlene was born, a beautiful baby daughter weighing in at seven and a half pounds.

The next few months, well, Charlene took up most of our time. It was a steady, uneventful time and for a while I was content with just being a family man. I loved our little daughter so much. It was probably the happiest period of my life.

I set up Custodis Security at the beginning of 1991. I got to learn all the details about running a legitimate business. And the loopholes too. Beardsley was organising the drugs side of things. I was to try and run the doors on as many clubs as I could and that way make sure it was always our drugs and our dealers that operated in those places. But it was much harder than when we were doing the raves. More competition. Lots of little power struggles going on in Essex. Beardsley ended up having a meet with Tony Tucker and they divided up some of the county, a sort of peace agreement. But to be honest things seemed to be getting heavier all the time. Beardsley didn't notice back then but the happy smiley time really had already gone. The music got faster and darker. The drugs got fiercer. Guns got easier to get hold of and loads of wannabes and coked-up chancers were running around Essex with automatic weapons.

And things started to get strained between me and Karen. After Charlene was born sex suddenly disappeared from the agenda to all intents and purposes. I didn't mind that so much but we didn't have very much else to get close to each other with. We didn't have very much in common. I could buy her nice clothes and a car and that but she wanted to be respectable. We'd moved into a fairly middle-class area and Karen wanted to keep up with that. I stuck out like a sore thumb, of course. When they found out that I ran a security firm I got an invitation to come along to the local Neighbourhood Watch scheme meetings but I didn't fancy that. I didn't really fit in with Karen's new friends and I felt that sometimes she was embarrassed about me.

Karen got up the duff again. Must have been that weekend we went away to Paris and left Charlene with the in-laws. I kind of wanted it to be a boy. Don't get me wrong, when Donna was born on 11 March 1992 I wasn't anything but overjoyed. I loved having two daughters. I just felt a little bit outnumbered, that's all.

In the autumn of 1993 I read this article in the local paper about a nine-year-old boy called Darren Tyler who was suffering from a a form of leukaemia that could only be treated in America. His family were trying to raise funds for this treatment. Something clicked inside of me and I decided I would help them. I thought that if I could get involved with doing some good people might see that I wasn't just some mindless thug. I figured that some charity work might give me a bit of respectability.

I started writing letters to people, celebrities and public figures, telling them of Darren's plight and asking for help. I wrote to Reggie Kray at Maidstone Prison and he wrote back. He remembered me and said that he was very touched by poor Darren's situation and that he wanted to get involved with some sort of fund-raising event. He sent me a list of contact numbers of friends of his that he thought might want to attend. These were gangland people but also pop stars and actors that he had known. His brother Ron was keen to get involved too and he phoned me from Broadmoor to offer his support.

I was well pleased that I was becoming acquainted with the Kray twins and gaining their respect. I thought that it would do my reputation good. Beardsley was a bit dismissive, though, when I told him. I thought that it might be because he had been involved with Jack 'The Hat' in the past but he denied that.

'It can't be bad being in with people that well known, can it?' I told him.

'Gaz, some of us are trying to avoid being well known. Know what I mean? The Twins always loved getting that attention but it didn't do them much good in the end, did it?'

I ignored that. I knew that like me a lot of people had a good deal of respect for Ronnie and Reggie. After a lot of phone calls and discussions it was decided that we would arrange a charity boxing show and dinner at a leisure centre in Romford. This bloke Harry Fraser got in touch soon after the decision was made saying that he had been appointed by the Krays to act as the promoter for the event. I wasn't entirely happy with this arrangement at first because I assumed that it would be me that would the promoter but I trusted the Twins' judgement and let Fraser get on with it.

The event was to be staged on 26 November, but the week before that unfortunately Darren died. He had been such a brave little fucker and I phoned his mother to offer my sympathies. And to assure her that the event would take place as a tribute to his courage and his memory. But when I next met with Fraser the first thing he said was: 'Well, what do we do with the money now, then?' I felt sick at this. Darren's family were heavily in debt from preliminary trips to the States and from paying for the extra care that their son needed and I told Fraser that all the cash raised should go to them. But I should have known then, from his attitude, that there was something dodgy about Fraser.

Both the twins were very sad at the news and sent tributes

to Darren that I read out at the event. We managed to sell over two hundred tickets at £50 a head and there was a raffle for a load of personal mementoes, some of them autographed, that had been donated by various celebrities. Charlie Kray attended, as did Tommy Patterson and his son Joe, the actor, and Ruby Ryder was there too. It was a great night and I was proud to have helped organise something like this. By my reckoning we had raised over ten thousand pounds.

But at the end of the night, when I went to collect the money, Fraser had scarpered. The hire of the leisure centre and the caterers had been paid but Fraser had made off with the rest. Subsequent attempts to contact him got no result. I was livid. I contacted Reg about it but in the end he said it would be best if the whole thing was forgotten. The press would have a field day if the Twins were seen to be associated with a charity rip-off. In the meantime I had to deal with Darren's family. I tried to explain to them what had happened but I got the silent treatment. I think they figured I was the one doing the ripping off.

The whole episode left me feeling bitter. Karen was not very sympathetic. I had been so involved in this charity event I had neglected my own family. It was about that time the rows began.

And the fact was that I had started to take a lot of drugs. It was an occupational hazard. Didn't really think about it much because everybody around me was at it. Nobody thought of themselves as being dependent or anything. People started taking more and more Es, trying to get that buzz you get from the first time you take it. Everybody saying the stuff was much better in the old days. I started taking more and more to sort of balance things out. Booze and puff to chill out. Coke and E to get up and feel confident. Then stuff to bring you back down again, ketamine or prescription drugs like temazepam or rohypnol. I never thought that I was a druggie. Oh no, I was in charge. I could control how I felt.

Well, that's what I thought. And I knew it wasn't exactly a healthy lifestyle and I should keep myself fit, so I started to get serious about going to the gym again. That's when I started taking the steroids. I was pushing forty and worried about keeping in shape but now I could train hard and get a really good muscle definition.

My relationship with Karen was getting worse and worse but we both just concentrated on leading our own lives. She had her own friends and my work meant that I was out most nights. I actually thought that I was stable with all the different drugs I was taking, like they were medicine to make me strong, keep me relaxed, get me high, level me off, help me work, help me sleep and so on. But I wasn't stable. I was like a chemical weapon ready to go off. A weapon of mass destruction.

I was on edge all the time. I started to worry about things all the time. I kept thinking that the house was being watched or I was being followed. I began to suspect that Karen was cheating on me. With Charlene at school and Donna at the nursery during the day, Karen started getting out of the house and doing things. An aromatherapy course and exercise classes. I didn't trust her. I felt sure she was having an affair.

I brooded over it for months. Got fixated on it. It got to be not if she was screwing someone else but who that someone else was. Any man she had contact with was a potential suspect as far as I was concerned. I was constantly checking in my mind who she spent time with, names of men she mentioned. Jason from two doors down who she'd got friendly with and was recently divorced, Barry, her step-aerobics instructor, and so on.

Some Saturday nights, if I was working, I might stay on for an all-night session somewhere and not get back home until the day after. This would piss Karen off and it would be another cause of us rowing. It wasn't as if she missed me, it was just that she'd worry something might have happened to me. So I agreed that I'd always let her know in advance if I wasn't coming home that night.

But the next time it happened, the beginning of November it was, I remember thinking, just as I'd put the phone down to let her know, this little thought: well, she knows the coast is clear now, doesn't she, Gaz? It was like a whisper in my ear. I couldn't get it out of my mind for the whole night. Her humping away while the old man was out.

I thought about going back to the house and catching them at it. Murderous thoughts. But I ended up just getting beasted on drink and drugs. A party at the house of one of the dealers until the early hours. Then some of us drove uptown to this chill-out club in Old Street. Twenty-four-hour party people – it seemed normal enough going on and on and on. It was nearly six o'clock on Sunday evening before I got back to the house.

'Don't know why you bother coming home at all,' Karen said. 'The girls have been wondering where you were.'

Charlene and Donna came through and wanted to play, jumping up and grabbing hold of me. But I was out of it.

'Sorry,' I said to them, pulling them off me. 'Daddy's very tired. He's been working hard.'

'Daddy's very off his face,' Karen hissed at me.

'Yeah, well, maybe Mummy's been having a good time too,' I whispered back.

'What's that supposed to mean?' she said out loud.

'I know what you're fucking up to!'

'Oh, great. Swear in front of the kids, why don't you?'

'Leave me alone.' I pushed past her and hauled myself up the stairs.

The next day it was my turn to pick up Donna from nursery and Charlene from school and then Karen from the sports centre. I'd slept through into the afternoon so I had a bit of charlie to try and perk myself up. Charlene's teacher came out and spoke to me by the school gates. Charlene's behaviour had become an issue for the school this term and the teacher was going on about how it was still a problem, she was being aggressive and disruptive. I hardly took in what she was saying. I felt bleary and irritable. I knew that Karen would blame me for this as well. *You hardly spend any time with them these days*, she was always saying.

Get to the sports centre and wait for Karen to come out. Watch her walking out of the front entrance talking with Barry the instructor. They look happy together. They are laughing.

They are laughing at you, Gaz. That voice whispering to me again.

They say goodbye. Barry holding up a palm, see you. Karen gently pats him on the arm then turns and walks out to the car park. A simple, delicate gesture. A gentle, intimate thing. She is still smiling until she sees where I'm parked and then her face flattens out again. She puts her bag in the boot and gets into the passenger seat.

Then I know. I know that it is him. Barry. That's who she's been fucking. Barry, Barry, Barry, Barry. Bet he preys on them. It's all women in those stupid classes.

Get home and the girls go into the lounge to watch children's TV. I follow Karen into the kitchen. I'm shaking. I'm wiped out from the weekend. Cold sweat running down the backs of my legs. I feel like a fucking zombie. Empty. Like there's nothing inside of me, just a pulse throbbing away, a vein on the side of my head twitching. Blood-red rage pumping into me. Filling me up. It's warm, oh yes, it's warm. *It's him*, says the voice. *Hmmm.*

'It's him,' says my voice. 'Isn't it?'

'What are you talking about?'

'It's Barry, isn't it?'

'What?'

'Is it good, then? With Barry?'

'Gaz, I really don't know what you're talking about.'

'You're fucking him, aren't you?'

'What?'

'Barry.'

She stares at me, green eyes wide, mouth open.

'Barry?' she says.

'Yeah.'

And then she laughs out loud. She's laughing at me. And I lose it. And I hit her. And she goes down. Laughter turning into screaming. And I keep hitting her. And the girls are crying as they come through the hallway hearing all this noise. And I hear this shouting. And that's when I think: who's that shouting? And I realise it's me. It's me shouting my head off.

And I stop.

And it goes quiet.

And Karen is looking up at me.

Her face swollen with hatred.

Christ.

And the girls are cowering together in the corner of the room.

And I stagger out of there. Get into my car and drive. I come back three hours later to an empty house. She's gone and taken the kids to her mum's. I go around there and Karen's mum tells me that Karen doesn't want to see me and I start rowing with her and she threatens to call the police. And the next day Karen gets that injunction thing out on me.

I come to some time in the afternoon. The smack's worn off and my body aches all over. Head's throbbing. The snow has come down heavily again. It's beautiful the way it covers everything and makes it look clean and new. I feel old and dirty. I lie there brooding about all the bad things in my life.

I'm so fucking stupid. I was going to go and do that Barry

bloke. I asked around about him and only found out he was gay, didn't I? That's why Karen was laughing at me.

The phone rings. I let it go on to the answerphone. *Gaz?* comes the voice. It's Karen. *Gaz, are you there?* What does she want? She sounds worried. I pick it up.

'Hello.'

'Thank God. You're there.'

'Yeah. What's the matter?'

'There was something on the news. I thought it was you.'

'What was on the news?'

'These blokes that got shot.'

'No, I'm all right.'

'Right. Well, then.'

'Hang on.'

'Look, I was just worried you might be dead. That's all.'

And she puts the phone down. Well, she's worried I might be dead. That's nice. Think about it. These blokes that got shot? What could that mean? Get up and my whole body is groaning at me. Go out and get a local paper.

GANGLAND CLUE TO MEN SHOT DEAD IN RANGE ROVER, is the headline in the *Echo*. Three men were shot in the head as they sat in a car after apparently being lured to a remote farm track in Essex. Fucking hell, I think. Look down the page to see if they say who it is but *their identities have not yet been disclosed*. Beardsley's got a Range Rover. Maybe he's one of them. A shudder goes right through me. Someone walking on my grave.

I'm walking up to my front door when I suddenly notice that someone's got out of a car parked up in front of the house and they're coming up behind me. Fuck, I think. I get my keys out and run for the door.

'Wait,' this bloke calls out. 'It's all right. I'm Old Bill.'

I turn around and this geezer's holding up this fob with a badge on it.

'Detective Sergeant Wilkinson,' he says.

'What do you want?'

'You seem a bit edgy, Mr Kelly. Expecting someone?'

'You got a warrant?'

'Just an informal chat.'

'I ain't letting you in here.'

'We can talk out here. You know what this is about, don't you?'

'No idea.'

'Come on, Gary. The whole of Essex is talking about it. The Range Rover shootings. Who do you think did it?'

'I don't know. I don't even know who it was that got done, do I?'

'Tony Tucker, Pat Tate and a guy called Craig Rolfe.'

This cozzer sees the look of shock on my face and he grins.

'Friends of yours?' he asks.

'Not particularly.'

'Seen your business associate recently?'

'And who would that be?'

'Simon Beardsley. I hear you and him have had a bit of a falling out.'

'I don't know what you're talking about.'

He comes up close to me and looks up and down the street.

'If I had been somebody else, say somebody who had a grudge, do you think you'd have made it indoors before I could have got to you?'

He hands me a card with his name and number on it.

'Think about it, Gary. Get in touch if you want to talk about it.'

Get inside and slam the door behind me. Some fucking clever little cozzer trying to frighten me. The thing is I do feel scared. All the details of the shootings are on the news. Heads nearly blown off with shotguns. Horrible. What if it was Beardsley that did it? Then I am in trouble.

And Pat Tate dead. My thirty grand gone. Shit. What am I going to do? After I've taken the money I gave to him from the Custodis account I've only got about three or four thousand. The phone keeps ringing. People thinking it might have been me shot dead in the Range Rover. And it might have been. I was all ready to go in with that lot. I feel sick. Get off my face again to keep my nerves going haywire. Try to stave off the nightmares but I don't get a good night's sleep.

Next day there's a bit of a thaw. Piles of dirty grey slush everywhere. *POLICE WARN OF GANG WAR AFTER DRUG MURDERS*, says the *Echo*. Maybe Beardsley's done it. What did he say? *Maybe now it's time for taking Tucker and his friends out of the game for good*. Try to stay straight. Clear headed. But by night-time I've got the shakes. I'm in a cold sweat. Feel like shit. Try to sleep but nightmares come. Wake up and I'm full of fear. Keep thinking that they're going to come and do me.

I've got to get away from this fucking place. I drive to the bank and draw out all that's left in all my accounts. Just about three and a half grand. It ain't much but I need every penny I've got. Tiffany's still owe me. I'm paid in arrears so I'm due a couple of weeks' work. I put a combat knife in the back of my trousers and a bottle of squirt in my pocket and head down there.

George is on the door. Looks edgy when he sees me.

'I'd better warn you,' he says. 'Beardsley's in there.'

Fuck, I think. But I ain't going to back down. I go in. Frank comes up to me. Fear in his eyes, sweating like a little pig.

'Gaz,' he says. 'I'm sorry. There's nothing I could do. Beardsley's running the door here now.'

'Never mind that. I want my money. Two weeks' worth.'

'All right, all right,' he stammers. 'I'll go and get it.'

Beardsley's at the bar. Team handed. Lording it over. He spots me and comes over with a couple of his guys in tow. All eyeballing me.

'What do you want, Gaz?' Beardsley snaps at me.

'This is nothing to do with you. I've just got some business with Frank.'

'I run this club now. You walked out of it. Now piss off.'

Frank's back with the money looking like he's about to have a heart attack.

'What's this?' demands Beardsley.

'Er, it's the money I owe Gaz.'

'You don't owe him nothing, Frank. Tell him to fuck off.'

Frank looks at me. Eyes wide. Mouth open.

'Give me the money, Frank,' I say.

He starts to hand it over. Beardsley makes a grab for it and before I even know it I've got the knife out and I'm holding it at Beardsley's throat. I grab his jacket and pull him slowly towards me.

'The money, Frank,' I say.

Frank tucks it into my pocket. Beardsley's men move forward a bit.

'Get back. Or I'll cut his fucking throat.'

'You are dead for this, Gaz,' Beardsley mutters through clenched teeth.

I put my arm around him and keep the point of the knife against his neck and shuffle out of the club with him.

'Steady on,' says George by the door.

'Shut up. I suppose you're working for this cunt now, are you?'

'Don't have much choice, Gaz. I got to eat.'

'Come after me, or mess with me again,' I say to Beardsley, 'and I'll fucking kill you.'

And I give him an almighty shove through the door and leg it to the car.

Get back to the house and put a load of stuff in the car.

Leave the fairy lights on and drive off. One last thing to do. Stop by Karen's mum's.

'You're supposed to stay away from me, Gaz,' she says when she comes to the door.

I hand her the keys to the house.

'You can move back in. I'm going.'

'What do you mean, going?'

'I'm getting away. There's nothing for me here any more.'

'Right, so you're just walking out on everything?'

'Well, you don't want me around any more. Do you?'

She looks me up and down. Shakes her head. I must look a right state.

'You're a mess, Gaz.'

'Yeah, well, maybe you're right. Maybe I do need to change. I'm sorry.'

'Bit late for that.'

'I want to see the girls.'

'They're in bed, Gaz.'

'Yeah, but I want to see them. You know, in the future.'

'Yeah, well, we'll see about that. Where you gonna go?'

'Dunno. Back to London, I guess. I'll let you know where I am.'

'Right.'

I try to explain. 'Look. I lost it. I'm completely fucking lost. I've . . . I've got to find it somehow.'

'What the hell is that supposed to mean?'

'I don't know.'

And we just look at each other for a couple of seconds. There's still a bit of bruising on her face where I hit her. I wish that there was something I could say. But I can't think of anything. So I just go:

'See you.'

And she just says:

'Yeah.'

And I turn around and walk back to the car. I start

driving west along the A13. Sodium fuzz above the gloomy marshlands. Glad to be away from this fucking county. Out of Essex. London calling, like that song by The Clash. Phone Dan on the mobile. I hope he's in this time.

4
offshore

I got Geoff to develop the film he had shot outside the churchyard and to bring around the contact sheets. I hoped he had no idea what he might have caught that day. I had no idea myself, not really. Eddie could easily have had some sort of hallucination, some manifestation of delusional paranoia.

I looked over the frames with a magnifying glass as nonchalantly as possible while Geoff looked on. All the time thinking: *is it Starks?* Geoff had got a few close-ups of the man's face. I moved the glass over one of them.

I had explained Eddie's erratic behaviour to Geoff by saying he thought that he had spotted somebody that had cuckolded him with his girlfriend while he had been in prison and it had driven him into a rage. I wasn't sure whether Geoff had fallen for that one. I was worried that his press photographer's nose might sniff that he'd inadvertently got something.

I'd had a good look at all the smudges that I had on file of Harry Starks. Police mug shots and celebrity line-ups. Even that one of him taken in 1979 when he was on the run in Marbella. I tried to study every aspect of his physiognomy. Of course, there were rumours that he had had plastic surgery but then Eddie had sworn that he had recognised him. I breathed out and looked down through the lens.

Heavily lined and gaunt featured, the face was crowned with grey hair. An old man. But it was him all right. A half-smile bringing out the scar on his right cheek, the telltale eyebrows that joined in the middle. I nearly laughed out loud. *Got you*, I thought. But I held it all in and feigned disappointment. I sighed and dropped the contact sheet on the table.

'Well, I don't think there's anything we can use here, I'm afraid,' I said.

'Who's this bloke, then?' asked Geoff.

'No idea. Just someone who Eddie thinks has been fucking his bird.'

'Looks familiar, though.'

'Yeah, well, maybe he's been featured on *Crimewatch*.'

Geoff went to pick up the contact sheets.

'Can I keep the contacts? Eddie wants a look at them. It might help to calm him down a bit.'

'Sure. What do I tell Victor?'

'Don't worry. I'll deal with Victor.'

And I knew what I would have to do. I would have to keep Victor away from all of this. I wasn't going to let him have any of it. This was *my* story. This was *truecrime* par fucking excellence.

You know, whenever a really good story came in at the *Sunday Illustrated*, Sid Franks, the news editor, used to shake his head and take in a little hiss of breath. He'd then let out a sigh that seemed part pleasure, part disappointment.

'This story is too good for our readers,' he'd declare. 'They just won't appreciate it.'

And that was exactly how I felt. This story was far too good for Victor. This was mine. This was what I'd been looking for. This could be the book. With Ronnie Kray dead, Starks was now the doyen of ancient gangland mythology. The last of the Old School and still at large. If I could find out where he was hiding, this could be my coup, as Eddie would put it. Something to retire on. The problem was Eddie, though. I would have to find a way to work with him somehow. Maybe he would be able to lead me to Starks. And we'd have to keep all of this to ourselves for the time being.

So I stopped returning Victor's increasingly irate phone calls. It was so soothing to hear his frustration as he ranted away into my answer machine. He repeated his threat to drop Eddie

Doyle completely and that suited me fine. All I needed to do now was to sort things out with Eddie.

I had one of the contacts blown up and I showed it to him.

'Well, it is him,' I said. 'But he was taking a hell of a risk showing up like that.'

'Yeah. Maybe he just couldn't resist the occasion.'

'I hope you haven't told anyone else about this.'

'Well . . .'

'What?'

'I did mention it to Ruby.'

'You did what?'

'She phoned me up. She was going on about the book, and it just slipped out.'

'It just slipped out?'

'Look, I'm sorry, Tony. I didn't mean it. We were just talking about old times. I'm not sure she believed me anyway. You're not the only one who thinks I'm paranoid, you know.'

'Well, look, maybe you should try and tell her that your eyes were playing up or something. And you can reassure her about her story. We won't be needing that now we've got this.'

'What do you mean?'

'I mean Harry Starks. Next to finding Lord Lucan this is the biggest story going.'

'Oh,' said Eddie petulantly. 'Thanks a lot.'

'I mean in terms of pure sensationalism, Eddie.'

He frowned at me.

'So what about my story?' he asked.

'Well, we'll get around to it. But we can do it your way, not that trashy tone that Victor wants. If we get this Starks story then we'll be made.'

'You mean work on it together?'

'Yeah. We could renegotiate our contract. Get a proper advance. Or we could go and see another publisher and pitch it to them. Fuck Victor.'

Eddie nodded slowly.

'Yeah, maybe,' he said. 'Maybe we should put the old memoirs on hold. I mean, maybe it's not over yet.'

'What's not over?'

'My story,' he said. 'This is unfinished business, Tony.'

I didn't like the sound of this.

'What do you mean?'

'Look, you want your precious story. I want something too. My fucking portion.'

'Eddie, I don't want to get involved in . . .'

'Don't worry,' he cut in. 'I'll sort that out myself. You want the story? Well, you can get the whole fucking story. And so can I. I want to know what happened to my money. Yeah, we can work together, Tony. We can both get what we want.'

'But . . .'

'It's all connected, Tony, don't you see? Starks, the bullion job, everything.'

'But I thought you didn't want to talk about all that.'

'I don't. You can have the story, Tony. It's all yours. I just want my cut.'

'This is ridiculous, Eddie,' I said, standing up. 'Absolutely ridiculous. To think that I'd get involved with something like this.'

I picked up the contact sheet and put it back in its envelope. I'd walk away, I thought. I'd cut my losses. I'd take the photo of Starks to one of the tabloids. The *Sunday Illustrated* would give me a good price for it and a little story. But I only had the contacts and if I tried to buy the originals off Geoff he'd get suspicious. He might work out what he'd got and sell them himself. So what would I do next? Crawl back to Victor Groombridge with my tail between my legs? Walk away from my last big chance? If I'd had any sense I suppose I would have done. This could get me into trouble. I'd spent decades avoiding acting on dangerous impulses. For what? Maybe it was just my sociopathic tendencies but I felt a sudden surge of childlike wonder. And it was such a good story, more than anything I wanted to find out what happened next.

I hadn't really thought through how I was going to collaborate with Eddie and I certainly hadn't banked on this. But this would have to be it. I felt an odd little thrill run through me. I was going to get into trouble again, I just knew it.

I dropped the envelope on the table and sat down.

'So?' asked Eddie.

'So,' I replied. 'We're both completely crazy.'

Eddie laughed.

'Where do we start?' I asked him.

'When I got put away I left my cut in the hands of people connected with Starks. Manny Gould, Manny the Money, we used to call him, Stark's old accountant. What do the Yanks call it? His fucking *consiglieri*. He was supposed to be running it and some of the old firm were meant to be keeping an eye on things. They used this dodgy Hatton Garden jeweller, Solly Blumberg, to resmelt the stuff. But then a whole load of it goes missing and Solly gets bumped off. So I come out after twelve years with nothing to show for it.'

'And you think that Starks knows where the missing gold is?'

'I don't know. Maybe he's trying to find out himself. Maybe he thinks I know. Maybe it's him who's having me followed. There is one person who'll know what he's up to.'

'Who's that?'

'Manny Gould, of course.'

His offices were in Charlotte Street. *Emmanuel Gould, FCA, FCCA*, read the brass nameplate by the door. Gould was a tubby little man with beetle brows. Hooded, buglike eyes blinked behind thick round spectacles. He shuffled through piles of books and files to show us through to his desk. Scuttling sideways, crablike, scooping up paperwork and moving it to and fro to clear a couple of chairs for us to sit down on.

'Please.' He gestured for us to sit as he clambered around his desk. 'Eddie,' he announced with a little shrug, a placatory gesture of the hands. 'It's been a long time.'

'It has, Manny,' Eddie returned. 'It really has.'

Manny sighed.

'What can I say?'

'I don't know,' said Eddie, leaning forward. 'What *can* you say?'

Manny hunched in his chair a little. He stroked his chin and looked at me.

'You haven't introduced your friend,' he said.

'This is Tony.' Eddie jerked a thumb in my direction. 'He's a writer, a journalist.'

Manny Gould frowned, his eyebrows twitching like antennae.

'Now, Eddie,' he said. 'What's all this about? I mean' – he shrugged, and gave a sour look – 'a journalist.'

'Don't worry, Manny. He's not here to do an exposé on you or anything. We're working on a book together.'

Manny's face opened up into a smile.

'A book, is it?' He shook his head slightly. 'Oy, a book.'

'We're working on Eddie's memoirs,' I said.

Manny stared at me, his eyes goggled in rimless magnification.

'And you are his what? His, what do they call it, his amanuensis? No, his recording angel?'

'He's my ghost writer,' said Eddie.

Manny cackled and with a little clap rubbed his hands together.

'A book, eh? Well, I hope when the account is settled, if you like, nothing seems out of place. Know what I mean?'

'Manny, it's all going to be done with discretion,' said Eddie.

'Discretion, yes, I like that.' He waved his hands, palms upward, at the stacks around him. 'See all of my books? Interesting accounts, I can tell you. There are so many stories here. I go over them sometimes, you know? That may seem preposterous to you but these are my journals. The things I've hidden. You know, it's always a question of balance. Of balancing the books. Sometimes a figure here, a figure there.'

Manny folded the air with his fingers.

'What we want to talk about is all off the record,' I told him.

'Good, good.' He nodded.

'We want to talk about Harry Starks,' said Eddie.

'Tch, Harry Starks.' He sighed. 'Everyone wants to talk about Harry Starks. Are you sure this is not for a book or an article? I've had many people asking me about Mr Starks over the years, you know.'

'We think you might know where he is,' Eddie went on.

'How should I know. He is on the run, Eddie. You know what that means? To be on the move all the time. How should I know where he is?'

'Because I've seen him.'

'Uh?' Manny exclaimed. His mouth hung open and the shutters of his heavy eyelids blinked slowly. 'What are you talking about?' he demanded.

'I saw him, Manny. At Ronnie Kray's fucking funeral. Now what's going on? Someone's having me followed. Is it him?'

'What's going on?' Manny retorted indignantly. 'What's going on? You come in here, with a journalist, asking me all these questions . . .'

'I just want to know.'

'No. I think you should leave, Eddie. I think you and your . . . your official biographer should take these ridiculous stories elsewhere. I think . . .'

Eddie pulled something out of his jacket pocket and reached over the desk to show it to Manny. It took me a moment to register that it was a pistol of some sort.

'Eddie,' I chided him. 'For fuck's sake.'

Manny's eyes bulged at the barrel of the firearm pointed at

his face. His mouth formed a perfect O, a bubble of sputum popped from his lips. Then he raised his hands slowly, more in a gesture of supplication than surrender, and tilted his head to one side.

'Now what's all this?' he demanded. 'For goodness' sake.'

'I've fucking had enough!' Eddie spat with sudden vehemence. 'I did all that time for you lot. Now I want some fucking answers.'

'Take it easy,' I implored him.

'You shut up,' Eddie ordered. 'I saw him, Manny. I've been out three months and no one has had the decency to even talk to me about what happened to mine.'

'Eddie.' Manny shrugged. 'I understood that you didn't want . . .'

'Oh yeah,' Eddie cut in. 'Eddie Doyle's going straight. Didn't have much choice, did I? I got to know about it all going missing years back. No chance of me making a deal to get a few years off my sentence, was there? I didn't have anything to fucking give them. So I keep quiet, try and do my time the easy way. Forget about it all. Wipe my mouth and just get on with it. I get out and I'm all ready to retire. Then I notice that someone's having me followed. And then Starks turns up. I want to know what's going on.'

'I don't know anything about you being followed, Eddie.'

'What about Starks?'

Manny grinned.

'Maybe he wanted to pay his last respects to dear old Ronald,' he said.

'I'm serious. Did you know he was in the country?'

'Well, yes.'

'You saw him?'

'No. And he is gone again already. Like the Wandering Jew, you know? Walking the earth, bearing witness to the error of our ways.'

'What's he up to?'

'He is putting his affairs in order.'

'What?'

'That is all I can tell you.'

'And would his affairs include the missing Hounslow bullion?'

'Please . . .' Manny gave a little downward wave with both hands. 'Put the gun down. Ha! "Put the gun down", that sounds like a bit of cheap dialogue.' He turned to me. 'Writer, you should be taking notes, eh?'

Eddie put the pistol back into his pocket. Manny rested his hands on his desk. He sighed.

'Well,' he began. 'Here we have it. So many people want to know where that missing gold went to.'

'Including Starks?'

'Nothing is directly connected to him, you know. His methods of asset protection are necessarily complicated, difficult to trace. That's the point, isn't it? But then when things go wrong and funds start to disappear . . .'

'You mean to say . . . ?'

'All I mean to say is that Harry lost a considerable sum himself from all of this.'

'He lost? He fucking lost? What about the boys that did the job in the first place? All that gold – it was us what had it away, Manny. It was our fucking job.'

'Yes, Eddie, your job. But our business. It's hard to deal with such an amount, as you well know. You know what the Customs people call fencing and money laundering? "Realisation". Good, no? And that's what it is, Eddie, realisation. You have to make it real, make it legitimate. It's like alchemy in reverse, turning all that nice shiny gold into something dull and everyday. Something that doesn't draw attention to itself.'

'Yeah, that's all very clever, but then it all gets fucked up at your end.'

'There was a breakdown in communication. Everyone was getting a bit jumpy. With all that was at stake.'

'Solly Blumberg,' said Eddie.

'Tch, that was a bad business.'

'Did Harry . . . ?'

Eddie let the question hang in the air. Manny drew in a breath and shook his head.

'No,' he replied. 'Not at all. Somebody messed up very badly there. Killing an old man like that. And with him dead no one knows where it went.'

'The gold?'

'Hmm,' mused Manny. 'Or something else.'

'What do you mean?'

'I mean, maybe it had already been turned into something else.'

'And you say Starks lost out on this?'

'Listen,' said Manny. 'I am not under any instruction from Harry on this. But if you are interested in recovering your assets, I could make some enquiries. We could try to find it, if you want.'

'I don't know,' Eddie said, shaking his head.

'If you want something from all of this.'

'Of course I fucking do.'

'Then we must look for it.'

'Yeah, but where do we start?'

'Right here, of course,' Manny declared with an open-palmed gesture. 'I told you, I look at my records, my accounts. There'll be a clue here, I'm sure of it.'

'I don't care about your precious accounts,' Eddie said. 'I just want my fucking money. Everyone seems to have done all right out of this except me.'

'That may be,' Manny said. 'But we do need to find it. And, you know, recirculate it legitimately. You'll need to cover your tracks, Eddie. You can't simply acquire a fortune from nowhere. You say you are being watched? Maybe it is the authorities are following your tracks. We need to be careful.'

'I want something now. Up front.'

Manny sighed.

'You mean you have not received any renumeration at all?'

'Not a fucking penny.'

'Well, that is remiss. Simon Beardsley should have furnished you with something.'

'Beardsley?'

'Yes, he was looking after some of the resmelting back then.'

'That fucking toerag?'

'I can assure you that he is far from being a toerag these days. A little clumsy in his methods maybe. He should be able to let you have something, on account as it were. In the meantime let me consult my archives.'

'Don't fuck me about, Manny.'

'I have no intention of doing so. We'll sort this out. I'll speak with Beardsley. And get in touch with other interested parties. And my books.' Manny rubbed his hands together with relish. 'I'll look through my books.'

As we were leaving Eddie checked the street from the doorway.

'Fuck,' he whispered sharply.

'What?'

'There.'

He nodded towards a car parked on the other side of the road.

'That's the fucker who's been following me. Come on,' he urged.

We raced across the street and into a little alleyway that led into Rathbone Street or Rathbone Place, I can't remember which. I turned back and managed to get a quick glance at the man in the car as he looked up.

'Come on,' he insisted, and I ducked into the alley after him. He zigzagged through the back streets of Fitzrovia, doubling back on himself until he was sure we were not being followed. He slowed down, turned to me and frowned.

'You think I'm paranoid, don't you?'

'No, no,' I panted, out of breath. 'The man in the car. I got a look at him. He reminded me of someone.'

'Who?'

'I can't think.'

'Well, try to remember, for fuck's sake.'

We walked on a little.

'You think Manny was telling the truth?' he asked.

'It's hard to tell.'

'And we still don't really know what Harry Starks is up to, do we?'

I shrugged. I didn't know what to make of it all. We passed a pub.

'Come on,' he said. 'I need a drink.'

Eddie took a sip of his large vodka and tonic. 'Maybe he was just taking the piss. You know, patronising me.' His right hand trembled slightly. He looked up at me, holding my gaze with his. A little of the murderous anger he had taken out on Manny still flickered in his eyes.

'Are you patronising me, Tony?' he demanded.

'Wouldn't dream of it.'

And at that moment I wouldn't have. Eddie's rage had impressed me. It was a reminder that this gaunt, nervous-looking man with grey hair was still something of a hard man. And he was desperate. It was that desperation, that fury and disillusion, which made me feel something for him. A sort of kinship, perhaps. Maybe I had been patronising him in the past when Victor had assigned me to him but he had gained my respect now. And I was intrigued by all that was unfolding. Our relationship had changed, I was no longer merely his ghost. We had embarked on a strange and danger-ous partnership. I felt excited by this. But could I trust him?

'What was with the gun, Eddie?' I asked him.

Eddie gave a nervous grin.

'It got results, didn't it?'

'Well, it got Mr Gould talking. But as you said, he didn't tell us everything.'

'Silly fucker. Going on about his books like he's the fount of all knowledge. Yeah, well, we're going to have to be a bit more careful with some of the other people involved in this.'

'I suppose so,' I muttered.

Something came to mind. My vision drifted into the middle distance. The blur of the fruit machine flashing in the corner of the pub.

'What's the matter with you?' Eddie was saying.

I focused back on him.

'I was just thinking.'

'What's the matter? That bloke in the car?'

'No. I've just had an idea.'

'What?'

'Just something I've got to look up, that's all.'

I'd have a look in my own books, my own records. Just as Manny Gould was consulting his accounts for clues, studying columns in ledgers like scripture for meaning, I resolved to do a little reading myself. I dusted down Teddy Thursby's diaries and flipped through the years. There were entries for 1984 that had always fascinated me though they had not made complete sense up until now. I began to read and make footnotes.

Friday, 11 May
Tangier

Arrive at Boukhalef airport at midday & then taxi to Hotel El Minzah. Suite agreeable enough. Me & Julian have lunch at the hotel then set out for a walk. Go up through the Grand Socco into the Medina. Hustlers homing in on us from every direction. Try to politely ignore them but Julian v. tiresomely starts to banter with them. I think somehow he imagines that they are attracted to him because of some great charm that he possesses. Maybe he sees something kindred; after all, he was once quite a little hustler himself. Though his looks have long gone. That petulant little pout of his twisted into an ugly sneer.

Get to the Petit Socco & settle on the terrace of the Café Central for a mint tea. Tangier isn't what it was. All the colourful expats replaced with scruffy backpackers & dreary tourists. We get lumbered with an annoying & totally unnecessary 'guide' called Mohammed who trails after us all around the Kasbah, insisting that we should visit his uncle's carpet shop. Julian hints at all kinds of filthy propositions with this wretched boy, who grins & plays along quite happily. I decide I've had enough of this after a while & paying off the lad with a ten-dirham note shout at J. to stop fucking around & show a bit more discretion.

Get back to the El Minzah quite exhausted. A note left at the desk: *Came around but you had gone out. Meet me in Dean's Bar noon tomorrow, H.*[1]

Read it v. surreptitiously. Julian curious but I haven't told him about this aspect of our jaunt. As far as he knows it's just research for the memoirs & a little holiday. Tried to get some work done this p.m., though J. was his usual lethargic self. Talked through the time I was first here in '21 when Archie Clark-Kerr was Consul-General. Pig-sticking on the Town Beach when my horse bolted & I nearly ran through a French cavalry officer with my spear & travelling south to Marrakesh with Walter Harris, the *Times* correspondent & adventurer. Tremendous fun being young & British back then.

Spot of dinner & a drink in the hotel bar. Julian announced that he was going out for a walk. Know exactly what he is up to & with his sense of propriety would not be at all surprised if he ends up left for dead in some alleyway.

[1] 'H' referred to here and elsewhere is clearly H. Starks. See corroborating evidence in note below.

Saturday, 12 May.

J. turns up late for breakfast looking unbearably smug. Starts telling me about last night's trade. Becomes petulant when I tell him that I'm not really interested. Says he has to listen to my dreary stories all the time, so I tell him that's what I pay him for.

Consider shaking him off & going to this rendezvous on my own but decide that it will be easier to take him along. Might shut him up for a bit.

It's just a short walk from the El Minzah to Dean's. Trust H. to pick this notorious drinking den for 'a meet', as he'd so succinctly put it. In its heyday in the '50s when Tangier was still an international zone Dean's attracted an extraordinary collection of high and low life. Expat pederasts, Soho bohemia, villains and *contrebandiers*, American beatniks. Dean was quite a character himself, half-caste. Some said that his mother was a Ramsgate landlady and his father a West Indian passing through Kent. Robin Maugham had told me that he had been a gigolo in London before the war and had come to Morocco after being caught up in a scandal involving the death of a Gaiety Girl in Brilliant Chang's opium den in Limehouse. All sorts of extraordinary stories surrounded him which, like H., he did little to play down & often clearly encouraged. H. had some dealings with him, I think. He had been in Tangier back then when he worked for Billy Hill.[2] In fact our paths must have crossed at sometime & probably in Dean's Bar.

Dean died back in the early sixties so I had no idea what to expect of what was left of his establishment as we passed through the beaded curtain into the tiny bar. The layout & decor of the place were largely unchanged but the clientele

---

[2] Gang boss referred to in Thursby's diaries, 12 February 1965: 'He [Harry Starks] had been in Tangiers in the fifties when he'd worked for Billy Hill, the king of the racecourse gangs.'

were all rather rough-looking Moroccans. We were the only Westerners in the place and were eyed up with some suspicion as we made our way to the bar. It had become a 'local', I suppose, like so many things in Tangier now that its cosmopolitan days seem over.

The piano, where Peter Lacy, former Spitfire pilot & Francis Bacon's lover, used to play all hours to pay off his gambling debts was gone. We got a couple of drinks, all the time being eyed by the sullen natives. Julian smiled & simpered, which didn't seem to help matters. I heard one of the drinkers mutter *maricones* & there were various derisive grunts in our direction. But then the beaded curtain clattered & the assembled eyes shifted to the doorway. H. had arrived.

All at once the atmosphere in the bar changed. As he walked in there were nods and smiles of greeting. He had a handsome and thick set Moroccan in tow. H. stood in front of me for a moment, just grinning. So much older than when I last saw him, though with a healthy tan and looking as charismatic as ever (Christ knows what I must have looked like to him, a warmed-up corpse, I suppose). 'Teddy,' he said finally, holding both my upper arms gently. 'I'm so glad you're here.'

We went through and sat at a table. Drinks & tapas were brought to us. H. nodded towards his companion, who he introduced as Mustapha. After a few drinks & some gossip over old times H. declared it was time to go. 'We need to talk,' he told me. 'I mean seriously. And I haven't got long in Tangier. It isn't safe for me here. It's not like the old days, eh? I've got a place I'm staying on the Mountain. Come back and have a chat.'

Mustapha drove us all up to the hill in the Marshan district to the west of the city that the British expats used to call the Mountain. Remnants of the old colony here & there, twisting lanes, dried-out gardens & disused tennis courts. What Cecil Beaton had once described as 'oriental Cheltenham', mostly faded now. The house that H. was staying at had a marvellous

view of the town & the bay from its terrace. H. insisted that
we should talk in private. I suggested that Mustapha might
show Julian some of the sights of Tangier. 'A little local colour.
It'll help to establish a background when you come to write
it all up.'

So off they went. H. made us some drinks & we got down
to the matter in hand. H. explained that he still used Tangier
as a base for some of his smuggling activities, using the rag
trade as cover. British companies use sweated labour out here
& shift the stuff back by HGV. But he had been, for the most
part, hiding out in the Dominican Republic since the extradition
treaty with Britain had broken down after the Falklands War.
'The Caribbean is a good place to operate,' he said. 'You can
hop from island to island.' 'Like a pirate,' I suggested. 'Funny
you should say that, Teddy. I mean, that's sort of what I
want to talk to you about.' He leaned towards me, beckoning
slightly with one hand. I too lowered my head as if in
conspiracy, though there was no one else in the room. 'Buried
treasure, Teddy,' he whispered hoarsely.

I couldn't help letting out a deep chuckle. I leant back and
took a sip from my glass. Same old H., I thought. He was
smiling at me. 'It's true, Teddy. There was this job that was
pulled, back in Blighty a year or so ago. Fifteen million in
bullion taken.[3] You might have heard about it.'

I nodded. He told me that the gold had been disposed of in
various ways and a sort of consortium had been formed. 'Those
of us that understood that kind of international finance' he
explained. But inevitably there had been some kind of falling
out & a substantial amount had gone missing.

'Of the gold?' I asked. 'That or money realised from it. No
one seems to know where it is.'

H. held two fists up then opened his hands. He said that
there were details of the missing loot hidden somewhere. 'You

---

[3] Clearly a reference to the Hounslow bullion job.

mean like a map?' I suggested. 'Maybe,' he sighed. 'Or an audit trail.' 'Fascinating,' I exclaimed, 'just like *Treasure Island*.' He grinned at that but then went on to suggest that I might help him with the recovery of these ill-gotten gains. I demurred but he was quite insistent.

'There're so many people I can't trust in this. The few I can are under surveillance or gone missing,' he said. I didn't like the sound of this. He tried to reassure me. 'Teddy, there's absolutely no risk involved for you. I just need you to pass on some information and maybe bring some back to me here.' He grinned that old shark smile of his and poured me another drink.

Julian & Mustapha arrived back. Later we all went out to a place called Scott's Disco in the Ville Nouvelle. Strange little club, rather tawdry with a mirror ball dangling over a tiny wooden parquet dance floor. Rather charming illustrations of Scottish regiments line the walls & two large oil paintings of beautiful Arab boys in full Highland dress take pride of place above the bar & on the wall opposite. We had a few drinks & the place started to fill up around one. The others started eyeing up the prospects in earnest but I'm really too tired, too old. Left them to it. Arranged to meet H. at Guitta's tomorrow for Sunday lunch. Mustapha drove me back to the El Minzah.

Sunday, 13 May
Go to morning service at St Andrew's, the little Anglican church built in a Moroccan style that nestles by the Grand Socco. The combination of a Moorish decorative style and an English country churchyard evokes some strange melancholy feeling in me. Looking up at its cedar ceiling carved by craftsmen from Fez, the Lord's Prayer scrolled in Arabic above the chancel, I'm moved by some feeling of nostalgia. But for what? God knows. The service itself a little vulgar, not really High Church enough for my liking. Bumped into Freddy Carruthers as I was coming out.

'Goodness, Teddy!' he exclaimed. 'I didn't know you were here. What are you doing in Tangier?'

Felt suddenly furtive, remembering the conversation with H. last night. Muttered something appropriate, though. Freddy came here in the early '50s after he was sent to prison for cottaging & his family couldn't bear the scandal of it all. We had a bit of a wander around the graveyard. They're all here. *Walter Harris, He Loved The Moorish People And Was Their Friend*, & there a cracked & overgrown headstone in the corner: *Dean. Missed by all and sundry*. Freddy asks about England & sniffs a bit as I reply. 'I'm never going back, Teddy,' he says. 'George Greeves[4] is dead, you know.' 'That evil old gossip.' 'Yes,' Freddie sighed wistfully. 'I do miss him.'

We got to the lich-gate & said goodbye. I headed up the Rue de Belgique towards Guitta's. Had a hell of a time finding it. A new mosque has been built opposite & any premises selling alcohol have to be screened from the holy place so a bloody great big wall has been built separating it from the street. Its entrance is now around the corner. Another reminder of how the blasted Islamicists have the run of things here now.

The place still has some of its old style. Run by an Italian family since the '40s, it is, I suppose, all that is left of the international zone days. A French-style house in an overgrown ornamental garden. Here, in its elegant if rather dilapidated dining room, the old guard come for their Sunday roast. Propped up like lizards in the sun, the dwindling gathering of exiles. H. is waiting by the colonnaded bar. The Moroccan waiter, resplendent in white tuxedo, black bow tie, tasselled fez & bottle-thick glasses, shuffles & wheezes heavily as he leads us to our table. Looks like he could drop dead any minute.

---

4 George Greeves (1900–1984), Reuter's Morocco correspondent, notorious pederast and gossip-monger. 'His stories are endless. He keeps up a constant stream of foul-mouthed commentary – life and death, nobody is saved' – Joe Orton.

'Christ,' I say to H. when we are seated. 'This really is God's waiting room.'

H. chuckles darkly. I suddenly have an awful vertiginous feeling, lost years falling away yet still farther to drop. An eternity, of course. Can't outstare the void. We have roast lamb & a very passable Côtes du Rhône. H. passes an envelope across the table to me. 'You know who to take this to,'[5] he says, 'and you know you mentioned *Treasure Island* last night.' 'Did I?' 'Yeah. And the funny thing is, it's come up before. It's a clue of some sort.[6] Have a think about it.'

I had no idea what he was talking about. I took the envelope. Suppose I don't have much choice about running this errand for him. After lunch we wandered out. Mustapha was waiting in a car for him. They dropped me off at the hotel. Julian was lounging about by the pool. He's done absolutely no work at all while we've been here. It's been me that has been busy writing things down. Lazy little bastard. I fear he'll never write this bloody biography & I'll be at the mercy of the vultures once I'm gone.

I searched through the rest of the diary to see whether there were any references to what was in the envelope that Starks had given to Teddy Thursby. There were none. I showed the extracts to Eddie. In giving my interpretation to some of the text I hoped that he might be forthcoming with some of his own opinions.

'How did you get your hands on this?' he asked.

'The diaries? Well, I was a friend of his literary executor.'

'So they belong to you now, do they?'

'Er, sort of. Look, never mind about that, have a look at this bit.'

I pointed out the sections that featured Harry Starks.

---

[5] Who is Starks referring to here? Manny Gould?

[6] *Treasure Island* as a clue? What can this mean? Note: reread R.L. Stevenson.

'Well, he doesn't seem to know where the fucking gold went to either,' was Eddie's only comment.

'What about *Treasure Island* as a clue?' I asked him.

'Well, it's a pretty fucking obvious literary allusion.'

'But could it mean anything specific?'

'You're obsessed with stories, Tony. This isn't a fucking story. What were the dates again?'

I handed him back the diary.

'Well,' he said, 'it's around the time Solly got bumped off, isn't it? That's the key to this whole thing. You know who had him done, don't you?'

I shrugged.

'The word always had it it was Beardsley. We should front him out about that.'

'But if it was him that had Solly Blumberg killed wouldn't that be dangerous?'

Eddie gave a flat laugh.

'I ain't afraid of him,' he snorted. 'I remember him when he was Harry Starks' pet hooligan, just a snot-nosed little Mod kid.'

Eddie was becoming increasingly filled with bravado and derring-do. I found his recklessness frightening but exhilarating as well. As much as he had insisted that 'this isn't a fucking story, Tony', that was how I felt. A wonderful, ridiculous story. An adventure. And I found myself drawn into it.

I felt restless. I spent the whole night reading *Treasure Island*. Stevenson's storytelling is so marvellous, fantastical, yet compelling and strangely touching. Conjuring the childlike wonder with action and danger. But I searched vainly for clues about the bullion robbery. Maybe Eddie was right, it was merely a clumsy literary reference.

A cold, grey dawn arrived and I staggered through the last chapters, my eyes burning with fatigue. Then, coming to the part where the treasure itself is finally uncovered, I came across a passage that seemed to jump out from the page at me and insist upon some sort of universal meaning. The sky began to blush with red a little and, in a manic state of over-tiredness, a crazed somnambulant lucidity, I mumbled the words out loud like an aubade:

> It was a strange collection, like Billy Bone's hoard for diversity of coinage, but so much larger and so much more varied that I think I never had more pleasure than in sorting them. English, French, Spanish, Portuguese, Georges, and Louises, doubloons and double guineas and moidores and sequins, the pictures of all the kings of Europe for the last hundred years, strange Oriental pieces stamped with what looked like wisps of string or bits of spider's web, round pieces and square pieces, and pieces bored through the middle, as if to wear them round your neck – nearly every variety of money in the world must, I think, have found a place in that collection; and for number, I am sure they were like autumn leaves, so that my back ached with stooping and my fingers with sorting them out . . .

As in a trance, or a waking dream where some occult or arcane knowledge is signified, these words and symbols blazoned themselves on my mind like emblems or a chart's legend. As if somewhere in the lines was a key, a map ('or an audit trail,' Starks had said). It was a discourse on the nature of treasure – no, on the nature of money itself. *Every variety of money in the world*, capital, international money markets, loot and possession. Money laundering, 'realisation', Manny Gould had called it, bullion transformed into commodities, treasure hidden in endless and numberless accounts. My mind reeled with labyrinthine exchanges and currencies. For an untransactable moment I had a clear notion of what was conceivable, that unpalpable pulse that throbs with meaning and clarity, only to reverberate into echoing reveries like coins clattering in an uncollectable jackpot. I slept and imagined an unconscious coinage of inscrutable sovereigns, money becoming immaterial, an abstract semantic, oaths in inscription, a future in sterling – *I promise to pay the bearer on demand* – a multiplication of possibilities. Change: I dreamt of coinage, obverse and reverse, treasured memories, a storehouse of properties. Everything suddenly made sense as I swooned into darkness.

I woke with an awful start, my feeble body jerking itself awake in the armchair. The book had fallen from my hands and my head was dull and empty. The illusory clarity faded into a forgotten, ungraspable dream.

We drove out to Simon Beardsley's mansion in Essex. Manny Gould had set up a meeting. Eddie wanted me to come along.

'Why?' I asked him, slightly daunted at the prospect.

'I need someone with me.'

'But why me?'

'Well, who else? The only people I can trust any more are either dead or inside. I can't trust anyone on the outside any more. Things have changed. Drugs, that's what it's all about these days. All these fuckers who made money out of us. This bent lawyer that was looking after Charlie and Ray's bit, you know, the guys who did the job with me, well, he ended up turning two million into five. Property boom, you know, that Docklands thing. I mean, we steal this stuff and yet there's other people who can make even more out of it just by sitting on their arses. Speculation. Of course, they caught up with him in the end. Got twelve years but he was out in five. That's white-collar crime for you. And you can be damn sure he salted some of it away somewhere. No, Tony, I can't trust any of them.'

'But you can trust me?'

'I don't know, Tony, I don't know. Fact is, you're harmless enough. And we're supposed to be working together, right?'

'Right,' I agreed, grudgingly.

'Don't worry,' Eddie said with a smile. 'There'll be no guns this time.'

'I'm very glad to hear it.'

'It's all about front, Tony. Just keep your mouth shut. It's all gonna be very polite and respectful. Face to face, that is.'

Eddie gave a mirthless cackle.

'Then we get done in when we least suspect it,' he said.

Beardsley's place was out in the country just the other side of Braintree. Electrically operated wrought-iron gates opened on to a gravel driveway. A large modern brick house with a ludicrous colonnaded portico. Greek urns and silly statues all over the place.

'Well,' said Eddie as we pulled up in front of this vulgar edifice, 'some people have done all right, haven't they?'

Beardsley was by the front door, holding back two demonic-looking Rottweilers. He nodded towards us and called out:

'Just let me put the dogs away.'

He dragged the slavering hounds into a side room then led us through.

'Good to see you, Eddie,' he said. 'I don't think I've met your friend.'

'This is Tony,' Eddie told him. 'He's a business associate.'

'Nice to meet you, Tony,' said Beardsley as we came into a huge reception room.

Eddie and Beardsley stood facing each other for a second, as if squaring up to one another. Beardsley was a muscular man in his forties with cropped hair, designer sportswear and lots of chunky gold jewellery. Eddie's frame was frail in comparison but there was an attempt at dignity in his deportment which was touching and impressive. Beardsley's head bowed slightly and he grinned to reveal yet more of the yellow metal.

'Eddie,' he said with a shrug. 'What can I say?'

Eddie Doyle smiled back.

'That's what everyone keeps asking,' he said.

'Drink?' asked Beardsley.

'I'd love a cup of tea,' said Eddie.

Beardsley made a pot and brought it through and we all sat down on a white suede three-piece suite. He reached under the glass-topped coffee table and pulled out a plastic carrier bag and handed it over to Eddie.

'What's this?' Eddie demanded.

'It's for you,' replied Beardsley.

Eddie peered inside the bag. He gave a short laugh then looked up at Beardsley.

'Is this a fucking joke?'

'Eddie . . .'

'What's in here? A couple of grand?'

'It's five thousand.'

'Have a fucking whip-round, did we?'

'Look, it's just something to tide you over.'

'Where's the rest of it?'

'That's just it. We don't know, do we. That business with Solly . . .'

'Yeah, well, maybe someone was a little bit hasty there. If Solly was still alive maybe he'd be able to tell us.'

'Or tell certain other people.'

'Did he tell you anything?' Eddie asked.

'What do you mean?'

'I mean before he was done in.'

'Nah. He was going on about having hidden the gold somewhere for safe-keeping. Said something about a map.'

'A map?' Eddie frowned and looked over at me.

'Yeah,' said Beardsley with a little laugh. 'He was really fucking losing it by then. Coming up with any kind of rubbish to buy himself more time.'

'Well, maybe you should have given him some.'

'Look, we didn't have a choice. He was about to grass.'

'That's what you think.'

'We couldn't take the risk. Honestly, Eddie, it all got fucked up and we had to cover our tracks. I don't know if we'll ever find out where the gold went to now.'

'It looks like you and half of Essex are fucking wearing it.'

Beardsley laughed again and with a sovereign-ringed paw toyed with the thick gold chain around his neck.

'You think it's a bit much?'

'I'm serious, Beardsley. And I'm not the only one.'

'What do you mean?'

'I mean I'm not the only one that might be interested in what went missing. Saw an old face recently.'

'Oh yeah?' Beardsley commented as he picked up his teacup.

'Harry Starks,' said Eddie softly.

Beardsley lost his grip on the cup handle and it clattered on to the glass table.

'Shit!' he exclaimed, standing up to avoid the spillage of tea. 'You're joking, aren't you?'

'I told you, I'm serious.'

'Shit,' he repeated, brushing at his trousers.

'A bit nervous, are we, Simon?'

Beardsley forced a smile.

'Just a shock, you know. I mean, Harry fucking Starks.'

'Yeah, and maybe he thinks you were a little hasty too.'

'Look, I can explain about Solly.'

Eddie stood up.

'Come on,' he told me. 'Let's go.'

He picked up the carrier bag.

'We're getting off now,' Eddie told him.

'You only just got here.'

'Well, you know, things to do.'

Beardsley followed us out through the hall.

'You really see Harry?' he asked.

'Large as life.'

'Fuck. Eddie, about Solly, we didn't have any choice. You've got to believe me.'

We were at the door. Eddie turned to Beardsley.

'Doesn't really matter what I believe, does it?' he said. 'So long, Beardsley. Be lucky.'

'You clock the reaction when I mentioned Starks?' Eddie asked me as we drove back to London.

'He was a little flustered.'

'I figure Beardsley's worried because he bumped off the only person who knew for certain where the gold was.'

'So where does that lead us?'

'Don't know. I'll tell you something, though, we're really in trouble now.'

'What do you mean?'

'You know, stirring things up like this. People are starting to get edgy and that's not a good thing.'

'Maybe we should, er, take things easy.'

'Too late for that, Tony.'

I got back to my flat and brooded over the situation. Eddie's attitude was becoming very disconcerting. He was an old man and yet was exhibiting all the recklessness of youth. It was ridiculous. And yet it struck me that maybe his behaviour was in keeping with his age. Why don't we become more desperate as the years advance? Why is it that the less we have to lose the more we cling on to what is left of a meagre existence? I also reflected that it was in Eddie Doyle's nature to take risks, to be always putting all of his energy into one big gamble. He was still a recidivist at heart. Rehabilitation would come only with the grave, it seemed.

And my sedentary life was now disturbed by action. I felt that I was losing control. I was no longer merely recording the facts but becoming part of the story itself. My head throbbed with the insane excitement of it all. I'd not felt so alive for years. I was myself being driven by an unpredictable narrative. Something was happening. And something would happen next. And, of course, I was beginning to lose track of what was the real story and what were plot lines of the imagination.

There was a plethora of references, fact and fable: underworld rumours, endless newspaper articles and *truecrime* accounts of the Hounslow bullion job, Teddy Thursby's chronicles and, in encrypted fiction, some obscure interpretation of *Treasure Island*. I picked the book up from where I had left it, lying on the floor, face down, with a cracked spine. I read the three or four pages that remained. The book's actual ending is somewhat disappointing, the journey home, a return to normality. Even Silver's escape is downplayed and anti-climactic. In its conclusion no words or phrases seemed to testify or offer the clue Starks had alluded to. I noted only that whereas with most fictions concerning treasure it is the loot which is jinxed, in Stevenson's tale it is where the hoard is buried, the island itself, which seems bewitched. In the end Jim Hawkins calls it 'that accursed island' and is only too happy to see the last of it slip from view over the blue curve of the horizon.

Was it the island itself which was of significance, rather than the treasure? Stories of isles, charmed or blessed, have been told since *The Odyssey* and perhaps before, with an ancient insistence that there is meaning and significance in how we navigate them. Symbol of alternative realities from Atlantis to Neverland, the island is also metaphor for the individual (Donne's attempted contradiction merely reminds us of how compelling is this image of isolation). We remember, perhaps, a primal insularity: the foetus a tiny atoll in an amniotic sea.

But if the clue is in the island, what is it? Some sort of code to where the treasure is buried? It all seemed rather fanciful given the brutal realities of the Hounslow job. I carried on reading. Stevenson wrote two appendices to *Treasure Island*. In the first, he explains that the writing of the story was preceded by the drawing of the map; in fact it was drafting an imaginary chart which gave the inspiration for the book itself, a narrative formed out of a prophetic topography. Beardsley had said that Solly had mentioned a map. But what could that mean? Was the tale itself in some way prescient of the treasure we sought? I couldn't see how. I read to the end and found nothing.

Wearily, I went back to the beginning. Not the start of the novel but its introduction, in my volume by a certain Frank Simpson, a professor of American literature. I scanned his little essay with not much enthusiasm until my eyes suddenly alighted on this short passage:

> There has been much scholarly debate as to the location of Stevenson's island. Does his fictional isle have an actual, geographical progenitor? Candidates range from the Isle of Pines off the coast of Cuba to the outline of Edinburgh as seen from the Pentland Hills. The most obvious geographical location is Norman Island in the British Virgin Islands. Overgrown and deserted but for a few wild goats, the largest of the uninhabited islands in the BVI has long been thought to be a site of buried treasure. More important, though, is the cultural placement of the island . . .

I didn't see it at first but then my mind had been island-hopping a whole archipelago of insular notions and deranged cartographies. Then it came into focus, a promontory suddenly visible against the horizon. *Land ho!* I almost said it out loud like a lookout spying *terra incognita*. Land fucking ho. It was so obvious. The British Virgin Islands, a remnant of Empire and a major site for offshore banking and money laundering. Eddie was right, *Treasure Island* was a literary allusion but also an analogy. Just as eighteenth-century pirates had buried their treasure in Caribbean islands, so modern-day equivalents do exactly the same thing but with shell companies and numbered bank accounts. The missing loot was offshore. It was somewhere in the British Virgin Islands.

I told Eddie of my findings but he wasn't convinced.

'Aren't you getting a bit carried away?' he demanded.

'Well, it's worth investigating, wouldn't you say?'

'I don't know. Let's hear what Manny has to say.'

'Can we trust him?'

'Probably not, but he's the expert in all of this. If anyone can put all of this together he can.'

'But what if it's a set-up? What do we do then?'

'I don't know,' said Eddie. 'But we can't afford not to talk to Manny. Let's hear what he says.'

So another meeting was arranged at the good offices of Emmanuel Gould, FCA, FCCA. I told him of my theory. The little accountant frowned across the desk at us; his black brows bristled with thought.

'A reference in Lord Thursby's diaries, you say? A literary clue? A little tenuous, don't you think?'

'That's what I told him,' said Eddie.

'But,' Manny continued, 'it could be offshore. And why not the BVI? My own research has had considerably less poetic licence, I'm afraid, but maybe it does connect with this rather, er, imaginative idea. Solly Blumberg's assets at the time of his death seem to have completely vanished. Liquidated or transferred somewhere. Now, although a substantial amount of the resmelted gold seems to have gone missing, Solly might already have sold it on and hidden the assets away.'

'Offshore?' I asked.

'That would make sense, supposing of course he had disposed of the bullion.'

'And supposing he did? How would that work?' I asked him.

'In terms of laundering it offshore?' Manny asked.

'Yes.'

'Well, there are three major stages in cleaning money. First is placement – you know, finding somewhere to put your assets, a financial system to get the money out of the country. Then what is called "layering", setting up a business, some sort of shell company, so you can disguise these funds as proceeds from legitimate business. Then finally "integration", with a complex web of money transfers, false loan repayments, income from investments. By this time it becomes exceedingly difficult to distinguish between legal and illegal wealth and all of this loot can come back looking squeaky clean. Oh yes, it all makes perfect sense, doesn't it? Only one problem.'

'What's that?' I asked.

'It didn't come back, did it?'

'No, it bloody didn't,' said Eddie.

'And there we have it. Money laundering is deliberately complicated, the audit trail has to be difficult to follow in order to keep the authorities off the trail, but when there's a breakdown in communication among those doing the laundering, well, then huge amounts can go missing, greedy people who are supposed to be involved in asset protection line their own pockets, and that is what might have happened.'

'Might have?'

Manny shrugged.

'We can't be sure. But in the BVI we got burned. There was an investigation. A joint operation, an Anglo-American thing, Scotland Yard and the DEA. This British tax lawyer, Joe Clement, had been salting away funds in the Isle of Man and the BVI. He had contacts with the Florida Mafia too. But he ended up doing a deal with the authorities in exchange for immunity from prosecution. Ended up on a witness protection programme. Assets were frozen, funds were confiscated.'

'Did that include proceeds realised from the Hounslow job?' I asked him.

'Perhaps. Unless they were transferred elsewhere on the island. That could be what this clue of yours is all about. That it's still hidden there somewhere.'

'But how on earth are we going to find it?' asked Eddie.

'We have to be methodical,' Manny announced. 'Try and find an audit trail from Clement's investment trust to another shell company.'

Manny got hold of a list of companies registered in the British Virgin Islands.

'I really don't know where to start,' he protested.

'Let me have a look,' I said.

He handed me the list. I didn't know what I was looking for but I felt that there must be another clue somewhere. And I found it. Flint Investments were listed with an address in Road Town, Tortola.

'You should check this one out,' I told Manny, pointing to it.

'Why's that?' Manny frowned at it, then his eyebrows shot up. 'Oh yes, of course, Flint, of course. Well, we might as well give it a try.'

'What are you two on about?' Eddie demanded.

Manny held up the list.

'See?' he said. 'Flint. Flint was the name of the pirate whose treasure was buried on the island.'

'Oh, for fuck's sake,' Eddie muttered.

But I was right. It took Manny a couple of days to find a link between Clement and Flint Investments and then we had another meeting in his office.

'So what do we do now?' Eddie asked.

'Well, I have taken the liberty of making contact with Mr Starks. He has people in that area who, shall we say, protect his interests, and they can go about attempting to recover whatever assets remain in this company.'

'What about my fucking interests?' Eddie demanded.

'Of course they will be represented too, Eddie.'

'And in the meantime I just sit on my arse while other people divide up my takings, as per fucking usual. Like I spent all my time inside doing.'

'I don't see what else we can do. We don't even know what is in Flint Investments, after all. It will be merely a shell company, maybe an empty shell.'

'All the more reason to find out ourselves.'

'You're not suggesting that we . . .' Manny began.

'No,' Eddie cut him off. 'Not you and me. Me and him.'

Eddie nodded in my direction.

'We'll go there and check things out ourselves.'

'Now, wait a minute,' I complained.

'Come on, Tony. We can't let Starks or anyone else take us for a ride again.'

'Take you for a ride, Eddie. This really isn't my problem.'

'No, but it was your fucking idea, Tony.'

'What?'

'This *Treasure Island* nonsense. Come on, a little holiday. It'll do you good.'

'I don't think so.'

'It'll be a good story. You can be Jim Hawkins and I'll be Long John fucking Silver.'

We flew into Antigua and got a connecting flight to Beef Island in the British Virgins then a taxi to Road Town. The sea was a deep gentian diffusing into the horizon; green hills sloped gently into cliffs and coves. A coastal road took us past clutches of porched wooden houses and one-room shacks. There were bigger houses as well with chain-link fences and concrete driveways.

'Look at some of these fucking mansions,' Eddie declared as we bumped along. 'You know, this is what I always dreamed of. Doing one last coup and retiring to a tropical island. That's what the Hounslow job was supposed to be all about.'

'And would you have done?'

'What?'

'I mean, if you'd got away with it.'

'What?' he said. 'Come away to somewhere like here?'

'Yeah.'

Eddie turned and gave me a look of exasperation or disdain.

'Of course not,' he said. 'It never works out like that.'

'So what will you do if you get some of your money back?'

'I don't know, do I? Look, will you stop spoiling it? I was enjoying myself for a minute there.'

Road Town was a busy little burgh. A boom town. The harbour was crammed with charter yachts, a fat cruise ship was coming in to dock. Amid the ramshackle dwellings, bars and shops were concrete-and-glass office blocks housing all manner of financial services. Herds of four-wheel-drives clogged the dusty streets. The wooded hillsides surrounding the town were studded with tiered condominia.

We checked into the Treasure Isle hotel on Waterfront Drive. Everywhere were tourist traps promoting the islands' glorious seafaring past. Tortola is the biggest sea yacht chartering centre in the world and the town had grown rich from the power of sail. And buried treasure in the form of international business companies and trusts drawn up here because of zero taxation and banking secrecy laws.

Our rooms overlooked the harbour. Eddie studied a guide-book.

'This ain't really Treasure Island, you know, Tony,' he announced.

He gestured out across the bay at a group of islands that rose out of the shimmering silvery sea on the horizon.

'It's out there,' he went on, checking a small map in the guidebook. 'Norman Island. And that little one,' he pointed, 'that's Dead Man's Chest where Blackbeard left fifteen men marooned to settle their differences with a cutlass and a bottle of rum.'

Eddie seemed in good spirits. I began to fear, with growing dread, that he was in a holiday mood.

'So what do we do now?' I asked.

'We wait for somebody to make contact.'

'Great.'

'Relax, Tony.'

Relax. The word always comes in the form of a command, doesn't it? A command that never fails to make me tense up.

'We can get a bit of sun while we're here,' he went on.

But I've never been that keen on bright sunlight. I've always felt that there was something reptilian about lounging about in it all day. And I found the heat oppressive and stupefying.

Eddie, on the other hand, lapped it up. He spent hours by the tiny hotel pool, sunbathing.

'What's the matter with you?' he demanded as I crouched in the shade, nursing a drink. 'It's therapeutic, you know. All this light. All this sky. It's what I missed most about being inside. Not being able to see the sky.'

There were a lot of people of retirement age staying at the hotel so Eddie and I didn't look out of place. There was a lot of ancient flesh on display which I frankly found quite sickening. Bulging out all over the place, flaccid and glabrous, oiled and reddening in the harsh ultraviolet. Eddie himself wasn't in too bad shape, though. His body sagged a little around the middle but his frame retained a taut muscularity. Semi-naked, his body had a jaunty ease in its movement. A quirky animal grace I could only envy.

I spent as much time as I could in my hotel room reading to the drone of the air conditioning. I missed my usual dull routine. I'm not cut out for vacations. I need a sense of order, an illusion of being in control of my surroundings. In the evenings Eddie insisted that we go out and try the local cuisine. Over-spiced fish that gave me heartburn. In one of the restaurants, a converted shack on the waterfront with reggae music throbbing away, I noticed someone at the bar looking over at us. It was the man in the car outside Manny Gould's, I was sure of it. As he saw me looking back at him he turned away, paid his bill and left. I nudged Eddie.

'Over there,' I hissed.

'What?'

He turned. The man had gone. A black youth cleared away a glass and wiped the counter.

'The barman?' Eddie whispered.

'No. There was someone else there a moment ago. The man who was following us back in London.'

'What? Are you sure you're not seeing things?'

'Yes.'

'I mean, the heat's been getting to you.'

'I'm perfectly sure, Eddie.'

Eddie sighed.

'Shit. You said you recognised him. Before.'

'Yeah, but I still can't think who he is.'

The next day Eddie booked us a day trip on a schooner going out to Norman Island. I really didn't want to go.

'Look,' Eddie insisted. 'We've got to make it look like we're holidaymakers. Especially if this bloke is checking up on us out here. Come on. We can go and see the real Treasure Island.'

The other day-trippers were amiable Americans and Canadians. They all seemed to be paired off.

'You notice everybody on this boat is a couple?' I said to Eddie.

'Yeah.'

'Do you wonder if they think that's what we are?'

'What?'

'A couple.'

I grinned at Eddie.

'Fuck off,' he muttered.

But Eddie could easily have passed as an ageing homosexual. Even in shorts and polo shirt he looked immaculately turned out. His neatly cut greying hair and well-kept body bore all the marks of an old queen who looked after himself. I, on the other hand, barely passed muster as human in this company. There was a camaraderie that I shrank from. People introduced themselves with that easy manner that North Americans seem so good at, making little comments about the places they came from. Eddie was outgoing and talkative, telling all manner of lies, no doubt. I retreated to a spot under an awning while the others chatted, slathering their skin with suncream, exposing themselves to the hideous sun.

The boat rolled to and fro as it cut through the water. My stomach lurched horribly. I felt an awful sense of unease, of uncertainty about the movement below me.

We moored off Norman Island. I stayed on board as the others went snorkelling. The only other people remaining apart from the crew were an antique couple from Indiana. The woman droned on incessantly about her ailments and operations in a slow, lazy Southern drawl. I was sorely tempted to throw the old bitch overboard. Luckily there was plenty to drink.

Eddie emerged later full of wonder at the secrets of the deep.

'It was fantastic, Tony. All these lairy coloured fish. And these spiney things . . .'

He went on, fervently describing a catalogue of grotesque marine biology. I'd begun to feel sick and it gave me no comfort to contemplate all of this gaudy life beneath the surface. But it was on the way back that I became really nauseous. I went below for a while but this only made things worse. It was hot and stuffy down there. The diesel engine was cacophonous, its fumes sickening. And the listing of the boat was more pronounced below the waterline.

I staggered back up top and spewed over the side vigorously. It was humiliating.

'Go on, my son,' Eddie urged. 'Get it all out.'

And the other tourists felt the need to join in with their own jocular encouragements.

When we got back to the hotel there was a message at the front desk. It was simply an address and a time to meet on the morning of the following day.

'Right,' said Eddie. 'This is it.'

The taxi took us to a condominium on one of the steep hillsides overlooking Road Town. The door to the apartment was opened by a dark-haired handsome man in his forties.

'I'm Hector Orosco,' he announced in a Hispanic accent.

'Where's Harry?' Eddie demanded.

'I'm here on Mr Starks' behalf,' Orosco replied.

'You mean he sent you down here to do his dirty work for him?'

'In a manner of speaking, yes.'

'Well, that's fucking typical.'

Hector Orosco grinned and shrugged.

'You know how it is,' he said.

'I certainly do, old son. Now, I hope you don't mind me asking, but who the fuck are you?'

'I'm a Cuban. I grew up with the fucking Revolution but I was not, shall we say, a very good little *comunista*. I got into trouble almost as soon as I could walk. I got sent to a work camp when I was a teenager. Re-education, they called it. Well, that didn't work and later it was jail. In 1980, during the Mariel boat lift – you know, when a whole crowd of people got sanctuary in the Peruvian embassy compound and the Yankees sent down boats to get them out of Cuba? – well, Fidel took the opportunity to throw out some people he didn't want, he insisted that they take the undesirables as well, prisons and mental hospitals were emptied, "anti-social elements", *escoria*, the government called us, you know, scum. So I ended up in Florida. Miami was a great town for somebody like me. But soon enough I get into trouble there and the Feds want to deport me back to fucking Cuba.'

'Yeah, right,' Eddie interjected. 'But what has this got to do with Starks?'

'I was coming to that, man. I left the States in a bit of a hurry. Ended up in the Dominican Republic. That's where I met Harry Starks.'

'When was this?'

'In 1983. Diplomatic links with Britain had been broken off after the Falklands War so it was a good place for him to operate. He had been running a marijuana smuggling operation from Morocco into Spain for some time but here was a chance to do something much, much bigger. For a while it was really beautiful, man. We had these five luxury yachts with uniformed crews and old folks we hired to look like rich retired people on a cruise. We even had this old guy who acted like he was really sick with a nurse who was actually a hooker from Key West. This way we could bring tons of grass from Colombia into Florida. And the sweetest part about it was here. Tortola. The BVI had really just opened up for offshore business. We linked up with this British tax lawyer, Joe Clement, and we could launder all our money through here. You see, nobody knew, nobody suspected. It was a very tight operation. But then the fucking Cuban mafia in Miami got to hear about it and they wanted a piece. Those bastard *gusamos* thought I still owed them. Then Harry got involved in this bullion thing, you know?'

'Yeah, I do,' said Eddie. 'It was my job.'

'Well, no disrespect, señor, but it brought us bad luck, you know. It drew some unwanted attention our way. Harry was trying to launder it through one of Clement's international business companies and before we knew it all of heaven fell down on us. The DEA were investigating the Florida Mob and the British cops were after the gold. They did a joint fucking operation. Clement, well, he was just a crooked businessman, no fucking *cojones*, you know? He soon broke down under interrogation. Did a deal in return for immunity. We had to finish the operation. But the thing is they never did find two things. The money from the bullion or the records they wanted incriminating the Miami Cubans. So we've got to work fast, you know? If the bloody Cubanos know that we're down here digging up paperwork that could put them away they will not be happy.'

'So what do we do?' Eddie asked.

'I've got the address of the registered agent for Flint Investments. A guy called George Peterson. We go and see him and get the records, find out where this bloody money is. But we have to move fast. So, *vámanos*. Let's go.'

Main Street, Road Town, is not a main street at all but a dusty winding back road. Lined with wooden shacks cheek by jowl with colonial buildings and concrete office blocks. A big-bellied cruise liner had just disgorged its cargo of American tourists and they wandered about Main Street's gaudy gift shops and restaurants, uniformed in baseball cap, shorts and T-shirts. They had a scorched look about them, their ruddy flesh glowing, blotchy and corpulent. Some looked as if they were suffering from a kind of radiation sickness, which indeed they were. More formally attired islanders went about their business with considerably more determination and dignity. A squawking hen led a row of chicks through a puddle in the gutter.

The address that Hector had was on the top of a two-storey wooden building accessed by stairs on the outside. We went up. Hector knocked on the door. A middle-aged black man opened it a crack and peered out into the daylight.

'What you want?' he demanded tersely.

'We're here to see Mr Peterson.'

'Him not here,' the man declared, and made to close the door.

Hector pushed against it with a greater force and the man staggered back into the office. We entered.

'You don't mind if we come in for a moment, do you?' said Hector.

'What you doing?' The man was indignant. 'This is private office. Me not supposed to let anyone in here.'

'Where's Peterson?' Hector asked.

'I tell you, man. Him gone. Now please, leave de premises at once, sir.'

He walked over to a desk and picked up the phone.

'Leave now, please. Or I call de police.'

'I wouldn't do that,' Hector suggested.

He had produced a pistol from somewhere and was pointing it at the man.

'What de bloodclaat?' the man shrieked, his eyes wide with shock.

'Put the phone down,' Hector insisted. 'OK. Now, where's Peterson?'

'Truly, man. Him gone.'

'And who are you?'

'Harrington Miller. Personal assistant to Mr Peterson.'

'OK, Harrington. We're going to search the office.'

But the office was empty of records. It had been cleaned out.

'Where is everything, Harrington?' Hector asked, putting his gun to Harrington Miller's head.

'Please, man . . .'

'All the files have gone. Peterson's gone. He's in some sort of trouble, isn't he?'

'Please.'

'Just leaving poor old Harrington to mind the store.'

'No, man. No trouble. All incorporated businesses correct under island jurisdiction.'

'Oh, I'm sure you're all above board with the local authorities. But maybe it's other jurisdictions that you're in trouble with.'

'I don't know what you mean, man.'

'Other less official jurisdictions, of course.'

'I just work for Mr Peterson. I don't know nothing.'

'And your boss just clears out and leaves you with an empty office. Not a very considerate employer. Where has he moved the files?'

'I don't know, man.'

'Come on, Harrington. You can do better than that.'

He pressed the pistol against Harrington Miller's temple.

'Him . . . him . . .' Harrington stammered. 'Him have a house up in the hills.'

'Give us the address.'

Miller scribbled something on a piece of paper.

'Your boss is up to something. What is it?'

'I don't know.'

'He's scared. Who is he scared of?'

'Please, man,'

'Come on, Harrington. What do you know?'

'I tol' you. Nothing.'

'That's not good enough.' He pressed the gun into his temple again. 'We haven't got much time. So tell us or I'll kill you.'

'Please.'

'Come on.'

Harrington Miller's breath was coming in sharp pants of fear.

'Please. Man. Nothing.'

'Oh, for God's sake. Tell us something. Anything.'

'Anything?'

'Yeah, anything.'

'I don't understand.'

'Tell us . . .' Hector mused. 'Tell us a story.'

'What?'

'You know, a story that you know.'

Hector was smiling.

'Me don't know no story.'

'Yes you do. Everyone knows a story.'

'Hector,' Eddie complained. 'What the fuck are you on about now?'

But Orosco lifted his free hand in a little wave.

'Come on,' he went on. 'Make it a good one and I won't shoot you.'

'Oh, Jesus Christ, man.'

'Harrington.'

'A story?' Harrington Miller asked.

'Yeah.'

'Right.' Miller took a few breaths and tried to concentrate. 'OK, mek me see . . .'

He let out a long sigh. He closed his eyes and his face relaxed, nodding slightly as if remembering something. A little smile played upon his lips. He seemed to go into some sort of trance. He opened his eyes and began:

'Back time in Spanish Town, Jamaica, I knew of dese tree brothers. Bad man, you see? Dem were bad breed roughnecks dat run tings an' nah business fi use fist or knife or gun 'gainst any man. Dem have a sistrin call Bella, an' in all de town she was de prettiest ting you ever see, but you fi see dem bredrin guard she most jealously 'gainst de attentions of any man. An' though so many desire she, Bella was all 'pon her own but for her brothers, wit' no husband, no man.

'But dere come one bwoy call Lawrence, a handsome yout', him have charm an' fine manners. Him a work for dem bredrin as small-time ganja dealer. When Bella see fi him looks and him demeanour it please she so much she heart jump an' she yearn after loving he. Lawrence too did fall for de beauty of she. An' since dem did sweet each other equal, dem were spiteful of de danger dem know an' soon come time when dem do what dem desire de most.

'Long time nobody catch on fi dem secret. Opportunities were many fi dem to spend time in each other's arms but soon come too de recklessness of pleasure an' de brothers did find out dere secret. Hateful of de shame dem felt der sistrin had suffer dey, so dem see it, at de hand of dis Lawrence, it vex dem an' mek dem act most drastically.

'Pretending everything normal, dem joke an' play friendly wit' Lawrence an' drive he out to dere ganja plantation. But dere dem shoot him dead an' bury he in de bush, down an'

187

dirty. Den dem chat 'bout how Lawrence gone America on special business. Bella kep' asking 'bout he an' soon de oldest bredrin get vex an' tell she: "Country woman, why ya keep aksin' 'bout dis yout'? What business ya have wit' he? Aks again an' ya get answer ya deserve. Seen?"

'She come all full of grief an' though she aks no more of de brethren, many time at night she call out to he wit' tears an' lamentation. One night she a bawl so hard that she cry she self to sleep an' in a dream Lawrence come inna form of a duppy.'

'A duppy?' Eddie asked.

'Yeah, man,' said Harrington Miller. 'Duppy. Ya know, a jumbie spirit. A ghost.'

'Right.'

'So Lawrence as a duppy come an' tell she what 'appen. Inna de dream him a chat 'bout de spot where him body was bury and de next day come an' in belief of her vision, she a get she an' go down dere deh. She sweep 'way de dead leaves dem dat cover him in burial an' wit' she own hands dig 'way at de shallow grave. De corpse not decay too much an' when she scrape 'way de earth from de head dere was still de handsome face of the yout' dat she had loved so much. If she de strengt' she would a tek him body 'way fi bury it proper but as she caan't do dat she do take a cutlass an' chop off him beautiful head, wrap it in one claat an' gwan with it.'

She tek it home an' after bathing it wit' de tears of she an' kissing it gently, she a bury it in a big earthenware pot. She den tek some sensimilla seeds an' a plant dem dere, watering dem wit' yet more tears. De plant catch quickly an' because a de richness of de soil from a de decomposing head, de weed dat come from dat vase was de sweetest an' de most mellow smoke dat one could have. She would pluck 'way de leaves nurtured by tears an' dry dem inna de sunlight. At night-time de most fragrant smoke would waft tru de house and though de bredrin were in most strong disapproval of what she a do as she smoke dis most fine ganja weed, dere seem little dat dey could do in dissuading she. Bella draw' way from de worl', come' way from de eyes of men an' de life in de town. An' she nah business 'cept fi tend she ganja pot. De beauty of she begin fade an' eyes come dark rimmed an' bloodshot. But Bella's one joy was de vase an' de deep green drug dat it bore. She feel dat when she smoke it, though her loved one gone, she a breathe his living thoughts an' drink from de very chalice of him mind. De ganja was sweet, so very sweet, an' it would a inspire de dullest an' most day-to-day of hearts. But Bella was in a state of ecstasy for she a grieve an' it sent she quite mad. 'De brethren soon get vex by her strange dotage an' as she fall ill dem take de sensimilla pot from de room while she a sleep. Discovering it gone, she a call out for it. Full of fever an' a ravin' in she sick bed she aks for nothing but she pot. De brothers were perplex by she, an' curious too. So dey pour de earth from out a de pot an' uncover de head. It was not so rot 'way an' dem could recognise it. In horror dem see dat it was Lawrence an' dat give dem mortal fear. So much shock an' dread dat all dey boldness at once vanish wit' terror dat dem murder might be discover. Dem bury de head an' swiftly leave town for fear.

'Bella remain behin' still crying out for de vase beloved of she to be return. She nah look so good an' a she wander de streets an' soon de whole town know of de strange yearning of she an' someone wrote a sad song dat's still sung, ya know.'

Miller started to sing a lilting, mournful tune:

> 'Who dat wicked man,
> Him what,
> Tief me sensimilla pot.'

Miller had been quite animated as he told his tale but now, as he came to the end, his head became once more conscious of the deadly device pressed against it and it warily stilled itself once more.

'Is that it?' asked Hector.

Harrington Miller nodded very gently.

'Yeah, man.'

'Well,' intoned Hector. 'What do we think, eh, amigos?'

'Yeah,' Eddie enthused. 'Nice one. Reminds me of something, though.'

Hector turned to me, still holding the gun against Miller's head.

'So,' he asked me. 'You're the writer. What do you think?'

I wanted to say that it was a marvellous retelling of the 'Isabella and the Basil Pot' story from Boccaccio's *Decameron*, better even than John Keats' long poem on the theme. But I figured that literary criticism at this moment in time wasn't exactly appropriate. So I just said:

'I think you should put the gun down, Hector.'

'What the fuck was all that about?' Eddie demanded when we were back on the street. 'Getting him to tell a story like that?'

'An interrogation method I learnt from the Revolutionary Police. They would keep us talking, saying anything, just so they could tell whether we were lying or not.'

There was a mischievous smile on Hector's lips.

'You're having us on,' Eddie insisted. 'You were just doing that out of badness.'

Orosco shrugged.

'Anyway,' he said. 'We have the address. We go there tonight, OK?'

Me and Eddie went back to our hotel with time to kill. We went out for an early evening drink. A bit of Dutch courage, Eddie had suggested, and I wasn't in the mood to disagree. We found a waterfront bar and settled down with a couple of rum and Cokes. Our pursuer turned up again. This time he made no attempt at subterfuge but instead started to walk towards our table, a little smile playing across his face.

'Good evening, gentlemen,' he announced. 'Frank Taylor. Mind if I join you?'

'Go ahead,' Eddie muttered with a bemused stare.

And it was then that I remembered who he was. Frank Taylor. A policeman, for God's sake. He had been connected to the Billy Porter case. A friend of his, a former partner, I believe, had been one of the officers killed in the Shepherd's Bush shootings. I had tried to interview him when I was writing the book but he hadn't wanted to talk. Eddie seemed to know who he was as well.

'Flying Squad, right?' he said, pointing a finger.

'Flying Squad, C1, C11, I was all over. But I'm not in the job any more, Eddie. I'm retired.'

'But you've been following me since I came out.'

'I've had you under surveillance, yes. You see I'm working for the insurers that covered the Hounslow job. My employers are interested in securing a return of assets, if you know what I mean. Nothing to do with police business. So we can be civil about this. In the true meaning of the word, if you get me.'

'I don't know what the fuck you're talking about, Frank.'

'Come on, Eddie. Don't take the piss. What are you doing in Road Town, for fuck's sake?'

'We're on holiday. Aren't we, Tony?'

'Yeah, and I'm the Queen of Romania. Look, I was with the Criminal Intelligence operation that tried to trace the way the Hounslow job was being laundered. Your bit of it took us to the Isle of Man and then here to Tortola. We did this joint thing with the DEA, Operation Panther it was called. Bit of a farce, to tell you the truth. The Yanks were lording it over, us lot were pretending to be the best detectives in the world, you know, this Scotland Yard reputation thing, but you know what the Met lads are like when they go abroad – messing about and getting pissed on expenses. And most ridiculous of all was this copper from the Isle of Man, where an investigation into this Clement guy had started, well out of his depth and desperate to make sure that nobody thought that he was a dumb swede. We got Clement to go QE and we managed to nick a few bodies. Good for PR but everyone knew we'd missed out on getting some of the really big faces.'

'Like Harry Starks?'

'Yeah, but to be honest he was small fry compared to some of the Florida lot. They were seriously heavy. You know their favoured way of disposing of anyone who crossed them? Take them out to sea, zip them up in a sleeping bag and chuck them over the side.'

'Nasty.'

'Yeah. Look, I don't know what exactly you're up to here, Eddie. I don't deal with the financial side of investigation. Never had any Fraud Squad experience. There's other people looking into that. My job is to keep tabs on you, maybe persuade you to cooperate. And to warn you.'

'Warn me?'

'Yes, Eddie. Have you been listening? All that time you were away, well, things changed. You and me, we're old school, right? Yeah, we're fucking dinosaurs. The Hounslow thing, well, it was a nice touch, Eddie, a fucking coup, but it was the end of an era. It's all drugs now. Drugs and white-collar stuff, all with very nasty people attached. And it's a lot heavier on our side these days too. The Yanks have got this war on drugs crusade, there's the DEA and the FBI, and you know the US Coastguard is bigger than the British Navy now. And even the Brits are getting involved, Customs and Excise, even MI6 now that they don't have to worry about the commies. And on your side, well, you don't really belong to that any more, trust me. There's some really horrible people out there and you don't want to get mixed up with them, believe me.'

'I'm touched by your concern, Frank.'

'I'm fucking serious, Eddie. I'm doing you a favour here, for fuck's sake. For old times' sake. I happen to think you've suffered enough. I'll let you into a little secret. When I was at C11 and we were just set to make a deal with Solly Blumberg, you know, just before he got topped, well, it wasn't for recovery of assets, I'll tell you that. It was for a substantial amount of the gold itself. Yeah. That would have looked so good, you know. The gold from the actual blag turning up. Rumour has it that it wasn't sold on. That it's hidden somewhere. One source claimed that it was buried in a warehouse in the East End but we never managed to find it. So maybe your share isn't out here, Eddie. And even if it is my employer's financial investigators aren't going to let you walk away with it. If they can trace any of their unrecovered assets to you they'll bring a civil action to secure an attachment of earnings for every penny that comes near you, bent or otherwise.'

'So that's what being civil means, does it?' demanded Eddie.

Frank Taylor gave a pained look and shook his head.

'As I said, I'm here to warn you. Go home, Eddie. Or have a bit of a holiday and try and keep out of trouble. And if you do want to cooperate . . .'

Taylor took out his wallet and slipped a business card out of it. He wrote something on the back of it.

'That's the number of my hotel. We can always do a deal, you know.'

'A deal?' Eddie looked incredulous.

'Yeah.'

'Like the old days?'

Taylor laughed.

'Well, not exactly, I'm afraid.'

'Then what do you mean?'

'As I said, my employers are simply concerned with the recovery of assets.'

'You mean I'd get a reward for returning some of the stuff I stole in the first place?'

'Well, we'd have to be fucking discreet about any arrangement we might come to. But let's say there would be room for negotiation. The main thing, of course, is that they'd be off your back. Otherwise, I promise you, they'll be checking up on your affairs for the rest of your life.'

Frank Taylor held out the card. Eddie didn't take it.

'I told you,' he said. 'We're here on holiday.'

Taylor put the card on the table and stood up.

'Suit yourself,' he said. 'But think about it.'

George Peterson's house was high up in the hills overlooking Road Town. I could see the cruise ship in the bay below picked out in a pointillism of lights. Across the vertiginous slopes the dark forest was decorated with condos lit up like jack-o'-lanterns. The night clicked and chirruped with little mechanisms of life. Hector went to the door and knocked. There was no reply.

Eddie had a good look around the house, checking out the security situation.

'So, we break in, no?' asked Hector.

Eddie winked at him.

'Leave this to me, old son,' he said. 'I think I can do this place. There's an upstairs window I should be able to get into.'

'What if there's an alarm?'

'I think I can sort that too. You stay here. I'll let you in.'

And with that Eddie launched himself into action with alacrity, climbing up the side of the house, finding footings somehow. He moved swiftly upwards undaunted by age or gravity. He was inside the house within minutes.

'Incredible,' muttered Hector.

He let us in through the front door.

'Harry Starks said you were a good thief,' Hector told him.

'Yeah, well, it's been a long time. But I've always been a climber at heart. And you never really lose the knack, you know?'

The front room of the house was littered with boxes and a couple of suitcases.

'Looks like this Peterson has been getting ready to move out,' Hector said.

'Yeah,' Eddie agreed. 'Let's have a look through this stuff.'

They quickly found the business records and we started to work our way through the paperwork. Hector started putting some of the files in a pile to one side.

'Jesus,' he said. 'There's over a hundred incorporated international business companies here.'

'And what's all that lot?' asked Eddie, pointing at the pile.

'That, my friend, is evidence. This could provide an audit trail for money laundered from drugs by the Florida Mob.'

'So what are you going to do with it?'

Hector grinned.

'Sell it to them.'

Finally Eddie found the Flint Investments files. He started leafing through them.

'Tony,' he said. 'Come and have a look at this. I don't really understand it.'

I went over.

'It looks like it's just a property,' he went on.

'Well, maybe it is,' I said. 'Plenty of people use offshore businesses to buy property.'

'You mean we come all this fucking way . . .'

'Shh!' hissed Hector.

'What?' Eddie whispered.

'There's a car outside.'

'Shit!' said Eddie softly. 'I hope it's not your friends from Miami.'

'Don't even joke about it, man,' Hector murmured, and took out his gun.

Footsteps. The sound of a group of people coming to the door. Banging.

'Police! Open up!'

'Come on,' Eddie urged. 'Out the back.'

But Hector had started to screw up some sheets of paper and stuff them into the pile of files he had made.

'What the fuck are you doing?' Eddie demanded.

'I've got to burn this, man. If they find out I let the police get hold of all of this I am dead.'

The banging on the door and the shouted commands came again. Hector took out a cigarette lighter and started a small bonfire on the floor.

'Shit,' he said, looking around. He went into the kitchen.

The police had started to break the front door down. Hector came back through with a bottle of something. He poured it over the smouldering pile and it erupted in a sheet of flame.

'Come on, Hector,' Eddie insisted, and we moved through to the back of the house. The police broke through the door but were immediately beaten back by the fire that now had started to take. In the panic and confusion that followed we managed to slip out the back and creep through the woods undetected.

It took hours to get back to Road Town. We had to keep off the main tracks and fumble through dense undergrowth. By the time we got to Waterfront Drive we were all scratched and tattered.

'What happens now?' Eddie asked.

'We get out, man,' said Hector.

'You think Miller went to the police?'

'No. I think it was part of a bigger operation. I think we should fucking get out of this place soon.'

'And George Peterson?'

Hector shrugged. He pointed out to sea.

'I've a feeling he might be out there somewhere.'

We walked down towards the marina.

'I chartered a yacht here,' said Hector. 'I think I know which bar the crew will be in. Gentlemen, I'm sorry.'

Eddie shrugged.

'That's the way it goes,' he said.

I was surprised at how calm Eddie was as we said goodbye to Hector. I was furious.

'Well, this has all been a fucking waste of time,' I said to Eddie back at the hotel.

'Not exactly, Tony.'

'What?'

'I worked it out.'

'Worked what out?'

He pulled something from his pocket.

'There is a map after all, Tony.'

'What?'

'This,' he said, holding up a crumpled piece of paper.

'What is it?'

'A property acquired by Flint Investments on behalf of Solly Blumberg. A warehouse in the East End purchased just a couple of months before Beardsley lost track of where the gold was. Think about it.'

'But why buy the property offshore?'

'Because of the business secrecy laws. He could have this place to stash the stuff and no one would know he owned it or would be able to trace it to him. Besides, it makes good business sense to buy property that way.'

'So what was Solly up to?'

'Maybe he was just have trouble resmelting and selling the stuff on. It was getting too difficult. Maybe Solly figured he'd sit on it for a while until all the fuss died down. Maybe he was about to do a deal with the Old Bill – remember what Frank Taylor said. It was for the gold itself and he mentioned a warehouse in East London.'

'So what are you going to do?'

He shrugged.

'I'm not sure yet,' he said with a grin. 'But I know where it is now.'

5
song of the smoke

For a while touring worked for me, travelling light with a sense of purpose in simply being on the move. It lifted me out of the brooding introspection of the rehearsal room into a line of flight. I could escape the dark thoughts I'd been having; motion freed me from the sense of being trapped. I was running away, of course. But I had this fear that my past was chasing me with some awful unknown destiny. Touring, on the other hand, broke life up into a simple series of destinations, crossing the country in a big red Mercedes van, the get-ins and get-outs, creating a show and then disappearing into the night. The bed-and-breakfast life, spare afternoons in provincial towns – I could breathe a little. I could concentrate on my performance and on being part of a group. And relax into the sense of a journey that was taking me. Taking me from myself.

But as I settled into the routine of the tour, and got that slightly deadening sense of familiarity with a part that comes after a few weeks, I began thinking again about the lack of resolution in my life. I mean, I couldn't go on running from it, or playing through it in performance, but what could I do? The play itself didn't help with this feeling of uncertainty. There is no happy end in *The Good Woman of Szechwan*. The gods ascend to heaven leaving Shen Te to deal with her difficulties on her own. An epilogue exhorts the audience themselves to change society, to consider: *what sort of measure you would recommend/ to help good people to a happy end*. This was the political message of the piece, after all. But it didn't leave much for me. I couldn't change the world. I couldn't even change myself. But there would have to be some sort of reckoning to

201

my life, some sense made of what had happened to me. I felt a horrible, sickening feeling whenever I thought of how Mum had taken that money from the man who had murdered Dad. I felt tainted by this ghastly attempt at atonement, poisoned by it. And as much as I tried not to think about Harry Starks he was always there, lurking in the shadows of my life. But I did try to forget him. I mean, there wasn't anything I could do about it now, was there?

I found myself in a sort of static orbit on tour. Gravity would get me in the end, I feared. At least my relationship with Jez didn't suffer from my being away. In fact, having periods of time apart made it special again. We had to struggle to find time for each other. Weekends together when he'd come up to visit when I was in Manchester or Newcastle or wherever. Time that was precious, unexplained. Sundays when we'd go to the pictures or for a walk together, not talking much about anything, just being with each other. For most of the time we'd be in bed together. The lack of time gave sex an urgency and passion.

Circumstances became romantic. Saying goodbye on railway platforms, brief notes and messages passed between us when I was on the road with simple unsophisticated sentiments, *love you, miss you*, the wonderful little banalities of affection. Jez had become quieter and more moody since the attack. But it was good to see him away from London. He could let go as well, let his guard down. He could drop his faux tough persona and just relax for a while.

When the tour came back to London winter was coming, the city was cold and grey. I felt the dread of return, of coming back down to earth; it felt like falling. We brought the show to the Bloomsbury Theatre for its final week. We got a few good reviews and my agent was pleased because a couple of important people had seen it. I might get some good work from this, he told me. But I was losing any enthusiasm I might have had for that. When the gods ascended for the very last time and I was left on the stage on my own I felt a genuine sense of despair. What the hell was I going to do now? No happy end for me, just a growing sense of doom.

I was able to spend some proper time with Jez but I found myself more distanced from him than when I'd been away. I still wanted to hold on to him, I could feel really secure with him sometimes. But maybe that was just the illusion that having a good-looking boyfriend could prove that I was a normal, desirable person. I couldn't feel good about myself. And I couldn't be totally honest with him. He was busy, he had finished the first draft of his screenplay and was starting on the rewrites. And he had already rewritten some bits of his own story. He became deliberately casual and offhand about how he had got his scar. *I got it in a ruck*, I overheard him telling someone. He talked and behaved in such an affected way now. But then, I suppose, so did I.

Who was I kidding, after all? I'd always carried that nagging fear around with me, that I'd be found out, sooner or later. Now I thought I might be heading for a breakdown, it didn't happen though I almost longed for it. Like Constance, who yearns: *I am not mad; would to God I were, for then 'tis like I should forget myself.* No, I was just crippled with grief and loss and an overwhelming sense of humiliation. I kept having this thought: *I want to get my own back*, without knowing what it could mean. I would have to do something, that was for sure.

And then one day it all just came to me, what I would have to do. I was going to a meeting at the National Theatre. There was a new play going on at the Cottesloe and the director wanted to see me. He'd seen me at the Bloomsbury and apparently had been impressed. This could be the big break, everyone kept telling me. It was a cold and windy day. I'd got the Tube to Waterloo and I was walking up to that big grey concrete building on the South Bank but as I got to the National I suddenly thought: *fuck this, I don't want to do this any more*. So I carried on walking, down to the river and along the Embankment.

My mind was racing but I began to think really clearly about my life. I would give up acting, I decided. I couldn't go on like this, just living through performance, sublimating all my feelings into the work. I'd never had a choice about the matter in the first place, Mum had put me on the stage. But it was him that had really made sure I had become an actress. Starks. It was him that had made me do it really, his blood money that had put me through stage school. He had been controlling me for all this time. He would turn me into a neurotic old woman, if I let him. I would have to stop him for good.

Of course, I still had to think about things in dramatic terms. That was how I had been taught, I couldn't escape that. My life was a drama after all, but what kind? I had to make my own terms now, determine it myself instead of being a passive player in it. I was classically trained, that was the only choice I'd made for myself, maybe because, in some instinctive way, that was the only level on which I could understand what had happened to me. That was all I really knew or trusted. I wasn't a populist like Jez.

This wasn't soap opera or pulp fiction, this was tragedy.

It was fucking Greek.

And then I knew, I suddenly knew, what it had meant when I had thought: *I want my own back*.

This was classical.

This was revenge.

No happy end, just a world where good people have to become bad in order to survive. Starks had made me what I was. And I would become bad. I would get my own back on him.

I had got to Lambeth Bridge, wind-burnt and slightly breathless. The muddy Thames swirled below. Seagulls wheeled above, keening, flying inland from a storm out at sea.

*   *   *

Of course, I had no idea how I was to go about taking my revenge. The decision itself was enough for now, it made sense of things. And little ideas started to form themselves in my head. Ruby had said that Eddie Doyle had seen Starks at Ronnie Kray's funeral. So he had been in the country quite recently, and maybe he could be lured back again by something. It sounded a bit like a B-movie plot but it was a start.

In the meantime I had to deal with the fallout from the other decision I had made. My agent was furious when he heard that I hadn't made the meeting at the National. But when I told him that I was giving up acting altogether it cut him dead. He suddenly went all quiet and concerned, as if someone had died or something.

And Mum found out somehow.

'Sweetie, you can't give up, not now that everything's going so well,' she told me on the phone.

She went on and on about not making such a rash decision. I couldn't help feeling just a little bit guilty. It was an old habit I'd soon get rid of, I hoped, but all her ambitions for me that she'd clung to over the years were going up in smoke.

'You can't just leave the business, baby.'

'It's what I want, Mum.'

'But it's your life. At least think about trying something connected to it, management or casting or something.'

I knew that she desperately wanted to keep some contact with her precious show business through me, so I went along with it to keep her quiet.

'OK, Mum,' I agreed. 'I'll think about it.'

I hadn't told Jez yet. He had finally finished his script and he wanted me to have a look at it. *Scrapyard Bulldog*, it was called. A 'caper movie', Jez explained. It had a deranged sense of plot and character, full of misspellings and outbursts of gratuitous violence. A gang of jewel thieves working for a gangster called Big Lenny lose their haul after a heist that goes wrong because they've been double-crossed. Or something like that. It was one movie cliché after another, full of exaggerated slang, borrowed wisecracks and cartoon-like action. And apart from a female card dealer called Lady-fingers (a nice little touch, I thought at first; turns out it was a direct steal from *The Cincinnati Kid*) no women in it at all.

'I thought you said there was a part in this for me,' I said to him.

Jez looked sheepish.

'Yeah. Well, there was. But she sort of disappeared with the rewrites.'

'Well, thank you very much.'

He sighed.

'Look, I'm really sorry,' he said.

I pretended to sulk. I was toying with him, as I often did, but also testing myself, seeing how manipulative I could be.

'I could go back to an earlier draft and try and rework it in again,' he suggested hesitantly.

'Could you, darling?'

'Well . . .'

He looked awkward and vulnerable. I knew that this was the version of the script he wanted. And it made sense. An absence of women was merely part of the absence of any sense of consequence to the actions in the screenplay. It was a complete parody of what had afflicted my life. Violence rendered as slapstick, tragedy made comic. One big joke, ugly and mocking. But there was something quite brilliant about it as well. It struck me that this was what so many people really thought about men like my dad. Jez had got something. The laughter of cruelty. But I'd have the last laugh, I thought.

'What's so funny?' asked Jez, and I realised I was smiling.

'Don't worry,' I told him.

'What?'

'I don't want a part in your film.'

'Oh.'

'In fact,' I went on, 'I don't want to act any more.'

'What?'

'I'm giving it up, Jez.'

'Why?'

Everyone was going to be asking me this question and I was in no mood to give a truthful answer. I needed an excuse. I remembered how I'd reassured Mum.

'It's too insecure,' I told Jez. 'I still want to be in the business but I thought I'd try to get work on the production side of things, or maybe casting.'

'But you're so good,' he insisted.

That was sweet of him.

'No, really, darling. It's such a bloody struggle. This will be for the best in the long term, believe me.'

'Well, if that's what you want.'

This seemed to satisfy him. He probably liked the idea of his girlfriend being in a more stable profession. And I could tell that his curiosity was already starting to wane. I knew that he wanted to know what I thought of the script. He coughed nervously.

'So, Julie, I know it's probably not your kind of thing but, well, what do you think of it?'

I smiled again and he looked at me edgily. An idea came; this was something I could use, something that could fit into my plot somehow. Hamlet came to mind, the play within the play, the dumb-show that he uses to expose Claudius's guilt. A pretentious and theatrical idea, maybe, but pretentiousness and theatricality were all that I really knew. *Scrapyard Bulldog* was a dumb-show all right, but Jez and Piers had been delving into the very places that I needed to investigate now. They had been making contacts with real villains. If I was involved with this project I could start networking in that way without raising suspicions. I could work with this script, I thought, it would give me a cover story.

'I think you've got something here, Jez. It needs a bit of work but you've got something.'

And what I meant was *I* had got something. I would be using him, of course. But that was how I'd have to operate from now on. Jez looked at me wide eyed.

'You really think so?' he asked incredulously.

'Yeah, it's got a real sense of, um . . .' I struggled to find a word. 'Energy.'

'Thanks.'

'In fact, I'd really like to work on it.'

'What?'

'On the production side, I mean. This could be the beginning of my new career.'

He was frowning.

'Wait a minute, Julie.'

'We could work as a team,' I went on.

'Well, Piers is going to be the producer.'

He looked anxious, suspicious even. I had to reassure him somehow. I had to make him part of my story. I had been going too fast.

'I could do the casting,' I suggested.

'We're not exactly at that stage yet.'

I couldn't be be too pushy. Jez was jealously protective of this little-boy's world that he had created with Piers and he was wary of letting a girl come and spoil the fun. I would have to prove myself useful. In the meantime I had to calm down. I was all wired up and I was making Jez uneasy. Be cool, I thought, be normal. Reassure him.

'Well.' I sighed. 'We should go out. Celebrate.'

'What?'

'This of course,' I said, holding up his script.

I needed to track down Eddie Doyle so I tried to get in

touch with Ruby Ryder. But she was out of town rehearsing *Cinderella* at the Theatre Royal Brighton. Christ, I thought, it's panto season already. I tried phoning and I left a couple of messages with the theatre management but in the end I thought that the easiest thing would be to get the train and go down and see her.

I walked through the back of the stalls as Ruby and some TV soap opera star were walking through the dance steps of a number together. Pantomime. I remember Mum putting me on the stage of the Yvonne Arnaud Theatre in Guildford when I was six or maybe seven. *Babes in the Wood*.

As they broke for lunch Ruby spotted me and came down.

'I got your message, darling,' she said. 'Are you all right?'

'I'm fine. I just want a quick word.'

'Well, let's go down to the front. Get some fish and chips, eh?'

We went to a seafood restaurant on the Esplanade. The seafront was empty and windswept. We chatted. Ruby asked about the tour, I asked her about the job.

'Fairy fucking godmother,' she said, wearily. 'I tell you, Julie, things aren't what they used to be in the theatre, you know. No respect for your elders these days. All my experience and these youngsters think I'm just an old has-been.'

I looked across the bleak promenade. The West Pier in the distance; derelict, skeletal.

'Anyway,' Ruby went on, 'you didn't come all the way down here to talk about the business. I know you better than that, Julie. What is it, dear?'

'I want to talk to Eddie Doyle.'

She sighed.

'This is about your dad, isn't it?'

'Well, you said Eddie had seen Harry Starks.'

She shrugged.

'I don't know, Julie. He's only just got out after twelve years. Maybe it's got to him. You know?'

She tapped her temple with a forefinger.

'Well, I'd like to see him.'

'So would I, dear.'

'What?'

'I told you he's writing this book, didn't I? God knows what's going to come out. I nearly got implicated in that bullion job, you know? He used my accountant to bank a load of cash just before he got arrested and they thought I had something to do with it. Nearly got my collar felt. I've been divorced from him for nearly twenty years and he still haunts me. And my career, you know. So, yeah, I want a word with him too, dear.'

'So you don't know where he is?'

'He's just disappeared. Out of the country, apparently.'

'Do you know where?'

'Somewhere in the bloody Caribbean, that's all I know. Look, I've got his home address and a telephone number but I've no idea when he'll be back. Sorry, dear.'

'No. Thanks, Ruby. For taking the time.'

She reached over the table and patted my hand.

'You're like family, dear. It's been hard what you've been through but try not to blame your mum.'

'She spoke to you about me?'

'Yeah, of course. Who else is she going to talk to? Look, it wasn't easy for women in that world back then. I should bloody know, dear. The things that happened, well, they were between men. That's how they lived.'

'And died.'

Ruby gave a little shrug and sighed.

'Yeah. Look, she feels bad about what she did, you know, taking that money, but try not to be too hard on her. She thought it was for the best.'

'I suppose,' I said.

'And she told me that you're getting out of the business. Is that true?'

Ruby was frowning at me but there was no judgement there. I knew, given her own experience, that she was the one person I didn't have to explain myself to.

'Yeah,' I said. 'Well, not out of it altogether. I don't want to act any more, Ruby. I was thinking of going into casting or something.'

'I don't blame you, dear. I mean, look at me, fucking pantomime at my age.'

'There's a chance of this telly series, though, isn't there?'

'Please. Don't ask. But if you do see Eddie, tell him he could fuck it up for me if there's another "Ruby and the Robber" exposé.'

'OK.'

'And good luck with whatever you decide on doing. Anything I can do to help.'

'Thanks.'

She patted my hand again.

'I mean it. Well,' she announced, 'I'd better be getting back.'

It was getting dark as my train came into London. As it clattered across the river by Battersea I turned to look at the lights on Chelsea Bridge. They looked so pretty. My eyes prickled with sadness. I blinked and the lamplight diffused through a film of tears. I felt pity for Mum for a moment. And for Ruby. And for myself. But I knew that I could not afford to feel like this. I'd worked it out and could start to feel a cold certainty about my actions. I wouldn't end up like them. I would become Shui Ta, become ruthless, use anything or anyone to get what I wanted. Use Jez, use Mum, use Ruby. And it suddenly struck me how I might use Ruby. I turned away from the pretty lights and looked over at the other side of the carriage. I caught a hollow reflection of my face in the darkened glass.

I'd arranged to meet Jez at a bar on Ladbroke Grove. When I got there he was with Piers. Piers seemed friendlier than usual towards me.

'Jez tells me you like the script,' he said, with a mischievous look on his face.

'Yeah, I do. And I've just had an idea.'

'Really?' asked Piers.

Jez frowned.

'About casting.'

'Look, Julie,' Jez butted in. 'I told you we're nowhere near casting it yet.'

'Well, let her say what it is,' said Piers. 'I'm interested.'

'It's just a little thing.'

'Go on,' Piers urged.

'Just a cameo really. Ruby Ryder for Ladyfingers the card dealer.'

Jez laughed dismissively. Piers had his hand on his mouth, thinking.

'Wait a minute,' he said. 'Yeah, that's fucking brilliant. You know, that would really work.'

'What are you talking about?' Jez demanded.

'Well, it fits in perfectly with the sixties iconic thing we're going for,' Piers enthused.

'Aren't we getting a bit ahead of ourselves?' said Jez. 'We haven't even got backing for this thing yet.'

'But maybe if we approach some people interested in being cast that might attract some interest. It would be great if we could get one of these rock stars who wants to act, you know, like Sting or someone. They'd bring in capital of their own then. Who else have you thought about?' Piers asked me.

'Well, Joe Patterson for the lead.'

'Who?'

'You know, *Borstal Breakout*.'

'Oh, yeah. What's he been doing since then?'

'His dad's a villain, isn't he?' asked Jez.

'And so was Ruby Ryder's husband,' said Piers. 'Yeah, this is great. There're all these references that we can play with.'

'Joe's an old friend, isn't he?' Jez said, with a slight edge to his voice.

'Yeah,' I retorted. 'So's Ruby.'

'You know Ruby Ryder?' asked Piers, wide eyed.

'She's a friend of the family.'

'That's fantastic! We've got to use her. She's such a camp icon. Authentic villainy meets old school show business. Yeah, we can be really postmodern with this film.'

Jez screwed up his face at this.

'You really talk shit sometimes,' he said to Piers. 'I'm going for a piss.'

'Well, he's got the hump,' Piers said as Jez walked off.

'What's the matter?' I asked.

Piers leaned across the table, confiding in me. 'He takes things so seriously. I mean, the script is great, but you know what? Look, for Christ's sake don't tell Jez I said this but I think it works as a comedy. A black comedy but a comedy nevertheless. Jez has got it into his head that he's written some dark *film noir* thing. And I don't want to disillusion him but I want him to do what he does in his pop promos. I want it to be fast, slick, over-cranked, you know?'

I didn't but I nodded along anyway.

'And I like your ideas about casting, Julie, it could really bring out the intertextualities in the script. Get the retro feel just right.'

'I'd like to get involved,' I said. 'But I think Jez is a bit wary.'

'Well, we need all the help we can get at the moment.'

Jez came back from the toilet and sat down silently.

'What about Big Lenny?' Piers asked me. 'We were thinking about Keith Allen.'

'Keith Allen?' I shook my head. 'Oh no, not him. You want someone with real menace. Someone convincingly scary.'

Piers laughed and nudged Jez.

'She's good, you know. She's really good. You know what?'

213

Piers held up a forefinger in front of his face. 'We should get a real villain to play Lenny.'

'Piers does talk a lot of bullshit,' said Jez when we were in bed together later.

'I'm serious about getting involved with this film.'

'Well, *he* seemed to like your ideas.'

'Are you saying that they were bullshit as well?'

'No.'

'Well?'

'I thought they were good choices. I just don't understand.'

'What?'

'What you're getting out of this.'

'I told you. A career move. Maybe casting is where my real talent lies.'

'But what about acting? You're giving it up just like that?'

'Yeah.'

'But it's been your whole life. There's got to be more to it than that.'

I wanted to tell him: my whole life is based upon a lie. But I didn't. I told him:

'I really do want to find something steadier. Maybe I could get work with a casting agency. Learn the job. But I do want to work on your film too.'

'Yeah, well, we've got to find the backers first.'

'Maybe I could help out there too.'

'You're awfully keen. It's not even your cup of tea.'

Jez was definitely suspicious. I had to be very careful with him now. I was acting out of character in getting enthusiastic about the script. And although I'd managed to keep so much from him he might easily guess that something was wrong from my mood. What I'd feared was happening: he was becoming inquisitive.

'And you never said you knew Ruby Ryder,' he went on.

'Didn't I?'

'A friend of the family?'

'Yeah, I told you, my mum used to work in the business.'

'You don't talk much about your family.'

'Well, you keep yours fairly quiet as well. You don't like people knowing that you're a nice middle-class boy when you're putting on that wide-boy act of yours.'

Usually this sort of attack on Jez's fake persona would shut him up. But he was having none of it this time.

'I'm just having a laugh,' he said. 'With you it seems like there's something that you're seriously trying to hide.'

So I changed tack.

'Well, after Dad died it was difficult.'

I put a little sob in my voice.

'I'm sorry,' said Jez. 'I didn't mean to . . .'

'It's OK. It's just hard to talk about, that's all. The accident tore us apart as a family, I guess.'

Jez slipped his arm around me and held on to me. I was becoming good at this cold, calculating act.

'I don't want to pry,' he whispered. 'But if you do want to talk about it I'm here, you know.'

I probably felt soft and warm in Jez's arms. But I was an impenetrable fortress. He wouldn't know the truth from me. I'd never break under questioning.

I'd put some of my research together. Bits of memory, things that had been said and references in true crime books. The timeshare business was, of course, all a front. He had been laundering money from pornography rackets and business frauds in London. It seemed my father got mixed up with a corrupt policeman called George Mooney who had retired to the Costa del Sol. Harry Starks had escaped from Brixton Prison in 1979. The story was that Dad had double-crossed Starks over money and also by tipping off the police as to where he was hiding out. Starks came to Spain and killed both Dad and the bent copper. And then he disappeared. There were all sorts of rumours as to where he might have gone and some sightings, though none actually confirmed. Eddie Doyle was the last person to have claimed to have seen him. But Eddie was still out of the country.

I went home to Mum's for Christmas and Jez went to his parents. I took Ruby's advice about not being too hard on Mum. I made it up with her. I realised it was a waste of time being confrontational about Dad and what had happened and that I couldn't really blame her for taking the money from Starks. It was just the two of us through to Boxing Day, which sounds a bit lonely, but that was what we were used to. All the times Dad was in prison or away and after he died it had been Mum and me most of the time. There was an intense, unexplained bond between us, which I had broken when I'd been direct with her about Dad but which re-established itself as we prepared Christmas dinner together in her kitchen, singing snatches of show tunes, retelling jokes that only me and her would understand, using private nicknames for things and people. I'd forgotten how close we had been and what a struggle it had been to become independent. It was drama school that had done it – received pronunciation, classical training. That had given me distance from her.

And I'd always known for as long as I can remember that I didn't want to end up like Mum. It was just that now I no longer let myself feel guilty about that. Or about her. Oh, I felt sorry for her in a way. She smoked too much, drank too much. She got depression. Ruby was right, I shouldn't be hard on her. I shouldn't waste my hardness on her.

After we had eaten we sat and watched telly for a while. Mum had a snooze on the sofa. For some reason I took all the old photo albums down from the shelf and leafed through them. Not many pictures of Dad and some pages with glue marks and shreds of paper where photographs had been deliberately taken out. One head-and-shoulders of him, sandy hair swept back, heavy jaw relaxed into a half-smile, a broken-nosed vulnerability about his face. I tore that one out myself and put it in my bag.

There were a lot of photographs of me. Posing for the camera from an early age. Julie in tap shoes and a ribbon in her hair. In a fairy costume, in a party dress, in a tutu. All eyes and teeth, wanting to please, to be seductive. Once I'd have been appalled and embarrassed by these pictures. I might have even felt indignant that Mum had forced all of this approval-seeking behaviour on to me. But I didn't really feel anything about them any more. The little girl in the pictures no longer existed. I gathered up the albums and put them back on the shelf.

Maybe there was a sense of loss, that I'd never get my childhood back, that I'd spent so much of my life putting on an act to hide the grief. I worried about feeling so cold and numb about things. But it felt like I could stand back and see my life for what it really was. After years and years of confusion I finally understood.

And I had something to occupy myself, something that might lead somehow to my purpose. If Jez was cautious about me becoming involved in the film, Piers was encouraging. Him and Jez had very different ideas about how *Scrapyard Bulldog* was going to work but Piers didn't want to get into a conflict about it.

'It's best if he doesn't really know what he's doing,' Piers confided in me. 'The humour in the script will only work if he takes it absolutely seriously.'

He had been hawking the script around film agents, trying to get representation. He hadn't had any luck.

'That cunt Nick Marsten at Curtis Brown said it was illiterate,' Piers said. 'They just don't get it.'

Piers had done most of the running in trying to stir up interest in the project, I think because he was aware of how sensitive to criticism Jez was and wanted to protect him from that. So instead he talked to me. He was using me as a way of mediating his relationship with Jez, but I didn't mind as it suited my plans perfectly.

I had suggested that I might proof-read the script and make it more legible. Jez always made a joke about the fact that he was dyslexic, though I suspected that his real feelings about this ran a little deeper. Piers had been adamant, though, that we shouldn't change a thing.

'It's a masterpiece of inarticulacy,' he declared. 'It's all going to work through the visuals, the references, the soundtrack. We've got to get a fucking solid soundtrack. It's the style of the thing that matters. That's where your boyfriend's genius lies, trust me.'

Piers and I became unlikely allies. He must have thought that I really went along with all his ideas. All these words he bandied about: *postmodernism, knowingness, retro chic* and so on. He thought that he knew what irony was. He really had no idea. And I would go along with it because I really did know what that term could mean. Together we would make sure that this film got made. That it was, in my mind, to be a parody – well, that seemed apt somehow. My plot was a tragedy; the play within the play would be a comedy.

Jez, of course, was completely unaware of this. He was strutting around with his wide-boy act which, in its own way, both me and Piers agreed, might be useful in stirring up interest in the project. It was amazing how many people seemed to be taken in. The scar helped. People couldn't help but notice it and it seemed to lend a real edge to Jez's tough-guy demeanour, some proof. Like it was written all over his face.

His connections helped too. They were trying to raise private finance and Jez's dad had plenty of contacts in advertising and the film world. They found someone who had directed commercials who was interested and could bring a huge amount of funding to the project, but he wanted to direct the thing himself. Piers had some contacts too; his father had been a successful record producer in the sixties and seventies.

Both of them belonged by birth to the media aristocracy. It was a world I knew nothing about but I wanted to learn about it. I also started to look at other ways that one could get funding and finance for feature films.

Though I'd never be able to network the way Piers and Jez could. They knew some seriously rich people and could feel relaxed with them. Piers knew this girl Georgina, the daughter of a fantastically wealthy banker, Albert de Brett. The plan was that he was going to try and persuade her dad to put some money up. A double date was arranged one Friday night at the Met Bar on Park Lane.

Georgina de Brett was blonde and petite. She had a husky posh voice and an insouciant manner. There was an easeful coquettishness in the way she behaved towards the men. The idea was that Piers would lead the charm offensive but it soon became clear that it was Jez she was more interested in.

They had people in common to talk about. Common for them, that is. The famous, the wealthy, the successful. Georgina never dropped names but rather floated them across the room with a lightness of familiarity. I didn't find much to say myself. I was scared of putting my foot in it somehow. All my words seemed leaden. I watched while she flirted with Jez and felt dull. I felt heavy and big boned, awkward.

The evening seemed to go well for them. Georgina promised that she would 'talk to Daddy'. Piers drove her home but she made a big fuss about saying goodnight to Jez. I did my best to hide my indignation. Nothing really matters to these people, I reasoned, and tried to adopt some of that indifference myself.

I worried about appearing useless in this rarefied world but I could prove myself in my knowledge of actors and casting. I'd suggested Joe Patterson for the lead part of Mickey and I'd arranged a meeting, ostensibly to talk about the film. I had my own reasons for getting in touch with Joe. His father Tommy had been a major South London face. He had spent time in

Spain before extradition had been restored. Maybe he'd know something about my dad and Starks.

Piers couldn't make the meeting in the end, he had a deadline to meet for *Sorted* magazine, so it was just me and Jez. I'd briefed Joe on the phone beforehand:

'Look, he doesn't know about my past.'

'And you don't want him to?'

'No, so can you please, just . . .'

'Listen, Julie, I know the drill. I'll keep my mouth shut about all of it.'

And he did. He talked a lot about his own underworld connections, though, and Jez lapped it all up. I could see him watching Joe's mannerisms and listening to his vocal intonations for future reference. Jez explained the script to him and Joe nodded impassively.

'Sort of a Tarantino thing, then, is it?'

'Yeah,' said Jez. 'But British, know what I mean? I want an authentic London gangland feel to it.'

Joe gave a flat laugh and sneaked a look across the table at me.

'So, have you done any film work since *Borstal Breakout*?' Jez asked.

'Nah. A bit of telly. Some theatre. But mostly ducking and diving. Know what I mean?'

Jez nodded and affected a knowing laugh.

'Yeah,' he said, standing up. 'Look, I've just got to . . .' He nodded towards the toilets.

'Seems like a nice boy,' said Joe once Jez was out of earshot. 'Bit of a plonker, though. Sorry, Julie, I don't mean . . .'

'It doesn't matter. Look, Joe . . .'

'So when are you going to tell him about "authentic London gangland"?'

'Not yet. I've just got to . . .'

'What are you up to?'

'Nothing, Joe, honest.'

'Are you in some sort of trouble?'

'No. Well.' I looked him in the eye. 'First things first. Have a look at the script. I know it might seem a bit, well, ridiculous, but it could just work. Could be a break, you know?'

Joe frowned, shrugged.

'And?'

'I want to see your dad.'

'You are in trouble, aren't you?'

'No, I just want to ask him some things. That's all.'

'Well, I'm seeing him tonight. There's this book launch we're going to. It's at somewhere called the Tardis Studios on Turnmill Street. I'll put you on the list. Heads up, your boyfriend is coming back. Be there around seven thirty, eight.'

The launch was for a book called *Basher* by Georgie Lewis, bare-knuckle boxing champion and gangland legend. The cover showed a battered physiognomy and a pair of huge sovereign-ringed fists with the strapline: *If I come at you you'll know about it alright!* Lewis himself was on display, having his picture taken in a whole series of line-ups. There were other famous villains present, mingling with journalists and media people. Freddie Foreman, Frankie Fraser, one of the Lambrianou brothers and Tommy Patterson. Nick Reynolds, the son of Bruce the Train Robber, had something to do with Tardis Studios. It struck me that there was a story here, what with me and Joe Patterson as well, about the children of famous criminals. A TV producer was probably already dreaming up a documentary proposal.

Except my story was different. My dad was dead. Joe came over and I was introduced to some of the faces. They knew who I was, they knew the truth about my life. This was the world I had tried to escape from. They were polite and respectful. I've never encountered a stronger sense of etiquette than among the people in this life. But there was a wariness as well. I was the daughter of McCluskey, 'Big Jock', who had died in dubious circumstances. Sins of the father. I remembered that voice on the phone I'd heard as a child: *Your dad was a grass*. But more than anything I think it was the superstition which put a little distance in their protocol. I was bad luck.

I noticed a frisson in the place caused by this roll-call of infamy. The media types were consumed with a hungry fascination for all this well-dressed villainy. An effete desire for brutal mythology. Jez and Piers were not alone, the room was full of gangster groupies, and it struck me then that their film could be a real success, something ugly in the culture that they had tapped into. That, I reasoned, would be their pay-off.

'Joe says you want a word.'

It was Tommy Patterson. Short and on the tubby side in a bespoke suit and designer-framed spectacles, he looked like a banker or a corporate lawyer. He was rumoured to have killed Jimmy Murphy back in the sixties but the body was never found. Legend had it that it ended up in the foundations of the Westway flyover.

'Yeah,' I said. 'Can we find somewhere quiet?'

We walked over to the far corner of the bar. Someone shook his hand and offered a salutation as we made our way through the crowd.

'Quite a circus,' I said.

'Yeah, well, everyone's getting book deals now.'

'You?'

He shrugged and looked a little sheepish.

'There's a real demand for the stuff, apparently.'

We sat down.

'So, what can I do for you, Julie?' Tommy asked.

'My dad,' I began, not quite sure what to say.

Tommy nodded slightly, waiting for more.

'Look,' I went on, 'you were in Spain.'

Shit, I suddenly thought. Maybe Tommy Patterson had something to do with my father's death. His face betrayed nothing, though. His features solid, impassive.

'Julie,' he said, as if reading my thoughts, 'I was on the Costa del Sol after your father was killed. I was there in the eighties up until the bastards deported me and I was dragged back here for a bit more of Her Majesty's pleasure.'

'I just want to know as much as I can about what happened.'

'Well, it was Harry Starks.'

'I know. I just want to, I don't know, put it all together. Part of my life has been blotted out.'

Tommy sighed.

'Maybe that's not such a bad thing. Don't get me wrong, Julie, but some things are best left alone. You know? Really, I mean it's bad what happened to your father. Really bad. But what's the use in going over it again? These days everyone wants to talk, air their problems, tell their story. Daytime telly people arguing with each other about who's to blame, why their lives are in such a mess. In my day we kept our mouths shut and got on with it. It's a better way, trust me.'

This attitude made perfect sense to my way of thinking, but I had to pretend otherwise.

'But you're selling your story, aren't you?' I demanded.

He smiled.

'Yeah. But I ain't exactly going to be telling it like it was. I'll just be giving the public what it wants. It's not even me, anyway, they'll get this writer bloke to do it for me.'

'Harry Starks has been spotted,' I said.

'What?'

'Ruby says Eddie Doyle saw him.'

'What, in the country?'

'Yeah. You know anything about that?'

'Look, Julie, I swear . . .'

'What do you know, Tommy?'

He laughed.

'What is this? I'll be asking for my brief next. Look, I've not had any dealings with Harry Starks since way back. I did see him in Spain a couple of times but I heard he was somewhere in the Caribbean. I don't know anything about him being in the country. Eddie and him, well, rumour had it that Harry was involved in laundering the Hounslow thing, you know, the bullion job.'

Ruby had mentioned the bullion job. Maybe this was what connected Eddie Doyle to Harry Starks. Maybe I could use that, use Eddie. But he was still abroad by all accounts. Tommy had started to eye me up a bit. I felt that he was beginning to get suspicious.

'Look, Julie,' he went on, 'all I know about what happened to Jock is what everybody else knows. I can't tell you anything else. Sorry, love.'

'It's just that I want . . .' I searched for a word. What would sound convincing? Oh, yeah. 'Closure,' I told him.

That was a good one, I thought, play the victim, cover your tracks. Tommy nodded solemnly at this. I got up to go. He stood and clasped both my hands in his.

'Well,' he said, kissing me on both cheeks, 'anything I can do to help.'

I made my way through the crowd to the exit and saw Piers coming in. *Shit*, I thought. He could find out about me. I hadn't even told Jez that I was going to this thing. He spotted me and looked surprised. I went over to him.

'What are you doing here?' I asked him.

'Well, it's work, sort of. It's a Groombridge Press launch. You know, they own *Sorted* magazine. More to the point, what are you doing here?'

'I'm with Joe Patterson.' I looked around for Joe. 'There he is. Let's go over and I can introduce you.'

'Where's Jez?' he asked as we went over.

'Er, he couldn't make it. Joe!' I called out above the dull roar of conversation.

Joe turned around and nodded in our direction.

'Excuse me,' I said, pushing my way through the group

around him. 'Joe, meet Piers. He's the producer for *Scrapyard Bulldog*.'

'How you doing?' said Joe, holding out his hand.

'We'd really like you in our film, Joe,' said Piers as he shook Joe's hand. 'Your work, well, it's fantastic.'

Joe shrugged.

'Don't know about that. Few and far between, I'd call it.'

'Well, *Borstal Breakout*, that was a classic, you know?' Piers went on. 'We really want to explore the iconography of Britishness in what we're doing. And you're really part of that, you know?'

'Don't know what you're talking about, pal,' said Joe with a smile.

Piers rattled with laughter.

'Great,' he said with a smirk. '"Don't know what you're talking about, pal", that's great.'

Joe frowned sidelong at me.

'Isn't this great?' Piers went on, looking around the room, his eyes bright with excitement. 'All these famous villains. Look, I'd better go over and say hello to Victor, you know, the boss. And I want to see if I can get an interview with Mad Frankie Fraser for the magazine. I'll see you later.'

And he was gone.

'Well, they're a right pair,' commented Joe. 'Your boyfriend and that one. What is it about nice middle-class boys that makes them so obsessed with the rough side of things?'

'I don't know, Joe. But there's something there to be cashed in on, you've got to admit it.'

'Maybe. But what are you getting out of this?'

'Look, it's just something I've got involved in. I think it could work.'

'Yeah, yeah,' said Joe dismissively. 'Same old Julie.'

'What do you mean?'

'Always playing her cards close to her chest.'

'Look, Joe . . .'

'It's all right. I know the routine. I've kept your secret before, you know. But this time . . .' He sighed. 'Just let me know what you're up to some time. Won't you?'

'Yeah,' I said. 'OK.'

'You speak to the old man?'

'I did. Thanks, Joe. I'm getting off now. Have a look at that script, won't you?'

'Yeah, yeah. I might just do it, you know. To tell you the truth I really need the work at the moment. You know what it's like.'

Piers reckoned that the budget for *Scrapyard Bulldog* could be kept down to a million pounds. Everything would be on a shoestring and the cast would have to agree to perform for deferred payment. It became my job to convince the actors we wanted that we had a potential hit on our hands. Piers was putting together private finance through his and Jez's contacts as well as going begging for donations of film stock and equipment hire. It was going to be a very tight shooting schedule, but Piers was confident that this would bring the best out of Jez. With little room to manoeuvre he would be forced into creating the fast, sharp and uncluttered style he had developed with his promos and advertising work.

Jez was not so sure. There was not much for him to do at this stage except brood over the script and worry about what Piers was turning it into. He became moody and seemed resentful of my enthusiasm. He no longer felt that he had control over the project, I guess. He exaggerated his yobbish act like a sullen child.

But I couldn't help feeling an excitement about how things did actually seem to be moving along. What could have been a tedious round of phone calls, appointments, meetings and lunches was fired up by my sense of a greater purpose. Even Jez had to admit to how good I became at selling this idea to people. But what, exactly, did all of this mean in terms of getting my revenge? I didn't know yet; I just had a gut feeling that I was on the right track.

We were getting close to securing the investment that we needed but there was a shortfall of around £200,000. It was my idea to apply for funding from the National Lottery. But when the form arrived it proved to be a real nightmare. We had to define the aims of our organisation, give a complete breakdown of our budget, determine a cash-flow forecast for the project, identify who would benefit and how from the project, and so on. But the real killer was on page seven: how will the project meet the needs of disabled people?

When I talked to Piers about this question he just laughed.

'Well, can't we just leave that bit blank? It doesn't really apply to us, does it?' he said.

'I'm not sure that's a good idea.'

'Well, we could say that we were raising awareness of disability. Danny the Debt Collector's victims get their legs broken, after all.'

'Piers, we've got to take this seriously. They're not going to hand over the cash unless we meet their equal opportunities criteria.'

'Oh, Christ. Well, I don't know.'

'Look,' I told him, 'I'll see what I can come up with.'

I phoned Sally, who had worked as a fund-raiser for Red Rag. She knew all about funding applications and the right language to use.

'Talk about raising access issues with the venues that are showing your film,' she told me.

'What else?'

'Well, does the theme of the film have anything to do with disability?'

I groaned, thinking about Piers' comment. *Scrapyard Bulldog* was probably going to be one of the least politically correct films ever made.

'There is an obvious thing you can do,' she went on.

'What?'

'Employ a disabled actor.'

I mentioned the idea to Piers. He laughed again.

'Well, you're in charge of casting,' he said. 'Just don't tell Jez. You know what he'll be like.'

Piers did an impression of Jez doing his wide-boy impression: '"I ain't having no fucking raspberry ripple in my film,"' he declared, jerking his shoulders about manically.

I laughed in spite of myself. Suddenly Piers went quiet.

'How is Jez?' he asked.

'What do you mean?'

'Well, he's not much fun these days. Seems to have the hump most of the time.'

'I think he feels that there's not much for him to do until we start shooting.'

'Yeah, but . . .' Piers said, then stopped. 'Look, I ought to mind my own business.'

'What is it?'

'Well, look, Julie, are things OK between you and Jez?'

'Yeah,' I lied quickly. 'Of course.'

'It's just that, well, I don't want to poke my nose in.'

'Get to the point, Piers.'

'I've liked working with you, Julie. I know in the past we didn't always see eye to eye . . .'

'Piers . . .'

'. . . but I'm responsible for making sure that nothing goes wrong with the project. If you two fall out it could bugger things up.'

'I don't know what you're talking about.'

'It's just something that's bugging me.'

'What?'

He sighed. 'That night of the book launch. Jez didn't know anything about it.'

'So?'

'Well, you were there with Joe but you hadn't told Jez. I talked to him about it and he was none the wiser.'

'And you told him I was there?'

'No, I thought it best not.'

'Because you think I'm having a thing with Joe Patterson?'

Piers shrugged.

I laughed out loud, with relief more than anything. For a moment I'd thought that Piers was on to me.

'Certainly not,' I told him.

'Right,' he said.

'It's the most ridiculous thing I ever heard.'

'OK, OK. I'm sorry.'

'So look,' I said, moving the subject on, 'we need to work out what we put in this bit of the form. Maybe we should say that we plan to employ a disabled actor.'

'Can you deal with this bit? I mean, you know all the politically correct stuff from that lesbian theatre company you were in.'

'It wasn't a lesbian theatre company, you little faggot.'

'Well, you know what I mean. I'm absolutely useless at this sort of thing. And besides, I've got a really big job on for *Sorted*.'

'Oh yeah?'

'Yeah. One of the main features for our "Cool Britannia" edition.'

This 'Cool Britannia' thing was everywhere. People talked about BritPop and BritArt, about 'Swinging London Mark II'. *Sorted*'s cover for May 1996 was a big-breasted girl in a Union Jack bikini.

Piers was convinced that all of this was going to make *Scrapyard Bulldog* a great success.

'We're in tune with the *zeitgeist*,' he announced.

He showed Jez and me the layouts for his features. LONDON CALLING TO THE UNDERWORLD, it was entitled. There were pieces on classic British genre celluloid: *The Italian Job*, *Get Carter*, *The Sweeney*, and so on. Photo shoots of real villains and wannabe gangsters who were signed up on the Groombridge Press payroll. An over-excited prose style, peppered with mockney patois, ran through the text and the captions. The Kray Twins' generation were served up as heritage culture. There was even a fashion spread.

'We've got to get the look right,' Piers insisted to Jez, pointing out some of the photographs of suited and booted male models.

Jez shrugged, unconvinced.

'It looks like just another Mod revival to me,' he said.

'Yeah, well,' Piers went on. 'It's an up-to-date retro chic. We need to get it in the clothes, the set design, the locations, everything.'

'I thought we were on a tight budget,' said Jez.

'Well, we should look into sponsorship, product placement, stuff like that. We can really sell this thing.'

'I don't know,' Jez muttered.

Piers turned to me.

'You see what I mean, don't you, Julie?'

'Yeah,' I agreed. 'Sure.'

We both looked at Jez. He shrugged again and gave a little grunt of resentment.

Later, when we were walking back to his flat, he complained to me:

'Piers just thinks this film's one big advert.'

'He just wants to get it made, Jez. We've got to think of every angle.'

'Maybe he thinks that's all I'm good for.'

'What?'

'Making adverts. He doesn't take me seriously. He doesn't take the script seriously.'

'Yes he does. It's just that he has to think about the more

superficial aspects of production at the moment. Once we start filming, well, you'll be in control.'

'Yeah,' said Jez, smiling a little. 'I guess. Look, Julie . . .'

He gazed at me imploringly.

'You take me seriously, don't you?' he demanded.

And I felt a sudden stab of anger. He was constantly wanting reassurance. This spoilt little child that I had given so much to and yet was still demanding. The past few months I'd spent all my time helping him get this stupid film made and I'd done nothing for myself. And I still had no idea of how I was to get what I wanted. My plans had gone nowhere so far.

'Oh, for fuck's sake!' I spat out at him.

Jez looked shocked.

'What's the matter?'

'It's always you we've got to be worrying about, isn't it?'

'I don't understand this, Julie.'

'Do you ever wonder how I'm feeling?'

'That's not fair.'

'Not fair?'

'No, it's bloody not fair,' he complained. 'You never tell me anything. If I ask you about yourself you just cut me off.'

'Well . . .'

'And then you accuse me of not being interested. That's fucking out of order.'

I didn't have anything to say to this. He was right, I guess. We walked for a while in silence.

'Sorry,' I said to him as we were coming up to his flat.

'I'm sorry too. I do go on, I know. The truth is I'm really nervous about the film.'

We were at the front of the house. Jez started up the front steps.

'Jez.'

He turned.

'What?'

'I'm not coming in.'

'What?'

'I think I need some time on my own.'

'Julie . . .'

He came down and tried to hold me. I turned away.

'I'm sorry,' I said.

'Julie, for God's sake, talk to me.'

I started to walk away. He called after me. But that was what I was afraid of: that I might talk to him. Tell him everything.

Next morning I felt bad about the way things had gone. I was so overcritical of Jez. He couldn't help the way he was and he did care about me in his own way. Maybe I could talk to him about myself a bit more. Not the truth, obviously, but I could share some of my feelings with him.

I really didn't have any idea of how I might do this. I didn't want to talk on the phone so I just went over to his place. I was walking down his street when I noticed somebody coming out of his front door. It was a woman. She turned to kiss Jez goodbye on the front steps. I came a little closer. As she skipped down the steps I could see that it was Georgina de Brett.

I stepped back. I didn't want her to see me as she sauntered across the road. And I wandered back to the Tube station in an angry daze.

I turned most of this anger on to myself, of course. I felt such a failure, a fraud. So much of what had attracted me to Jez in the first place was his class. That being with him could make real my own pathetic aspirations. But I was fooling myself. I could never be like this Georgina girl. I could never have her easy sophistication. And I realised with an awful bitterness that I was jealous of what she was as much as anything.

It was no use trying to escape what I was. I needed to confront it head on and destroy what had ruined my life, but

I'd made no actual progress. I'd spent all this time working on the film but I still had no real idea of what I was going to do. Then Ruby phoned.

'Hello, darling,' she said. 'I've seen the script.'

'What do you think?'

'It isn't much of a part, dear.'

'Well, it's a cameo, isn't it.'

'Yeah, I suppose. Look, I'll do it.'

'Thanks, Ruby.'

'My agent isn't happy about this deferred payment thing, you know.'

'I'll talk to him.'

'Another thing.'

'What?'

'You still want to talk to Eddie Doyle?'

'Yes.'

'Well, he's back. And if you do go and see him . . .'

'Uh-huh.'

'Can you say to him that if he is selling his story can he spare me any more grief.'

'Won't that be better coming from you?'

'I can't go through it all again, Julie. It's all too much. We'll just end up having a row or something. I just want him to know, that's all. If I arrange a meeting with him, will you do that for me, darling? Tell him that I've spoken to my lawyers.'

We met in the afternoon, in a pub in New Cross. Eddie was tall and thin. He wore a blue suit with an open-necked shirt. His face was lined and hollowed out from prison but he was still handsome in a gaunt sort of a way.

'So you're Jock McCluskey's girl,' he said.

'Yes.'

'Pleased to meet you, darling. Last time I saw you you were about this high.'

He patted an imaginary girl on the head then held out his

hand. As he shook mine his grey-blue eyes took me in. His head shook a little, thinking of all the years maybe, all the sentences passed down. We sat.

'Ruby said you wanted to meet me.'

'Ruby's not happy about the book, Eddie.'

Eddie sighed.

'Is this what this is all about?'

'Well, not just that. But Ruby wanted me to tell you.'

'Ruby could have come herself. I don't know why she's getting so high and mighty.'

'She's serious, Eddie. She's seen a lawyer.'

'Oh, for Christ's sake.' He leaned forward. 'Well, look, tell her she doesn't have to worry. It's all done with.'

'Right.'

'So,' he went on tersely. 'Is that it?'

'No, look, Eddie, I'm sorry. We haven't really started out very well, have we? I just wanted to get that out of the way. I promised Ruby I'd tell you.'

Eddie sat back in his chair and looked me up and down again.

'What do you want, darling?'

'I want to talk.'

'About your dad?'

'Yeah. You knew him, didn't you?'

'Yeah.'

'What did you think of him?'

'What did I think?'

He smiled.

'What's so funny?'

'Well, to be honest with you, darling, Jock scared the shit out of me.'

And I laughed too. Out of relief, really, that someone could be honest about my dad.

'Hard as nails, your dad,' Eddie went on. 'A lot of London firms used Glaswegians back then. They had a reputation, see.'

He gave a little chuckle. 'No one wanted to mess with your old man.'

'But somebody did.'

Eddie's smile suddenly dropped.

'Yeah,' he muttered. 'Well.'

He couldn't think of anything to say but he slid a hand across the table and patted mine gently. 'Those were bad times, darling. It must have been hard for you.'

'People say he was a grass.'

'Well, people say lots of things. You don't want to listen to most of them.'

'But I want to know what happened.'

Eddie sighed.

'There's not much I can tell you, love.'

I could feel the conversation coming to a dead end. No one wanted to talk about my dad's murder. It was bad business. So I resolved to keep Eddie drinking. Keep him drinking, keep him talking. He told a couple of anecdotes about my father. He asked about my work and I told him about the film. He had some ideas about some of the technical details in the heist part of the script. He was on his fourth vodka and orange when I got back to the matter in hand.

'Ruby says that you saw Harry Starks.'

'What?'

He frowned at me. His voice slightly blurred with the booze.

'Well, did you?'

'Look, Julie . . .' He looked nervously around the half-empty pub. 'Let's not talk about that, not here.'

'I want to know where he is, Eddie.'

'I wish I knew that, darling. I really do.' Eddie looked down and muttered: 'That bastard owes me.'

I shook him by the arm.

'Well, he fucking owes me too!' I hissed.

Eddie stared at me, shocked out of the slight stupor of the alcohol. He touched my hand, which was still clawing at his arm.

'Steady on, girl,' he whispered.

'We've got something in common, then, haven't we? What do you mean, he owes you?'

'Well, it's the same old story, isn't it?' He looked around the room again. 'You know what we used to call people like Starks? Thieves' ponces, that's what we called them. People like me would take all the risks and the gangsters, the heavies, they'd always want their cut.'

I remembered what Ruby had told me.

'You mean like the bullion job?' I asked him.

He put a finger to his lips.

'Not here, darling. We can't talk about that here.'

'Where, then?'

Eddie drained his drink and slammed it clumsily on the table. He sighed.

'What do you want, Julie?'

'I want what's mine.'

He nodded slowly. I think he thought I meant money.

'Come back to the flat,' he said. 'We can talk there.'

It was still a bright sunny day as we walked up to Deptford to where Eddie lived. He started to tell me a story on the way.

'A long time ago, and I mean a long time, late fifties, I used to do big houses in the country with a couple of other fellas. It was easier back then, not so much security as you get nowadays, and I was fit enough to shin up the drainpipes. Anyway, we'd sized up this place in Surrey. Big stately pile, it was. There'd been this photo spread about it and the guy that owned it in the *Tatler*. I always kept up with the society pages back then, my "trade publications," I'd call them. Very nouveau this bloke was so we figured there'd be plenty of tom, you know, jewellery, and all the other trappings of conspicuous wealth. The main problem, though, was dogs. He had four really nasty Dobermans loose in the grounds at night. Now I'd read somewhere that what dogs were really scared of was the smell of tigers or lions because they're like their natural predators. So what I did was I got talking to one of the keepers at London Zoo, took him for a drink and persuaded him to let me have a bag of lion shit. Can't remember for the life of me what I told him I wanted it for but I do remember that we negotiated a price and decided that the going rate for lion shit was three quid a pound. Not a bad little earner for a zookeeper back then. Anyway, he meets me after work the next day with a big bag of the stuff and I pay him off. So, when we get to this house we've got the ladder against the wall and I'm up at the top of it waiting for these vicious dogs to turn up. And sure enough, just as soon as my head's over the wall, there they all are, the hounds of hell, teeth bared, growling, eyes all fiery and full of murder. I duck back down and get the bag and sling the contents over the wall at them. Suddenly it all goes quiet and I stick my head over again, hoping to see the dogs fleeing as they get a whiff of this fearsome lion scent. But instead they're merrily rolling about in it like it's the sweetest stuff in the world. And I realised that although this trick might work with dogs in Africa where they know what a lion smells like it ain't going to be much use here where they've never had so much as a whiff of one.'

We got to his flat. It was on the second floor of a concrete-and-brick low-rise block. A lot of the other dwellings were boarded up.

'Well, this isn't exactly stately,' he said as he turned the key in the lock. 'Come in and see how crime pays.'

I followed him through into the kitchen. He put the kettle on.

'Cup of tea?' he asked.

I nodded. He picked up a mug from the draining board and peered into it.

'We could join forces,' I said.

'What are you talking about?'

'We could both get our own back on Starks.'

'What?'

'There must be a way. He's come into the country before. Perhaps we can find a way so he does it again.'

He put the cup down and turned to me. He held on to both my arms. His bony hands shuddered a little at the contact.

'You don't want to know about this.'

'Yes I do.'

'Look, girl, he's dangerous.'

'I know that.'

'Do you? Do you really know?'

'What do you mean?'

'I mean, I know what a lion smells like.'

'What?'

'That story I told you. I know what to fear. I know the smell of it.'

He let go and dropped his arms by his sides. He shrugged and said:

'I've had lion shit all my life.'

A thin smile, milky blue eyes staring at me once more. I reached out and touched his chest. He shivered.

'You don't want to get involved,' he said. 'Trust me.'

And I knew then what I needed to do. I needed to involve myself with him, manipulate him, like all the others. I touched his face. I kissed him gently on the lips. His breath came in little sobs.

'What? What is this?'

'Come on,' I murmured, drawing closer to him.

'Please, don't.'

He tried to pull away from me but he needed to be held

so much he couldn't resist. His thin body quivered against mine.

'It's just been so long,' he hissed. 'So bloody long. Look, I don't think I know how to do this any more.'

'Don't worry,' I said, and led him into the bedroom.

I was gentle with him. He wanted to be touched more than anything else. And to touch. After we had made love he buried his face in my breasts and cried for a bit. Then he rolled off me and lay on his back. His face was wet and slack with relief. I stroked his greying hair gently.

'Tell me,' I told him softly. 'Tell me everything.'

A car horn sounded in the street below. The minicab that Eddie had called for me. I left his flat just before midnight. He shuffled to the door to see me out in a sort of trance. His brittle frame yielded a little, softened with booze and sex and talk.

'Goodnight, Julie,' he said hoarsely.

I kissed him on the lips.

'I'll phone you soon,' I told him. 'I've got some ideas.'

'Julie . . .'

'No, Eddie. I'm in on this. We've going to do this together. You promised.'

He blinked slowly. His tired face nodded.

'OK,' he whispered.

'I'll phone you,' I repeated, and turned to leave, to clatter down the stairwell into the dark blue night.

'McCluskey?' asked the minicab driver.

Eddie had given him my real name.

'Yeah,' I said, and got into his car. I gave him my address and we pulled away. I had a plan now.

This involved getting Piers and Jez to agree to have Eddie as a technical consultant on the film. I suggested it to Piers first.

'Eddie Doyle, eh?' he said. 'Well, you are well connected.'

'Not really. I know him through Ruby.'

'And Tommy Patterson too.'

'Well, that's because of Joe.'

He gave a flat little laugh.

'It's hard to know where crime ends and showbiz begins, or should that be the other way around? So postmodern and ironic, isn't it? It's hard to know whether somebody is acting or not.'

His voice had suddenly got an edge to it.

'What do you mean?'

'I mean, it's hard to know whether somebody has actually stopped acting or not. Or if they're just acting all the time.'

'Piers, what the fuck are you getting at?'

'I'm getting at you, Julie. I've got it, you see.'

'Got what?'

'You. I've got you. I know who you are, darling. I know all about you.'

I stared at him. He laughed again.

'It's incredible. It's quite a story, Jules. Big Jock McCluskey's daughter.'

'Piers, listen . . .'

'I thought something was up at that book launch. I thought you were cheating on Jez, that has why you were so cagey. Then, when I phoned up Frankie Fraser to get a quote for the "London Underworld" piece for *Sorted* and mentioned that I met him there, he says, "I didn't expect to see Jock McCluskey's daughter." That's you, isn't it? He'd noticed you, you see. Your dad was a gangster. You've kept this quiet.'

'I can explain.'

'And in a way you have been cheating on Jez, haven't you? I mean, he knows nothing about this, does he?'

'No, but . . .'

'That's out of order, Jules. This is all fucked up.'

'Just let me explain.'

Piers folded his arms and tipped his head back slightly.

'Go on, then.'

'You've done your homework so you know all about my father, right?'

'Right.'

'Then you know what happened. I was ten years old when he was murdered, Piers. Just a little girl. Think of the effect of that. I was made to feel guilty and ashamed all the time as I was growing up. I had to tell lies about my past. I got used to that, Piers. I always wanted to get away from the badness in my life. I wanted to be a nice middle-class girl. People like you and Jez, you don't know what it's like not to have that sort of security in your life. To always feel that there's something wrong with you. That's why I covered things up.'

'Yeah, but . . .'

'Everyone likes to pretend. I mean, you and Jez with the wide-boy act.'

Pier gave a little laugh.

'Yeah, well, it is funny that all the while you were pretending, we were . . .'

'But with me . . .' I went on.

'I mean it's, you know . . .'

'Don't say it.'

'What?'

'That fucking word.'

Piers shrugged.

'What I mean to say is,' I continued, 'that I needed to pretend. That's why I started acting.'

'And Jez never guessed anything?'

'Well, you know how self-obsessed he is.'

'I suppose. Still, it must be difficult if you're having a relationship with someone and keeping all of this a mystery.'

'Piers, I've been doing it all my life. Even before my father died. What do you think I told kids at school?'

He frowned.

'I still don't get it.'

'What?'

'Well, wanting to keep that part of your life covered up and then getting involved with the film. I mean, doesn't it just bring up bad memories?'

'I'm just coming to terms with things. The film, well, it's like part of that. It's, you know . . .' I searched for the right word. 'Cathartic.'

'Hmm.' He nodded. 'I guess.'

I could tell that he wasn't altogether convinced.

'So, are you going to tell Jez?'

'I will. I just need a bit more time. I want things to work out between us. You won't tell him, will you? Not yet.'

'He's my best friend, Julie. It's going to be hard keeping something like this from him. It puts me in a difficult situation.'

I thought about telling Piers about Jez and Georgina de Brett. But that would only complicate things.

'Just give me some time,' I said. 'Let's get this film into production first. We don't want to mess anything up, do we?'

'No, we don't. But look, I want something in return.'

'What?'

'I want your input on the script. It still needs a polish.'

'What?'

'Look, *Scrapyard Bulldog* is really going to work if it plays with gritty reality and a sort of knowing surface. Strikes me you'd be an expert.'

'You're a calculating bastard.'

'And you're a clever bitch. A good working combination, if you ask me. You want me to keep quiet, then that's the deal.'

'But how am I going to be able to do it without Jez knowing?'

'Well, you said about using Eddie Doyle as a consultant. It can be done through that, can't it? I mean, I'm sure Eddie has some suggestions himself, but it's your ideas I'd be interested in. So, what do you say?'

6
double jeopardy

Well, the East End had really fucking changed. Dan was working in Shoreditch and Hoxton, turning old warehouses into plush apartments, artists' studios, galleries. All those grotty old buildings were turning into desirable properties. I couldn't believe it. And Dan was coining it.

I kipped at his for a few days. He had this big Victorian house in Mile End that he had converted himself. It was lovely. Really sophisticated. He had Marcia, his wife, two teenage kids, his own business. Dan was pretty well fixed. All very grown up and respectable now. It was like he'd got all his badness out of his system. All his naughtiness. Me, well, I was back to square one, wasn't I?

I told Dan about my marriage breaking up. I didn't go into the gory details, though.

'Maybe you're having a mid-life crisis, Gaz,' he said.

'I don't like the sound of that.'

'It could be a good thing. You know, a chance to change.'

'Change? What's so good about change? The way things are going I'll be asking for it. You know, like a fucking beggar.'

'You'll be all right, Gaz. You just need to sort yourself out.'

He was right there. I did some labouring for him, which came in handy. There was plenty of work about. A big property boom around the corner, Dan was sure of it. I found a flat for myself above a shop on the Roman Road and set about thinking what I was going to do next. Dan offered me a regular job with his firm but I said no. I knew that it wasn't my style. I didn't have a trade and I was too old to learn one now.

Christmas was coming up. A depressing time if you're on your own. A couple of days before it in a supermarket I saw this pensioner with half a chicken and a packet of mince pies in her basket. All she could afford, I guess. It's a hateful fucking time if you've got no one.

Karen let me come over Christmas Day morning to give the girls their presents. Charlene was giving me the silent treatment. Donna was shy of me at first then got all playful when the presents came out. Karen was coldly polite. She put on a bit of a show so as not to upset the kids. When we were alone together in the kitchen I tried to have a word. She didn't want to know.

'I've spoken to a solicitor,' she said.

Well, a Merry Christmas to you too, dear, I thought.

I drove back to London at midday. The city was quiet. Dead. Everyone stuffing themselves, getting pissed and having a double dose of *EastEnders*. Dan had invited me over to his for Christmas dinner. I couldn't face that somehow. I made up some excuse. I didn't want him to know I was all on my tod. I didn't want anybody's pity but my own.

No work about so I spent the next week on my own watching telly and getting off my face on booze. I'd decided to stay off drugs for a bit, but I just ended up drinking like a fish. I mooched about this little flat, hardly going out. I didn't bother to wash or shave for days. I kept churning things around in my head, but none of it seemed to make any sense any more. I started to think that maybe Dan was right and I was having some sort of a breakdown. Maybe I was just losing my bottle. I had horrible moments of panic and paranoia. Nightmares. The booze helped blot it out but I'd get the shakes in the mornings and start to worry about things again.

Dan came around and it was embarrassing. The place was in a right fucking state. I didn't want to let him in at first but he just barged past me at the door.

'Jesus Christ, Gaz,' he said, looking at me and around the flat. 'What's the fuck's the matter with you?'

I sighed.

'I don't know, Dan,' I said. 'I guess I've just fucking lost it.'

'Come on, Gaz. Don't talk like that.'

'No, it's fucking true.'

'Look, Gaz, you can pull it together. I know you can. You're just going through a bad patch.'

He patted me on the arm. He was being so nice to me I almost couldn't bear it. I felt all choked up as if I was going to start crying or something. Like that time at that MOVE meeting. Part of me wanted to let go but I was scared. I was worried that I might just fall apart completely.

But it was all right. I was able to hold it all together. I wanted to tell Dan how much I appreciated him as a friend and how much I took for granted all the times he had stood by me, been there when I'd come out after a sentence and all that. I wanted to say sorry for that time that we didn't speak to each other. But I didn't know how to. So I just patted him on the arm back and managed to croak:

'Thanks, mate.'

'Look. Smarten yourself up and come out with us tonight. That's what I came round for.'

'Tonight?'

'Yeah. Of course. It's New Year's Eve, isn't it?'

I didn't even know. I really had hit rock bottom. But suddenly I thought: well, maybe I can't get any lower, maybe it's time to start coming back up again. A new start.

'Yeah,' I said. 'All right.'

'We're going to this place south of the river. The Groove Corporation, it's called. One of these new super-clubs. It's supposed to be the dog's bollocks.'

We got to this club just before midnight and there was this huge queue even though Dan had got tickets. I went up to the door and sure enough there was someone I knew there, by the crash barriers. It was Jason, who had worked for me back in the rave days. I had a quick chat with him and he waved us through.

The Groove Corporation was a converted warehouse but not like those warehouse venues of the past. It had all been tarted up, with different levels with bars and dance floors on. It was huge and someone had spent a fortune on it. I had a wander around. I was staying sober so I noticed how most people were off their faces, pilled or coked up, as usual. But there was something different about the atmosphere of the place, something cold and calculated like some sort of institution. A big fun palace but one that was carefully controlled and regulated. There was a separate VIP area with a balcony that overlooked the main dance area. I saw somebody standing on their own with a glass in their hand, not looking down but out across the whole building. I recognised him. It was Ben Holroyd-Carter.

I went to the entrance of the VIP area. There were two doormen there. Nobody I knew and as I clocked them I knew that they didn't know me from Adam neither. No flicker of recognition or anything. I was known by a lot of doormen but not these two, it seemed. But I did have a reputation.

'Gaz Kelly,' I said.

One of the blokes looked at the clipboard.

'Sorry, mate,' he said.

'I'm with Ben Holroyd-Carter,' I tried.

Clipboard laughed and turned to his partner.

'Sure you are, mate,' he said. 'We all are.'

'You know who I mean?'

'You having a laugh? You mean our boss, don't you? The bloke what owns this place.'

So Holroyd-Carter ran this gaff. Always wondered what happened to him. Clipboard shook his head slowly and turned to the other one again.

'You think they'd try something a little more subtle, wouldn't you, Dave?'

I tried not to get riled by this. I took a breath.

'Look, mate, I ain't taking the piss. I'm an old friend of your guvnor's. Just tell him I'm here and he'll want to see me.'

This bloke stared at me for a second then shrugged.

'OK,' he said. 'I'll have a word. Who was it again?'

'Gaz.'

'Gaz? Gaz who?'

I don't think Holroyd-Carter ever knew my second name.

'Geezer Gaz,' I said. 'Tell him Geezer Gaz is here.'

He was off and back in five minutes with a stupid smile on his face.

'Go on through,' he said.

I wandered into this poncey party that was going on. The VIP lounge was all big sofas, glass tables and lairy light fixtures. There were fit birds everywhere and I recognised someone off the telly in a loud suit. Holroyd-Carter was in the corner surrounded by people, holding court, like. I sort of hovered, not wanting to interrupt the group, who were all yakking and laughing away. I felt a right cunt. Suddenly I was spotted.

'Gaz!' he called out, and waved to me. '*Geezer* Gaz.'

I walked over. He was taking the piss, I thought. Everybody turned around to look at me. Gawping, like I was some strange animal or something.

'Now, Piers,' he continued, turning to somebody next to him. 'You'll be interested in Gaz, here. He's the geezer. Aren't you, Gaz?'

I tensed up. I felt like giving him a slap.

'You want to watch your fucking mouth, Ben,' I told him.

And the group all burst into laughter, like this was a comedy routine or something.

'See what I mean, Piers?' Everyone was hanging off his every fucking word. He turned to me. 'Piers here is a writer. He'll be after you for material.' He turned back to Piers. 'Gaz here was one of my . . . well, let's say associates, when I used to run the Paradise raves.'

'All double-barrelled names and double-barrelled shotguns back then, wasn't it?' this Piers bloke says.

'Yes, very funny. Thinks he's got a way with words. You write anything about my nefarious past I'll fucking sue you for every penny.'

Laughter. Holroyd-Carter came closer to me.

'All legitimate now, you see, Gaz,' he said. 'So, how are you, Geezer? Happy New Year. Old acquaintance be forgot and all that, what?'

'Don't take the piss out of me,' I hissed at him.

His eyes flashed some of their old fear for a second. But only for a second.

He sighed. 'Gaz, I wouldn't dream . . .' He trailed off. 'Look. Let me show you something.'

He led me through the lounge and up some stairs. We ended up in this huge office, like a big glass cage suspended in the roof of the building. There was a bank of television monitors, you could see every part of the club.

'Welcome to the Groove Corporation,' he said.

'Well, you've done all right, haven't you?'

'Oh yes. Of course, you're a part of it, Gaz.'

'What do you mean?'

'I mean, well, I learnt so much from people like you. About exploitation. Of course, your methods were a little primitive. Look, Gaz, I'm not taking the piss. What I mean is, well, how have I got all this? Legitimately, mind, completely legitimately. You want to know?'

I shrugged.

'Yeah, I guess.'

He led me over to one of the windows. He pointed.

'It's about exploiting the market. Yeah, you had some good ideas about that. But I have to say you lacked finesse. There's about two and a half thousand bodies down there. There's a finite number of people we can physically get into the club, but you see the Groove Corporation isn't just a club. It's a brand.'

He walked over to a desk. There was a pile of stuff on it. He started picking things up and throwing them across the room.

'The *Groove Corporation Club Mix* CD. The *Ibiza Club Mix*. Groove Corporation T-shirts. *In the Groove* magazine. We can sell it in so many ways. Franchising, sponsorship. It's a bloody gravy train, Gaz. More than you ever imagined. What do you do? You squeeze every last drop out of them. Look, here's a really simple example.'

He led me over to one of the monitors. He pointed to the screen that showed the doors.

'See those people queuing? Why are they queuing, Gaz?'

'To get into the club.'

'No. They're queuing because I want them to queue. We could get them into this place much quicker, you know. But I want a queue. You know why? Well, it's sort of an advertisement for the club, makes the place look like it's popular. But also because in weather like this you're going to need a coat if you're standing around. And a coat means you've got to use the cloakroom. That's five thousand every weekend just keeping the queue slow. It's the little things, Gaz. Oh, and in case you're wondering about who runs the door here, well, that is something I learnt off you. I keep rotating companies, I make sure that no one firm gets too entrenched here. And sure, they can run their dealers, but only as long as they are very, very discreet about it. This is a respectable business, Gaz.'

'I can see that.'

'You still working for Beardsley?'

'Well, not exactly.'

'Sounds like it's pretty heavy in Essex.'

'That's why I've moved back to the Smoke.'

'Well, it's all happening here. People are calling it "Swinging London" again, you know, like back in the sixties.'

'Who are?'

'You know, the media. It's a boom time, Gaz. And the Groove Corporation is the *zeitgeist*.'

'The what?'

'The spirit of the times, Gaz. Cool Britannia rules the waves and all that shit.'

I didn't try to follow what Holroyd-Carter was fannying on about at this point. But what he had explained about his business operation was clear enough. He'd got it all sewn up nicely. All above board. And he was too big for the likes of me to threaten any more.

'Don't suppose you'd consider using me to run security here, would you?'

Well, it was worth a try. Holroyd-Carter smiled.

'Times have changed, Gaz.' He rubbed his chin. 'Still, something might come up. Something that might require your particular talents. You know?'

'Oh yeah?'

'You never know. Here.' He handed me his business card. 'See you, then, Ben.'

'Keep in touch, Gaz,' he called after me, and I went back to find Dan and Marcia.

My New Year's resolutions were: come off the drugs and the booze for a bit; start going to the gym again regular but keep off the steroids; get back in business somehow. There were bits of door work and debt collecting here and there but I'd lost all the contacts I'd had through Beardsley. Word had got around about our falling out. And people kept asking about the Range Rover shootings. All sorts of theories about who done it. Funny, but some faces and some firms would like to give the impression that they had something to do with it. Stick their own names up, as it were. Not to the police, of course, but to other villains. It was like claiming a bit of clout. And what with all the double-crosses and rip-offs that were going on it might be useful for people to think that you'd wiped out those three. And it kind of made sense to me. A bit of moody respect could come in handy.

I heard that Essex Constabulary still wanted to have a word with me about it. But I was staying away from that manor. I wanted to keep my head down and find some sort of earner. Something a bit more easy going. I thought about Charlene and Donna. I wanted to provide for them but I wanted them to grow up with a father they could be proud of. To be honest I was tired of the life I had led. But what could I do?

Dan reckoned I should invest in property.

'Do a conversion. Buy up some empty warehouse space in EC2 and I could do it up as a loft apartment. It would suit you for now and you could sell it on in a couple of years and make a fortune.'

'You reckon?'

'I'm telling you, Gaz, prices are set to go right up around here.'

'But why would anyone want to live in fucking Shoreditch? When you and me were growing up everyone wanted to get away from the East End. If they had any sense.'

'Well, it's central enough. And it's fashionable, Gaz. It's become a fashionable area.'

'But what am I going to buy property with? I'm boracic at the moment.'

'Well, you could remortgage your house in Essex, couldn't you?'

I'd have to sort this out with Karen. She'd moved back into it but it shouldn't be a problem. I phoned her up and told her about the idea.

'Well, there's a few things we need to sort out, Gaz,' she said. 'Give me your address, there's something I need to send you.'

I told her where I was staying.

'How are the girls?'

'They're OK, Gaz.'

'I really want to see them.'

'Look, I've got to go.'

Then something turned up. I was doing this door job at a club in the West End and this doorman called Sean said that there was some film work going out at Shepperton Studios. They were looking for big, evil-looking blokes and he reckoned I'd be just the ticket. We went out there and sure enough I got the job. I was one of the extras in this American action film called *Red Mercury*. Our scene was set in a Russian nuclear power plant and we played the henchmen of a mad ex-KGB colonel who have surrounded the hero, played by Hollywood star Rick Sanchez. He offs us all single-handedly, of course. It was three weeks' work at a hundred pounds a day plus overtime. I couldn't believe at first that it would take so long to shoot something that would last just a few minutes in the actual film. But everything took so long. Most of the time we were standing around waiting for the film crew to set things up. So I got talking to people. There was a lot of work around. The stunt men were on a good whack but I wouldn't fancy that. All that bravado was never my cup of tea. The proper actors didn't tend to mix with the extras and the stars sort of lived in a world of their own, in trailers or on chairs with their names on. Sean had been an extra in loads of films. 'Noddy work', he called it.

'Just keep your head down, Gaz,' he told me.

I wasn't quite sure what he meant by that.

But I really liked it. It was a piece of piss. An early start usually, picked up in a minibus from Charing Cross Station. We'd arrive just as the caterers were setting out breakfast. Then make-up and wardrobe. We waited to be called on to the set and Phil, the assistant director, would tell us what to do. Then it would be action, lots of takes, then more waiting as the camera was moved or whatever. The film crew themselves seemed a bit aloof. There was this pecking order among them that I couldn't quite figure out but it had something to do with that list of credits at the end of a film when all those strange names like 'best boy' and 'key grip' come up on the screen.

Then, on the fourth day that I'd been working on the film, I found out what Sean had meant. There was a close-up scene between Rick Sanchez and a couple of the henchmen who were actual actors and had some lines to say. We were on the set as background. Phil came over to us from the huddle he'd been in with the director and the cameraman.

'We need somebody to be in the next shot,' he said.

I didn't want to push myself forward really, but all the other guys were backing off for some reason. I looked at Sean and he sort of nodded at me but I couldn't work out what he meant.

'I'll do it,' I said to Phil, and I followed him over.

'Right,' said the director to me. 'Just stand there and look dangerous. That's fantastic.'

I'll tell you something. I've seen Ricky Sanchez in a couple of films but I didn't realise he was that short. Nice bloke, though. Friendly. He made these little jokes in between takes and said 'Thanks a lot, guys' to us when we finished.

I was dead chuffed at the end of the day. I was actually going to be recognisable in this film. But when I saw Sean in Wardrobe when we were getting changed he shook his head at me.

'What's the matter?' I asked.

A runner had come in with the call sheets for the next day's shooting and my name wasn't on it.

'Sorry, Gaz,' said Sean. 'But I told you to keep your head down, didn't I?'

'I don't understand.'

'Well, look. You're an extra, right? You end up in shot in one scene, they can't use you in another, can they?'

'Why not?'

'Because if you turn up in another scene the audience will be thinking,' That geezer who was killed a couple of minutes ago seems to have come back to life.' It's called continuity.'

I felt such an idiot on the minibus back to London. But sort of pleased as well. I was actually going to be on-screen in this film, even if it was just for a few seconds. Charlene and Donna would be able to see their dad in a Hollywood movie. Though with all the violence in this film they couldn't go to the pictures to see it for a fair while. Maybe I'd get it for them when it came out on video.

'Don't worry, Gaz,' Sean told me. 'There'll be other work. Look, I could have a word with my agent, if you like.'

'You got an agent?'

'Yeah. He just does extra work, walk-ons and modelling. Strong characters are his speciality. Heavies, you know. Bodybuilders and big ugly-looking geezers like you and me.'

The David Merriman Agency was run from a mansion flat on Streatham High Road. The door was opened by this sullen-looking bloke with dyed blond hair. He showed me through to a large living room stuffed full of furniture and poncey ornaments.

'David will be with you in a minute,' said this bloke, and he disappeared.

Sean had given me the SP on David Merriman.

'He's gay and he goes for the big butch types. So, you know, use that to your advantage.'

'What do you mean?' I'd asked him.

'You know. Play along.'

Play along. I didn't like the sound of that. I had a shufti around the room. It was like *Antiques* bloody *Roadshow* or something. Little fucking china figurines everywhere. The door opened and this podgy little queen swanned in with a fixed smile on his gob and a little sausage dog waddling after him. He had an orange suntan and his hair seemed to be perched on his round face like a bird's nest. Probably a wig, I thought.

'Hello,' he said, all sing-song like. 'David Merriman.'

He held out his hand and I shook it. Limp and clammy it was.

'Gaz Kelly.'

His watery blue eyes glared at me like he was sizing me up.

'You're a friend of Sean's.'

'That's right.'

The little dog started yapping at me.

'Quiet, Portia,' he said, patting it on the head. 'She gets jealous of anybody else getting the attention, you know. Well, Sean was certainly right about you. Big lad, aren't you.'

He looked me up and down.

'Good body?'

'Sorry?'

'Your body, it's in good shape?'

'Yeah,' I said. 'I guess.'

And I reckoned it was. I'd been to the gym every day since New Year.

'Well, let's have a look at it, then.'

'What?'

'For purely professional reasons, Gary. After all, I can't take you on unless I know what I'm representing.'

The fixed smile widened. I felt like punching the fucker but I remember what Sean had said. *Play along.*

'What, here?'

'Don't worry, we won't be interrupted.'

So I got my kit off. He asked me whether I'd done much work and I told him about *Red Mercury*. He pursed his lips.

'Well, we don't do much extra work. A bit of modelling. Walk-ons and small parts.'

I was down to my underpants.

'But in your case, well, who knows?'

His greedy little eyes were staring.

'Let's have a little look at that, shall we?'

I coughed.

'You don't mind, do you?'

'Of course not,' I lied, and pulled them off as well.

'Oh yes, very nice.'

The dog barked again.

'Portia, stop it!'

He slapped her on the back, all the time ogling me.

He sighed. 'Well, put your clothes back on and we'll have a little chat.'

I sat with him on this leather settee and he went through all sorts of things that I needed to do. I needed to get some photographs done. And I needed an Equity card.

'How do I get one of those?'

'Well, cabaret is the best way. Do you have an act of any sort? Any special skills?'

'Er, no.'

'Can you sing?'

'Not really.'

'Well, you could try stripping, you know. That's how Sean got his. Have a word with him.'

'You never told me about that,' I said to Sean when I saw him next.

'Well, you didn't ask, did you? It was a long time ago.'

'You don't do it any more, then?'

'Nah,' he said, slapping his belly. 'Not exactly in shape for it now, am I?'

'Well, I don't fancy it. Can't you just join this fucking union?'

'Nah. You need contracts, you need to prove that you're a professional.'

'Can't that be fixed?'

'Yeah, I guess. It wouldn't be the first time.'

'You know anyone who could straighten it for me?'

'I'll ask around.'

And I started thinking about it myself. Beardsley would have known someone probably. Then I suddenly thought about Fat Wally, who'd been an associate of his back in the old days. Walter Peters had been a big player in the Soho porn rackets in the past but he now ran the Comedy Club, which had started out at the Stardust, Harry Starks' old place, and had now moved to Leicester Square. Wally had done eighteen months for assisting a fugitive when Starks had escaped from Brixton Prison and gone on the run in the late seventies. I knew he still ran a few shops and peep shows around Brewer Street, so I headed up there.

LIVE NUDE GIRLS, said one of the signs. This tart trying to hustle up trade outside.

'Only five quid, love, lots of lovely girls,' she says.

'Are you sure they're live?'

'Oh, a comedian. Come on, darling, you want to see a show? It's starting any minute.'

'I want to see Fat Wally.'

'Fat Wally? Who's he?'

'You know.'

'And who might you be?'

'I'm a friend of his.'

She shrugged her bare shoulders and cocked her head towards an alleyway farther up the street.

'He's in the shop at Walker's Court.'

There was a big sign that said PRIVATE SHOP. In the window were displays of fetish gear and pictures of half-dressed birds gaping away. I went through the multi-coloured plastic fly screen into this dimly lit place and saw Wally, his fat arse perched on a stool at the back of the shop. I went over. He was flipping through a copy of *Loot*.

'Wally,' I said.

He looked up from the paper. Frowned at me.

'It's Gaz. A friend of Beardsley's,' I lied, hoping he hadn't heard about what had happened.

He squinted, then nodded. We'd only met a couple of times.

'Oh yeah,' he said. 'Gaz. What can I do for you, Gaz?'

'Well, I wondered if you could fix something for me.'

Wally's eyes darted about the shop dramatically. There was only one sad fucker in the corner but he leaned forward and spoke out of the side of his mouth.

'Let's go to my office,' he whispered.

He hopped off the stool with surprising agility for a man of his size.

'Oi! Marcello!' he called down into the basement. 'Come up here and mind the store. I've got some business to attend to.'

Wally's office was above the shop. He sat on the edge of his desk. He lit a cigarette and puffed at it manically.

'How's Beardsley?'

'He's all right.'

'So, what can I do you for?'

'I want an Equity card.'

Wally burst into laughter at this. His huge belly heaving and bouncing up and down on the desk.

'I'm serious. I've heard that I can apply as a variety artist if I have enough contracts. You could fix the contracts for me. I'll make it worth your while.'

'So you're going into acting, Gaz?'

'Yeah.'

Wally chuckled a bit more, then stopped. He looked me up and down.

'Well, you'd be good for playing heavies, you know. You look the part.'

'That's what I was thinking. I've already done this film out in Shepperton.'

'Can you do stand-up?'

'What?'

'You know, stand-up comedy.'

'No. Look, what I was meaning was fixing it to look like I did, not actually doing it.'

'Don't worry, it's a piece of piss. All these cunts that play my club, they're always whining on about how hard stand-up is. Wankers. All it takes is bottle. I reckon you'd be a natural.'

'What are you talking about, Wally?'

'I need a compère for Tuesday nights. The cunt I had down for it has gone and got a telly job. It's an open mike, like the old days. A try-out spot for anyone who wants a go. Can get a bit rowdy. You'd be just right for it. All you'd have to do is introduce the acts and keep the punters in order. Then you'd get an Equity card legit.'

'I don't know, Wally.'

Wally slammed a palm against the desk.

'I got it!' he declared. 'You could be like a comedy bouncer. It would be like you were running a door. Look, give it a try.'

'Well . . .'

'I tell you, Gaz, a lot of people get their big break from doing stand-up.'

I liked the sound of that.

'Yeah,' I said. 'All right.'

'Nice one.'

'So,' I went on, curious, 'how is the comedy business?'

'It's doing all right. Just opened another club up in Manchester. Got plans to open them all over. You know, university towns, students love this shit. Got a live TV series lined up: *Friday Night at the Comedy Club*.'

'You still running the sex shops and peep shows, though?'

Wally heaved a deep sigh.

'Ah, Gaz, Soho is not what it was,' he lamented. 'What we used to rake in from that business in the old days you would not believe.'

He slipped off the desk and went to a grime-caked window. You could just make out the lights of Brewer Street below.

'No,' he went on. 'Soho is all being cleaned up now. I've got a couple of shops, a basement cinema, a peep show. They tick over but there's not the demand that there once was. You know what I hear? People are making pornography themselves. You know how cheap video equipment is these days. Or this new computer thing, you know, this fucking Internet. Diabolical. It's putting the retail trade out of business. And you know what? We actually get raided for the hard-core stuff, I mean really raided. Taken to court and everything. Can't do deals with the Old Bill any more. It's terrible. Have you seen Old Compton Street?'

I shrugged. He was going into one.

'It's become fucking fashionable. Full of poofy coffee bars. It's horrible.'

He went on like this for a bit longer. And I thought about this stand-up thing. I'd never figured on doing comedy. I was thinking about hard-man roles and so on. Me and Wally agreed to meet at the club the following day and sort out what I would be doing.

As it turned out Geezer Gaz, the Comedy Bouncer was a great success. I wanted to use 'doorman' instead of 'bouncer' because no self-respecting doorman would ever call himself a bouncer, but Wally said that that was what the punters called us and besides it had a better ring to it. I'd come on in all the gear, black leather coat, big gold chain, wraparound sunglasses, headset and clipboard. I'd announce the acts like they were on the guest list, and when they got booed off I'd come and escort them off the stage like I was chucking them out.

I have to admit I was nervous at first. There was a lot of heckling. Wally gave me some put-down lines but in the end I generally just said shut it or I'd threaten them like I would if I *was* running a door. They seemed to like that. Afterwards Wally told me that it had worked. Staying in character, he called it. The fact was I wasn't expected to be funny, just to bring these sad fuckers onstage and take them off again. I could make the odd joke or comment but being the compère was like an authority role and the humour was in going over the top a bit about how I kept the audience in check. They enjoyed being ordered about by me and then they would take it out on the next poor bastard who was up on stage.

So I got a provisional Equity card and I started to get work. Walk-ons mostly. I was a builder in the caff in *EastEnders*, a soldier in the English Civil War in a BBC2 costume drama, a doorman in a Channel 4 comedy sketch show. David Merriman got me a lot of work. As Sean had said, he had a soft spot for big muscular guys, so the thing to do was to keep in his good books. I would go around to see him every week. He was lonely really. Just little yapping Portia for company. He offered to teach me how to speak lines and that and I thought it would be silly to refuse. He even got me singing, saying it was a good way of developing the voice. He'd get a bit queeny with me, making all these queeny-type comments and suggestions, and I'd go all stern with him. Which he seemed to like. It was like a silly little game. No harm in that if it could get me work.

And it paid off. He put me up for a small part in *The Bill*. Playing a villain, of course. I got to be in three scenes and I worked out OK. I was dead nervous but it wasn't that difficult really. I was playing myself, after all. And I had remembered what Merriman had told me about acting for the screen, about not doing too much but concentrating on what was going on in the character's head.

And I was dead chuffed. Charlene and Donna would be able to see their dad on the telly. But that was all they would see of him. I hadn't had any contact with them in months. I'd tried to send Karen money and stay in touch with her but it just hadn't turned out that way. The fact was that I wasn't making very much out of this acting lark, most of the time I was between jobs.

And Dan had found this place for me just off Old Street. A 'shell', he called it. Just a unit in a disused warehouse. A big open space with cast-iron pillars and a loading bay. We went around it with an estate agent.

'It's got a lot of character,' this spotty kid in a cheap suit and too much hair gel was saying. 'Lots of original industrial features.'

'Is that a good thing?' I whispered to Dan. He nodded.

Industrial features? I remember thinking. Why would anyone want industrial features?

They wanted ninety thousand for it.

'You can probably knock them down to eighty,' Dan told me.

'It's a lot of cash for a bit of an old warehouse.'

'I'm telling you, Gaz, give it a year or so and it will have doubled in value. If you can get hold of a big cash deposit, twenty or thirty grand, you can get an unsecured mortgage and you're laughing.'

Christ, I wish I hadn't blown that thirty large on that stupid deal with Pat Tate. I mean, it looked like you could make more money these days dealing property than dealing drugs. I'd have to try and mortgage the house. Or sell it. I tried to get hold of Karen. I left a message on her mobile.

Then something came through the post from her. Or rather, her solicitors. So that was why she wanted my address. It was a divorce petition. The grounds she gave were unreasonable behaviour and desertion. She wanted full custody of the kids. I phoned her up.

'Gaz, I want this done through the solicitors. I don't want to talk to you about it.'

'Karen . . .'

'And you'll want to get a solicitor yourself. If you're going to contest it.'

'Well, of course I'm going to contest it.'

'What, "unreasonable behaviour"? Good luck, Gaz.'

'But what about desertion? You left me, remember.'

'Yeah, but I'm back in the house now. And you've been gone since Christmas.'

'Yeah, but I had to get out of Essex, didn't I?'

'Why don't you tell the court all about that? I'm sure they'll be most impressed.'

'Karen, please. Don't stop me seeing the girls. Please.'

'Gaz, don't you see it's for the best? I don't want them to grow up around people like you. I want them to have a proper start in life.'

'There's someone else, isn't there?'

'That's got nothing to do with it. Gaz, I want this sorted out all proper and legal. I'm not going to argue with you about it any more.'

'Karen, wait.'

'I'm going to put the phone down.'

'Wait. There is something we need to talk about.'

'What?'

'The house. We need to sort out selling it.'

'Why?'

'So we can divide up the money from it. Half and half. That would be fair, wouldn't it?'

'Why would I want to do that, Gaz?'

'Well, if we're splitting things up, you know.'

'But why would I want to sell my house?'

'What? You mean our house.'

'No, Gaz. I mean my house. It's all in my name, remember?'

'But I bought it.'

'Yeah, with whose money?'

'My money, of course.'

'But that wasn't your money, was it, Gaz?'

'What are you talking about?'

'You stole it. Or got it from selling drugs. That's why you put it in my name.'

'Karen, for fuck's sake.'

'No, you listen now. I'm taking what I can. I can't trust you to pay maintenance, can I? I can't trust you to stay out of prison. So I want something I can be sure of for me and the girls. So I'm taking the house.'

'You bitch.'

'Goodbye, Gaz.'

So everything was fucked up. It was my fortieth birthday in a week's time and what did I have to show for it? I had nothing to my name except the motor, and I figured the way things were going I'd have to sell that. All that money that had passed through my hands, where had it all gone? Where had all the time gone?

Dan had got a nice house and a family, everything that had been taken away from me. He'd made it all legitimately too. But I didn't have the mentality for that. Working, it's always seemed like a mug's game. That's why this acting seemed like a good thing. A way of making lots of money without too much slog. But it just hadn't worked out like that. And I thought it might be a way of proving to Karen and the kids that I could go straight, but she just didn't take me seriously any more.

I'd got to do something, I thought. A little job or two to get enough cash to buy property like Dan had suggested. Then I'd have something, at least. I brooded about all of these things as the big four zero loomed. I didn't want to do anything on the day, I mean, what the fuck was there to celebrate? But Dan remembered and he wanted him and Marcia to take me out for a meal or something. I know he meant well but I didn't want him to be treating me again. It would just be a reminder of how down on my luck I was. So I said it was my turn to take them out. I wanted to feel flash again. It was my fucking birthday and I wanted it to be like I still was somebody. And I suddenly thought of Holroyd-Carter's club, the Groove Corporation. I could get us into the VIP room and maybe arrange it so we were treated like honoured guests and that. I phoned up Holroyd-Carter. He sounded pleased to hear from me and he put us all on the guest list.

On the night it felt good to be walking past the queue on the main door and having that little rope thing unhooked for us so we could walk into the VIP lounge. That's all I've ever wanted really, to feel special. A waitress brought over a bottle of champagne for us.

'With the compliments of Mr Holroyd-Carter,' she said.

I looked over at him in the far corner of the room. He caught my eye and raised his glass.

'I'm just going to go over,' I told Dan and Marcia.

Holroyd-Carter was talking to this bloke in a suit and a red tie.

'Happy birthday, Gaz,' he said. 'This is Paul.'

'All right.' I nodded to him.

'Pleased to meet you.'

'Gaz here is one of your floating voters, Paul. A real Essex man.'

Holroyd-Carter was taking the piss again.

'I ain't from Essex,' I said.

'Paul works for the Labour Party, you see.'

'I thought you supported the other lot, Ben,' I said.

'Well, they're on their way out. And Labour's a party of free enterprise now, isn't it, Paul?'

'Free enterprise and social justice,' this bloke Paul declared.

'What do you think of that, Gaz?' asked Holroyd-Carter.

'Sounds great,' I said.

'I've really got to get off now, Ben,' Paul said. 'So I'll tell Peter that you're interested.'

'You do that, Paul. And give him my regards.'

Holroyd-Carter nodded towards Paul as he left.

'Good to get in with the new bosses. Know what I mean, Gaz?'

'Yeah,' I said. 'I suppose.'

'They want to be young and groovy, well, I can help them with that. And you know what they say? A favour for a favour. So how are you?'

'All right. I guess.'

'How does it feel? To be forty?'

'I don't fucking know.'

To be honest I felt like a failure but I wasn't going to tell him that.

'And how's business?' he asked.

'I'm trying to go straight, Ben.'

'Yeah? And how's that going?'

'Well, you know.'

'Maybe you could do with a bit of capital.'

'What do you mean?'

'Well, you remember I said that something might come up?'

'Yeah.'

'A friend of mine wants a job doing.'

'What sort of job?'

'A little delivery.'

'I don't know.'

One of the club staff came over. Holroyd-Carter nodded towards him.

'You'll have to excuse me, Gaz. Think about it, though, won't you?'

I went back to Dan and Marcia. Marcia was having a good time. She'd just talked to someone who was in *EastEnders*. Dan started talking about property again.

'You want to put an offer in for that place we saw soon, Gaz,' he told me.

'Yeah,' I muttered.

I looked around the room. Everyone was having a good time. Acting flash. At the end of the night I found Holroyd-Carter.

'I'll do it,' I told him.

He handed me a little piece of paper.

'Phone this number,' he said.

Two weeks later and it was all set up. It seemed simple enough. Deliver a package, collect some money and that was that. But there was something about it that didn't seem right. I couldn't really afford not to do it, though. There was a couple of grand in it for me. I decided to cover myself a bit, just in case.

I got the driver to pick me up at half past ten in the evening at the Elephant and Castle. Beforehand I'd gone in to the Groove Corporation and made sure that the CCTV cameras had got me on tape by the main entrance. It would be an alibi if I needed it. The video would show the time and the date on it. I would come back later and make sure I was filmed leaving so I could say I'd been in the club all evening. I made my way through the premises and left by a fire exit and went to the rendezvous to be picked up.

We got to the place just before eleven. It was a ground-floor flat in a terraced house in Tottenham. I went up to the front door but when I knocked it swung a little. It had been left open. Well, I should have just got right out of there but I was curious. Stupid, more like. I went in and tiptoed along the front hall. I could hear the TV turned up loud in the front room. I tapped on this door. Nothing. I barged in there. This bloke was lying sprawled on the settee, his eyes wide open. It was Beardsley. It was fucking Simon Beardsley staring up at me. I thought at first that he must be stoned or something. He didn't move or flinch or anything. Then I realised that he wasn't looking at me at all. He wasn't looking at anything. He was dead. There were these patches of blood on his chest and loads more of it all down the settee and on the floor.

I couldn't work this one out at first. Then I heard police

sirens coming closer. Then I knew the whole thing had been a set-up with me as the fucking mug punter. Time to go. I dropped the package on the floor. Then I picked it up again. It would have my dabs all over it.

A squad car was coming around the corner as I made it on to the pavement. The driver had fucked off, of course, so I started to leg it and ran straight into this old bloke.

'Oi!' he shouted. 'Watch it!'

The police car was squealing up the street behind me. This old fellah's bony hands gripped my arms.

'What's going on?' he said.

'Sorry, sir,' I told him. 'I'm a police officer. We're after someone.'

He let go and I pushed past him and ran as fast as I could. As I turned the corner at the end of the street I could hear car doors slamming and voices shouting into the night. A pub up ahead was crowded with closing-time traffic. I lost myself in the drunken mob as another squad car came shooting past. An Asian bloke next to a battered motor nodded at me.

'You want cab?' he asked.

I was out of breath. I nodded and got into the back. I got him to take me back to the Elephant, back to the Groove Corporation. I wiped down the package and chucked it out of the window. When I got to the club I thought about finding Holroyd-Carter. I felt like killing the little fucker. But that wouldn't do me much good. I knew what I had to do was to fix my alibi, so I just crept in there and made sure I was on tape leaving the club at about 2 a.m.

I was arrested a couple of days later. They asked me all of these questions that I just went 'no comment' to. Then I was put on an identity parade. The bloke I'd nearly knocked down had got a look at me but it had been dark. I was in a line with a load of other big bald-headed blokes. Must have been fun for the cozzers to round up that lot. I just hoped that the old fellah would point out one of the other skinheads by mistake.

I was put back in the cell and had plenty of time to think. I needed to work out what they might have on me. An ID perhaps. They'd done a forensic check on all of my clothes but I should have been clean. The main thing was the motive. I was well in the frame there. It was common knowledge that me and Beardsley had a grudge against each other. Someone had topped Beardsley and wanted a fall guy. Holroyd-Carter had fingered me for them, the bastard. Finally they dragged me out to an interview room again.

'Well, Gary,' this detective said with a big smug smile on his chops. 'We have a positive identification of you at the scene of the murder. Do you have anything to say about that?'

'No comment.'

'I draw your attention to the fact that if you refuse to answer or make comment at this time it may prejudice any other evidence you give at your trial. Do you understand?'

'No comment.'

'You were a business associate of Simon Beardsley's, were you not?'

'No comment.'

'Up until last December, that is. I understand you had something of a dispute concerning security arrangements at Tiffany's nightclub in Southend. Do you want to tell us anything about that?'

'No comment.'

'All right, Gary, let me jog your memory a little. We have a statement here from Frank Whitehead, the manager of the aforementioned club. I won't read it all out now but simply draw your attention to the fact that he says that on the ninth of December 1995 a serious argument occurred between you and Mr Beardsley at the club. Do you want to give us your version of the events of that evening?'

'No comment.'

'Right. Well, according to Mr Whitehead's statement the argument culminated in you saying to Simon Beardsley, and I quote: "Come after me, or mess with me again, and I'll fucking kill you." Anything to say about that, Gary?'

'No comment.'

'OK. The time by my watch is 2325 hours and I am now charging you with the murder of Simon Beardsley. Do you wish to say anything?'

Of course, I could have told him I'd been set up but they'd hardly believe that. Even if I told them the whole story of how Holroyd-Carter had put me in touch with these people they'd never believe that I hadn't actually done the killing. It would just have got me further into the shit. I had to prove that I hadn't been there at all. What I did have was the CCTV alibi but I had to be a bit clever with that. The tapes were in Holroyd-Carter's possession and if he knew about them he might fuck about with them or get them mysteriously wiped or something.

'No comment,' I said.

I was remanded in custody and sent to Belmarsh. I got into the papers this time because the episode of *The Bill* with me in it had been broadcast the same week and some clever journalist picked up on it. TV VILLAIN CHARGED WITH MURDER, was the headline. The kind of publicity I could do without, I thought at the time.

They made me a Double A Category prisoner, which was like letting me and the rest of the world know that they considered me a really dangerous hitman. The Double A Cat Unit at Belmarsh is like a prison within a prison, and it's meant for those who the state consider to be the most dangerous prisoners in the system. In there with me were some very big serious villains, a couple of major Yardie faces, some

IRA blokes and a lot of other nutters: a hijacker, an animal rights activist and some fellah who threatened to put anthrax in the water supply. So I had hit the big time, criminal-wise. I almost felt privileged. But having that much security around you can only be prejudicial to the trial process. The jury's going to see you coming in and out of court being treated like you're Public Enemy No. 1 – well, it ain't a good start to the proceedings, is it?

There was surveillance everywhere in the unit. My cell was bare and sterile. Stainless-steel sink, stainless-steel mirror, stainless-steel table, stainless-steel seat. Like a bloody cage. You get to know who'll stick by you pretty quickly when you're inside. I remember one old con telling me that at the end of the year he'd count his Christmas cards and he'd know how many friends he had left. He'd done five years and at the last count he'd had four cards. Dan came to visit and kept in touch, which I really appreciated.

Strangely enough my agent, David Merriman, came to see me. I thought he'd want to drop me like a stone once I'd been charged but he was very supportive. I think he got a bit of a thrill coming on visits, to tell you the truth. The thought of all those dangerous men banged up probably gave him the horn.

My committal hearing came up. I got taken through to the magistrates' court attached to the prison. The police presented their evidence, which was being identified at the scene of the crime and a bit of forensic. They'd found this particle that related to the firearm used in the murder in the pocket of my jacket when they'd arrested me. My brief seemed confident that we could challenge both of these bits of evidence. But the main thing was my alibi. I'd kept shtum up until now, but I had only seven days to file a notice of alibi to be submitted to the trial when it went to the crown court.

I had to get the tapes, but if we applied to Holroyd-Carter

for them he might fuck about with them. I realised that I had to make some sort of deal with him. It's bloody difficult to get messages in or out of Belmarsh because they monitor everything. In the end I used David Merriman as a go-between. I got him to tell Holroyd-Carter that if he fucked about with the tapes I'd start telling the whole story of what really happened. But if he just handed them over I'd keep quiet and if I walked I wouldn't take any revenge on him.

When Merriman came to see me we had this code when we talked about the CCTV evidence. We called it the 'show reel', which is what actors call a tape they have of clips of them in whatever they've been in. So if anyone was listening in they'd think that we were talking about my acting career.

'The show reel's ready, Gary,' he told me.

And we were on. I submitted the tapes as evidence and a trial date was set. I started writing letters to the celebrities and public figures I'd contacted when I'd done that charity event for that kid with leukaemia, Darren Tyler. Some of them remembered me and sent back messages of support. Dan and some other friends started this 'Gary Kelly Is Innocent' campaign. David Merriman was telling lots of his friends in high places that he reckoned that I was being fitted up. So there was going to be quite a lot of publicity buzzing around my trial.

But just as I was beginning to feel a little bit confident and determined about my situation I got the decree nisi of my divorce sent to me. I'd been expecting it but it still came as a blow. It took the wind right out of me, to tell you the truth. It was like everyone was out to get me. I'd been set up by Holroyd-Carter or whoever, fitted up by the police over the forensics, and now I was being stitched up by my own fucking wife, for Christ's sake. It nearly sent me loopy. Talk about paranoia. I nearly gave up. I thought about ducking my nut and changing to a guilty plea. Get it over with. Darker days,

I thought about topping myself. Almost impossible in Double A Cat in Belmarsh. There's nothing you can get hold of to do yourself in and you're being watched nearly every minute of the day. It was like someone was taking the piss with my life. I felt like the whole world's mug punter.

7
london calling

When we got back from Tortola we lay low for a while. Things had got quite out of hand out there and Eddie said that he needed time to think about what to do next.

'I've got to act very carefully now,' he said.

'Yes, but you know where the gold is now, don't you?'

'Where it might be. Look, certain people might be watching me. Waiting to see what I do next. I don't want to lead anybody to where it is, do I?'

Weeks passed and nothing happened. I began to suspect that he was avoiding me or, worse than that, had forgotten me altogether. After all I had done for him this really annoyed me. Indifference is the worst insult of all. He was up to something, I was sure of that, and he was excluding me.

And I had become quite attached to him. It's never been an easy thing for me to do, to connect with someone. I feel a sort of autism towards the world in general, but I had found myself drawn to Eddie Doyle. He was the opposite of me in so many ways. He was a man of action, full of blood and passion. Maybe it was that I could feel and engage with things vicariously through him. Maybe I really had become his ghost in a way that I could not have foreseen.

Then the news came of Beardsley's murder. I had a meeting with Eddie. I expected him to be edgy, another person connected to the Hounslow job had been killed, but he seemed calm and collected.

'Right,' he said. 'I know what I'm going to do now.'

'And do you mind letting me know what that might be?'

'All in good time, Tony. First up we go and see Manny.'

'What's the matter with you?' I demanded.

'What do you mean? There's nothing the matter with me. I'm in a good mood, Tony.'

'Well, that's just it. This Beardsley fellow has just been bumped off and you don't seem rattled at all. Wait a minute, you didn't have anything to do with it, did you?'

'Of course not, Tony. What do you take me for?'

'You don't seem worried by it.'

'I'll watch my back. Don't worry, everything's going to plan.'

Something was up. And I had no idea what it might be. Eddie was acting strangely, that was for sure. Something about him had changed since we'd got back to England. He seemed relaxed, his usual agitation and paranoia gone somehow, his manner and demeanour apparently carefree, jocular even. He seemed untroubled, which was unlike the Eddie Doyle I knew, and that perplexed me. If I didn't know better about human nature I would have said that he was happy.

Manny Gould, on the other hand, was in an entirely different mood.

'I expected that you gentlemen might have come to see me sooner.'

'Sorry, Manny,' Eddie retorted. 'We were just getting over the merry dance your client has been leading us.'

'Well, it was a complex situation, granted, but weren't you supposed to bring some paperwork for me to have a look at?'

'It wasn't there, Manny. Solly never sent the assets from the gold that went missing out there. It was never smelted down. It's still here, somewhere in London. And you know that. So does Starks.'

'We were never completely sure. It was, shall we say' – he shrugged – 'a process of elimination.'

'Elimination, yeah, that's a good one, Manny. That's what it's been about all along, hasn't it? Except that it's been people that have been eliminated. What's this with Beardsley?'

Manny shrugged again.

'I really don't know. This Essex business, I believe. It's like the Wild West out there.'

'Are you sure your esteemed client didn't have a hand in it?'

'Of course I'm sure.'

'Well, Beardsley certainly had the wind up about Harry.'

'He had nothing to do with it.'

'Whatever. The good news is I might just know where it is now.'

Manny's eyes goggled.

'Where?' he demanded.

'Not so fast, my old son. We play these things my way this time. You tell your boss that he can have it all, for the right price.'

'How much is there?'

'We don't know yet. Ask him how much he's prepared to gamble and he can have the lot. A fixed price. I just want to walk away from all of this with a bit of cash for once.'

Manny nodded cautiously.

'All right. I'll make some enquiries.'

'And tell him I want to meet him there. Where it's hidden.'

'What?'

'You heard. I'll let him know the time and the place when I'm ready.'

'You really don't expect that Harry will just come into the country at your beck and call, do you?'

'That's exactly what I expect.'

'But he'd be taking a hell of a risk doing that.'

'Well, we've all been taking risks. He's done it before. Tell him I want him alone, too.'

'I don't understand,' I told Eddie when we left Manny's offices. 'Why do you want to bring Starks in on this? You could take the gold yourself, couldn't you?'

'And be stuck with the stuff again, Tony? Do me a favour.'

'And what about Frank Taylor? What are you going to do about him?'

'I can sort him out. Do a deal. Like the old days. In the meantime I'm sorting out cover for the operation.'

'Let me get this straight. You're going to deal with Starks and Taylor. That doesn't make sense.'

Eddie laughed.

'I'm going to do the right thing, Tony.'

I didn't like the sound of this.

'I don't understand, Eddie.'

'It'll all come clear in the end. You'll get the big scoop on Starks, don't you worry. You want your story, don't you? Well, you'll get it all right.'

I tried to work out what Eddie was playing at but I was baffled by it all. I soon found out what his 'cover' was, though. He was working as a consultant for a film company called Cutthroat Productions, advising them on some gangster movie called *Scrapyard Bulldog*. I went to see him in their small run-down office in Soho.

He was going over a section of dialogue with a young man I vaguely recognised.

'Hello, Tony,' said Eddie. 'You remember Piers, don't you?'

I tried to place him.

'All right, mate?' said the youngster. 'We met at Ronnie Kray's funeral.'

Then it came back to me. He had worked on *Sorted*, Groombridge's infantile lad magazine.

'How's Victor?' I asked, shaking his hand.

Piers chuckled.

'He's well pissed off with you, mate.'

The use of *mate* rankled. No bloody respect. As did the reminder that my so-called career was on its uppers. This youth probably saw me as some pathetic washed-up old hack.

'So, what are you up to, Eddie?' I asked.

'Eddie's our consultant on this film we're making,' Piers interjected. 'We want to get the details right, you know, the authenticity of the piece.'

'They're paying me for my expertise,' said Eddie.

'Yeah,' said Piers. 'Eddie's the real thing.'

'Isn't he just,' I muttered.

Just then a couple came into the office. A tall red-headed woman and a blond-haired man.

'We could always build a set of the warehouse,' Blond was saying.

'It'll cost too much,' Redhead replied. 'Look, we've gone through this before. It'll be easier and cheaper to find a place and do it on location.'

'Yeah, you keep saying this but you haven't found anywhere, have you?' said Blond.

'Well, it's where the main part of the action happens, you want it to be right, don't you?' said Redhead.

'Of course I want it to be right.'

'Well then, it might take a bit of time to find the right location.'

'But if we built it we wouldn't have to worry, would we?'

'I've told you, we can't afford it. We've got to keep the budget down.'

Blond sighed.

'I shouldn't have to worry about this, you know,' he complained. 'Just find somewhere soon, can't you? I want to know how I'm going to shoot this bloody thing.'

'Here's the happy couple,' Piers announced.

'Who's this?' Blond demanded.

'He's a friend of Eddie's,' Piers explained. 'Tony, meet Jez Scott, he's the director. And Julie Kincaid, my co-producer.'

'All right, mate?' Jez said, cocking his head back a little to show a scar on his right cheek.

'Pleased to meet you,' said Julie.

I tried to meet her eye and noticed her shoot an anxious glance at Eddie.

'Welcome to Cutthroat Productions,' said Piers. 'You've met all the staff now.'

'Yeah, well,' said Jez. 'Eddie, if you'll excuse us we need to have a meeting.'

'You want me in on it?' asked Eddie.

'No, just me, Piers and Julie. You can go for lunch if you want.'

'What do you say, Tony? I'll buy you lunch, put it on my expenses for once.'

As we were leaving the office Eddie had a quick exchange with the red-headed girl. It was something about an arrangement to meet up and talk about something in the script. The other two men were already engaged in some deep conversation of their own and they paid no heed to a strange sort of casual intensity between Eddie and this woman Julie. It wasn't in the words that they said to one another but rather the intimacy of space between them. I saw Eddie touch her ever so lightly on the shoulder as he took his leave.

'Well, you have fallen in with a young crowd,' I said to Eddie in the restaurant.

'Yeah,' he replied. 'I guess.'

'And that Jez and Julie, they're a couple?'

'Yeah.'

'Quite a family business, isn't it?'

'What's that supposed to mean?' Eddie snapped.

'Nothing,' I replied.

I hit a nerve there, I thought. Eddie poured himself some more wine.

'So you worked it out, then?' he asked.

I sighed.

'This warehouse location is the place where the gold's buried.'

'Yeah.' He grinned. 'Good, isn't it?'

'Brilliant.'

'Gives me time to find out if it really is there. And if the film company approaches the estate agents managing the property about renting it as a location there's no suspicion about what we might be up to and nothing that can get traced back to me.'

'And everybody thinks that it's just being used to make a film.'

'Yeah, it's a low-budget number. You know they got lottery money for it?'

'Really?'

'Yeah. Imagine that. Lottery money for some stupid B-movie.'

'And that's what it is?'

'*Scrapyard Bulldog*? Yeah, it's a bit silly to tell you the truth. Imagine all those people wasting their money on scratch cards for something like that. I'm supposed to be putting the realistic criminal element into it.'

'Well, you're certainly doing that.'

Eddie laughed.

'And they have no idea how realistic?' I asked.

'No. What do you think I am, stupid?'

'Well, the girl seemed very keen on using the warehouse.'

'Yeah,' said Eddie, a little cagily. 'She's a bright kid.'

'Not too bright, I hope.'

Eddie put his glass down.

'What are you getting at?'

'Nothing, Eddie. It seems you've got everything sewn up. I'm just not sure how I fit into this any more.'

'You'll get your story, don't worry.'

'Yeah, you already said that, but how?'

'You'll find out soon enough.'

'You seem very confident, Eddie.'

'I am.'

'Yeah. You seem, I don't know, happy.'

'I am, Tony.'
'Something's happened.'
Eddie smiled.
'Don't be so suspicious. Can't a fellah be happy?'

No, I thought to myself, he can't. He must be up to something. I had time on my hands so I decided to find out what was really going on. Eddie's guard was down now. He wasn't an easy person to follow, his instincts were sharp. But I managed to tail him driving out to the warehouse in East London that Solly had the deeds for. The red-headed girl Julie was with him. Location hunting, I suppose, is what these film people would call it. And Eddie was setting up his 'cover,' as he called it. But there was something wrong about how the pair of them behaved with each other. Something playful, mischievous.

There was no sign of Frank Taylor shadowing him so perhaps Eddie had done some sort of deal with him. Taylor hadn't exactly been incorruptible during his time on the job, after all. I started watching Eddie's flat. I saw the girl Julie arrive at it late at night and leave early in the morning. So this was what it was all about. There was something going on between them. And this was why he seemed so happy. The poor old fool was in love.

And I felt an odd sense of betrayal. Of jealousy even. It was pathetic, I know, but it seemed to mock the loneliness and desolation of my life. I felt left out. I thought about confronting Eddie about this new dalliance of his but decided to wait. I wanted to find out as much as I could for myself. I wanted to outwit him, to outflank him.

I got in touch with Piers. We arranged to meet for a drink. I told him that I wanted his advice on how I might get back with Victor. He must have seen me as a charity case. He said he'd have a word, whatever that meant. The conversation moved on to his project fairly swiftly. People always want to talk up what they're doing. I asked him about the director, Jez. It turned out they were old pals, they had gone to school together. Then I brought up Julie.

'Yeah,' Piers explained. 'She used to be an actress, then she wanted to get involved in casting and stuff on this film. I wasn't sure it was going to work but she's been great. Bit of a dark horse, really.'

'You can say that again.'

Piers frowned at me. He'd had quite a lot to drink by then.

'You mean, you know about her?' he mumbled.

I didn't know where this was leading so I just shrugged and nodded.

'Shit,' he went on. 'Well, you would, wouldn't you?'

I smiled and pretended I knew what he was talking about.

'Of course you would. I mean, you were a crime journalist, after all.'

What did this mean? I let him carry on.

'I told her people were going to find out. The thing is . . .' He sighed. 'Well, Jez doesn't know and she really wants to keep it a secret from him.'

'Well, I suppose she would.'

'But I can't see why. He's going to know sooner or later. Eddie knows.'

I laughed.

'Well, he would, wouldn't he?' I said.

'What's so funny?' Piers demanded.

And then I realised that he was talking about something else altogether. But what? I got Piers another drink. A large one.

'So what did she tell you about it?' I fished.

'Well, just that she'd tell Jez in her own time. Look, I really shouldn't be talking about this. I promised Julie. You won't tell anyone, will you? I mean, anyone who doesn't know already. I think she's always wanted to put it all behind her, you know. It must have been a tough time.'

'Yeah, I guess so,' I agreed, without any idea with what.

I thought about letting Piers know about Julie and Eddie's affair. That would really stir things up. But I decided against it. I had the advantage of knowing something that he didn't and nearly knowing something that he did. There would be time enough to find out what it was.

In the meantime I prepared myself for the big story. I had a thick file on Harry Starks and loads of old clippings. I had done him for *Murder Monthly* back in the '80s. Then there were all the references in Teddy Thursby's diaries. Some of the real meat had been hacked out of the journals when he and Julian had been working on the official biography, but there was plenty of stuff that I could use. I just had to find a way of incorporating it without revealing its source.

I would go to Victor with it. I didn't really want to deal with Groombridge again but I still owed him for the advance on Eddie's book and I was still technically under contract with him. But I knew that I could renegotiate something really sweet for a book this big. I began to muse about serialisation rights, film and television options.

Eddie had promised me the Starks story. I had no idea how he was going to deliver but I'd make sure he kept his side of the bargain somehow. I'd lost a lot of trust in Eddie. Since he'd been seeing this wretched girl I'd been completely cut out of things. It struck me that maybe she was the key to what Eddie was planning. Something about her nagged at me but I couldn't work out what.

Maybe I was just haunted by the loss of Eddie's companionship. Not that we'd become friends or anything. But there had been a semblance of contact with a fellow being. I felt foolish and resentful at this weakness.

My life had been a series of timid adjustments to loneliness. But I'd managed never to let anyone get to me. I had been utterly ruthless in the past. I had repressed my desires. I had murdered them. Now all that was left was the slow surcease of feeling. Vigilance, that was all that was left for me now. To be able to watch.

So I reverted to my dull world of calm and morbid preoccupation. All these adventures, this senseless running around, were not really my style at all. I'd given up on real life, after all. It was an argument that I'd lost years ago. I found that I preferred the ghost life. Controlling events in the way they are recorded. This was my own *truecrime*.

The genre at large was growing. A turgid swelling in the publishing market. As Victor had prophesied, all sorts of Kray associates and hangers-on had come out of the woodwork since Ronnie's death. The Groombridge Press seemed to be issuing hagiographies of small-time crooks with an almost religious fervour. Every week another simple soul endowed with miraculous physical prowess would be staring out of the shelves of WH Smith's. Each cover photo an icon of brutality along with some charming aphorism of violence. *Basher: The Story of a Bare-Knuckle King*: '*If I come at you you'll know about it alright!*'. These were Victor's Unspoiled Monsters.

And news came that the man held for Simon Beardsley's murder had been released after police evidence had fallen apart at his trial. It was suggested by the defence that forensics could have been contaminated as one of the arresting officers had been present at the crime scene, a positive identification of the suspect was in some doubt, and the defendant was able to supply an alibi in the form of a CCTV tape of him attending a nightclub at the time of the crime. The case got most attention in the media for a comment made by the defendant on leaving the dock. Gary Kelly had announced to the waiting press pack outside, presumably thinking that he was now protected by the double jeopardy rule: 'Yeah, I done it.' The *Sunday Illustrated* ran an exclusive interview with TV VILLAIN GAZ KELLY (apparently he had found time to do some acting between his nefarious activities) in which he spouted no end of ghastly braggadocio.

I felt strangely envious of this ridiculous thug. He could admit to his crimes. He could boast of noble savagery, claim a revenge on the modern world that we all secretly long for. I couldn't admit to mine, could I? And who would be interested? My sordid little secrets. I hadn't been a particularly successful psychopath. I'd got away with it, that was all.

And I had a job to do. I was *truecrime*'s faithful amanuensis, recording the sins of others. I would judge the readers' thirst for evil by the dryness of my own palate. I still had a taste for it. As I researched Harry Starks' story, the secret of what Eddie was up to with this girl Julie, what Piers had alluded to, nagged at me. Then it came to me quite by chance. I'd spent all day at the Newspaper Library in Colindale checking a few facts, near snow-blind from hours spent straining my eyes in the white light from the microfilm reading machine. I was looking at the reports on the Costa del Sol murders and there was a photograph in The *Daily Mirror*, a snatch shot of Jock McCluskey's wife and daughter coming out of their house. The wife was covering her face but the daughter had been caught with her full face into the lens, looking bewildered but with a half-smile on her face as if unable to stop herself posing for the camera. A ten-year-old girl stared out at me. The picture quality was poor but there was something about that face. The caption gave her name as Julie.

It's a complicated process confirming somebody's real name with their stage name. Equity has a register but they have rules of confidentiality. I knew someone from my *Sunday Illustrated* days who specialised in this sort of thing. It took him a couple of days but I was sure now that Eddie and this girl really were up to something: Julie Kincaid and Julie McCluskey were the same person.

I'd arranged to have another drink with Piers. I wanted to pitch the Starks book to Victor and I thought that he might be a good go-between since relations between me and Groombridge had completely broken down.

Piers had just come from a casting session when we met. He seemed possessed by some intense manic energy that was quite disturbing. Some sort of horrible animation. Pop-eyed with pinprick pupils, his mandible mechanically clenching and twitching. Cocaine, I concluded. The drug for ventriloquists' dummies.

They had just hired this goon Kelly to play a heavy in this moronic film of theirs.

'It's great, Tony,' he jabbered gleefully. 'We've got a real villain playing a villain.'

'And I don't suppose all of this publicity over the murder case will do any harm.'

'No. Not at all. Quite the reverse, I reckon. I've already got him doing a column for *Sorted*. He's got a lot of great stories.'

'Well, I've got a really good story, Piers. I want you to let Victor know that I've got something big for him.'

'Yeah, yeah.' He nodded. 'Sure.'

He grinned like an idiot. His mouth an awful rictus. I could tell that he wasn't really listening.

'Of course,' I went on, 'your co producer, Julie Kincaid, well, she's got a really good story, don't you think?'

'Not half.'

He looked around, his burnt-out eyes scanning the room distractedly.

'I mean what with her father being murdered.'

'Yeah.' He continued chewing. 'Terrible.'

'Don't you think that you could use that?' I asked him.

'Well, I've been trying, on the quiet, mind. It would be a terrific angle. But you know what women are like.'

'No,' I said emphatically.

'What?'

His face froze into a frown for a second.

'I have *no* idea what women are like,' I insisted.

He broke into a spasmodic giggle.

'No,' he squealed. 'Neither do I.'

It was time to confront Eddie. We met for lunch at an Italian restaurant in Frith Street.

'You've been avoiding me, Eddie,' I said as we made our way through the main course.

'Now, now, Tony,' he chided me. 'I've been busy. You know that.'

'You certainly have, Eddie. So have I.'

He put his knife and fork down and glared at me.

'What the fuck are you on about now?' he demanded.

'I know,' I said.

'You know what, exactly?'

'I know about you and this girl.'

'You . . .'

'And I know who she is.'

'Let me tell you something.'

'It's quite a story, Eddie.'

'You don't know nothing, Tony.'

'Oh, I don't blame you. A young attractive girl like that.'

'Just shut up!' he hissed.

'And her old man done in by our friend Mr Starks.'

Eddie drew himself up suddenly. His chair scraped back, cutlery clattered, a wineglass tipped over. The room was alerted to the commotion and turned as one in our direction. A waiter came over.

'Is everything all right, sir?' he demanded.

Eddie slowly sat back down.

'Yeah,' he muttered. 'No problem.'

He looked at me across the table. Nostrils flared slightly. Blue-grey eyes full of contempt. I shrugged.

'I'm sorry,' I said. 'I just want to know what's going on, that's all.'

'What do you get out of all this?'

'You've lost me now, Eddie.'

'Snooping around. It's just another story to you, isn't it?'

'Well, that is the general idea, Eddie, yes.'

'There are other kinds of stories, you know. Good stories.'

'Oh yes. Happy ever after. All that. Spare me the details. You promised me an ending of a different sort. I want to know what it is now.'

'You're sick, you know that?'

'Yes I do, actually.'

'What?'

'I'm not a normal person, Eddie. I've never had a normal feeling in my life. I've led a vicarious life. Always watching. Never taking part.'

'What are you talking about?'

'I'm trying to explain. I'm sorry if I'm a little insensitive to this, um, affair with this girl. It's just that I don't . . .' I sighed. 'Well, I've never . . .'

I made a futile gesture with my hands. Eddie stared at me.

'You've never . . .' He frowned. 'You've never had a relationship?'

I laughed out loud.

'A relationship? Isn't that a wonderful word? No, not in the way that you mean.'

'I don't believe you. You must have.'

'Oh, I've tried to, you know.' My mind flashed memories of those awful moments. 'I did some things in the past but you couldn't call them normal.'

Eddie shook his head sadly.

'That's . . .'

'Tragic? No. It's a joke. My whole life's a fucking joke. I don't want your pity, Eddie. I've enjoyed your company. It's been exhilarating. But it's been an arrangement. That's all I can deal with really. Arrangements. And if an arrangement gets broken, well, it really upsets my world. Don't you see?'

Eddie sighed. Shrugged.

'I guess.'

'Now, you're up to something with this Julie. Let me rephrase that. You have made some sort of arrangement with her. Yes?'

'I'm in love with her, Tony.'

'Hmm.' I nodded, trying my hardest to look understanding.

'You know what happened to her dad. Well, she wants justice for that.'

'Really?'

'So the plan is that we arrange a meet with Starks to collect the gold and he gets handed over to the police.'

'He's a dangerous man, Eddie.'

'I know that. I can handle him.'

'And the gold?'

'I've made a deal with Frank Taylor. It's going back. The lot of it.'

'You really are in love with her, aren't you?'

'Yeah. And I'm sick of the bullion. It's destroyed too many people's lives. So you can be there, Tony. When they take Starks. You can have your story after all.'

8
the night shoot

I fell in love with Eddie though I hadn't really meant to. It took me by surprise, which is what it should do, I suppose. All my life had seemed foretold up until this point, determined by a fixed narrative. But love is a random event. At first he was just part of the plan, just another person I was using, another player in the drama. Then it happened. I found out that I really did like being in his company, I could relax with him. I think Eddie was the first person in my life I could truly be myself with. There had been so much deception in the past, I'd always had to put on such a front to the outside world. But when we were together, just me and Eddie, it was like we were hiding from them, not from each other. I felt safe with him. Safe enough to be me.

We tried to tell each other everything, and we both had a lot to let go of. All those years in prison had taken their toll on Eddie. But it was like we had both been released. So many things that I'd never said to anyone. So many issues I could talk through, just as I was supposed to have done in those counselling sessions. But this wasn't therapy. This was love.

And I really didn't want to think about me and him in these modern analytical terms. I knew how some professional might see it, you know, that my affection for Eddie was the need for a sort of father substitute or something. But it wasn't that. Besides, Eddie was nothing like Dad. There was something familial between us, we were connected to each other's pasts in a way. And I mean, Ruby had been like an aunt to me. But I saw nothing incestuous in how I felt about Eddie. My Electra complex was classical, not Freudian. I simply wanted revenge for my father. I wasn't looking for any other kind of motivation, but it bothered me, I'd made no allowances for something like this happening. And when I found myself wanting him I was scared. Scared of some twisted psychology inside of me maybe, but mostly scared of weakness. I didn't want to let go of my anger. I needed it. And I didn't want to feel that I was somehow making up for the absence of Dad. There was only one thing that could do that.

But I gave in to Eddie. He loved me with such a passion. It was overwhelming at first, then I felt it fire something inside of me. Something real. I'd never felt like this before. Love had been about superficial attraction, determined desire for what I felt I should feel. It had made sense. I had wanted Jez because he was the sort of boy I had wanted to want. I didn't want to want Eddie. It didn't make sense. It just happened.

And it wasn't only emotional love. I found I desired Eddie physically as well. Jez had a commodity of good looks but there was something bland and milk-fed about him. A gym-toned body, the inevitable musculature of repetitive exercise. His physical hardness meant nothing, a duplication of images from *GQ* or *Men's Health* magazines. Even his scar had healed into a perfect ellipse, like a design feature. Eddie really was hard but his body was soft and lithe. He was peppered with marks, scribbled with lines, pushing sixty but still in good shape. Prison had kept him thin, there was a sprightliness about him, an agility retained from his cat-burglaring days. A sad smile in his gauntly handsome face that could break my heart. And he had style, not flashness, not this new-lad affectation, but a sombre elegance, an *éminence grise*.

But with me he was self-conscious about his body, about his age. He recoiled from my touch sometimes, drew in to himself. But I wanted to see him. To know him.

One night after we had made love I put on the light and drew back the sheets.

'What are you doing?' he asked.

'Let me look at you.'

'Julie . . .'

I traced my fingers along his weathered skin. Marbled with broken veins and liver spots.

'For Christ sakes, girl, I'm an old man.'

I brushed my lips along the contours of his ribcage.

'You're my old man,' I said.

'I'm your lucky old man.'

'Tell me a story,' I urged him.

'I'm tired, babe.'

'Go on.'

'I don't know. I've told you all my best ones.'

'Then make something up.'

'Well . . .' He sighed.

'What?'

'Put the light out, darling. It's hurting my eyes.'

I found the switch. The room went back to near-darkness. Just a milky wash from the street lights outside.

'I was thinking about something,' Eddie went on.

'What?'

'A story. I only remember the beginning bit.'

'Tell me.'

'It's in *The Thousand and One Nights*. I only know the start of it. This fisherman finds a bottle, right? He opens it up and whoosh! This bloody great genie comes out of it. And this genie says: "Right, you're done for, little man," and the fisherman goes: "Please don't kill me! How come you want to kill me when I've just released you from this bottle?" And the genie explains that he's been trapped in the bottle for three hundred years. And he says that in the first hundred years he vowed that whoever set him free he would give eternal riches to. A hundred years passed and no one came. In the second hundred years of his imprisonment the genie promised that he would open up all the buried treasures of the earth to the person who would free him. Still no one came. Then after three hundred years this genie had had enough. He was full of rage and anger. He said: "Fuck this! I'm going to kill the first fucker who sets me free." So . . .'

Eddie paused. A siren wailed in the distance.

'Yeah?' I whispered.

'Well, that's it.'

'What happened to the fisherman?'

'I don't remember. I was just thinking about the first bit of the story. About what happens to the genie when he's trapped in that bottle all those years. It just reminds me of being inside. At first you can kid yourself it's OK. I can do the time, you think. I can do five, no problem. Then you get a parole knock-back. Then another. All your optimism about life gets burned out of you. By the time you get out you're just full of bitterness and hatred about everybody. It's like it's too late, you know, your release date never really comes. All your feelings are still banged up. The time to feel good about things has gone.'

'And is that how you feel?'

'It's how I used to feel, Julie. I scarcely even knew how much anger I had inside of me. It was like it had gone solid or something. I never thought that I'd feel properly happy again. Until . . .' There was a catch in his voice. He swallowed. 'Until I met you.'

He reached out to me in the darkness. I touched his face. It was wet with tears.

'You let me out,' he said. 'You set me free proper.'

He kissed me.

'And I want to give you all the buried treasures of the earth for that.'

'You don't want to kill me, then?' I asked.

Eddie laughed.

'No, I don't,' he said. Then his voice went flat and cold all of a sudden. 'I want to kill someone else.'

'Shh,' I said, holding him close to me.

There was something that I wasn't telling him. I didn't tell him that I meant to kill Harry Starks. I really didn't want to keep anything from Eddie but I knew that I couldn't tell him that. He would try to stop me. Or worse. He would try to do it himself. Another spell in prison would kill him. What would I get? Life with a recommendation to serve fifteen, at the worst. Life, that's what I'd be getting. My own life back. It didn't matter if I had to spend some of it in Holloway.

But I knew this would upset Eddie. He might not go along with the plan at all if he knew how it would all end. And I needed to get to Starks. So we agreed that the plan was to hand over Starks once we had lured him back into the country. And it was all nearly set up now. We had found the place, the warehouse where the gold was hidden. Eddie had done a deal with the retired policeman who was working for the insurers. All we had to do was convince Jez to use it as a location.

My relationship with Jez held together all through this time. I had to make it work, somehow. I couldn't afford to let it fall apart, not now. Everything had to run smoothly. So I had to be very secretive and arrange things carefully. Piers was suspicious, which didn't help at all, but Jez was busy covering up his own infidelity and struggling to keep up the façade. He was never as good at lying as I was.

We still had sex. And it was good in an efficient, workout sort of way. I detected something competitive about it now. Maybe it had always been there and I'd just not noticed it before. I still ended up on top, though. Jez would put up a fight but I knew that was what he liked. I suspected that frail little Georgina didn't quite indulge him like this.

Eddie didn't like the fact that I was still sleeping with Jez. I tried to talk about it with him but it didn't help things. I couldn't explain to Eddie that what we had was deeper and more real than what passed between me and Jez. It was about understanding, but I couldn't put it into words. Then it came to me: the way that in the Bible 'to know' is used to describe sex. That was how I felt with Eddie. It was pure knowledge. It was something that he and nobody else could give to me. I'd been knowing all my life, I'd had to be. But now I was known. It was wonderful to be known.

And I wanted to talk to Jez, he had a right to know about me too. I resolved that as soon as I could I would tell him. It wouldn't be long now. In the meantime we carried on with the happy deceptions of many a young couple. I still found affection for him and he still needed me, for support more than anything else. Not just all the practical stuff but emotional support as well. He had all sorts of anxieties and doubts about the film and we were coming up to the time when it would be up to him to come up with the goods. I got the impression that this girl of his was a little too demanding of him. You know, I actually worried that she wasn't right for him.

Finally I had got to understand Jez properly. I suppose I felt detached and less annoyed with him than I had in the past. When I'd gone through the script again, as Piers had suggested, it struck me how often the insults in it had to do with sexuality. It was full of men calling each other 'faggots' or 'poofs'; at one point a character talked of ''aving me pants pulled down'. At first I simply thought, well, public school homophobia, what a dead give-away. But then I realised it made sense in relation to this 'crisis of masculinity' and the 'feminisation of culture' some of the broadsheet pundits had been going on about. It was something Piers could vaguely articulate, though he much preferred to pretend to enjoy talking about football or the semiotics of action movies. I had thought that this crisis in masculinity was all a bit of a joke. I thought of Dad's generation, his world – they could have done with some of that. It would have seemed a luxury.

But Jez didn't intellectualise, he was an instinctive embodiment of these contemporary ideas. Maybe that was where the heart of his talent really lay. I got to know that he acted hard because of a crushing sensitivity that he had to hide from the world. In the time leading up to shooting he opened up to me about his schooldays. He'd been a nervous, pretty little teenager. Because of his dyslexia he'd had to attend special classes. Other boys called him 'spaz' or 'Special Needs Scott'. Even the teachers had made jokes at his expense. All the arrogance of the working class over-achiever that I was had meant that I had failed to see that he'd had a hard time too. And *Scrapyard Bulldog* was to be his revenge as well as mine. Revenge against all of the people who had taunted him and put him down. Revenge of the middle-class thick kid.

We went to see the warehouse. Me, Jez, Piers and Eddie. I was really nervous that Jez wouldn't like it. He didn't say anything for a long time. He walked about the place, looking at it from different angles. He stared up at the light that streamed in from the broken skylights, diffusing through the motes of dust that hung in the air. He stood in the middle of it and looked around once more. He nodded slowly.

'It's great,' he declared.

'Isn't it just?' muttered Eddie wryly.

'We can do at least three of the main interior set-ups in here,' Jez was telling Piers.

I caught Eddie's eye. He saw the look of relief on my face and gave me a wink.

'So, what's the deal on this place?' Jez asked.

'Well . . .' Eddie shrugged. 'We've approached the agents managing it. Cutthroat Productions could get it for a very reasonable rent.'

'Yeah?'

'Yeah. So what do you think?'

Eddie looked across at me nervously.

'I think we use it,' said Jez.

I winked at Eddie. Jez was still in his own world, walking around, lining up shots.

'It's fantastic,' he said, his blue eyes twitching with ideas.

We were nearly ready to shoot and he had come alive after months of brooding. I was happy for him.

Scrapyard Bulldog started filming on 2 September 1996. The first action to be shot was a poker game scene. This was Ruby Ryder's cameo as the card dealer Ladyfingers. The set was in the warehouse and it was not much more than a huge green baize table with lampshades suspended above it.

There was a real buzz on-set when Ruby arrived. She'd never been a big star but she had this very British sort of fame. She was an icon of sorts, and I knew that I had been right in suggesting her for the part. She could bring just the right sort of charisma to the film. Some of the cast and crew came up to her during lunch asking for autographs. She joked about it.

'I'm a cult,' she announced loudly in that camp way of hers. 'I'm a complete cult.'

A handsome but nervous young man was escorting her when she arrived. His name was Greg. She got me to look after him.

'Met him doing panto,' she explained to me.

'He seems nice.'

She sighed.

'Oh, he is, darling. Too nice. He's a sweet, sensitive boy. It was lovely when we first started seeing each other but it's hard for him. He has to deal with this larger-than-life persona of mine. He hasn't been getting the work lately and you know what that can do to your confidence at the best of times. I'm worried that I'm cutting his balls off. It doesn't help Eddie being here either.'

'You knew he was a consultant on the film.'

'Yeah, but I didn't know he was going to be on the set, did I?'

Ruby and Eddie cautiously approached each other. Little signals, polite nods and tentative greetings. Then Eddie broke into a huge grin, threw his arms open wide and with a hug kissed her on both cheeks.

'You look fantastic, Ruby,' he said.

Ruby tensed a little in his embrace then smiled and let her shoulders drop.

'Yeah, yeah,' she said. 'Mind the make-up.'

I must confess I felt a tiny twinge of jealousy seeing them both laughing together. I'd seen photographs of them as a couple back in the sixties. They had both looked so glamorous back then.

The set was lit and a smoke machine started up.

'Oh, this is atmospheric,' enthused Ruby, then hissed out of the side of her mouth at me: 'Ain't exactly big-budget, is it?'

But she never complained out loud. She was a professional of the old school. Always smiling, never being difficult or superior.

A real card sharp was used to do the close-ups of the fanning and shuffling of the cards in the scene. This dealer was a man but his hands had been made up and dagger-sharp bright pink false nails applied to the ends of his fingers. Ruby came off the set and we chatted together.

'Well, Eddie looks happy,' she said.

'Yes, I suppose so.'

'No, I mean really. I've never seen him so happy. Not since . . .'

She looked me in the eye.

'What's going on?' she asked.

'What do you mean?'

'I mean, I saw the way he looked at you earlier. And it reminded me of something. I remember he once looked at me like that.'

Just at that moment Piers came over.

'We've got a problem with the dealer,' he told me.

'What?'

'We need to shave his forearms.'

'What?'

'They're too hairy.'

Ruby giggled.

'Well, get them shaved, then,' I said.

'Yeah, but . . .'

'What?'

'Well, I haven't asked him yet. I wonder if you could.'

'Oh, for Christ's sake.'

'I just thought it would be be better coming from you.'

I sighed.

'OK,' I agreed. 'I'll be over in a minute.'

'And try and make sure he doesn't ask for extra for it,' Piers called out as he walked away.

'Ruby,' I muttered.

'Look, I should mind my own business. But something's going on, isn't it?'

I shrugged, nodded.

'Well, he's still a charmer.'

Yes, I thought. *But it was me that charmed him.*

'He's trouble, you know,' she said.

No he's not. I'm trouble.

We wrapped around eight that evening. It had been a good day's work and a good start to the film. Ruby's presence had really lifted everyone's spirits. There was a sense of occasion about the shoot. A strange feeling that we could actually be on to something.

Jez congratulated Ruby as she was leaving the set. He looked awe-struck.

'Thank you so much, Ruby,' he said. 'You were fantastic.'

His voice was all polite and posh for once; he really looked quite sweet.

I walked her and Greg out to their car.

'Look, dear,' she said to me as Greg walked on ahead. 'I didn't mean to pry.'

'It's all right.'

'I mean, I'm one to talk with my toyboy here.' She nodded at Greg, who was out of earshot. 'He's thirty-two, you know. Looks younger, doesn't he?'

'Ruby . . .'

'Yes, dear.'

'Don't tell Mum. Not yet.'

'I wouldn't dream of it, darling. Just you be careful with that one, that's all.'

'Of course I will,' I lied.

Scrapyard Bulldog was shot on a tight schedule. Everyone involved on it was working hard for little money and few creature comforts. Early mornings and occasional night shoots at the warehouse. Jez was using all sorts of special effects and state-of-the-art camera tricks he'd learned from doing adverts and pop promos, over-cranked and under-cranked steadicam shots. Most of the action seemed either to be speeded up or in slow motion, gaudy colours awash with a dirty brown filter. Characters were established by freeze-frame and voice-over. The dialogue pattered in staccato cross-over, like music-hall routine. Piers had been right, it was shaping up as a knockabout comedy with glossy slapstick ultra-violence. But it moved along with a twitchy, juvenile exuberance that made up for what it lacked in substance with pure flash.

The acting, such as there was any, was of variable quality. Joe Patterson's performance had a gravitas that was unfortunately entirely out of place with everything around him. There was far too much naturalism in what he was doing, it looked like a real character had found himself in the middle of a cartoon. I suspected that his heart wasn't really in it. I watched him struggle with the script, vainly trying to find something that he could believe in. Most of the rest of the cast looked like male models on a particularly frenetic fashion shoot with guns as designer accessories. Resplendent in Crombies, suits and Gabicci polo shirts that never seemed to get messed up despite all the mayhem around them. Again Piers was right – this look was tailor made for the new-lad audience the film would be courting. A paean to power dressing and male grooming, they would see more glamorous versions of themselves on-screen, it would be sexy for them, a swaggering advertisement for their deep dreams of sartorial brutality.

But the real surprise of the film was Gaz Kelly, who played the heavy. When we looked at the rushes something astonishing came across in his portrayal of Big Lenny. There was a luminosity in his presence, as if he was lit from within. A real coruscating rage that leapt out of the celluloid at you. It was a stylised performance but instinctive too. A heightened super-realism, an exaggerated choreography of menace that was somehow persuasive and convincing, like Cagney or something. He wasn't great at delivering lines but his physicality drew your attention like a magnet.

There had been some worries about casting Kelly. He had a real criminal past and had only just been released from prison after being acquitted on a murder charge. But Piers was sure that this could only be good publicity for the film. 'Authenticity,' he insisted, for the millionth time.

Eddie was less convinced by Gaz's villainous credentials.

'He ain't really one of the chaps,' he commented. 'Talks himself up. More of a wannabe, if you ask me.'

'Maybe that's it,' I said, suddenly knowing why Gaz worked so well on screen. 'He's been playing at it all his life. That's why he comes across so well.'

Eddie and I didn't have much time to be together during the filming at the warehouse. And we had to concentrate on the plan. He had found where he thought the gold was buried. There was a mismatched patch of cement on part of the floor that he had gone over with a metal detector one night when the warehouse was deserted. Once the shooting was finished we'd meet with Starks there and dig it up.

We were rapidly approaching what Jez would call the denouement.

Jez was absorbed in his work, walking around in almost a trance state. I found myself being close to him throughout. We had become used to each other and could work side by side with a quiet unspoken understanding. But I wanted to settle my account with him somehow, I owed him that much.

After the final day's filming at the warehouse I went back with him. We were burned out and over-tired but ended up having energetic sex until the small hours. There was a sense of release, a feeling of abandonment, of letting go.

'I need to tell you something,' I said afterwards.

'I'm really tired, babe,' he groaned.

'This is important,' I insisted. 'I'll get you a drink. You're going to need it.'

I got a bottle of wine from the fridge and poured us both a glass. I sat on the edge of the bed.

'You know my real name's McCluskey,' I began.

'Yeah.'

'You ever wonder who my father was?'

'You never really talk about him, just the car accident.' He sat up in the bed. 'What's all this about, Julie?'

'My dad was from Glasgow.'

I sighed. I didn't know how to tell this story. I didn't really want to, to be honest, I just wanted Jez to know. So I picked up the true crime book *London Underworld* from the side of his bed, found the reference to Dad and handed it to him.

'That's my dad,' I told him, pointing at the relevant passage.

Jez read slowly, tracing each word with a finger, frowning at the text.

'It's all there,' I said. "Big Jock" McCluskey. Like one of your bloody characters. No mention of me or Mum, of course. But no one's very much interested in that, are they?'

Jez looked up from the book, his face agape with wonder and curiosity.

'You?'

'Yeah, me.'

'Why didn't you tell me before?'

'I might have done if things had been different. I've been trying to get away from this darkness all my life. Then I find that my nice middle-class boyfriend is obsessed with it. It's hardly reassuring for a girl, you know.'

'But you said you liked the film. You got involved in it, for Christ's sake.'

'*Scrapyard Bulldog* doesn't exactly bear much relation to reality, Jez.'

'You don't think it's any good?'

I laughed. It was so typical of him to be thinking about his stupid movie even at this moment.

'It's not the real thing,' I told him. 'But who on earth would be interested in the real thing? I wanted you to succeed, Jez, that's why I helped out. And I think you will. They'll all fall for it just like you have.'

I started to get dressed.

'There's something I need to do now. I'm going to go.'

Jez sat up in bed.

'I worried about you, you know,' he said.

'I know you did.'

'I knew something was up. But you never talked to me. I wish you'd talked to me.'

'I'm sorry.'

He pouted sulkily.

'It's not nice to be lied to.'

'Well, we haven't exactly been telling the truth to each other for a while, have we? I know about Georgina.'

'What?'

'Oh yeah.'

'I can explain about that.'

'Please, Jez. It doesn't matter. I don't blame you. Though I don't think she's right for you, somehow. A nice posh bird like I used to want to be. But a bit drippy. You need a strong woman in your life. Someone older maybe.'

As I got ready to leave Jez followed me about the flat in a bewildered state.

'So,' he said. 'So, what happens now?'

'I told you. I'm leaving. This is goodbye, Jez. Good luck with it all.'

I got to the door and turned to look at him one last time. Blue eyes staring helplessly. Little boy lost.

'You'll be all right, Jez,' I said, and kissed him on the cheek.

On the way over to Eddie's I thought: that's it, I'm saying goodbye to people. I thought about Mum, about explaining things to her. But she would understand, I reasoned. I was doing this partly for her, after all, but then my stomach sank suddenly and I realised I was scared. But this was a useful fear, like stage fright. It would keep me focused.

```
INT. A WAREHOUSE. NIGHT.
P.O.V. from above. EDDIE is standing in a pool of
light. Sound of warehouse door opening, footsteps.
We see a shadow of a man at first, then HARRY STARKS
enters, stepping into the light.
                    HARRY
        Well, this is atmospheric, isn't it?
```

I can't help seeing it like this. I accused Jez of a lack of realism and here I am losing it myself. I've got to concentrate. I'm hidden in the darkness, up above on a gantry by a loading bay. The set hasn't been completely dismantled yet and we've used one of the film lights to illuminate the building. So the place does look theatrical, cinematic. I'm waiting in the wings. Waiting for my cue. I feel I should be meditating clearly on the matter at hand, not lost in the illusion of it. Maybe

*it's all this time I've been spending on this bloody film.
It's got to me. But maybe that's how I'm going to cope
with this. A sense of detachment so that I can go through
with it . . .*

'Yeah,' Eddie replied. 'We've been using this place for
a film.'

'Was that the cover, then?'

'Something like that.'

'I've parked the van outside. Is it here, then?'

'Well, we'll soon find out, won't we?'

Eddie had marked out a rectangle on the mismatched patch
of cement where the metal detector indicated the gold might
be. He lifted a pickaxe.

'We're going to have to do it by hand, I'm afraid,' he said.
'You want to start?'

Starks shrugged. Eddie handed him the pickaxe.

'About time you got your hands dirty,' he said.

They set to work, digging. Taking it in turns to break up
the cement with the pickaxe. Pulling out chunks of it by hand.
When the hole was big enough they went at it with a spade as
well. I don't know how much time passed but finally Eddie
stopped and called out.

'Hold up!'

He lay on the ground and reached into the hole. He pulled
at something. It wouldn't budge. He got up again and pointed
at a certain part of the excavations.

'Give that bit another whack,' he said.

And Starks swung the pickaxe down. This time Eddie
reached down and pulled what looked like a brick at first.

'Shit,' he groaned. 'I'd forgotten how much these things
weighed.'

He brushed the dust off it and it gleamed as it caught
the light.

'Fuck me,' Starks gasped.

They set to work pulling out the rest of it.

'Nobody else knows about this, do they?' Starks asked.

Eddie shook his head.

'They're all dead, Harry.'

'Is that the lot?'

'Looks like it.'

'Right. Well, let's get it loaded up in the van.'

When they had finished Starks brought a hold-all into the warehouse and dropped it on the floor.

'You want to count it?' he asked Eddie.

'I'll have a look,' he replied.

He crouched down, unzipped the bag and had a rummage inside.

'Looks about right,' he said.

Starks grinned.

'All in a day's work. Well, Eddie, that's about it, then.'

He moved towards Eddie with his hand out. Eddie pulled out his gun and pointed it at him.

'Not quite, Harry.'

'What the fuck?'

His hands instinctively went up in front of him.

'Keep those hands up.'

'Stop fucking around.'

'I'm quite serious, Harry.'

Starks sighed and shook his head.

'Oh, Eddie. We're both too old for this carry-on.'

Eddie reached into the front of Starks' jacket. He pulled out a pistol.

'Well, we both came prepared, didn't we, Harry?' he said, backing slowly away from him.

'Look, let's talk this through.'

'Now the keys, Harry.'

'You what?'

'The van keys. Throw them over here.'

Starks tossed them over and they chimed on the concrete floor.

'You're making a big mistake, Eddie. You won't get away with this.'

'I don't plan to.'

'What?'

'You'll find out. There's someone here who wants a word.'

That was my cue. I came down the stairs and walked towards the light. I got my first good look at Starks. From above, with thick shadow framing him, he had seemed impressive. Close up under the light's glare he looked worn out. He hadn't aged as well as Eddie. His face had sagged and gone puffy around the eyes. There was a haunted look about him. I'd been ready to meet a monster but here I was face to face with just a sad old man.

'This is Julie,' Eddie announced. 'Julie McCluskey.'

'Oh yeah?'

I had to clear my mind of any feelings of sympathy or empathy. I had to concentrate on how ruthless he had been.

'You don't even know who I am, do you?' I demanded. 'I don't suppose you remember.'

'Sorry, love, I haven't had the pleasure. Look, Eddie, can you tell me what the fuck is going on?'

Eddie handed me Starks' gun and fished in his pocket for his mobile phone. He started to call up the ex-cop Taylor and this journalist Tony I'd met at the offices that time to tell them we were ready. I pointed the pistol at Starks. It would be good to kill him with his own gun, I thought.

'Look, darling, do you mind not pointing that thing at me?'

'Shut up,' I said, feeling the weight of it, steadying it with both hands. 'I want you to think very carefully. I want you to remember what you did.'

'I don't know what you're talking about, darling,' he said.

'Well, just have a think, eh?'

He frowned at me. Eddie had finished talking into the phone. He switched it off and put it back in his pocket.

'They're on their way,' he said.

'Who are? Some team you've got waiting to have me over? I didn't think that was your style, Ed.'

'This is even less like my style. You see, I'm handing the gold back.'

'Back? What do you mean back?'

'To who it belongs to.'

'You silly cunt. What do you want to go and do that for?'

'Just doing the right thing for once.'

Starks started laughing.

'Oh, fuck me, Eddie, now you really are having a laugh.'

'Yeah. And here's something even funnier. We're going to hand you up and all.'

'Now wait a minute . . .'

'You see, this is Julie McCluskey. You know, Jock's daughter?'

Starks went wide eyed and open mouthed for a second. He stared at me.

'Fuck,' he rasped under his breath.

'Yeah,' I said. 'Just another of your victims. I've had to live all my life under the shadow of what you did to my father. I want you to think about that.'

'And you're going to hand me up for that? Well, listen . . .'

'No,' I said. 'You listen. We're not going to hand you up.' I steadied the gun again, pointing it at his incredulous face. 'I'm going to kill you.'

'Julie!' Eddie exclaimed.

'Just like you did Dad.'

'Julie,' said Eddie. 'Wait a second.'

I knew that with every moment of delay it would become harder to pull the trigger. But I wanted him to know what he had done before I killed him.

'I want you to think about it. You ruined my life, Harry Starks.'

'Put the gun down, Julie,' Eddie was saying.

'No. This is how it's done, isn't it? No going to the police or worrying about the implications of killing another human being. This was the way it was done, wasn't it?'

'Julie, they're going to be here any minute,' Eddie went on. 'Put the gun down, for Christ's sake.'

'Oh, I don't worry about being caught. I don't mind going to prison for this. I just want him to know what he did and why he's going to die for it.'

At that moment Starks lunged forward. Eddie turned and kicked his legs from under him. Starks tumbled to the floor on all fours.

'Sorry about that, Harry,' said Eddie. 'Julie, please, don't do this.'

'Shut up, Eddie. I want my fucking own back.' I pointed the gun at the crawling figure on the ground. 'You stay down there,' I told him.

'Jesus fucking Christ!' Starks spat out, looking up at me. 'Look, girl, I didn't fucking do it!'

I needed him to admit what he had done. I needed to hear it from his own lips.

'Liar!' I shouted. 'You took my life away from me. Now you're going to pay for it.'

Starks rocked back on to his knees and rubbed his hands. He shook his head.

'Well, go on, then, girl. Shoot me,' he said with a shrug.

'Julie, please,' Eddie implored.

I aimed the pistol at his head. *Shoot him*, I thought. But I wanted him to break down and confess and he wasn't doing that.

'But I'm not the one that killed your dad,' Starks went on.

'I don't believe you.'

'Then shoot me. Get it over with. I'm a dead man anyway.'

I started to imagine what it would be like to shoot somebody. Would it be like a Tarantino film or those weird violent Japanese gangster movies Jez was so keen on? It would be easier imagining it like that than facing the real horror of it. But then I'd be doing just what I had criticised Jez for, glorifying violence. Was that what I was doing? No, no, I thought, I musn't start to feel doubt now. Just do it, not think about it, just get it over with. Just then Taylor and Tony came into the warehouse.

'What the fuck's going on here?' the ex-cop demanded with a shocked look on his face.

The journalist stood by with a bemused smile.

'She wants to kill me,' Starks announced.

'Things have got a bit out of hand,' Eddie explained.

'I just want you to admit it,' I said to Starks.

'But I wouldn't be telling the truth, darling.'

Taylor edged his way towards me.

'Now steady on, girl,' he said. 'Admit what, exactly?'

'That he killed my father.'

'Who?'

'Jock McCluskey.'

'I didn't do it,' Starks insisted.

'Big Jock?' the ex-cop demanded. 'You're Big Jock's daughter?'

'Yeah,' I said. 'Have a big gawp, the lot of you. I'm Little Julie. I'm the one that was robbed of a dad and paid off with stage school fees. What was that about?'

'It was what your mother wanted.'

'What was it? Guilt? Compensation for what you did?'

'Wait a minute,' Taylor said.

'It was nothing like that. Jock was on the firm. It was like a responsibility.'

'Responsibility? You don't know the meaning of the word.'

'Hold on,' Taylor went on.

'I want you to understand what responsibility is. Admit it.'

'He didn't kill your dad,' said Taylor.

'What?' I demanded.

'Just calm down a second and let me explain.'

'Who the fuck are you anyway?' Starks asked.

'Frank Taylor. I used to be in the Job. Remember? We met a couple of times.'

Starks squinted at him.

'You worked for Vic Sayles?'

'Yeah. And I was part of the team that put you away in '69.'

'Thanks a lot.'

'My pleasure. Got a commendation for that.'

'Sorry to interrupt the reunion, gentlemen,' I said. 'But you say he didn't kill my father. How do you know?'

'Well, I worked with George Mooney, too. He was the retired detective that got killed about the same time as your father.'

'Yeah, I know about him. Go on.'

'I worked with him on an internal investigation into corruption amongst officers in South London. The Operation Skeleton inquiry. It was a cover-up, we wanted to avoid more widespread hookiness being brought out into the open, you know, this "firm within a firm" thing, and we managed to restrict the inquiry to three detectives low down the scale who were going to take the fall for it. Thing is, there was this one guy, a detective sergeant called O'Neill. He didn't want to duck his nut and threatened to start coughing up all sorts of nasty stories. So Mooney organised him being paid off to skip the country. Ended up in Morocco for a while then the Costa del Sol when the extradition was dropped. Did a bit of business with Mooney when he went out there on retirement. Anyway, O'Neill comes back in the eighties and gives himself up. Did a bit of bird. He had all sorts of stories. And one of them was that it was Mooney that had Jock McCluskey killed and pinned it on Harry here.'

'How do you know he was telling the truth?'

Taylor shrugged.

'Well, he did have a grudge against the Met, that was for

sure, but certain details he gave us, that no one else could have known about, tallied with the investigation done by the Spanish police. But no one wanted to dig it all up again, it wouldn't have looked good. So we stuck to the official line, that Starks had done it.'

'Thanks a lot,' muttered Starks.

'Well, you did kill Mooney, after all,' said Taylor.

'I didn't even do that, mate.'

'Really? Then who . . . ?'

'You would never believe me if I told you.'

'That's enough!' I shouted. 'I don't believe this. I won't believe it.'

I lined up the gun again. My hands were trembling. Starks held his hands up in supplication. He looked like a demented holy martyr kneeling on the floor.

'Then shoot me,' he said. 'You might be doing me a favour.'

They were trying to take this away from me. I had to do it now. My finger quivered against the trigger.

'I'm a dead man anyway.'

'You said that before. What do you mean?'

'I got cancer. Inoperable. I got a year. Two maybe. It ain't going to be a pretty end. Might as well get it over with.' He sighed. 'To tell you the truth I'm sick of running. Always fancied dying on my native soil. I was born just up the road from here, you know.'

I started to shake.

'Julie,' Eddie said softly.

I let my arms drop. It wasn't fair. There would be no revenge now. No restitution. No meaning to it all. Just another unsolved crime. Another unsolved life.

'Why?' I started to sob. 'Why can't you be the man I want to kill?'

Tears came. Eddie walked over and put an arm around me.

'Shh,' he whispered. 'It's all right now.'

'No it's not!' I wailed. 'I can't be. It'll never be all right now.'

Harry Starks got up off the floor and brushed himself down. Eddie turned and pointed his gun at him.

'So what happens now? You want to take me in?' asked Starks.

'Julie?' Eddie asked.

'I just want you to go away,' I said to Starks.

'Frank?'

'I'm retired, Eddie. I don't need another commendation. I do want the gold, though.'

Eddie crouched down and picked up the van keys. He handed them to Taylor.

'Move the van somewhere else, could you? You know, so it can be officially recovered somewhere away from here. Don't want anyone implicated.'

'Right,' he said. 'Thanks, Eddie. See you, Harry.'

And he walked out.

'Well,' said Starks, making for the bag. 'I'll just get my things and be off.'

'Uh-uh.' Eddie held the gun up. 'I think that's mine.'

'Oh, be reasonable, Eddie.'

'I think I deserve it after all I've been through.'

Starks stood there, thinking for a minute. He shrugged.

'Well, let me have a little back. I'm a bit short, to tell you the truth.'

Eddie motioned with the pistol.

'Go on, then. Help yourself.'

Starks grabbed a couple of bundles of cash and stuffed them in his pockets.

'I had a set-up with the gold that could have tied me over until the end,' he said. 'Now all my Caribbean contacts are burned. I'm diving for scraps, if you want to know.'

'Where are you going to go now?' Eddie asked.

'Northern Cyprus, I guess. No extradition there. Look,

Julie,' he said to me. 'I'm . . . I'm really sorry about your dad but . . .'

'It was all a long time ago.'

'What?'

'That was what you were going to say, wasn't it? That's what everyone says, don't they? It was all a long time ago. A lifetime. My lifetime.'

I looked at him. He had the weary look of a hunted man. But there was something about the eyes. They still burned with some kind of energy, the charm everybody had spoken of. But no, I wasn't going to fall for this. He might not have killed Dad but he'd certainly killed other people's fathers.

'Look, what I mean is . . .' he began.

'Please,' I cut in. 'Just go.'

'Right, then,' he said.

'Wait a minute,' Tony suddenly announced. 'You're not going to let him get away, are you?'

'Who's this fucker?' Starks demanded.

'What about my story?'

'He's a writer,' said Eddie.

Starks burst out laughing.

'A writer? That's a good one. Well, you've had a good story here tonight. Shame no one's going to believe you.'

He started to walk out. The clatter of the van starting up could be heard in the distance.

'Wait,' said Tony.

'Be lucky!' Starks called out as he left.

'Eddie?' Tony demanded.

'What are you going to do? Go after him?'

'But . . .'

'Leave it, Tony. It's over.'

Eddie took Starks' gun from me and put it in the bag. He zipped it up.

'Come on, sweetheart,' he said.

I wiped my face.

'What?'

'Let's go.'

'Go? Where am I going to go now?'

'Give me your gun, Eddie,' Tony was saying.

'What?'

'Give me the gun now and I'll be able to catch him. There's still time.'

'Don't be so ridiculous.'

I heard them argue behind me as I walked out of the warehouse. Nothing made sense any more. Where would I go now? I didn't know. I just started to walk. A purple dawn streaked the sky above the back streets of the East End. The morning star burned bright and low over the city.

'Julie!' Eddie called out after me.

But I just kept walking. I felt like a ghost, empty, lost in the yawning emptiness of the morning. What I'd imagined as tragedy had turned out as farce. A bad joke that echoed hollow with the pitiless laughter of comedy. I'd been so stupid. There was no ending, no resolution, no denouement. I thought that I was being so bloody clever but I'd ended up acting out what I thought I'd despised. I'd deluded myself that my life was some great classical drama and it had merely become like a scene in a cheap gangster movie.

I'd thought I'd had some answer, that I'd found a name for my pain. And now that had been taken away and only the pain remained. A rage had burned away inside me and it hadn't left much behind. What the hell was I supposed to do now?

I'd got to Victoria Park by the time Eddie caught up with me, carrying the bag. The sun was coming up behind the tower blocks of Hackney.

'Julie,' he panted, out of breath. 'Wait a minute.'

For a while we just walked together in silence.

'Hang on,' he said, after a while. 'Just got to do something.'

He went over to the canal and dumped the guns in the muddy water.

'Look,' he said when he came back. 'I don't expect you to feel . . .'

'Please, Eddie, not now.'

'I just want you to know that I love you.'

I didn't know what to say. I didn't know what I could feel about another person any more. And what could my feelings towards Eddie mean now? Maybe that was part of the problem, too, maybe it was just me clinging to the past I thought I wanted to escape from, maybe that was why I, too, had wanted some of this stupid 'authenticity'.

'There's a fair bit of cash here, babe. We could maybe, you know, make a new start somewhere.'

'A start?'

'Yeah, you know.'

'I can't make any plans, Eddie. My life isn't just going to start somewhere. I don't know who I am any more or what I'm going to do, for God's sake.'

'I'm sorry. You want me to go?'

'I don't even know that, Eddie.'

'Right,' he said, and we fell into silence once more.

London was waking up. Joggers and dog walkers were making their way around the park. It was just another day and all over the city people were getting ready for it. People with their own private grief and damaged childhoods, with their own lonely little feelings of despair.

'There is something we can do, you know,' Eddie said.

'Please . . .'

'No, nothing heavy, darling, honest. I was just thinking.'

'What?'

'We could go and get breakfast somewhere,' he said with a sad smile. 'I don't know about you but I'm starving.'

9
the voice of society

I hadn't planned to say what I did to the press after my trial, it just sort of happened. I was relieved to be getting off, that was for sure, but I still felt angry about it all. And there was this huddle of press outside. All these microphones and cameras being shoved in my face. Not that I minded all that attention but I thought: *It's my turn now, you fuckers.* I'd been fucked around so much in the last few months. It was my turn to do the fucking around. So when some cunt asked me what I thought of the judgement I just said:

'It's fine by me because I done it.'

And there was a bit of an uproar at this.

'You mean to say you admit to the murder of Simon Beardsley?' someone else asked.

Well, I know you can't be tried twice for something you've been acquitted for. That's the double jeopardy rule. And I thought: *Yeah, this will give them something to chew on.*

'Yeah,' I said. 'I done it.'

The press had a field day over that. I was all over the papers. There was even a question asked in the House, apparently. The *Sunday Illustrated* ran a big two-page exclusive interview. It was with this guy Keith who I'd fed that story to back in Essex. There was a big photo spread, like a hall of infamy. There were pictures of me at that charity thing I'd organised, lined up with a few tasty faces. There was one of me next to Tony Tucker and Pat Tate taken at the Epping Forest Country Club. A blurred photo of me with Reggie Kray that I'd had done surreptitiously when I'd visited him at Maidstone Prison one time. They even dug up an old picture of me as a skinhead back in the Earthquake days. I was presented as a dangerous and well-connected gangster. Of course, they had to condemn me and all that. But that only made it better. I'd become notorious, a celebrity villain.

And all for something I hadn't actually done.

The police requested an informal interview with me. I didn't have anything to lose so I went along. It was weird, all these cozzers with this pained look on their faces. That I'm-not-angry-I'm-disappointed look I used to get in the headmaster's study. Only I wasn't bending over this time.

'We can't see why you did it, Gary,' said one. 'I mean, it makes everyone look bad.'

'No, mate,' I told him. 'I reckon it makes me look fuck-ing great.'

There was a lot of shaking of heads and tut-tutting. A senior officer went on to say, in no uncertain terms, that from now on they would be on my case, checking my every move and so on. My card was marked, right? He fannied on about the 'public interest' and all that. One thing was clear: I'd have to watch myself. I'd thought about getting back at that little toerag Holroyd-Carter but I'd have to go easy on that score. Bide my time, maybe. But when they were finished with me I couldn't resist one last crack at their expense.

'Well,' I said, 'I know I don't have any statement to sign or anything, but do any of you gentlemen want my autograph?'

And David Merriman was well pleased with me. All these offers started to come in. He told me that this poofy writer Oscar Wilde once said that there wasn't any such thing as bad publicity. I got a small part in this BBC drama playing a drug dealer. The Channel 4 sketch show that had used me as this doorman character did this series of scenes with me in this mocked-up prison cell, ranting away. Then a part in a feature film came up.

Merriman wasn't so sure about *Scrapyard Bulldog* at first. It was low-budget and they were only offering what they called deferred payments, which meant that if it went tits up we could end up with fuck-all. In the end he negotiated a tiny percentage of the gross takings, which turned out to be a very clever move on his part.

My role in the film wasn't very big. But it was a good one. I had a couple of key scenes and my character sort of dominated the film. I was playing this big nasty evil bastard called Big Lenny. And everyone on the film seemed well pleased with the way I came across.

It was touch and go during the shooting. Because it was so low-budget it had to be shot from week to week. Sometimes we'd have the weekend off because there wasn't enough money to film on the Saturday. There were times when most people thought it just wasn't going to happen. But the director, this young guy Jez Scott, he just had so much drive. A real sense of self-belief which I respected.

The film had a real struggle to get a distribution deal at first. Then this buzz started going around about it. *Scrapyard Bulldog* was released in the spring of 1997. The premiere was a real event, loads of stars turned up at it. I could hardly believe it. There were these famous actors coming up to me afterwards, congratulating me. The reviews were pretty mixed but a lot of them, even some of the bad ones, said that I was the best thing in it.

Then things really started to kick off. I was everywhere. I already had this little column in *Sorted* magazine, 'A Word from the Geezer'. I didn't actually write it. I just sat down with this journalist every month and talked about the old times, stuff about the naughtiness in my past, stories from the rave scene days, things like that. Then bingo! My column would appear with a fearsome-looking byline photo.

Scrapyard Bulldog became a big hit, it grossed over £12 million at the box office with video sales to come. So I was going to be in pocket what with this percentage point thing. And everyone wanted a piece of me. I did photo shoots for

Esquire magazine and *GQ*. Interviews with *Arena* and *Maxim*. I even got on the telly on *TFI Friday* with Chris Evans. Offers come in all the time for advertisements and promotions.

I got to go over to the States for the American premiere. The film didn't go down as well over there but things look good for the video market. The main thing was that I got to meet some of the influential casting agents from Hollywood. I've had meetings about a part in a new action movie called *Hotwire*. There are no lines as such but it's a featured role and as David Merriman pointed out: 'It's your strength of character they're after.'

Back home I've got a theatre show lined up, a cabaret thing called *An Evening with the Geezer*. And Merriman keeps going on about this new thing called 'reality TV'. I don't know what it is but he reckons I'd be good for it.

So now I'm a celebrity. I'm in the VIP lounge of life. The best thing about success is that all your failures become part of it too. Like they were just part of your struggle to get to the top of your game.

And being pretty well fixed financially means that I've been able to make a proper settlement with Karen. She can't stop me seeing the kids now. And even if I don't see as much of them as I'd like to, they'll grow up knowing who I am because I'm famous now. They've got a dad they can look up to and be proud of. Some of that fame stuff even rubs off on Karen, and though she'd never admit it in a million years I reckon she doesn't mind that one bit.

And I've got to look the part too. I go for style rather than fashion. These days it's Versace suits, silk shirts with the collars worn outside the jacket and lots of personal jewellery. Tasteful, though. It's not showing off how much you got that's important, it's having a sense of refinement. I always say you can't buy class, you can only buy flash.

The thing about being a celebrity is that you get to meet

a lot of other celebrities. And at first it throws you because there you are standing right next to someone famous. Then you get used to it. You realise that you're in the same boat. You're not like some fan gawping at them from a distance. You belong there. You can have a proper conversation with them. They're as surprised to see you as you are them. And you get respect. Just for being famous. It doesn't seem to matter too much these days what you're famous for. It's just celebrity, and everyone wants it.

And it's funny being recognised, in the street or out and about somewhere. You get used to that too. It becomes a pain sometimes when someone always wants to stop you and say something or come over to say hello. Even being looked at all the time gets to be like a drain on your energy or something. Your life becomes public. That's where you exist now. Where you become real. But I tell you what, you worry most when you don't get noticed. It sets off a little fear, deep down inside, that you might just suddenly become invisible again.

I still think about the bad times now and then. It gives me the fear, to tell you the truth. I'm lucky to have got out when I did. Now I've got the lifestyle of a top-class villain with none of the danger. So I hope. I still keep looking over my shoulder. Plenty of faces out there with grudges to bear. Cozzers on the lookout to fit me up for something. I think of those boys shotgunned to death in the Range Rover. I see Beardsley's face staring out at nothing, lying in a pool of his own blood.

And I'm not the big, bad gangster that I'm made out to be. Nowhere near it really, never was. But I talk it up for public consumption. I ain't the baddest, but for the mugs, the punters, I'm the best bad guy they're ever going to get. And they love it.

I sometimes wonder why. I'm like the voice of something that they're frightened of but want to hear at the same time. I'm living the dream because I'm living their nightmare. And they can sleep easily in their beds knowing that I'm playing it out for them.

That's why I have people coming up to me all familiar. Normal, boring, straight-life people want to shake my hand, touch me, because I'm real to them. More real than their own lives. The Geezer has no doubts, no fears, no day-to-day worries, according to them. They have all these frustrations. Something goes wrong, hassle from the bank manager, a row with the boss, and they dream about how someone like me would deal with it. And everyone seems to want to act like a geezer these days. For most of these blokes mouthing off in these poncey bars that have sprung up all over London, the Geezer is their deepest fear and their biggest fantasy.

Some people come on with this anti-authority thing. But I don't buy that. I ain't anti-authority. Christ, authority was my job description when I was working the doors or collecting debts. That's what a gangster is, an authority figure. No, some people have this Robin Hood idea about villainy. Wealth distribution or something. That's bollocks. I've never known a proper villain to operate like that. I ain't exactly sure that old Robin Hood himself had that MO. I mean, in all the films and that you don't see much of him divvying up the swag with the peasants, do you? What did he do, have a fucking means test or something? No, it's just another alibi. And a useful one too. It keeps people from remembering that all the really big crime – not the petty stuff, mind, but what I was into – it's about trying to get rich and powerful, and most victims of crime are poor.

Everyone likes the idea of getting hold of something for nothing. The cash, the loot, the bling-bling. But there's something more to it. I remember that trip to Madame Tussaud's with Dan when we were kids and him joking about me ending up in the Chamber of Horrors. Well, it didn't end up like that. Instead it's like I'm one of the guides, showing them around. Except the Chamber is that little room in their heads where all the bad stuff is stored. I give people permission to have those nasty thoughts. Ambitious, greedy thoughts. Thoughts of violence. I'm the voice for them.

Everything changed for me in 1997. So many things happened. But there were all sorts of things going on around me too. Tony Blair came to power and invited all these fashionable people to Downing Street. Rock stars and comedians and what have you. No, I didn't get an invite, but guess who I saw a picture of in the paper, standing next to the new PM with a glass of champagne in his hand and a smug grin on his face? Ben Holroyd-Carter, that's who. I guess he's become too well connected and powerful to touch now. Not that I've really seriously thought about if for a while anyway.

But I still think about Beardsley's murder. Was Holroyd-Carter directly involved in it? Was it some Essex firm or was it about the Hounslow bullion job? I guess we'll never know now. The missing gold did turn up in the end. It was recovered by the police from this abandoned van in the East End just after we finished shooting *Scrapyard Bulldog*. Funny that.

Harry Starks surrendered himself to British justice in September. He's terminally ill with cancer. He had been hiding out in northern Cyprus but he he didn't fancy the health service there once he started to get really ill. He said he wanted to die on British soil, so he gave himself up. He's currently in the hospital wing of Belmarsh Prison, ready to croak his last words.

Dan was right about the property boom. It's crazy what they're asking for somewhere in the East End these days. He's become quite rich now and we're proper friends again after all this time. He still takes the piss out of me but he says I need it. He reckons there's far too many people telling me what a great bloke I am.

I've become quite good friends with Jez Scott too. I went on a shooting weekend with him and some of the other guys from the film the other week. Turns out he's pretty handy with a shotgun, not a sawn-off, mind, but, you know, these proper sporting models. I had a great time on this pheasant shoot. It was proper weekend in the country, great food and plenty of booze in this big old mansion. And blasting away at these birdies is a great laugh, I can tell you. Doesn't seem legal to have that much fun with a firearm. Jez is getting ready to make another film with a proper budget this time. I'm lined up for a part.

And to top it all, I'm writing a book. Yeah, that's right, a fucking book. Gaz Kelly, chucked out of school at fifteen without even a CSE to his name, is going to become a fucking author. I can't wait for it to come out and I can show all those teachers who thought I was an illiterate yobbo.

Of course, there's going to have to be a writer involved. I've been a bit concerned over this, about how it's going to work out. But my publisher, Victor Groombridge, has set me straight.

'Don't worry about the writer,' he told me. 'Writers aren't important. Two-a-penny hacks, most of them. No, Gaz, it's the subject that's important. And let me tell you, you are a fantastic subject.'

Which has put my mind at rest. You see, I want my story told the right way. I want to be in control of my material, you know what I mean? Certain things that happened in my life, well, I'd sooner skirt around some of them. The marriage break-up, for example, especially that business with the court injunction. The stuff about me cracking up on drugs, some of my criminal activities that haven't been taken into account, and that. And I want it played so that the violence was always against people who had it coming to them.

And Victor sees it my way. I've got a nice little advance on the book. It's going to be called *The Geezer*. The art department have already done a mock-up of the cover. A big photo of me looking fierce in all my shaven-headed glory in a tasty white sharkskin suit I had made recently.

So he arranges a meeting with the writer I'm going to work with at the Groombridge Press. I arrive a little early and I wait outside Victor's office while he has a quick chat with this bloke. I can just hear their voices so I go up to the door to listen in. Old habits die hard. I can hear their conversation.

'Let me do the Starks book, Victor.'

'I told you, no.'

'But he's about to die, for God's sake. I could get it done quickly. We could have it in print in time for the funeral.'

'I can just imagine your God-awful over-wrought prose style. Like that Porter book that never sold any copies. You're better at ghosting, Tony, trust me.'

'But I've got stuff that nobody else knows about. Stuff you'd never believe.'

'I've heard it all before. Anyway, I've already got somebody working on a Starks book. No, you do this. You fucked me about, Tony. Now you pay for it. You still owe me an advance, you know.'

'I know, Victor. But please, not this.'

'Think of it as penance.'

'But *The Geezer*. It's like that other one of yours, *Basher*. They sound like comic-book titles.'

'I get very tired of your superior attitude, you know? I mean, you're hardly some great literary talent youself, are you? And do you know how many copies of *Basher* we sold? In hardback? Over a hundred fucking thousand. And *The Geezer* is going to be even bigger. I'm cleaning up in the true crime market, Tony. And I'm offering you a chance to be part of it.'

'Why?'

'Because of your gutter press instincts. You have all these pathetic pretentions but this is what you're good at. I suspect you'll make a good job of it. Oh, you'll hate it, of course. But that'll be good for your soul. Maybe you'll learn a little humility.'

'And if I say no?'

'You'll have a solicitor's letter in the morning concerning the recovery of an outstanding advance.'

'I see.'

'Then we're agreed, then. Here. Go on, shake my hand. There. Isn't publishing a civilised business? Well, I'll just go and fetch our noble subject.'

I hear him coming to the door so I go and sit down again. The door opens.

'Ah, Gaz,' says Victor. 'Please. Come in.'

This writer bloke stands up as I enter.

'Gaz,' Victor continues. 'This is Tony Meehan, your ghost writer.'

He gives this little smile as he shakes my hand but he doesn't look too happy.

'I was thinking that maybe you two could get acquainted,' says Victor. 'Have a sort of preliminary session. You can use the boardroom. Then we can all go for lunch somewhere.'

So me and Tony go through to this room with a long table and chairs around it. It looks like he's not been having a good day so I start telling him a few things to try to cheer him up. You know, little jokes and asides that I think might work well with the book. He nods and smiles, so I know I'm on the right track. It's got to have a sense of humour, after all. One of the publicity girls brings some coffee through and we finally get sat down at the end of the table. Tony gets out a notepad and a little tape recorder.

He sighs, switching it on. 'Right, let's get started, shall we?'

JAKE ARNOTT

The Long Firm

Meet Harry Starks: club owner, racketeer, porn king, sociology graduate and keen Judy Garland fan. There is a business like showbusiness – it's what Harry does. Fronting violence with rough charm and cheap glamour; performing menace while trying to jump the counter into legitimacy.

'This gangster novel set (mainly) in sixties London is one of the smartest, funniest and original novels you will read all year. It is a gloriously accomplished re-creation of the city in the era of the Kray Twins when aristocratic politicians mixed freely with gangsters, rent boys and actresses of dubious repute in a decadent demi-monde. Arnott is quite brilliant at excavating the cultural minutiae of the time to bring the period vividly to life'
John Tague, *Independent on Sunday*

'Truly fascinating . . . Arnott's ability to powerfully resurrect an era is astonishing'
Jimmy Boyle, *Guardian*

'This is pulp fiction so polished as to be immaculate'
James Harkin, *New Statesman*

'*The Long Firm* manages to hook you from the first. It is compulsive reading, powerful writing with an evocative feel for the bleaker side of the Swinging Sixties'
Dominic Bradbury, *The Times*

'Outstanding . . . Arnott's recreation of the decadent, dangerous atmosphere of the times is immaculate. His prose is as smooth as a seersucker suit, as sweet as a purple heart. Suck it and see.'
Robert MacFarlane, *Observer*

'Gripping . . . slumming it doesn't get much better than this'
Mark Sanderson, *Time Out*

'One of the most impressive first novels I've read in years.'
Simon Shaw, *Mail on Sunday*

SCEPTRE

JAKE ARNOTT

He Kills Coppers

'Brilliant . . . you won't be able to put it down.'
Mark Sanderson, *Sunday Telegraph*

'Easily as good as, if not better than, the superb *Long Firm*.
Arnott returns to the world of 1960s gangsters, except this
time it's the cops as well as the robbers who take centre stage.
The novel is a stylish tour-de-force, Arnott's taut lucid prose
moving the reader effortlessly from the 1966 World Cup to
the 1980s and the age of Thatcher's Boot Boys and the
Battle of the Beanfield. Smashing.'
Julia Bell, *Big Issue*

'A wonderful mix of period detail and atmosphere, this is a fine,
evocative novel'   Stuart Price, *Independent*

'Many thought that Jake Arnott's debut, *The Long Firm*, was
good but not quite as good as the hype tried to convince us it
was. Frankly, Hemingway, Hammett and Greene together would
have been hard pressed to come up with anything that good.
His eagerly awaited follow-up, *He Kills Coppers*, has arrived –
and it's better . . . a fine piece of work that can only increase
Arnott's reputation further.'
Jim Driver, *Time Out*

'Arnott's tough and streetwise novel packs a powerful punch'
Simon Shaw, *Mail on Sunday*

'Incendiary stuff.'   Neil O'Sullivan, *GQ*

'The story and its characters ride perfectly within the setting,
to the benefit of both . . . It propels Arnott even further into a
league of his own. You don't have to be a crime fan to enjoy
Arnott's books, you just have to be interested in the lives of
ordinary, fallible people.'
Christopher Fowler, *Independent on Sunday*

'Told from the point of view of each of the three
central characters . . . they embody a dark and unhappy
Englishness. Although we know these lives will all intersect
at some point, it's a tribute to Arnott's mastery of plot
that the twist is wholly unexpected.'
Sukhdev Sandhu, *Daily Telegraph*

SCEPTRE